LEWIS CARROLL

Jabberwocky and Other Nonsense

Collected Poems

Edited with an Introduction and Notes by
GILLIAN BEER

PENGUIN BOOKS

PENGUIN CLASSICS

Published by the Penguin Group
Penguin Books Ltd, 80 Strand, London WC2R ORL, England
Penguin Group (USA) Inc., 375 Hudson Street, New York, New York 10014, USA
Penguin Group (Canada), 90 Eglinton Avenue East, Suite 700, Toronto, Ontario, Canada M4P 2Y3
(a division of Pearson Penguin Canada Inc.)
Penguin Ireland, 25 St Stephen's Green, Dublin 2, Ireland (a division of Penguin Books Ltd)
Penguin Group (Australia), 250 Camberwell Road, Camberwell, Victoria 3124, Australia
(a division of Pearson Australia Group Pty Ltd)
Penguin Books India Pvt Ltd, 11 Community Centre, Panchsheel Park, New Delhi – 110 017, India
Penguin Group (NZ), 67 Apollo Drive, Rosedale, Auckland 0632, New Zealand
(a division of Pearson New Zealand Ltd)
Penguin Books (South Africa) (Pty) Ltd, Block D, Rosebank Office Park,
181 Jan Smuts Avenue, Parktown North, Gauteng 2193, South Africa

Penguin Books Ltd, Registered Offices: 80 Strand, London WC2R ORL, England

www.penguin.com

Published in Penguin Classics 2012
003

Set in 10.25/12.25 pt PostScript Adobe Sabon
Typeset by Jouve (UK), Milton Keynes
Printed in Great Britain by Clays Ltd, St Ives plc

ISBN: 978-0-141-19594-0

www.greenpenguin.co.uk

ALWAYS LEARNING   **PEARSON**

Contents

JABBERWOCKY AND OTHER
NONSENSE

Chronology

(See Further Reading section for a fuller publications list.)

1832 *27 January*: Charles Lutwidge Dodgson born in Daresbury, Cheshire, the third of eleven siblings. Educated at home until 1844.

1835 Charles Dickens, *Sketches by Boz*, first series.

1837 Queen Victoria's accession to the throne.

1840 Marriage of Victoria and Albert.

1841 *Punch* started.

1843 John Ruskin, *Modern Painters*, vol. 1 (vol. 2, 1846; vols. 3 and 4, 1856; vol. 5, 1860).

1844 Robert Chambers, *Vestiges of the Natural History of Creation*.

1844–5 Attends Richmond School.

1845 *Useful and Instructive Poetry*, a family magazine.

1846–50 Attends Rugby School.

1847 Karl Marx, *Communist Manifesto*.

1848 Revolutions across Europe. Formation of the Pre-Raphaelite Brotherhood. William Makepeace Thackeray, *Vanity Fair*.

c. **1848** *The Rectory Magazine*.

c. **1850–53** *The Rectory Umbrella*.

1851 *January*: Comes into residence as an undergraduate at Christ Church, Oxford. Mother dies 26 January, the day before his nineteenth birthday.
The Great Exhibition.

1852 Takes Moderations examinations; awarded 1st Class in Mathematics, 2nd in Classics.

John Henry Newman, *The Scope and Nature of University Education* (later editions, *The Idea of a University*).

1853 Frederick Denison Maurice, *Theological Essays*.

1853–6 Crimean War.

1854 Takes 1st Class degree in Mathematics.
George Boole, *Analysis of the Laws of Thought on which are founded the Mathematical Theories of Logic and Probability*.

c. **1855–62** *Mischmasch.*

1855–98 Senior Student (i.e. Fellow) of Christ Church.

1856 *March*: Buys a camera, lenses and chemicals; "ready to begin the art" by May. *25 April*: Becomes acquainted with the Liddell family. Meets Alice Liddell in spring and first photographs the three Liddell sisters, "not patient sitters".

1857 Indian Rebellion.

1858 First photographic exhibition at the Victoria and Albert Museum, organised by the Photographic Society of London.

1859 Charles Darwin, *On the Origin of Species*.

1860 Bishop Wilberforce–T. H. Huxley debate in Oxford on Darwin's theory of evolution.

1861 *22 December*: Ordained Deacon.

1861–5 American Civil War.

1862 *4 July*: River trip with the Liddell sisters from Folly Bridge, Oxford to Godstow, during which Carroll first tells them the story of Alice.
Christina Rossetti, *Goblin Market and Other Poems*.

1863 *June*: Break with Liddell family until Christmas; henceforth on less intimate terms.

1864 Gives Alice Liddell a handwritten manuscript of "Alice's Adventures Under Ground", illustrated with his own pictures.

1865 *Alice's Adventures in Wonderland*.

1866 *Aunt Judy's Magazine* started. William Rowan Hamilton, *Elements of Quaternions*. Algernon Charles Swinburne, *Poems and Ballads*.

1867 Takes trip to Russia, recounted in his Russian Journal (published posthumously).

1868 *June*: Father dies.
Disraeli becomes Prime Minister.

1869 *Phantasmagoria and Other Poems*.

1869–73 Gladstone is Prime Minister.

1870–71 Franco-Prussian War.

1871 Abolition of religious tests at Oxford, Cambridge and Durham. Edward Lear, *Nonsense Songs and Stories*; Charles Darwin, *The Descent of Man*.

1872 *Through the Looking-Glass, and What Alice Found There.*

1874–9 Disraeli is Prime Minister.

1875 First Gilbert and Sullivan operetta, *Trial by Jury*, opens at the Royalty.

1876 *The Hunting of the Snark.*

1877 F. J. Furnivall's edition of Shakespeare.

1879 Walter Skeat, *Etymological Dictionary of the English Language* (concluded 1882).

1880–84 Gladstone is Prime Minister.

1882 Virginia Woolf born.

1883 *Rhyme? And Reason?*

1885 Salisbury is Prime Minister (until 1891). Fall of Khartoum, Sudan. First volume of the *Dictionary of National Biography*, ed. Leslie Stephen.

1888 W. B. Yeats, *Fairy and Folk Tales of the Irish Peasantry.*

1889 *The Nursery "Alice". Sylvie and Bruno.*

1892–3 Gladstone's last Prime Ministership.

1893 *Sylvie and Bruno Concluded.*

1898 *14 January*: Dies of pneumonia at his sisters' house in Guildford. *Three Sunsets and Other Poems.*

Introduction

Lewis Carroll's imagination is always at play, ricocheting across previous poems, reversing and viewing askance the assumptions embedded in poetic forms and poetic language. He wrote poems for fun and to give pleasure, often to other particular people. Occasionally he wrote more anguished, serious or personal poems and, indeed, many of the poems he composed have a poignant undertone despite their high spirits. A great many of his poems have been lost to view, though those in the *Alice* books and *The Hunting of the Snark* remain well known. This, the first collected and annotated edition of his poems, brings into the light a fresh array of often brilliant verses and provides contexts that reveal the full force of his wit and, occasionally, his sadness. He began writing young, as part of a large family, eleven children in all, and he lived for much of his childhood at the parsonage in Daresbury, Cheshire, then after the age of eleven in the Rectory at Croft-on-Tees, Yorkshire. The first years of his life were spent at home in a group of children varying in age and gender, but all dependent on each other for their daily entertainment. He went to school when he was twelve years old, having been tutored by his father until then, and he seems to have enjoyed boarding at the quite free-and-easy Richmond School. Rugby School, where he went at fourteen, was a shock: "I cannot say that I look back upon my life at a Public School with any sensation of pleasure, or that any earthly consider-ations would induce me to go through my three years again."[1]

Throughout all that time, and beyond, he was Charles Dodg-son and nobody else. Lewis Carroll first became part of his life in March 1856, accompanying the poem "Solitude" in the magazine *The Train*. It was not a well-known name, however, until the publication of *Alice in Wonderland* in 1865 when he was thirty-three years old. He had been writing poems, and in some cases publishing them, ever since his boyhood. Indeed, some of the poems in the *Alice* books are based on these earlier verses. For simplicity, and because his pseudonym has overtaken his own name in renown – rather as his parodies did the earlier poems of others – I usually refer to him in this edition as Lewis Carroll, or even Carroll (shortened to "LC" in the Notes). I am nevertheless conscious that this is not an entirely satisfactory solution: there is a specific timbre to the early poems before he had adopted the pen name; his poems sparked by Oxford university controversies were definitely known to be from the pen of the redoubtable Reverend C. L. Dodgson, Student of Christ Church (when they were signed at all); and much later in his life his many occasional poems were written in correspondence that was signed C.L.D. or C. L. Dodgson or Charles L. Dodgson. In the early family collections and in the university magazine *College Rhymes* he used a variety of initials: V.X., B.B., F.L.W., J.V., F.X., Q.G., K., R.W.G. He signed many of his more serious early poems C.L.D. alongside place and date of composition, and those initials and that information are here included where inscribed at the end of poems. In his later years when the *Alice* books had given him some celebrity he tried, rather intermittently, to keep Charles Dodgson and Lewis Carroll apart. He would sometimes refuse to answer letters from unknown people addressed to Lewis Carroll, but he used the name when he wanted to give publicity to a cause, such as the anti-vivisection movement. And he disliked people pronouncing his family name as "dodge-son" as much as he disliked people dropping the "g" out of the spelling of the name: "Dodson" is traditionally the family's preferred pronunciation, avoiding the possibility of dodgy puns, to which his ears were always alert.

Early Poetry

During his boyhood Carroll took the lead in the various games and pursuits of the family, in magic lantern and marionette shows, and particularly in the making of family magazines.

The first of these, *Useful and Instructive Poetry* (1845) was written entirely by him and especially for his younger brother and sister, Wilfred and Louisa, when Charles was thirteen and they were seven and five. The poems are uproariously dissident, neither useful nor instructive, and often very funny:

> "Sister, sister, go to bed,
> Go and rest your weary head,"
> Thus the prudent brother said.

> "Do you want a battered hide
> Or scratches to your face applied?"
> Thus the sister calm replied.

> "Sister! Do not rouse my wrath,
> I'd make you into mutton broth
> As easily as kill a moth."

> The sister raised her beaming eye,
> And looked on him indignantly,
> And sternly answered "Only try!"

> Off to the cook he quickly ran,
> "Dear cook, pray lend a frying pan
> To me, as quickly as you can."

> "And wherefore should I give it to you?"
> "The reason, cook, is plain to view,
> I wish to make an Irish stew."

> "What meat is in that stew to go?"
> "My sister'll be the contents." "Oh!"
> "Will you lend the pan, Cook?" "NO!"

> *Moral:* "Never stew your sister."

Moralising and moral tags amused him throughout his writing career. Indeed, the poems in *Alice in Wonderland* delight in reversing the piety of pedagogic verses and Alice is exasperated by the moral tropes of the Duchess: " 'How fond she is of finding morals in things!' Alice thought to herself." The high-spirited anarchism of these early verses is already underpinned by considerable technical formal skill, as here in the triple rhyme verses and the easy way dialogue is folded into the lines. They are neat as well as outrageous.

The second magazine, *The Rectory Magazine*, includes contributions from several of the Dodgson children under pseudonymous initials. The whole is described on the title-page as "a Compendium of the best tales, poems, essays, pictures &c that the united talents of the Rectory inhabitants can produce, Edited and printed by CLD", although only his poems are included in this edition. The magazine ran to nine numbers. The next four of these domestic magazines unfortunately are not known to have survived; only their names remain: *The Rectory Comet*, *The Rosebud*, *The Star* and *The Will-o'-the-Wisp*. So *The Rectory Umbrella*, the seventh of these family magazines, is the next extant and comes from the period 1850–53. All the contents, as indeed he complains, are by CLD, the rest of the contributors having fallen by the wayside. Perhaps he outshone them or they simply enjoyed his prowess. However, in *Mischmasch*, covering 1855–62, the eighth and last of the magazines, two contributions from other members of the family are present: "The Mermaids" by Louisa and "Blood" by Wilfred. "The Mermaids" is an elegant if rather insipid poem, and "Blood" a rip-roaring and unironic celebration of violence. The volume includes "She's All My Fancy Painted Him" which appears transmogrified in the courtroom scene of *Alice in Wonderland*, as well as a "Stanza of Anglo-Saxon Poetry", with notes, dated 1855, and later to be known as the first stanza of "Jabberwocky" in *Through the Looking-Glass* more than fifteen years later. These early volumes are decorated with Carroll's witty and sometimes grotesque pen-and-ink drawings, which often take the poems' jokes further. He continued to draw for his friends' amusement alongside poems offered to them although he never ventured to publish the drawings, considering himself too crude and untrained an artist. A few of them are included in this edition to give the flavour of his verve as a draughtsman.

Mischmasch was put together when Dodgson was already in his twenties, making it clear that he valued these early productions as part of the family's history and present, quite apart from his relish for the verses. Four of the family were still children when he was already a Student (that is a Fellow) of Christ Church at Oxford, and his mother had died suddenly only two days after he went up to Oxford as an undergraduate in 1851. As the eldest son Charles had a special position in the family and knew that when his father died he would be in some large measure responsible for the well-being of all his siblings who remained unmarried. In the event, only one of his sisters married and she returned to share a house with the rest of the sisters after her husband's death. One sister did decide to live alone, Henrietta, who set up house in Brighton and Carroll quite frequently visited her there. But six adult sisters lived together in a house in Guildford where Lewis Carroll spent many of the university vacations throughout his life and where he died in 1898. There is a sense in which the shared girlhood or childhood never quite dispersed and Carroll's strong identification with his sisters continued. That identification is an element in his unusual enjoyment of the company of children, particularly girls, whom he entertained with many of the same delights that he had shared in his own childhood: verbal games and zany poems, paper-cutting, the dressing-up box and the marionette theatre. Two of his three younger brothers did marry and have children, while the youngest of the family, Edwin, became a missionary on Tristan da Cunha. The female household in Guildford alternated with the male college community of Christ Church to give Carroll throughout adulthood, constant company and also some solitude. They also gave him two very different readerships for his occasional verses.

Professional Life and Poetry

Charles Dodgson was throughout his adult years a mathematics don at Christ Church, Oxford, specializing in logic. He wrote extensively about mathematical ideas and problems, always following Euclidean orthodoxy. He was not regarded as a particularly innovative mathematician, though he was friends with a number of important innovators such as J. J. Sylvester and Augustus De Morgan. However, his work on proportional representation, "Principles of Parliamentary Representation", has proved to be of very considerable importance for twentieth-century attempts to produce fairer voting systems.[2] He taught undergraduates, who were at first all men, as well as later giving voluntary lectures in logic at two women's colleges, Lady Margaret Hall and what was then St Hugh's Hall (now St Hugh's College), and at the Oxford High School for Girls. He supported higher education for women but he thought that they would thrive better in a university of their own.

Dodgson was also a cleric, though not in full orders. His position at Christ Church indeed depended on his being a bachelor and a clergyman. He read very widely in works of theology and was affected by the ideas of Christian Socialism, though he was in some ways socially conservative. He experienced his faith personally. The poem, "After Three Days", subtitled "Written after seeing Holman Hunt's picture of 'Christ in the Temple'", written in 1861, recounts a dream in which he is among those in the temple when the twelve-year-old Jesus joins in debate with the elders. It reaches a climax of intensity as he imagines gazing into the face of the young Christ:

> Look into those deep eyes,
> Stirred to unrest by breath of coming strife,
> Until a longing in thy soul arise
>   That this indeed were life:
>
> That thou couldst find Him there,
> Bend at His sacred feet thy willing knee,
> And from thy heart pour out the passionate prayer,
>   "Lord, let me follow Thee!"

The language of the seventeenth-century poet-priest George Herbert with its heartfelt direct address is here realised, but sequestered within a dream.

Lewis Carroll's friendships with members of the Pre-Raphaelite movement, particularly the Rossettis and Holman Hunt, had their effect in both his parodic medieval comic verses and his more troubled poems such as "Stolen Waters", which imagines a destructive and obsessional love. Its title is drawn from Proverbs: "Stolen waters are sweet and bread eaten in secret is pleasant" (9:17). He also knew John Ruskin, the great social and aesthetic critic and supporter of the Pre-Raphaelites (who discouraged him about his drawing and who himself acted as drawing master to Alice Liddell). Ruskin was for a time resident at Christ Church so that the two men had opportunities for conversation. Ruskin's name turns up in several of the poems, particularly in "Hiawatha's Photographing", where he has been misunderstood by the son of the house who has set about organising himself in curves, imagining that he is following Ruskin's edict on beauty.

> Curves pervading all his figure,
> Which the eye might follow onward,
> Till they centred in the breast-pin,
> Centred in the golden breast-pin.
> He had learnt it all from Ruskin,
> (Author of The Stones of Venice,
> "Seven Lamps of Architecture,
> Modern Painters," and some others);
> And perhaps he had not fully
> Understood the author's meaning;
> But, whatever was the reason,
> All was fruitless, as the picture
> Ended in a total failure.

Perhaps unexpectedly, "Hiawatha's Photographing" is the only one of Carroll's poems that engages fully with his other great enthusiasm: photography. In the later version of the poem (in this volume) in *Phantasmagoria*, he contrives a brilliantly exact description of the cold collodion method of developing photographs, working within the constraints of Longfellow's metre which he is mimicking. Henry Longfellow's epic and much-parodied poem *The Song of Hiawatha* is written in a metre that is both lulling and engrossing (see Notes). The second of Carroll's three stanzas about the processing of photographs runs thus:

> Secondly, my Hiawatha
> Made with cunning hand a mixture
> Of the acid Pyro-gallic,
> And of Glacial Acetic,
> And of Alcohol and water:
> This developed all the picture.

There is much to be written, and much that has been written, about Lewis Carroll's enthusiasm for photography: it gave him access to a great range of people, such as the Tennysons and Darwin to whom he offered a photograph for inclusion in *The Expression of the Emotions in Man and Animals*, and it formed a pervasive element in his friendships with young girls. However, for an edition of his verse it scarcely figures as a topic beyond the invention of "Hiawatha".[3] One might argue that the acrostics in which he delighted particularly in his later years have something of the same function as photographs in establishing intimacy and distance at once. Both demand intricate technique and both provoke a particularly strong and yet controlled relationship between subject and practitioner: the photographer looks through a lens at a distance, all attention focused on the one person, who is highly conscious of being that focus; the poet offers poems that have in them beneath the surface a verbal message that speaks directly to that person alone, her name concealed and revealed in the letters of the verses (see "Poems for Friends"). Reciprocity is hidden but essential in both practices. But beyond that, it is not easy to uncover parallels. Carroll was a man who relished a variety of forms for his creativity, including most particularly mathematics; poetry and photography were among the most compelling, yet without a manifest relation between them.

Another group of poems, the Oxford satirical poems, have

lost a good deal of their appeal since they are bound up with long-gone controversies of seething importance to members of those close-knit communities during Carroll's, or Dodgson's, long residence in college. Some still have enough play in them to entertain, such as "The New Belfry of Christ Church, Oxford", which provoked him to witty revisions of *King Lear* and *The Tempest* and some syllogistic comedy. As ever, he writes with panache and variety so that even though the cause is long forgotten the wry humour survives.

> Five fathoms square the Belfry frowns;
>   All its sides of timber made;
> Painted all in greys and browns;
>   Nothing of it that will fade.
> Christ Church may admire the change –
> Oxford thinks it sad and strange.
> Beauty's dead! Let's ring her knell.
> Hark! now I hear them – ding-dong, bell.
>
> ("Song and Chorus")

That neat comma added to Ariel's "ding dong bell", so that it becomes "*ding-dong, bell*", shifts the scale of mourning from a father lost, but unexpectedly equals it with "Beauty's dead!", the bell muffled in this raw new belfry. Instead of loss and fading, as in Ariel's song in *The Tempest*, here the threat is permanent ugliness: "*Nothing of it that will fade*" instead of "Nothing of him that doth fade / But doth suffer a sea-change / Into something rich and strange" (i, 2, 400-402). Christ Church, Dodgson here muses, is stuck with a permanent monstrosity without transformation. This present edition gives only the verses from these Oxford controversies but they have their full zest in their setting of prose argument and debate, too extensive for inclusion here.

The third and most famous group of his poems is addressed not only to a known but to an unknown readership. *Alice's Adventures Under Ground* is still addressed to a known reader,

the young Alice Liddell, and that first version remained
unpublished for many years.[4] But after that comes the publica-
tion of *Alice's Adventures in Wonderland* (1865), *Through the
Looking-Glass, and What Alice Found There* (1872), *The
Hunting of the Snark* (1876), and much later, the two-volume
novel *Sylvie and Bruno* (1889) and *Sylvie and Bruno Con-
cluded* (1893). In *Alice's Adventures in Wonderland* Carroll's
skill as a parodist becomes part of a larger psychological adven-
ture as Alice struggles to recall the pious verses with which she
descended into Wonderland only to hear them emerge as ex-
uberant violence, sometimes from her own mouth. In *Through
the Looking-Glass* some nursery rhymes remain intact –
"Humpty Dumpty", "Tweedledum and Tweedledee", "The
Lion and the Unicorn" – while alongside them Carroll gives the
full "Jabberwocky" and "The Walrus and the Carpenter", to
say nothing of Humpty Dumpty's maddening song that ends
with conjunctions, leaving the reader stranded on the brink of
obscure crisis:

> And he was very proud and stiff:
> He said "I'd go and wake them if———"
>
> I took a corkscrew from the shelf:
> I went to wake them up myself.
>
> And when I found the door was locked,
> I pulled and pushed and kicked and knocked.
>
> And when I found the door was shut,
> I tried to turn the handle, but———
>
> There was a long pause.
> "Is that all?" Alice timidly asked.
> "That's all," said Humpty Dumpty, "Good-bye."

(Centenary Edition, 192)

If the joke there is emptiness, the White Knight's song a little later is full: of feeling, of absent-mindedness, of Wordsworthian condescension and exasperated encounter. Its subject matter parodies Wordsworth's poem "Resolution and Independence", a prolonged account of a meeting between an insistent questioner and an old leech-gatherer, in which the questioner is depressed and alone. He is obscurely heartened by the old man's wisdom, drawn out of him by indefatigable queries: "What occupation do you there pursue?" "How is it that you live, and what is it you do?" Carroll gets the mismatch between the questioner's high and self-absorbed thoughts and the leech-gatherer's own account with its hints for alms: Carroll wrote to his uncle Hassard Dodgson in 1872 that the poem had always amused him, "by the absurd way the poet goes on questioning the poor old leech-gatherer, making him tell his history over and over again, and never attending to what he says. Wordsworth ends with a moral – an example I have *not* followed" (*Letters*, i, 177). Carroll's poem is in fact a reworking of an earlier poem of his own that had appeared anonymously in *The Train* in 1856. One of the marvellous turns in the *Alice* books is the way that such earlier poems are reinvented by embedding them in particular characters, or – as with "She's All My Fancy Painted Him" – in a particular situation. That poem in the *Comic Times* (1855) grows menacing when set anew (and abbreviated) at the end of *Alice in Wonderland*.

His last two works of fiction, *Sylvie and Bruno* and *Sylvie and Bruno Concluded*, with their constant miasmic shadings across different forms of reality and dream, accommodate an extraordinary variety of poems with no attempt to drive them through the narrative, even to the degree that occurs in the two *Alice* books. But the poems are generated out of the characters in the book and are appropriate to each one in particular rather than flowing straight from Lewis Carroll. These books, indeed, are full of buried treasure and the poems represent an arresting new phase in Carroll's creativity, more sardonic, more extreme and more moving than his earlier parodies. Indeed, almost none of the poems in these late novels is parodic. At one extreme

of feeling we have the idealised song of Sylvie and Bruno with
its chorus:

> For I think it is Love,
> For I feel it is Love,
> For I'm sure it is nothing but Love!

> ("A Fairy-Duet")

These stressful verses, urging love, are contrasted with venge-
fully logical poems such as "Peter and Paul", where Peter is
trapped by a loan never in fact given; or the Gardener's Song
that crops up again and again with new verses always structured
by "He thought he saw" and "He looked again": for example:

> He thought he saw an Albatross
>   That fluttered round the lamp:
> He looked again, and found it was
>   A Penny-Postage-Stamp.
> "You'd best be getting home," he said:
>   "The nights are very damp!"

Or:

> He thought he saw a Garden-Door
>   That opened with a key:
> He looked again and found it was
>   A Double Rule of Three:
> "And all its mystery," he said,
>   "Is clear as day to me!"

The Gardener's Song marks the point where whimsy and
grotesque become untranslatable, even indistinguishable. The
delight and the exasperation felt by the listeners in the book
(and probably by the reader) can't be separated. The everyday
and the exotic, postage-stamp and albatross, oscillate in these
purest forms of nonsense. Carroll shifts speech-registers with-
out remark while always respecting the demands of metre and

rhyme: that calm provokes the sense of something uneasy, even unconscionable, that many readers experience even as they delight in the dexterity of the verse.

There was a further constituency of individual readers for whom he wrote his most occasional verse: the array of child-friends he gathered across the years, some of whom remained his friends into adulthood. The verses he wrote for these young girls (for all these poems were addressed to girl children or adolescents, sometimes as a family group) tended to be games in themselves, with hidden names and riddles. The ingenuity of the acrostics follows tight rules. Intimacy and bounds are both respected in these agile inventions. They vary from fond and simple compliments like this small poem addressed "To Miss Margaret Dymes" where the first letter of each line spells her name:

> Maidens, if a maid you meet
> Always free from pout and pet,
> Ready smile and temper sweet,
> Greet my little Margaret.
> And if loved by all she be
> Rightly, not a pampered pet,
> Easily you then may see
> 'Tis my little Margaret.

– to elaborate double acrostics, like the one addressed to Agnes and Emily Hughes, where each verse not only hides their names but is also a riddle (p. 294). Clearly, Carroll delighted in these codes and riddles as he delighted in the company of the girl children who were his friends: the fun and play was curbed and yet made more exhilarating by intricate rules. The inhibition of rhyme and the control of acrostic sorted well with his exquisite affection for the children – affection that knew its own bounds, and the necessity for those bounds. Very often these little poems occur in a letter, on the flyleaf of a book he is giving, or as a way of greeting or parting: they are presents, more personal and so more valuable than toys or trinkets, and clearly received as such by many of the girls who were given them and who kept them into adulthood. They are also teases, quite often apparently scolding as much as praising the child who is their inspiration. In the double acrostic poem below, each verse, after the first one, is a riddle (with the answer beside it) and the names of the little girls addressed provide the first and last letters of each answer: Trina and Freda.

> Two little girls near London dwell,
> More naughty than I like to tell.
>
> Upon the lawn the hoops are seen:
> The balls are rolling on the green. **TurF**
>
> The Thames is running deep and wide:
> And boats are rowing on the tide. **RiveR**
>
> In winter-time, all in a row,
> The happy skaters come and go. **IcE**
>
> "Papa!" they cry, "Do let us stay!"
> He does not speak, but says they may. **NoD**
>
> "There is a land," he says, "my dear,
> Which is too hot to skate, I fear." **AfricA**
>
> ("Two little girls near London dwell")

But it was not solely children who inspired Carroll to his knottiest verses. Building on a system invented by Dr Richard Grey in 1730, Carroll worked out mnemonics for logarithms, the dates of kings or the specific gravities of metals and resolved that information into couplets by means of a code. The couplets are often as difficult to recall (at least for anyone but Carroll) as the information itself; or, rather, the relationship between a couplet like "Columbus sailed the world around / Until America was found" and the buried date 1492 can only be understood by learning the cipher system.[5] These "Memoria

Technica" crop up in unexpected places, often in the diaries
and in letters, and I have offered a few of them only.

After the *Alice* books Carroll's poetry takes a rather differ-
ent turn, away from parody, into the darker *The Hunting of the
Snark* (1876). Behind that poem lie travellers' tales and explor-
ation, including the loss of Franklin's expedition in search of
the Northwest Passage, which so preoccupied Victorian society
in the 1850s, and Coleridge's *Ancient Mariner*, and even some-
thing of *Frankenstein*. *The Hunting of the Snark* came to
Carroll first through its intact last line: "For the Snark *was* a
Boojum, you see." Quite what this means remains a mystery
except that, as Alice says about "Jabberwocky":

> "Somehow it seems to fill my head with ideas – only I don't
> know exactly what they are! However, *somebody* killed *some-
> thing*: that's clear, at any rate—"

> (Centenary Edition, 134)

At the end of the *Snark* that observation is reversed: *something*
killed *someone*, it would seem. "For the Snark *was* a Boojum":
that italicised "*was*" suggests that the snark being a boojum
confounds a host of unnameable possibilities. Late in his life
Carroll insisted that he "didn't mean anything but nonsense"
in the poem, but he was intrigued by the readings that clustered
around it, such as that it represented the search for happiness
or for the absolute. In a letter to the Lowrie children he made a
remark crucial to understanding how his creativity worked despite
the precision with which he wrote and rhymed:

> As to the meaning of the Snark? I'm very much afraid I didn't
> mean anything but nonsense! Still, you know, words mean more
> than we mean to express when we use them; so a whole book
> ought to mean a great deal more than the writer meant. So, what-
> ever good meanings are in the book, I am very happy to accept as
> the meaning of the book. The best that I've seen is by a lady . . . –
> that the whole book is an allegory on the search after happiness.

Elsewhere he is more succinct: "My dear May, In answer to your question 'What did you mean the Snark was?' will you tell your friend that I meant that the Snark was a *Boojum*. I trust that you and she will now feel quite satisfied and happy."[6]

The *Snark* is unusual in being composed intact rather than clustered around shards of his own or other writers' previous poems, as in his many parodic works. Here it seems to have spun backwards out of that single impenetrable line. As so often, Carroll was fortunate in his illustrator, and Henry Holiday well captured the bluntness and the obscurity of the poem.

Carroll's Reading and His Parodies

Carroll read poetry of many kinds with delight. He kept abreast of a great deal of recent and contemporary poetry, as well as being deeply familiar with the English and Latin classics. He loved William Blake's *Songs of Innocence and Experience*. He was much attracted by Christina Rossetti's *Goblin Market and Other Poems* (1862) and came to know her well. In his personal Scrapbook now available online from the Library of Congress, he has pasted in two of her poems. He owned Adelaide Procter's *A Chaplet of Verses* (1862) and her two-volume *Legends and Lyrics* (1858–61), possibly in the 1866 edition that included an illustration by John Tenniel, his inspired collaborator as the illustrator of both the *Alice* books. Carroll owned Swinburne's highly controversial collection of poems *Poems and Ballads* (1866). He read William Morris's *The Defence of Guinevere, and Other Poems* (1858) when it first came out, and he owned *The Poetical Works of Edgar Allan Poe* (1853). Of course he read Tennyson at large and owned at least twenty-six collections of his work, including the German translation of "In Memoriam". But he also read now little-known writers such as William Motherwell, both his collection of ballads *Minstrelsy Ancient and Modern* (1827) and his *Poetical Works* (3rd edition, 1849) and Robert Pollok's large epic *The Course of Time* (1829), which went through many editions and which, Charlie Lovett notes, "was issued in 1857 in an illustrated edition which included pictures by John

Tenniel".[7] He read also the works of humorous poets like Bon Gaultier[8] and Praed, and his copy of the two-volume *The Poems of Winthrop Mackworth Praed* (1864) was offered for sale in 1965. And every week he read *Punch* with its wealth of comic verses. Later in his life he greatly enjoyed Gilbert and Sullivan's operettas with their witty verses and catchy tunes and their friendly satire on social mores. The list could be greatly expanded and those interested will find many other examples in Charlie Lovett's excellent bibliography, *Lewis Carroll Among His Books* (2005).

Carroll was above all a superb parodist. Parody is a curious form, relying as it must at the outset on what it will overturn and perhaps obliterate. Many of the poems he parodies would have been well known at the time but are unknown to us now, the more so because his version has usurped their standing. An example is the poem by David Bates discussed below ("Speak Gently!"); another is Robert Southey's didactic poem "The Old Man's Comforts and How He Gained Them", which lies behind "'You are old, Father William'". They were in authority then; his version is in authority now. Inevitably the loss of the original in our reading takes away a level of debate and of comedy. Sometimes their shadows do still haunt his poem; occasionally both versions still survive alongside each other, as "Twinkle, twinkle, little star" does beside "Twinkle, twinkle, little bat". In the annotations I have tried to offer long-enough extracts from the originating poems to give their flavour.

Parody is a game rather than an accusation. Carroll's parodies often show a certain affection or at the least a quizzical appreciation of the originals. He is amused by the moralising urgency of many of the verses and he eases the demands they make on children, or he encourages the child reader to vengeance without consequences. One of the most famous of the poems that turn "hoarse and strange" in Alice's mouth is "How doth the little crocodile" – the first line ends in the Isaac Watts poem with "the little busy bee", in Alice's recollection it is "the little crocodile". By keeping close to all the linguistic patterns of the Watts poem Carroll gives zest to his disruptive new version.

Bee and crocodile both have appetites; the verses display each of them to the child reader: "How doth". Both claim to improve things and make them shine; the Watts is on the left below, the Carroll on the right:

How doth the little busy bee	How doth the little crocodile
Improve each shining hour;	Improve his shining tail,
And gathers honey all the day	And pour the waters of the Nile
From every opening flower.	On every golden scale!

The glamorous crocodile allures the child, as had the gentler "opening flower" and honey; the first lines of both second verses share upbeat words: "skilfully" and "cheerfully", "neat" and "neatly". Then the still smiling crocodile shows his claws and relaxes, while the bee "labours hard":

How skilfully she builds her cell!	How cheerfully he seems to grin,
How neat she spreads the wax!	How neatly spreads his claws,
And labours hard to store it well	And welcomes little fishes in,
With the sweet food she makes.	With gently smiling jaws!

Left dangling in the outer memory of early readers would be all the injunctions of Watts's third and fourth verses, which the child is expected dutifully to make her own but which have here vanished entirely from the script:

In works of labour or of skill,
    I would be busy too;
For Satan finds some mischief still
    For idle hands to do.

In books, or work, or healthful play,
    Let my first years be passed,
That I may give for every day
    Some good account at last.

Alice abandons the transformed poem halfway through, feeling betrayed by her unconscious, or by the rules of another world.

She fears she is not who she thought she was. She has different *words* inside her: perhaps after all she has been changed for the dreary and unfortunate little Mabel, who has so few presents and a "pokey little house" and "ever so many lessons to learn". But perhaps she is the crocodile too. The crocodile isn't working; he just sits there welcoming the little fishes into his jaws, a vision of leisure. There is something sumptuous about the Carroll image of the spangled crocodile, satisfied, unjustified.

The poems in the *Alice* books include a lot of cheerful violence, but it is usually pantomime violence where everything survives on the page. An exception is perhaps the fate of the trusting little oysters at the end of "The Walrus and the Carpenter":

> "O Oysters," said the Carpenter,
>   "You've had a pleasant run!
> Shall we be trotting home again?"
>   But answer came there none –
> And this was scarcely odd, because
>   They'd eaten every one.

The reader shares Alice's indignation. Carroll much later made amends to the oysters (and conventional morality) by adding verses for Savile Clarke's operetta based on *Alice* which makes it clear that the Walrus and the Carpenter both suffered horribly from indigestion that night (see Notes).

Strikingly, "The Walrus and the Carpenter" is one of the few poems in the *Alice* books that is not a direct parody. Carroll remarked that though the metre was shared with Thomas Hood's "Eugene Aram", it "is a common one" and "I don't think 'Eugene Aram' suggested it more than the many other poems I have read in the same metre."[9] It would be interesting to understand what it was about the metre that set the narrative going: perhaps the relatively free, insouciant rhyme-scheme (abcbdb) with three different unrhymed words at line-ending (1, 3, 5) alongside a rhyming word in lines 2, 4, 6. The laconic voices of the walrus and the carpenter, casual and sinister – and running so readily through the metre without strain – are the main source of the humour.

Sometimes Carroll turns over an apparently pious poem to reveal its underside. So, David Bates's innocuous-seeming "Speak Gently! It is better far / To rule by love than fear" lies behind "Speak roughly to your little boy" ("[The Duchess's Lullaby]"). But every one of the ten stanzas of the Bates begins: "Speak gently" and the effect becomes bludgeoning rather than persuasive. Moreover there is a sickly pleasure in the reminders of mortality:

> Speak gently to the little child!
>   Its love be sure to gain;
> Teach it in accents soft and mild;
>   It may not long remain.

So, you can afford to be lenient, as the child will probably soon die. Carroll, in contrast, leads us to rejoice in the resilience of the pig-baby.

Entries in Carroll's diaries during the 1850s reveal some earlier disquiet about parody and satire. Reading Bon Gaultier's parodic *Ballads of Crewe* for the first time in 1856, before he owned a copy, he thought them "very clever", but that they "spoil the beautiful originals". Nevertheless he bought the book and throughout the 1850s was composing parodies of his own.[10] Indeed, a number of his parodies of Scottish ballads and medieval verse owe quite a lot to the fashion provoked by Bon Gaultier. For Carroll was not a lone star. Parody was one of the most popular forms of verse in Victorian England and Tennyson, for one, was persistently imitated. Theodore Martin's "The Lay of the Lovelorn", for instance, is a brilliant imitation of the metre and general grumpiness of "Locksley Hall", written in the voice of a drunk man, while Cuthbert Bede (Edward Bradley) captures in "In Immemoriam" the strained empyrean, vapid or vatic, that always lies threateningly close to Tennyson's sonorities. Cuthbert Bede opens his poem thus:

> We seek to know, and knowing, seek:
> We seek, we know, and every sense
> Is trembling with the great intense,
> And vibrating to what we speak.[11]

Carroll's "The Three Voices" mimics the high tones of Tennyson's "The Two Voices". So, Tennyson:

> This truth within thy mind rehearse,
> That in a boundless universe
> Is boundless better, boundless worse.
>
> Think you this mould of hopes and fears
> Could find no statelier than his peers
> In yonder hundred million spheres?

Carroll's long "Three Voices" figures an oppressive female sage who spouts forth somewhat similar wisdom to the cowed poet as they pace the moonlit shore:

> "Thought in the mind doth still abide;
> That is by Intellect supplied,
> And within that Idea doth hide.
>
> "And he, that yearns the truth to know,
> Still further inwardly may go,
> And find Idea from Notion flow.
>
> "And thus the chain, that sages sought,
> Is to a glorious circle wrought,
> For Notion hath its source in Thought."
>
> When he, with racked and whirling brain,
> Feebly implored her to explain,
> She simply said it all again.
>
> ("The First Voice")

Carroll clearly enjoyed his own poem, which first appeared in *The Train* in November 1856; he published it again not only in *Mischmasch*, but in *Phantasmagoria* and then, much later, in *Rhyme? And Reason?* Most of his extended parodies were written during the earlier years of his career, sometimes as part of a family magazine and sometimes as contributions to Oxford controversies, poems such as "The Deserted Parks" and "The Elections to The Hebdomadal Council", collected in *Notes by an Oxford Chiel*. He sought publishers for many of them, though the Oxford ones often anonymously, and he relished the opportunity to contribute to the various journals that concentrated on comic writing: strikingly, only one of his poems was accepted by *Punch*. It was "Atalanta in Camden Town", published anonymously on 27 July 1867. The poem is a very loose parody of Swinburne's *Atalanta in Corydon*. Carroll was a weekly reader of *Punch* and also kept a scrapbook (almost certainly with more volumes than the one now in the Library of Congress[12]) in which he preserved poems and items that particularly caught his fancy. Among these items are a number of poems both serious and frivolous from *Punch*, including "The Bards of Burns: A Lay of Crystalle Palace", from which he may have taken the idea of poetic "Fyttes" for *The Hunting of the Snark*".[13]

Carroll's writing rapidly became itself a source for parody and imitation. On 16 March 1872, less than three months after the publication of *Through the Looking-Glass*, *Punch* had a full-page cartoon "The Monster Slain", praising the barrister J. Coleridge, and an accompanying poem that claimed to "translate" "Jabberwocky" into the English of the law courts; it opens:

> 'Twas May time, and the lawyer coves
> Did gibe and jabber in the wabe,
> All menaced were the Tichborne groves,
> And their true lord the Babe.

The still-continuing rush of translations of "Jabberwocky" was begun as early as February 1872 by Robert Scott's skilful German pseudo-translation. And pasted in to one of the scrapbooks kept by Carroll's lifelong friend and colleague at Christ Church, J. Vere Bayne, there appears a witty new version by A. C. Hilton of "The Walrus and the Carpenter", now named "The Vulture and the Husbandman" by Louisa Caroline, a play on Dodgson's pseudonym, and describing the horrors of the Viva-Voce examinations at Cambridge where examiners ask unforeseen questions and "plough" (that is, fail) all the undergraduates:

> "The time has come," the Vulture said,
>   "To talk of many things
> Of Accidence and Adjectives,
>   And names of Jewish kings,
> How many notes a Sackbut has,
>   And whether shawms have strings."
>
> "Please, Sir," the undergraduates said,
>   Turning a little blue,
> "We didn't know that was the sort
>   Of thing we had to do."[14]

Carroll's wit is sprightly, versatile and penetrating. He brought to bear his skills as a logician to undercut logic and his fascination with ordinary objects to pursue the mystery in things. Sudden plangency emerges from in the midst of his humour. His serious poems, such as "Only a Woman's Hair", "Faces in the Fire" and "The Path of Roses", meditate, often painfully, on love lost and women's dilemmas. And some poems, such as "Stolen Waters", show a mind troubled by the impossibility of feeling without recoil. But he wrote most often for fun, his own and ours, and the ingenuity of his humour becomes the more remarkable the more you read him. As I prepared this edition more jokes would swim to the surface under my eyes, often jokes hidden in jokes. Some were recondite, many purely verbal, and some spun out of the music of the verse.[15] Carroll had a particularly clever ear for speech and his devotion to the theatre probably helped him to poise the climax of a scene even within a very short poem. His rhymes conspire: they bring out the absurdity of language, where sounds and semantics can't be reconciled. He had a fine metrical ear that can choose just the rhythms that will most express the implications of his verse. He was devoted to popular song and he relished its way of meaning more than the writer or the composer knew: "She's All My

Fancy Painted Her,"[16] for example, keeps shifting and turning in his mind, echoing down through years of his writing, sometimes ridiculous, sometimes poignant. He was not a social satirist in his verse, although in life he was quite a considerable controversialist on university matters and a man with strong views on social issues such as vivisection and the treatment of children employed in theatre, as well as against the doctrine of eternal punishment. Much of his verse is poised on the brink of insurrection, threatening to topple us into chaos but vibrating within the safety net of prosody. You have a treat in store in these gathered verses.

NOTES

For complete publication details, see Further Reading.

1. Stuart Dodgson Collingwood, *The Life and Letters of Lewis Carroll* (London: T. Fisher Unwin, 1898), p. 30. Collingwood was the son of Carroll's sister Mary.

2. See Duncan Black et al., *A Mathematical Approach to Proportional Representation: Duncan Black on Lewis Carroll* (Dordrecht: Kluwer, 1996).

3. Carroll's early comic essay "Photography Extraordinary" includes verses that demonstrate how to "develop" literary styles on the model of photographic prints, and his short story "A Photographers Day Out" humorously recounts a disastrous day of photographing.

4. See the Centenary Edition for the complete text of *Alice's Adventures Under Ground*, pp. 249–91, which includes the earlier "mouse's tale" poem and some variants on the Mock Turtle's songs.

5. Falconer Madan explained it thus in the first *Lewis Carroll Handbook* (Oxford: Oxford University Press, 1931): see note to "Memoria Technica".

6. Hatch, p. 241.

7. Lovett, p. 240. The information in this paragraph is all derived from this invaluable book.

8. *A Book of Ballads*: see note 10.

9. Letter to his uncle Hassard Dodgson, 14 May 1872, *Letters*, i, p. 177.

10. *Diaries*, ii, 44; entry for 26 February 1856. Bon Gaultier's *Book of Ballads* was first published in 1845; a new edition with several new ballads appeared in 1849 illustrated by Alfred Crowquill, Dickie Doyle and John Leech. Carroll owned the 1859 edition. Bon Gaultier was the pseudonym; from Rabelais of Theodore Martin and William Edmonstoune Aytoun. Aytoun was also the scourge of the "Spasmodic" school of poets.

11. *A Century of Parody and Imitation*, ed. Walter Jerrold and R. M. Leonard (Oxford: Oxford University Press, 1913), pp. 258–65 and 273.

12. View *The Lewis Carroll Scrapbook* at the Library of Congress, Global Gateway.

13. *Punch*, xxxvi, 29 January 1859, p. 48.

14. A pen addition by Bayne tells us that the poem was written by Arthur Clement Hilton, Cambridge (J. Vere Bayne *Scrapbooks*, volume 2, Christ Church Library). I am grateful to the Christ Church Librarian for permission to consult and quote from these volumes. Hilton, who was a brilliant parodist, edited two numbers of a magazine, *The Light Green*, largely written by himself and a take-off of an Oxford magazine, *The Dark Blue*.

15. Sometimes these further jokes are buried in the form of the poem, as in the discovery that the form of the stanzas in the mouse's tale is that of "a 'tail rhyme' – a rhyming couplet followed by a short unrhymed line" (*Annotated Alice*, p. 36).

16. See note to "She's All My Fancy Painted Him".

Further Reading

Poetry collections by Lewis Carroll (Charles L. Dodgson) and his prose works containing poems

Useful and Instructive Poetry, intro. Derek Hudson (London: George Bles, 1954), composed *c.* 1845

The Rectory Magazine, edited by Lewis Carroll (Printed by C. L. Dodgson, 1850; facsimile reprint, Austin: University of Texas Press, 1975), composed *c.* 1848

The Rectory Umbrella and *Mischmasch*, foreword Florence Milner (London: Cassell, 1932; reprinted Dover Publications: New York, 1971), *Umbrella* composed *c.* 1850–53, *Mischmasch c.* 1855–62

Alice's Adventures in Wonderland (London: Macmillan, 1865)

Phantasmagoria and Other Poems (London: Macmillan, 1869)

Puzzles from Wonderland, in *Aunt Judy's Christmas Volume* (1871)

Through the Looking-Glass, and What Alice found There (London: Macmillan, 1872)

Notes by an Oxford Chiel (Oxford: James Parker, 1874)

The Hunting of the Snark (London: Macmillan, 1876)

Rhyme? And Reason? (London: Macmillan, 1883)

A Tangled Tale (London: Macmillan, 1885)

Alice's Adventures Under Ground, facsimile (London: Macmillan, 1886)

The Nursery 'Alice' (London: Macmillan, 1889)

Sylvie and Bruno (London: Macmillan, 1889)

Sylvie and Bruno Concluded (London: Macmillan, 1893)
Three Sunsets and Other Poems (London: Macmillan, 1898)

Poems printed individually, and not collected in these volumes,
    will be found in this edition in "Other Early Verse" and
    "Poems for Friends"

Journals to which Lewis Carroll (C. L. Dodgson) contributed poems

All the Year Round (1860)
Aunt Judy's Magazine (1870, 1871)
College Rhymes (1862, 1863)
The Comic Times (1855)
Jabberwock (Boston, 1888)
The Monthly Packet (1880–82)
Oxford Critic (1857)
Punch (1867)
Temple Bar (1861)
The Train (1856, 1857)
The Whitby Gazette (1854)

Manuscript collections

Important collections of Lewis Carroll related materials are
held at the following libraries though not all of them include
poems:

Alfred C. Berol Collection, Fales Library, Elmer Holmes Bobst
Library, New York University, New York City (Berol); The
British Library; Christ Church Library, Oxford; Harcourt
Amory Collection and Houghton Library, Harvard University;
Helmut Gernsheim Collection, Harry Ransom Humanities
Research Center, University of Texas at Austin; Library of Con-
gress, Washington DC; The Morris L. Parrish Collection,
Princeton University; New York Public Library; Beinecke
Library, Yale University; and the Dodgson Family Collection
Archive, Surrey History Centre, Guildford.

Reference works

Short citations used in the Introduction and Notes are given in round brackets below.

The Letters of Lewis Carroll, ed. Morton N. Cohen, 2 vols. (New York: Oxford University Press, 1979) (*Letters*)

Lewis Carroll Among His Books: a descriptive catalogue of the private library of Charles L. Dodgson, ed. Charlie Lovett (Jefferson, NC: McFarland, 2005) (Lovett)

The Lewis Carroll Handbook, being a New Version of "A Handbook of the Literature of the Rev. C. L. Dodgson", by Sidney Herbert Williams and Falconer Madan (Oxford, 1931), revised and augmented by Roger Lancelyn Green (1970), now further revised by Denis Crutch (Folkestone, Kent: Dawson, Archon Books, 1979) (*Handbook*)

Lewis Carroll's Diaries: The Private Journals of Charles Lutwidge Dodgson (Lewis Carroll), ed. with notes and annotations by Edward Wakeling, 10 vols. (Luton, Beds; Clifford, Herefordshire: The Lewis Carroll Society, 1993–2007) (*Diaries*)

A Selection from the Letters of Lewis Carroll to His Child-Friends, ed. Evelyn M. Hatch (London: Macmillan, 1933) (Hatch)

Later editions and anthologies

Alice's Adventures in Wonderland and *Through the Looking-Glass, and What Alice Found There*, ed. Hugh Haughton, Centenary Edition (London: Penguin, 1998) (Centenary Edition)

The Annotated Alice, with an introduction and notes by Martin Gardner, Definitive Edition (London: Penguin, 2000) (*Annotated Alice*)

Collected Verse of Lewis Carroll (London: Macmillan, 1932) (*Collected Verse*)

The Complete Works of Lewis Carroll, with an introduction by Alexander Woollcott (London: Nonesuch Press, 1939) (This useful edition is not in fact complete)

The Hunting of the Snark, with an introduction and notes by Martin Gardner (London: Penguin Classics, 1995)

Lewis Carroll Observed: A Collection of Unpublished Photographs, Drawings, Poetry, and New Essays, ed. Edward Guiliano (New York: Clarkson N. Potter, 1976)   (Guiliano)

The Lewis Carroll Picture Book. A Selection from the Unpublished Writings and Drawings of Lewis Carroll, together with reprints from scarce and unacknowledged work, ed. Stuart Dodgson Collingwood (London: T. Fisher Unwin, 1899)   (Collingwood)

Lewis Carroll's Games and Puzzles, compiled and ed. Edward Wakeling (New York: Dover, 1992)

The Magic of Lewis Carroll, ed. John Fisher (Harmondsworth: Penguin, 1975)   (Fisher)

The Mathematical Recreations of Lewis Carroll: "Pillow Problems" and "A Tangled Tale" (New York: Dover, 1958)

The Pamphlets of Lewis Carroll: The Oxford Pamphlets, Leaflets, and Circulars of Charles Lutwidge Dodgson, compiled, with notes and annotations by Edward Wakeling, vol. 1 (Charlottesville: University Press of Virginia for the Lewis Carroll Society of North America, 1993)   (*Pamphlets*)

Rediscovered Lewis Carroll Puzzles, compiled and ed. Edward Wakeling (New York: Dover, 1995)

Under the Quizzing Glass: A Lewis Carroll Miscellany, ed. R. B. Shaberman and Denis Crutch (London: Magpie Press, 1972)

Related works

A Century of Parody and Imitation, ed. Walter Jerrold and R. M. Leonard (Oxford: Oxford University Press, 1913)

The Poets and Poetry of the Century: Humour, Society, Parody and Occasional Verse ed. Alfred H. Miles (London: Hutchinson, 1894)

The Tenth Rasa: An Anthology of Indian Nonsense, ed. Michael Heyman with Sumanyo Satpathy and Anuschka Ravishankar (New Delhi: Penguin Books India, 2007)

Some further suggestions

Morton N. Cohen, *Lewis Carroll: A Biography* (London: Macmillan, 1995)

Stuart Dodgson Collingwood, *The Life and Letters of Lewis Carroll* (London: T. Fisher Unwin, 1898)

Eleanor Cook, *Enigmas and Riddles in Literature* (Cambridge: Cambridge University Press, 2006)

Richard Foulkes, *Lewis Carroll and the Victorian Stage: Theatricals in a Quiet Life* (London: Ashgate, 2005)

Martin Gardner, *The Universe in a Handkerchief: Lewis Carroll's Mathematical Recreations, Games, Puzzles, and Word Plays* (Berlin: Springler-Verlag, 1996) (Gardner, *Universe*)

Karoline Leach, *In the Shadow of the Dreamchild: The Myth and Reality of Lewis Carroll*, 2nd edition (London: Haus, 2009)

Robin Wilson, *Lewis Carroll in Numberland: his fantastical mathematical logical life; an agony in eight fits* (London: Allen Lane, 2008)

Jenny Woolf, *Lewis Carroll: discovering the whimsical, thoughtful and sometimes lonely man who created "Alice in Wonderland"* (London: Haus, 2010)   (Woolf)

Note on the Texts

Carroll paid scant heed to the authority of cold print. He was always revising his poems, tweaking this line or that, sometimes writing in or taking out whole sections, as he did with "Hiawatha's Photographing". He was also quaintly attached to certain poems and had no compunction in publishing them again and again in different collections: so for example, the poem called "The Dream of Fame" appeared first in the magazine *College Rhymes* in 1861 and then, retitled as "Three Sunsets", in *Phantasmagoria* (1869) and with only minor changes as the title poem in *Three Sunsets* (1898). When we reach the late-verse volumes *Rhyme? And Reason?* and *Three Sunsets*, they turn out to contain a very great deal of earlier work. One motive for this republication seems to have been his wish to keep his more serious poems current. This persistent revising and republication means that there can be no single "authoritative" version of the poems. That impossibility may be appropriate to Carroll's unsettled and unsettling creativity though it makes for problems for the editor.

This is not a variorum edition where every nuance and turn of revision is recorded, so the reader may find a well-known poem suddenly turning strange. Where there are large differences between versions I have noted them, and in two cases I have included both versions entire, as with "She's All My Fancy Painted Him". I have turned to Carroll's own collections of his poetry as my main source for those poems that were published during his lifetime, but of course that does not do away with variants, especially as some poems snake through from collection to collection. On the other hand, the juvenilia were not published until the twentieth century.

I have taken the first edition of *Phantasmagoria* (1869) as copy-text for all the poems gathered in that volume, many of which had already been published elsewhere earlier in magazines, often in somewhat different versions. But 1869 is a useful mid-point for his oeuvre, falling as it does between the publication of *Alice's Adventures in Wonderland* (1865) and *Through the Looking-Glass, and What Alice Found There* (1872). More importantly, *Phantasmagoria* gathers together the poems that Carroll valued up to that date, in the version that he then preferred. Some poems published there turn up again, revised, in the late collections *Rhyme? And Reason?* and *Three Sunsets*, as I have indicated in the Notes.

Since the poems come from many sources, mostly printed, house styling has been standardised for the reader's enjoyment. Carroll's own notes for a poem follow it rather than being printed as footnotes (some are very long, e.g. "The Elections to The Hebdomadal Council" – where the note numbers were in square brackets and preceded final punctuation); spelling is regularised (grey/gray, recognise/recognize); an extra space before some punctuation is omitted; quotation marks are doubles (with singles inside as needed); dashes are spaced N-dashes, with longer dashes for emphasis; Carroll's hyperapostrophes in contractions are omitted (e.g. wo'n't, ca'n't).

In his later years many of the fresh springs for his verse were friendship and the entertainment of particular people. So it is in letters or on the flyleaves of his books that most of the new poems appear, outside *Sylvie and Bruno* and *Sylvie and Bruno Concluded*. Because many of the poems were written to an occasion or a person they pop up like mushrooms, and for that reason also this is a Collected Poems, not a Complete Poems. There is now a wonderful ten-volume edition of the *Diaries*, edited with extensive notes by Edward Wakeling, but four volumes of Carroll's early diaries are simply not extant. The two-volume edition of the *Letters*, edited by Morton Cohen in 1979, does not attempt completeness though it is invaluable for what it does contain. Evelyn Hatch's 1933 selection from among the letters that Carroll wrote to his child-friends includes a number of further poems and also has the value that she had been one of his child-friends and can contextualize the letters in a particular way. Further collections such as that of Carroll's nephew Stuart Dodgson Collingwood, *The Lewis Carroll Picture Book* (1899), yield more verses and there are occasional verses scattered in libraries and private collections. This is particularly true of the small gifts of acrostics and riddles. This edition is drawn entirely from printed sources, as listed in the Further Reading. All illustrations are from my collection. I am grateful to the Trustees of the Estate of C. L. Dodgson and to A. P. Watt as their agent, for their permission to use for this edition all those poems still in copyright.

I must also express my gratitude for the work of all those scholars past and present whose endeavours make an edition such as this possible: above all, the editors of the original and the two subsequent revisions of the invaluable *Lewis Carroll Handbook*, Sidney Herbert Williams, Falconer Madan, Roger Lancelyn Green and Denis Crutch (1931, 1970, 1979); Morton N. Cohen; the work of Martin Gardner in *The Annotated Alice* (Definitive Edition, 2000) and elsewhere; the editor of *Lewis Carroll Among His Books*, Charlie Lovett (2005); and Edward Wakeling, whom I also thank most warmly for his individual advice and information.

I am grateful to the Librarians of Cambridge University Library, the Sterling Library and the Beinecke Library at Yale University, the British Library, Christ Church Library, the Houghton Library of Harvard University, and the Berol Collection at the Fales Library, New York University. The Yale Center for British Art has been a most hospitable and inspiring base for much of the research I have conducted on Lewis Carroll over the past five years and I am particularly grateful to Director Amy Meyers and Associate Director of Research Lisa Ford, as I am to my son Zachary Beer for his comments and support.

The edition is dedicated to our grandchildren, Sam, Ella and Sophia, with love.

Frontispiece to *The Rectory Umbrella*

Poems from Family Magazines

Useful and Instructive Poetry (1845)

My Fairy

I have a fairy by my side
    Which says I must not sleep,
When once in pain I loudly cried
    It said "You must not weep."

If, full of mirth, I smile and grin,
    It says "You must not laugh,"
When once I wished to drink some gin,
    It said "You must not quaff."

When once a meal I wished to taste
    It said "You must not bite,"   10
When to the wars I went in haste,
    It said "You must not fight."

"What *may* I do?" At length I cried,
    Tired of the painful task,
The fairy quietly replied,
    And said "You must not ask."

    Moral: "You mustn't."

The Headstrong Man

There was a man who stood on high,
  Upon a lofty wall;
And every one who passed him by,
  Called out "I fear you'll fall."

Naught heeded he of their advice,
  He was a headstrong youth,
He stood as if fixed in a vice,
  Or like a nail forsooth.

While thus he stood a wind began,
  To blow both long and loud,
And soon it blew this headstrong man,
  Right down among the crowd.

Full many a head was broken then,
  Full many an arm was cracked,
Much they abused headstrong men,
  Who sense and wisdom lacked.

For this mishap he cared naught,
  As we shall shortly see,
For the next day, as if in sport,
  He mounted in a tree.

The tree was withered, old, and grey,
  And propped up with a stake,
And all who passed him by did say,
  "That branch you're on will break."

Naught heeded he of their advice,
  He was a headstrong youth,
He stood as fixed in a vice,
  Or like a nail forsooth.

While thus he stood the branch began
    To break, where he did stand, 30
And soon it dropped this headstrong man
    Into a cart of sand.

The sandman vainly sought for him,
    For half an hour or more,
At last he found him in a trim
    He ne'er was in before.

For sand his face did nearly hide,
    He was a mass of sand:
Loud laughed the sandman when he spied
    The branch where he did stand. 40

"Why, what a foolish man thou art,
    To stand in such a place!"
Then took some sand from out his cart,
    And flung it in his face.

All wrathful then was sandy-coat,
    Wrath filled his sandy eye,
He raised his sandy hand and smote,
    The sandman lustily.

Full soon upon the ground he lay,
    Urged by the sandman's fist, 50
These words were all that he could say,
    For those to hear who list.

Moral:

'If headstrong men *will* stand like me,
    Nor yield to good advice,
All that they can expect will be,
    To get sand in their eyes."

Punctuality

Man naturally loves delay,
  And to procrastinate;
Business put off from day to day,
  Is always done too late.

Let every hour be in its place
  Firm fixed, nor loosely shift,
And well enjoy the vacant space,
  As though a birthday gift.

And when the hour arrives, be *there*,
10 Where'er that "there" may be;
Uncleanly hands or ruffled hair
  Let no one ever see.

If dinner at "half past" be placed
  At "half past" then be dressed,
If at a "quarter past" make haste
  To be down with the rest.

Better to be before your time,
  Than e'er to be behind;
To ope the door while strikes the chime,
20 *That* shews a punctual mind.

Moral:

"Let punctuality and care
  Seize every flitting hour,
So shalt thou cull a floweret fair,
  E'en from a fading flower."

Charity

While once in haste I crossed the street,
  A little girl I saw,
Deep in the mud she'd placed her feet,
  And gazed on me with awe.

"Dear sir," with trembling tone she said,
  "Here have I stood for weeks,
And never had a piece of bread,"
  Her tears bedewed her cheeks.

"Poor child!" said I, "do you stand here,
  And quickly will I buy,   10
Some wholesome bread and strengthening beer,
  And fetch it speedily."

Off ran I to the baker's shop,
  As hard as I could pelt,
Fearing 'twas late, I made a stop,
  And in my pocket felt.

In my left pocket did I seek,
  To see how time went on,
Then grief and tears bedewed *my* cheek,
  For, oh! My watch was gone!   20

  Moral: "Keep your wits about you."

Melodies

I

There was an old farmer of Readall,
Who made holes in his face with a needle,
They went *far* deeper in,
Than to pierce through the skin,
And yet strange to say he was made beadle.

II

There was an eccentric old draper,
Who wore a hat made of brown paper,
It went up to a point,
Yet it looked out of joint,
The cause of which *he* said was "vapour."

III

There was once a young man of Oporta
Who daily got shorter and shorter,
The reason he said
Was the hod on his head,
Which was filled with the *heaviest* mortar.

His sister named Lucy O'Finner,
Grew constantly thinner and thinner,
The reason was plain,
She slept out in the rain,
And was never allowed any dinner.

A Tale of a Tail

An aged gardener gooseberries picked,
From off a gooseberry tree;
The thorns they oft his fingers pricked
Yet never a word said he.

A dog sat by him with a tail,
      Oh! *such* a tail! I ween,
That never such in hill or dale,
      Hath hitherto been seen.

It was a tail of desperate length,
      A tail of grizzly fur,   10
A tail of muscle, bone and strength
      Unmeet for such a cur.

Yet of this tail the dog seemed proud
      And ever and anon,
He raised his head, and barked so loud,
That tho' the man seemed *something* cowed,
      Yet still his work went on.

At length in lashing out its tail,
      It twisted it so tight,
Around his legs, 'twas no avail,   20
      To pull with all its might.

The gardener scarce could make a guess,
      What round his legs had got,
Yet he worked on in weariness,
      Although his wrath was hot.

"Why, what's the matter?" he did say,
      "I can't keep on my feet,
Yet not a glass I've had this day
      Save one, of brandy neat.

"Two quarts of ale, and one good sup,   30
      Of whiskey sweet and strong,
And yet I scarce can now stand up,
      I fear that something's wrong."

His work reluctantly he stopped,
    The cause of this to view,
Then quickly seized an axe and chopped,
    The guilty tail in two.

When this was done, with mirth he bowed,
    Till he was black and blue,
40   The dog it barked both long and loud,
    And with good reason too.

Moral: "Don't get drunk."

A quotation from Shakespeare with slight improvements

Warwick.   Wil't please your grace to go along with us?
Prince.   No I will sit and watch here by the king.
                  [Exeunt all but Prince Harry.]
  "Why doth the crown lie there upon his pillow
  Being so troublesome a bedfellow?
  Oh polished perturbation! golden care!
  That keepst the ports of slumber open wide
  To many a watchful night – sleep with it now!
  Yet not so sound, and half so deeply sweet,
  As he whose brow with homely biggin bound
  Snores out the watch of night."

10 King.   Harry I know not
    The meaning of the word you just have used.
Prince. What word, my liege?

King.   The word I mean is "biggin."
Prince. It means a kind of woollen nightcap, sir,
    With which the peasantry are wont to bind
    Their wearied heads, ere that they take their rest.

King. Thanks for your explanation, pray proceed.
Prince. "Snores out the watch of night. Oh majesty!
  When thou dost pinch thy bearer thou dost sit
  Like a rich armour, worn in heat of day
  That scalds with safety."
King.   Scalding ne'er is safe   20
  For it produces heat and feverishness
  And blisters on the parched and troubled skin.
Prince. Pray interrupt not. "By his gates of breath
  There lies a downy feather which stirs not."
King. I knew not that there was one, brush it off.
Prince. "Did he suspire that light and weightless down
  Perforce must move."
King.   And it *hath* moved already.
Prince. It hath *not* moved. "My gracious lord! my father!
  This sleep is sound indeed, this is a sleep
  That from this golden rigol hath divorced   30
  So many English –"
King.   What meaneth rigol, Harry?
Prince. My liege, I know not, save that it doth enter
  Most apt into the metre.
King.   True, it doth.
  But wherefore use a word which hath no meaning?
Prince. My lord, the word is said, for it hath passed
  My lips, and all the powers upon this earth
  Can not unsay it.
King.   You are right, proceed.
Prince. "So many English kings; thy due from me
  Is tears and heavy sorrows of the blood
  Which nature, love, and filial tenderness,   40
  Shall, oh dear father, pay thee plenteously:
  My due from thee is this imperial crown
  Which as –"

King.   'Tis *not* your due, sir! I deny it!
Prince. It *is*, my liege! How dare you contradict me?
    Moreover how can you, a sleeper, know
    That which another doth soliloquise?
King. Your rhetoric is vain, for it is true:
    Therefore no arguments can prove it false.
Prince. Yet sure it is not possible, my liege!
50 King. Upon its possibility I dwelt not
    I merely said 'twas true.

Prince.   But yet, my liege,
    What is not possible can never happen,
    Therefore this cannot.

King.   Which do you deny
    That I have heard you or that I'm asleep?
Prince. That you're asleep, my liege.

King.   Go on, go on,
    I see you are not fit to reason with.
Prince. "Which as immediate from thy place and blood
    Derives itself to me. Lo, here it sits, –
    Which heaven itself shall guard, and put the world's
        whole strength
60 Into which giant arm, it shall not force
    This lineal honour from me: this from thee
    Will I to mine leave as 'tis left to me."

Brother and Sister

        "Sister, sister, go to bed,
        Go and rest your weary head,"
        Thus the prudent brother said.

        "Do you want a battered hide
        Or scratches to your face applied?"
        Thus the sister calm replied.

"Sister! Do not rouse my wrath,
I'd make you into mutton broth
As easily as kill a moth."

The sister raised her beaming eye,   10
And looked on him indignantly,
And sternly answered "Only try!"

Off to the cook he quickly ran,
"Dear cook, pray lend a frying pan
To me, as quickly as you can."

"And wherefore should I give it to you?"
"The reason, cook, is plain to view,
I wish to make an Irish stew."

"What meat is in that stew to go?"
"My sister'll be the contents." "Oh!"   20
"Will you lend the pan, Cook?" "NO!"

   Moral: "Never stew your sister."

The Trial of a Traitor

There *was* a strange being in*to* the North,
       And, oh, he was strange to see;
His chin was as broad as the Firth of Forth,
       And as deep as the Zuyderzee.

Ne did his chin conceal his knees,
       Ne did it show his waist;
Eke was it like a peck of peas,
       In human skin encased.

The neighbours oft had viewed his chin
          With admiration mute;
"Soothly," said they, "we will begin,
          This man to prosecute.

"Who knows but that this chin may hide
          A sword or pike or gun?
Perhaps the Government," they cried,
          "He'll murder one by one!"

His warrant duly was enrolled,
          "His body ye shall seize,
And in safe custody shall hold,
          Till further notices."

The constables, a grimly pair,
          Marched on their mission fell,
They took their victim by the hair,
          And dragged him to his cell.

The lifelong night upon the stones
          In fetters was he layn,
Whilom his sighs and eke his moans,
          Betoken grief and pain.

The morrow morn the magistrate
          Granted an interview.
His hair was short, though *very* straight,
          To*ward* the skies it grew.

The magistrate he raised his hand,
          Ne from his seat he stirred,
"A*side*," said he, "I pr'y thee stand,
          A*non* thou shalt be heard."

"*Soothly*," said he, "and that will I
    For *cer*tes am I weard."
He sunk into a chair hard by,
    And rubbed his frizzled beard.   40

The evidence was fairly tried,
    The jury left the dock,
Upon their verdict to decide:
    The key turned in the lock.

"Not *guilty*." The j*udge* forward bent,
    His hair of eighty frosts,
"You see the prisoner's innocent,
    So you must pay the costs."

      Moral: "Pay the costs."

The Juvenile Jenkins

The juvenile Jenkins was jumping with joy,
As he sported him over the sandy lea;
In his small fat hand there was many a toy
And many a cake in his mouth had he.

But the juvenile Jenkins he heard a voice
Which made him with horror thrill through
    and through,
"Come into the house, don't make any noise,
For I have got a parcel for you!"

The juvenile Jenkins he entered the door,
And, lo, on the table the parcel lay,   10
He wiped his feet on the mat on the floor,
While his mother reluctantly did say,

"Perhaps it may be a sock or a mitten:"
He covered her face with his kisses soft,
As he read the directions upon it written,
"The juvenile Jenkins."

   Moral: "A present from Croft."

Facts

Were I to take an iron gun,
And fire it off towards the sun;
I grant 'twould reach its mark at last,
But not till many years had passed.

But should that bullet change its force,
And to the planets take its course;
'Twould *never* reach the *nearest* star,
Because it is so *very* far.

The Angler's Adventure

As I was ling'ring by the river's stream
Striving to lure the shoals of glitt'ring fish
With hook and line, methought I had a dream,
That what I caught was placed upon a dish.

No tail it had, it could not be a beast,
No wings, it could by no means be a bird.
Its flesh, when tasted, proved a luscious feast,
And yet, methought, its name I'd never heard.

Speckles it had of most enchanting hue,
An unknown foreign creature it appeared;
It might be anything, perhaps a Jew,
I almost wondered it had not a beard.

While thus I slept and dreamed, I felt a twitch
Which almost pulled my fishing rod away,
I started to my feet. Oh! what a rich
Vision of splendour in the water lay!

The creature of my dreams! most wonderful,
Struggling most violently on the hook,
I landed it with one most desperate pull,
Ere that I ventured on its form to look.   20

In every item it did correspond
Exactly with what I in sleep had seen,
It seemed in fact almost to go beyond
The former in the grandeur of its mien.

I scarce could fancy that there did exist
A creature which in beauty so surpassed.
I pondered o'er each fish and bird and beast,
And puzzled out its name, I thought, at last.

By thinking over Buffon's history,
And Bewick's Birds, and Isaak Walton's book,   30
I seemed to penetrate the mystery,
The name of that which hung upon my hook.

Remembering Isaak Walton's own instructions
And other anglers' who have gone before us,
By algebra, and eke the help of fluxions,
I made it out, it was a Plesiosaurus!

"Is it not so?" I said unto my maid,
She wrung her hands as through the room she strode,
"Take it away! Oh master mine," she said,
"It is, it is, it is, it is a toad! ! ! ! ! ! ! !"   40

Moral: "Don't dream."

A Fable

The Khalif Emir sat upon his throne,
He ravaged all the land till he was left alone.
The Brahmin Mufti came his throne before,
He told a tale all full of learned lore;
"An ancient owl he sat upon a tree,
A younger owl, and he would married be,
He asked him for a boon and dowry fair,
Since he to all his property was heir.
He said, 'My son, I have it not to give
But if one year our khalif he should live
I'll give you, dearest duck, as sure as fate
One hundred farms all waste and desolate.'"
He ceased his tale: he gazed upon his face,
He saw his tears come trickling down apace,
He thought upon it for an hour or more,
He did what he had never done before,
He changed his conduct, he the people bless'd
          (No more he made them weep)
And the land was steeped in happiness
          (Full eighteen inches deep.)

Moral: "Change your conduct."

Rules and Regulations

A short direction
To avoid dejection:
By variations
In occupations,
And prolongation
Of relaxation,
And combinations
Of recreations,
And disputations
On the state of the nation

In adaptation
To your station,
By invitations
To friends and relations,
By evitation
Of amputation,
By permutation
In conversation,
And deep reflection
You'll avoid dejection.   20

Learn well your grammar,
And never stammer,
Write well and neatly,
And sing most sweetly,
Be enterprising,
Love early rising,
Go walks of six miles,
Have ready quick smiles.
With lightsome laughter,
Soft flowing after.   30
Drink tea not coffee;
Never eat toffy.
Eat bread with butter.
Once more, don't stutter.
Don't waste your money,
Abstain from honey.
Shut doors behind you,
(Don't slam them, mind you.)
Drink beer, not porter.
Don't enter the water,   40
Till to swim you are able.
Sit close to the table.
Take care of a candle.
Shut a door by the handle,
Don't push with your shoulder
Until you are older.
Lose not a button.

Refuse cold mutton,
Starve your canaries,
Believe in fairies.
If you are able,
Don't have a stable
With any mangers.
Be rude to strangers.

Moral: "Behave."

Clara

Solemnly sighing,
Like one a-dying,
The countess Clara on her pillow lay:
Along the pillow white,
Through the drear, drear night
Her golden ringlets thickly cluster,
"Woe's me, woe's me!"
Thus did she sadly say,
"My punishment is just; what can be juster?
Yet am I wretched and in misery.
Why hath he left me here alone?
Why doth he thus delay his coming?
I hear no sound but the fitful drone,
Of the beetle idly humming.
I live in woe and hopeless love,
And gaze on the lovely moon above.
The yellow moon, the yellow moon!
She looketh down aloft,
And through the dark and murky night
She sends her whispers soft.

With rays of light through the murky night
She makes the dark as noon,
Oh! would I were a screech owl now,
To woo the yellow moon!

*

"Through distant lands of pleasantness
        A region of despair,
I wander on in weariness
        And madly tear my hair.
Is it not so? Do not I hear his voice
Ah me! My heart, rejoice!   30
Woe! woe! woe! woe!
My brain it reels, my heart is all on fire,
As curls the smoke from yonder village spire!"
        Alas, oh! no!
Sudden she hears a thundering charger's stamp
She hears a horseman tramp
She hears a vacant tone
Still wild and wilder grown
"Ha! ha! ha! ha!
Some beer there, ho!   40
Who said so? hey?
Answer you baseborn churl!
One, two, three, four,
I took you for a door,
But still you are an earl!
Stay!
Fetch me the bottle, 'tis not empty yet!
What? Will you fret?
I didn't do it, no!
I'll bet you two to three I win –   50
What's that?
Fish up that fish without a fin –
Fetch me my walking stick and hat –
Who trod upon the collar of my coat?
I do not care a groat.
Fill, fill the cup –
Let's have a sup!
Have not I rid the livelong night?
Dear me! I cannot stand upright!"
At the sound of his voice, and at his tone,   60
The Lady Clara gave a moan,
Thus said she, "Oh!

Oh! what a go!
What did he say? I did not understand.
The gaiety, the sadness of the land
Through bounding binnocks ever flows
Like the red rose!
The smoke it curls, the chimney topples near!
The stars all quake for fear!
70   Ah me! I make my troublous moan,
But he is wild and wilder grown,
       His wrath is hot,
       Oh, is it not?

"I shriek with agony's attack,
       I scream with sudden pain,
I would I were a maniac!
       I would I were insane!"

Through the dim darkness of the night,
She saw a vision bright,
80   An aged, hoary monk,
Thus he the silence broke,
And thus he spoke,
Extending forth his shrivelled hand,
It seemed a mountain, dimly grand,
That did before the Lady stand.
"Weep not for him, Lady fair!
Tear not off thy golden hair!
Do not scream, and do not faint,
Utter not thy loud complaint,
90   He's only swallowed too much beer,
       He'll not come to any harm,
Don't waste time in useless fear,
       And indulge not in alarm!
Go down and let thy guilty husband in."
       Thus spake the monk,
"He's only been a drinking too much gin,
       And got dead drunk!"

       Moral: "Woo the yellow moon."

A Visitor

Well, *if* you must know all the facts, I was merely reading a
    pamphlet
When what should I hear at the door but a knock as soft as a
    Zephyr.
I listened and heard it again, so, as loud as I possibly *could*
    call,
I shouted, "Don't stand waiting there, come in, let me know
    who you are, sir!"
Mild he entered the room, with his hat in his hand and his
    gloves off,
And a meek gentle bow he performed, while my anger was
    rapidly rising,
"Who *are* you?" I angrily cried, and with hand on his heart
    as he bowed low,
In the gentlest of terms he replied, "Your servant, Sir
    Pokurranshuvvle."
Didn't I just ring the bell, "here, Tom, Dick, George, Andrew!"
    I bawled out,
   "Come here! Show this stranger the door!" 10
   My summons they heard and they did it:
   Soon to the door was he guided; once more he
   Turned to me and bowed low,
And so, with his hand on his heart, with all possible meekness
    departed.

The Rectory Magazine
(c. 1848)

Tears

For more than sixty years,
    Less than a hunderd,
I lived in sighs and tears
    And often wondered,

If I should ever be
    An indiwiddle,
Brim-full of jollity,
    Playing a fiddle.

I played a broken fife,
    And sung in a dull key.
Thus I remained for life
    Wretched and sulky.

As It Fell Upon a Day

As I was sitting on the hearth
    (And o! but a hog is fat!)
A man came hurrying up the path,
    (And what care I for that?)

When he came the house unto,
His breath both quick and short he drew.

When he came before the door,
His face grew paler than before.

When he turned the handle round,
The man fell fainting to the ground.   10

When he crossed the lofty hall,
Once and again I heard him fall.

When he came up the turret-stair,
He shrieked and tore his raven hair.

When he came my chamber in,
    (And o! but a hog is fat!)
I ran him through with a golden pin,
    (And what care I for that?)

J.V.

Terrors

See the planets as they rise,
    Each upon his starless way,
Look on us with angry eyes,
    Do they not appear to say,

"Stupid fellow! Hold your tongue!
    Seek not thus to goad us on!
You in fact are much too young,
    To offer your opinion!

"Seest thou not the mountains swell?
    Seest thou not the trees draw near?"   10
Ah me! I hear an angry bell!
    Ah me! I see a waving spear!

Is not that an angry snake?
    Lo! he twists his writhing tail!
Hear the hisses he doth make!
    See his yellow coat of mail.

Distant howls still louder grown,
    Angry mutterings sounding near,
All proclaim with solemn tone,
20   Something dreadful coming here!

Lo! it comes, a vision grim!
    Puffing forth black coils of smoke!
While amid these terrors dim
    I listened, thus the monster spoke,

"Clear the line there! Clear the rails!
    Stop the engine! hold there! steady!
Stoker! hand me up those pails!
    Euston station! tickets ready!

"Tickets ready! tickets! tick –"
30   Thus it spoke, and thus I acted;
Left these scenes of terrors quick,
    And rushed home like one distracted.

B.B.

Woes

With rapid start,
And forward dart,
As when it left the cannon,
Along the ground,
With swift rebound,
The cannon-ball it ran on.

Through hill and dale,
Through many a vale,
Through country, town, and village:
    Now onward borne,   10
    Through fields of corn,
Rich recompense for tillage.

Still hop, hop, hop,
No pause nor stop,
O'er precipice and mountain,
    Through briar and brake,
    Through pool and lake,
By stream and sparkling fountain.

Across the plain,
Along the main,   20
Of ocean loudly roaring,
    Now here, now there
    Now in the air
Like swallow lightly soaring.

And still hop, hop,
No pause nor stop,
The cannon-ball it ran on,
    With swift rebound,
    Along the ground,
As when it left the cannon.   30

Along the ground,
Through hill and mound
It passed, no pause nor warning,
    When, see! oh see!
    Beneath a tree,
A lion grimly yawning!

Deep yawning, grim,
Of massive limb,
And jaws with blood be-spattered:
While all around,
Upon the ground,
White skulls and bones were scattered!

With rapid bound,
Along the ground,
The cannon-ball did fly on,
No pause, nor stop,
Till it entered, pop!
The deep throat of the lion.

Two chokes, one howl,
A stifled growl,
It died without a struggle:
And the only sound
That was heard around
Was its last expiring guggle.

B.B.

Yang-ki-ling

His highness Yang-ki-ling,
Great China's mighty king,
Upon his throne was sitting,
Around him courtiers all,
Lay prostrate in the hall,
In attitude most fitting.

"Approach, Feefifofum!
Great western traveller, come!
Of science learned lover!
Among my cooks not one,"
Thus spake the crowned one,
"Can a new dish discover!

"Of bird-nest soup I'm tired,
A dish, though much admired
Which yet well bears omission:
Baked puppies and stewed snails,
Like oft-related tales,
Disgust on repetition!"

He spoke: "Sire", Fum replied,
"I've travelled far and wide,"   20
His robe with terror crumpling,
"But in all the world combined
No better dish could find,
Than an English apple-dumpling!"

F.X.

Misunderstandings

If such a thing had been my thought,
        I should have told you so before,
But as I didn't, then you ought
        To ask for such a thing no more,
For to teach one who has been taught
        Is always thought an awful bore.

Now to commence my argument,
        I shall premise an observation,
On which the greatest kings have leant
        When striving to subdue a nation,   10
And e'en the wretch who pays no rent
        By it can solve a hard equation.

Its truth is such, the force of reason,
        Can not avail to shake its power,
Yet e'en the sun in summer season
        Doth not dispel so mild a shower

As this, and he who sees it, sees on
  Beyond it to a sunny bower –
No more, when ignorance is treason
20 Let wisdom's brows be cold and sour.

 Q.G.

Screams

Grim was the scowl of his face that day,
  As he led me by the wrist:
Ever and anon he paused on the way,
  And beat me with his fist.

Dread was the sneer of his evil leer,
  Dread was the glance of his eye,
My heart within me shrunk for fear,
  And my parched mouth was dry.

With massive club he beat me down,
10 He kicked me as I lay,
And cried, "get up you lazy clown,
  Don't keep me here all day!"

A rascal by me chanced to rove,
  I would I could have shot him!
He asked another, "Who's that cove?
  And why's the Peeler got him?"

His friend replied, as on they went,
  "He's rather gone in liquor,
He prigged the shiners off a gent,
20 And neatly nabbed his ticker."

 B.B.

"Peeler".. Policeman .. "shiners" .. money .. "ticker" .. watch ..

Thrillings

Uncertain was his hazy pace,
    His blood shot eye was dim:
I gazed in wonder on his face,
    In wonder gazed on him.

All haggard was his cold-pale cheek,
    All haggard was his brow:
Me thinks again I hear him speak,
    Me thinks I hear him now.

As he paced across his lonely room
    With tightly clenched fist,   10
As his glaring eyes did hideous loom,
    Through the blackly gathering mist.

As with desperate hand he struck his brow,
    And stamped upon the floor,
Me thinks I hear his accents now,
    In solemn tone once more,

"I gave my pen a careless flirt,"
    He said midst deep-drawn sighs,
"And the scratchy thing the ink did spirt,
    Right into both my eyes."   20

B.B.

The Rectory Umbrella
(c. 1850–53)

Ye Fatalle Cheyse

Ytte wes a mirke an dreiry cave,
    Weet scroggis[1] owr ytte creepe,
Gurgles withyn yᵉ flowan wave
    Throw channel braid an deip.

Never withyn that dreir recesse
    Wes sene yᵉ lyghte of daye,
Quhat bode azont[2] yt's mirkinesse[3]
    Nane kend an nane mote saye.

Yᵉ monarche rade owr brake an brae,
    'An drave yᵉ yellynge packe,
Hiz meany[4] au', richte cadgily,[5]
    Are wendynge[6] yn hiz tracke.

Wi' eager iye, wi' yalpe an crye
    Yᵉ hondes yode[7] down yᵉ rocks:
Ahead of au' their companye
    Renneth yᵉ panky[8] foxe.

Yᵉ foxe hes sought that cave of awe,
    Forewearied[9] wi' hiz rin,
Quha nou ys he sae bauld an braw[10]
    To dare to enter yn?

Wi' eager bounde hes ilka honde
      Gane till that cavern dreir,
Fou[11] many a yowl[12] ys[13] hearde around,
      Fou[11] many a screech of feir.

Like ane wi' thirstie appetite
      Quha swalloweth orange pulp,
Wes hearde a huggle an a bite,
      A swallow an a gulp.

Y[e] kynge hes lap frae aff hiz steid,
      Outbrayde[14] hiz trenchant brande;   30
"Quha on my packe of hondes doth feed,
      Maun deye benead thilke hande."

Sae sed, sae dune: y[e] stonderes[15] hearde
      Fou many a mickle[16] stroke,
Sowns[17] lyke y[e] flappynge of a birde,
      A struggle an a choke.

Owte of y[e] cave scarce fette[18] they ytte,
      Wi pow[19] an push an hau'[20] –
Whereof Y've drawne a little byte,
      Bot durst nat draw ytte au.[21]   40

1 Bushes. 2 Beyond. 3 Darkness. 4 Company. 5 Merrily. 6 Going, journeying. 7 Went. 8 Cunning. 9 Much wearied. 10 Brave. 11 Full. 12 Howl. 13 Is. 14 Drawn. 15 Bystanders. 16 Heavy. 17 Sounds. 18 Fetch. 19 Pull. 20 Haul. 21 All.

The Storm

An old man sat anent a clough,[1]
      A grizzed[2] old man an' weird,[3]
Deep were the wrinks in his aged brow,
      An' hoar his snowy beard,
All tremmed[4] before his glance, I trow,[5]
      Sae savagely he leared.

The rain cloud cam frae out the west,
    An' spread athwart[6] the sky,
The crow has cowered[7] in her nest,
    She kens the storm is nigh,
He folds his arms across his breast,
Thunder an' lightning do your best!
    "I will not flinch nor fly!"

Draggles[8] with wet the tall oak tree,
    Beneath the dashing rain,
The old man sat, an' gloomily
    He gazed athwart the plain,
Down on the wild and heaving sea,
Where heavily an' toilsomely
    Yon vessel ploughs the main.

Above the thunder cloud frowns black,
    The dark waves howl below,
Scarce can she hold along her track,
    Fast rocking to an' fro,
And oft the billow drives her back,
And oft her straining timbers crack,
    Yet onward she doth go.

The old man gazed without a wink,
    An' with a deadly[9] grin:
"I laid a wager she would sink,
    Strong hopes had I to win;
'Twas ten to one, but now I think,
    That Bob will sack the tin."[10]
Then from the precipice's brink
    He plunged headforemost in.[11]

1 Probably a bank. 2 Grizzled. 3 Wizard-like. 4 Trembled. 5 = I wot, I ween, meaning nearly the same as "I know." 6 Across. 7 Crouched. 8 Hangs heavily. 9 Or, murderous. 10 Pocket the Money. 11 Imitated from the conclusion of Gray's "Bard," only finer.

Lays of Sorrow – Number I

The day was wet, the rain fell souse
    Like jars of strawberry jam,[1] a
Sound was heard in the old hen-house,
    A beating of a hammer.
Of stalwart form, and visage warm,
    Two youths were seen within it,
Splitting up an old tree into perches for their poultry
    At a hundred strokes[2] a minute.

The work is done, the hen has taken
Possession of her nest and eggs,   10
Without a thought of eggs and bacon,[3]
(Or I am very much mistaken:)
    She turns over each shell,
    To be sure that all's well,
    Looks into the straw
    To see there's no flaw,
    Goes once round the house,[4]
    Half afraid of a mouse,
    Then sinks calmly to rest
    On the top of her nest,   20
First doubling up each of her legs.

Time rolled away, and so did every shell,
    "Small by degrees and beautifully less,"
As the sage mother with a powerful spell[5]
    Forced each in turn its contents to "express,"[6]
    But ah! "imperfect is expression,"
    Some poet said, I don't care who,
    If you want to know you must go elsewhere,
    One fact I can tell, if you're willing to hear,
    He never attended a Parliament Session,   30
    For I'm certain that if he had ever been there,

Full quickly would he have changed his ideas,
With the hissings, the hootings, the groans and
    the cheers.
And as to his name it is pretty clear
That it wasn't me and it wasn't you!

And so it fell upon a day,
        (That is, it never rose again,)
A chick was found upon the hay,
Its little life had ebbed away.
40 No longer frolicsome and gay,
No longer could it run or play.
"And must we, chicken, must we part?"
Its master[7] cried with bursting heart,
        And voice of agony and pain.
So one, whose ticket's marked "Return,"[8]

When to the lonely roadside station
He flies in fear and perturbation,
Thinks of his home – the hissing urn –
Then runs with flying hat and hair,
50 And, entering, finds to his despair
        He's missed the very latest train![9]
Too long it were to tell of each conjecture
        Of chicken suicide, and poultry victim,
The deadly frown, the stern and dreary lecture,
        The timid guess, "perhaps some needle pricked him!"
The din of voice, the words both loud and many,
        The sob, the tear, the sigh that none could smother,
Till all agreed: "a shilling to a penny
        It killed itself, and we acquit the mother!"
60   Scarce was the verdict spoken,
        When that still calm was broken,
A childish form hath burst into the throng;
        With tears and looks of sadness,
        That bring no news of gladness,
But tell too surely something hath gone wrong!

"The sight that I have come upon
  The stoutest[10] heart would sicken,
That nasty hen has been and gone
  And killed another chicken!"

1 i.e. the jam without the jars: observe the beauty of this rhyme.

2 At the rate of a stroke and two thirds in a second.

3 Unless the hen was a poacher, which is unlikely.

4 The hen-house.

5 Beak and claw.

6 Press out.

7 Probably one of the two stalwart youths.

8 The system of return tickets is an excellent one. People are conveyed, on particular days, there and back again for one fare.

9 An additional vexation would be that his "Return" ticket would be no use the next day.

10 Perhaps even the "bursting" heart of its master.

Lays of Sorrow – Number 2

Fair stands the ancient[1] Rectory,
  The Rectory of Croft,
The sun shines bright upon it,
  The breezes whisper soft.

From all the house and garden,
  Its inhabitants come forth,
And muster in the road without,
And pace in twos and threes about,
  The children of the North.

Some are waiting in the garden,   10
  Some are waiting at the door,
And some are following behind,
  And some have gone before.

But wherefore all this mustering?
    Wherefore this vast array?
A gallant feat of horsemanship
    Will be performed today.

To eastward and to westward,
    The crowd divides amain,
Two youths are leading on the steed,
    Both tugging at the rein:
And sorely do they labour,
    For the steed[2] is very strong,
And backward moves its stubborn feet,
And backward ever doth retreat,
    And drags its guides along.

And now the knight hath mounted,
    Before the admiring band,
Hath got the stirrups on his feet.
    The bridle in his hand.
Yet, oh! beware, sir horseman!
    And tempt thy fate no more,
For such a steed as thou hast got,
    Was never rid before!

The rabbits[3] bow before thee,
    And cower in the straw;
The chickens[4] are submissive,
    And own thy will for law;
Bullfinches and canary
    Thy bidding do obey;
And e'en the tortoise in its shell
    Doth never say thee nay.

But thy steed will hear no master,
    Thy steed will bear no stick,
And woe to those that beat her,
    And woe to those that kick![5]
For though her rider smite her,

As hard as he can hit,
And strive to turn her from the yard,
She stands in silence, pulling hard   50
    Against the pulling bit.

And now the road to Dalton
    Hath felt their coming tread,
The crowd are speeding on before,
    And all have gone ahead.
Yet often look they backward,
    And cheer him on, and bawl,
For slower still, and still more slow,
That horseman and that charger go,
    And scarce advance at all.   60

And now two roads to choose from
    Are in that rider's sight:
In front the road to Dalton,
    And New Croft upon the right.
"I can't get by!" he bellows,
    "I really am not able!
Though I pull my shoulder out of joint,
    I cannot get him past this point,
For it leads unto his stable!"

Then out spake Ulfrid Longbow,[6]   70
    A valiant youth was he,
"Lo! I will stand on thy right hand,
    And guard the pass for thee."
And out spake fair Flureeza,[7]
    His sister eke was she,
"I will abide on thy other side,
    And turn thy steed for thee."

And now commenced a struggle
    Between that steed and rider,
For all the strength that he hath left   80
    Doth not suffice to guide her.

Though Ulfrid and his sister
        Have kindly stopped the way,
And all the crowd have cried aloud,
        "We can't wait here all day!"

Round turned he, as not deigning
        Their words to understand,
But he slipped the stirrups from his feet,
        The bridle from his hand,
And grasped the mane full lightly,
        And vaulted from his seat,
And gained the road in triumph,
        And stood upon his feet.

All firmly till that moment
        Had Ulfrid Longbow stood,
And faced the foe right valiantly,
        As every warrior should.
But when safe on terra firma
        His brother he did spy,
"What *did* you do that for?" he cried,
Then unconcerned he stepped aside
        And let it canter by.[8]

They gave him bread and butter,[9]
        That was of public right,
As much as four strong rabbits,
        Could munch from morn to night,
For he'd done a deed of daring,
        And faced that savage steed,
And therefore cups of coffee sweet,
And everything that was a treat,
        Were but his right and meed.

And often in the evenings,
        When the fire is blazing bright,

When books bestrew the table
   And moths obscure the light,
When crying children go to bed,
   A struggling, kicking load,
We'll talk of Ulfrid Longbow's deed,
How, in his brother's utmost need,
Back to his aid he flew with speed,   120
And how he faced the fiery steed,
   And kept the New Croft Road.

1 This Rectory has been supposed to have been built in the time of Edward the sixth, but recent discoveries clearly assign its origin to a much earlier period.

A stone has been found in an island formed by the river Tees, on which is inscribed the letter "A," which is justly conjectured to stand for the name of the great king Alfred, in whose reign this house was probably built.

2 The poet entreats pardon for having represented a donkey under this dignified name.

3 With reference to these remarkable animals see "Moans from the Miserable," page 12.

4 A full account of the history and misfortunes of these interesting creatures may be found in the first "Lay of Sorrow" page 36 [Penguin edition, p. 35].

5 It is a singular fact that a donkey makes a point of returning any kicks offered it.

6 This valiant knight besides having a heart of steel and nerves of iron, has been lately in the habit of carrying a brick in his eye.

7 She was sister to both.

8 The reader will probably be at a loss to discover the nature of this triumph, as no object was gained, and the donkey was obviously the victor, on this point, however, we are sorry to say, we can offer no good explanation.

9 Much more acceptable to a true knight than "cornland" which the Roman people were so foolish as to give to their daring champion, Horatius.

The Poet's Farewell

All day he had sat without a hat,
 The comical old feller,
Shading his form from the driving storm
 With the Rectory Umbrella.
When the storm had passed by, and the ground was dry,
 And the sun shone bright on the plain,
He arose from his seat, and he stood on his feet,
 And sang a melting strain:

   All is o'er! the sun is setting,
10   Soon will sound the dinner bell;
   Thou hast saved me from a wetting,
    Here I'll take my last farewell!
   Far dost thou eclipse the Maga-
    zines which came before thy day,
   And thy coming made them stagger,
    Like the stars at morning ray.
   Let me call again their phantoms,
    And their voices long gone by,
   Like the crow of distant bantams,
20   Or the buzzing of a fly.
   First in age, but not in merit,
    Stands the Rectr'y Magazine;
   All its wit thou dost inherit,
    Though the Comet came between.
   Novelty was in its favour,
    And mellifluous its lays,
   All, with eager plaudits, gave a
    Vote of honour in its praise.

   Next in order comes the Comet,
30   Like some vague and feverish dream,
   Gladly, gladly turn I from it,
    To behold thy rising beam!

When I first began to edit,
    In the Rect'ry Magazine,
Each one wrote therein who read it,
    Each one read who wrote therein.
When the Comet next I started,
    They grew lazy as a drone:
Gradually all departed,
    Leaving me to write alone.   40
But in thee – let future ages
    Mark the fact which I record,
No one helped me in *thy* pages,
    Even with a single word!

But the wine has left the cellar,
    And I hear the dinner bell,
So fare thee well, my old Umbrella,
    Dear Umbrella, fare thee well!

Mischmasch
(c. 1855–62)

The Two Brothers

There were two brothers at Twyford school,
    And when they had left the place,
It was, "Will ye learn Greek and Latin?
    Or will ye run me a race?
Or will ye go up to yonder bridge,
    And there we will angle for dace?"

"I'm too stupid for Greek and for Latin,
    I'm too lazy by half for a race,
So I'll even go up to yonder bridge,
10   And there we will angle for dace."

He has fitted together two joints of his rod,
    And to them he has added another,
And then a great hook he took from his book,
    And ran it right into his brother.

Oh much is the noise that is made among boys
    When playfully pelting a pig,
But a far greater pother was made by his brother
    When flung from the top of the brigg.

The fish hurried up by the dozens,
20   All ready and eager to bite,
For the lad that he flung was so tender and young,
    It quite gave them an appetite.

Said he, "Thus shall he wallop about
      And the fish take him quite at their ease,
For me to annoy it was ever his joy,
      Now I'll teach him the meaning of 'Tees'!"

The wind to his ear brought a voice,
      "My brother, you didn't had ought ter!
And what have I done that you think it such fun
      To indulge in the pleasure of slaughter?   30

"A good nibble or bite is my chiefest delight,
      When I'm merely expected to *see*,
But a bite from a fish is not quite what I wish,
      When I get it performed upon *me*;
And just now here's a swarm of dace at my arm,
      And a perch has got hold of my knee!

"For water my thirst was not great at the first,
      And of fish I have had quite sufficien–"
"Oh fear not!" he cried, "for whatever betide,
      We are both in the selfsame condition!   40

"I am sure that our state's very nearly alike
      (Not considering the question of slaughter),
For I have my perch on the top of the bridge,
      And you have your perch in the water.

"I stick to my perch and your perch sticks to you,
      We are really extremely alike;
I've a turn-pike up here, and I very much fear
      You may soon have a turn with a pike."

"Oh, grant but one wish! If I'm took by a fish
      (For your bait is your brother, good man!)   50
Pull him up if you like, but I hope you will strike
      As gently as ever you can."

"If the fish be a trout, I'm afraid there's no doubt
    I must strike him like lightning that's greased;
If the fish be a pike, I'll engage not to strike,
    'Till I've waited ten minutes at least."

"But in those ten minutes to desolate Fate
    Your brother a victim may fall!"
"I'll reduce it to five, so *perhaps* you'll survive,
    But the chance is exceedingly small."

"Oh hard is your heart for to act such a part;
    Is it iron, or granite, or steel?"
"Why, I really can't say – it is many a day
    Since my heart was accustomed to feel.

" 'Twas my heart-cherished wish for to slay many fish,
    Each day did my malice grow worse,
For my heart didn't soften with doing it so often,
    But rather, I should say, the reverse."

"Oh would I were back at Twyford school,
    Learning lessons in fear of the birch!"
"Nay, brother!" he cried, "for whatever betide,
    You are better off here with your perch!

"I am sure you'll allow you are happier now,
    With nothing to do but to play;
And this single line here, it is perfectly clear,
    Is much better than thirty a day!

"And as to the rod hanging over your head,
    And apparently ready to fall,
That, you know, was the case, when you lived in
        that place,
    So it need not be reckoned at all.

"Do you see that old trout with a turn-up-nose snout?
    (Just to speak on a pleasanter theme,)
Observe, my dear brother, our love for each other –
    He's the one I like best in the stream.

"To-morrow I mean to invite him to dine
    (We shall all of us think it a treat,)
If the day should be fine, I'll just *drop him a line*,
    And we'll settle what time we're to meet.

"He hasn't been into society yet,
    And his manners are not of the best,   90
So I think it quite fair that it should be *my* care,
    To see that he's properly dressed."

Many words brought the wind of "cruel" and "kind,"
    And that "man suffers more than the brute":
Each several word with patience he heard,
    And answered with wisdom to boot.

"What? prettier swimming in the stream,
    Than lying all snugly and flat?
Do but look at that dish filled with glittering fish,
    Has Nature a picture like that?   100

"What? a higher delight to be drawn from the sight
    Of fish full of life and of glee?
What a noodle you are! 'tis delightfuller far
    To kill them than let them go free!

"I know there are people who prate by the hour
    Of the beauty of earth, sky, and ocean;
Of the birds as they fly, of the fish darting by,
    Rejoicing in Life and in Motion.

"As to any delight to be got from the sight,
110   It is all very well for a flat,
But *I* think it all gammon, for hooking a salmon
        Is better than twenty of that!

"They say that a man of a right-thinking mind
        Will *love* the dumb creatures he sees –
What's the use of his mind, if he's never inclined
        To pull a fish out of the Tees?

"Take my friends and my home – as an outcast I'll roam:
        Take the money I have in the Bank –
It is just what I wish, but deprive me of *fish*,
120   And my life would indeed be a blank!"

Forth from the house his sister came,
        Her brothers for to see,
But when she saw that sight of awe,
        The tear stood in her ee.

"Oh what bait's that upon your hook,
        My brother, tell to me?"
"It is but the fantailed pigeon,
        He would not sing for me."

"Whoe'er would expect a pigeon to sing,
130   A simpleton he must be!
But a pigeon-cote is a different thing
        To the coat that there I see!

"Oh what bait's that upon your hook,
        My brother, tell to me?"
"It is but the black-capped bantam,
        He would not dance for me."

"And a pretty dance you are leading him now!'
        In anger answered she,
"But a bantam's cap is a different thing
        To the cap that there I see!   140

"Oh what bait's that upon your hook
        Dear brother, tell to me?"
"It is my younger brother," he cried,
        "Oh woe and dole is me!

"I's mighty wicked, that I is!
        Or how could such things be?
Farewell, farewell, sweet sister,
        I'm going o'er the sea."

"And when will you come back again,
        My brother, tell to me?"   150
"When chub is good for human food,
        And that will never be!"

She turned herself right round about,
        And her heart brake into three,
Said, "One of the two will be wet through and through,
        And t'other'll be late for his tea!"

Croft. 1853

The Dear Gazelle

THE DEAR GAZELLE
ARRANGED WITH VARIATIONS

espressivo
" I NEVER loved a dear gazelle,"
Nor aught beside that cost me much ;
High prices profit those who sell,
But why should *I* be fond of such ?

p.p   *cres :*
" To glad me with his soft black eyes,"
My infant son, from Tooting School,
Thrashed by his bigger playmate, flies ;
And serve him right, the little fool !
con spirito

A Tempo
" But when he came to know me well,"
He kicked me out, her testy sire ;
And when I stained my hair, that Bell
Might note the change, and thus admire

dim :   *cadenza*   *D.C.*
" And love me, it was sure to die "
A muddy green, or staring blue,
While one might trace, with half an eye,
The still triumphant carrot through.
con dolore

CH: CH: 1855.

She's All My Fancy Painted Him
A Poem

This affecting fragment was found in MS., among the
papers of the well-known author of "Was it You or I?" a
tragedy, and the two popular novels "Sister and Son," and
"The Niece's Legacy, or the Grateful Grandfather."

> She's all my fancy painted him
>   (I make no idle boast);
> If he or you had lost a limb,
>   Which would have suffered most?
>
> He said that you had been to her,
>   And seen me here before;
> But, in another character,
>   She was the same of yore.
>
> There was not one that spoke to us,
>   Of all that thronged the street;
> So he sadly got into a 'bus,
>   And pattered with his feet.
>
> They sent him word I had not gone
>   (We know it to be true);
> If she should push the matter on,
>   What would become of you?
>
> They gave her one, they gave me two,
>   They gave us three or more;
> They all returned from him to you,
>   Though they were mine before.
>
> If I or she should chance to be
>   Involved in this affair,
> He trusts to you to set them free,
>   Exactly as we were.

10

20

It seemed to me that you had been
        (Before she had this fit)
An obstacle, that came between
        Him, and ourselves, and it.

Don't let him know she liked them best,
30   For this must ever be
A secret, kept from all the rest,
        Between yourself and me.

From *"Photography Extraordinary"*

"the milk-and-water School of novels"

"Alas! she would not hear my prayer!
Yet it were rash to tear my hair;
Disfigured, I should be less fair.

She was unwise, I may say blind;
Once she was lovingly inclined;
Some circumstance has changed her mind."

"the matter-of-fact School"

"Well! so my offer was no go!
She might do worse, I told her so;
She was a fool to answer 'No.'

10   However, things are as they stood;
Nor would I have her if I could,
For there are plenty more as good."

"the Spasmodic or German School"

"Firebrands and daggers! hope hath fled!
To atoms dash the doubly dead!
My brain is fire – my heart is lead!

Her soul is flint, and what am I?
Scorch'd by her fierce, relentless eye,
Nothingness is my destiny!"

From *"Wilhelm Von Schmitz", chapters 3 and 4*

[*"What though the world be cross and crooky"*]

What though the world be cross and crooky?
Of Life's fair flowers the fairest bouquet
I plucked, when I chose *thee*, my Sukie!

Say, could'st thou grasp at nothing greater
Than to be wedded to a waiter?
And didst thou deem thy Schmitz a traitor?

Nay! the fond waiter was rejected,
And thou, alone, with flower-bedecked head,
Sitting, didst sing of one expected.

And while the waiter, crazed and silly,   10
Dreamed he had won that priceless lily,
At length he came, thy wished-for Willie.

And then thy music took a new key,
For whether Schmitz be boor or duke, he
Is all in all to faithful Sukie!

["His barque hath perished in the storm"]

His barque hath perished in the storm,
    Whirled by its fiery breath
On sunken rocks, his stalwart form
    Was doomed to watery death.

*["My Sukie! he hath bought, yea,
Muggle's self"]*

My Sukie! he hath bought, yea, Muggle's self,
Convinced at last of deeds unjust and foul,
The licence of a vacant public-house,
Which, with its chattels, site, and tenement,
He hands us over, – we are licensed here,
Even in this document, to sell to all
Snuff, pepper, vinegar, to sell to all
Ale, porter, spirits, but – observe you well –
"*Not* to be drunk upon the premises!"
Oh, Sukie! heed it well! in other places,
Even as thou listest, be intoxicate:
Drink without limit whiles thou art abroad,
But never, never, in thy husband's house!

The Lady of the Ladle

The Youth at Eve had drunk his fill,
Where stands the "Royal" on the Hill,
And long his midday stroll had made,
On the so-called "Marine Parade" –

(Meant, I presume, for seamen brave,
Whose "march is on the mountain wave";
'Twere just the bathing-place for him
Who stays on land till he can swim –)
Yes he had strayed into the town,
And paced each alley up and down,   10
Where still, so narrow grew the way,
The very houses seemed to say,
Nodding to friends across the street,
"One struggle more and we shall meet."
     And he had scaled that awful stair
That soars from earth to upper air,
Where rich and poor alike must climb,
And walk the treadmill for a time –
That morning he had dressed with care,
And put pomatum on his hair;   20
He was, the loungers all agreed,
A very heavy swell indeed:
Men thought him, as he swaggered by,
Some scion of nobility,
And never dreamed, so cold his look,
That he had loved – and loved a Cook.
Upon the beach he stood and sighed
All heedless of the rising tide;
Thus sang he to the listening main,
And soothed his sorrow with the strain: 30

Coronach

"She is gone by the *Hilda*,
     She is lost unto Whitby,
And her name is Matilda,
     Which my heart it was smit by;
Tho' I take the *Goliah*,
     I learn to my sorrow
That 'it won't,' says the crier,
     'Be off till to-morrow.'

"She had called me her 'Neddy',
          (Though there mayn't be much in it,)
And I should have been ready,
          If she'd waited a minute;
I was following behind her
          When, if you recollect, I
Merely ran back to find a
          Gold pin for my neck-tie.

"Rich dresser of suet!
          Prime hand at a sassage!
I have lost thee, I rue it,
          And my fare for the passage!
Perhaps *she* thinks it funny,
          Aboard of the *Hilda*,
But I've lost purse and money,
          And thee, oh, my 'Tilda!"

His pin of gold the youth undid,
And in his waistcoat-pocket hid,
Then gently folded hand in hand,
And dropped asleep upon the sand.

Lays of Mystery, Imagination, and Humour

Number 1

The Palace of Humbug

I dreamt I dwelt in marble halls,
And each damp thing that creeps and crawls
Went wobble-wobble on the walls.

Faint odours of departed cheese,
Blown on the dank, unwholesome breeze,
Awoke the never-ending sneeze.

Strange pictures decked the arras drear,
Strange characters of woe and fear,
The humbugs of the social sphere.

One showed a vain and noisy prig,   10
That shouted empty words and big
At him that nodded in a wig.

And one, a dotard grim and grey,
Who wasteth childhood's happy day
In work more profitless than play.

Whose icy breast no pity warms,
Whose little victims sit in swarms,
And slowly sob on lower forms.

And one, a green thyme-honoured Bank,
Where flowers are growing wild and rank,   20
Like weeds that fringe a poisoned tank.

All birds of evil omen there
Flood with rich Notes the tainted air,
The witless wanderer to snare.

The fatal Notes neglected fall,
No creature heeds the treacherous call,
For all those goodly Strawn Baits Pall.

The wandering phantom broke and fled,
Straightway I saw within my head
A Vision of a ghostly bed,   30

Where lay two worn decrepit men,
The fictions of a lawyer's pen,
Who never more might breathe again.

The servingman of Richard Roe
Wept, inarticulate with woe:
She wept, that waited on John Doe.

"Oh rouse", I urged, "the waning sense
With tales of tangled evidence,
Of suit, demurrer, and defence."

40   "Vain", she replied, "such mockeries:
For morbid fancies, such as these,
No suits can suit, no plea can please."

And bending o'er that man of straw,
She cried in grief and sudden awe,
Not inappropriately, "Law!"

The well-remembered voice he knew,
He smiled, he faintly muttered "Sue!"
(Her very name was legal too.)

The night was fled, the dawn was nigh:
50   A hurricane went raving by,
And swept the Vision from mine eye.

Vanished that dim and ghostly bed,
(The hangings, tape; the tape was red:)
'Tis o'er, and Doe and Roe are dead!

Oh, yet my spirit inly crawls,
What time it shudderingly recalls
That horrid dream of marble halls!

Stanza of Anglo-Saxon Poetry

```
TWAS   BRYLLYG ,  AND  Yᴱ  SLYTHY   TOVES
DID  GYRE  AND  GYMBLE  IN  Yᴱ  WABE :
ALL  MIMSY  WERE  Yᴱ  BOROGOVES ;
AND  Yᴱ  MOME  RATHS  OUTGRABE .
```

This curious fragment reads thus in modern characters:

TWAS BRYLLYG, AND THE SLYTHY TOVES
DID GYRE AND GYMBLE IN THE WABE:
ALL MIMSY WERE THE BOROGOVES;
AND THE MOME RATHS OUTGRABE.

The meanings of the words are as follows :

BRYLLYG (derived from the verb to BRYL or BROIL).
"the time of broiling dinner, i.e. the close of the afternoon."
SLYTHY (compounded of SLIMY and LITHE). "Smooth
and active."
TOVE. A species of Badger. They had smooth white hair,
long hind legs, and short horns like a stag: lived chiefly on
cheese.
GYRE, verb (derived from GYAOUR or GIAOUR, "a
dog"). "To scratch like a dog."
GYMBLE (whence GIMBLET). "To screw out holes in
anything."
WABE (derived from the verb to SWAB or SOAK). "The
side of a hill" (from its being *soaked* by the rain).
MIMSY (whence MIMSERABLE and MISERABLE).
"Unhappy."
BOROGOVE. An extinct kind of Parrot. They had no
wings, beaks turned up, and made their nests under sun-
dials: lived on veal.

MOME (hence SOLEMOME, SOLEMONE, and SOLEMN). "Grave."

RATH. A species of land turtle. Head erect: mouth like a shark: the fore legs curved out so that the animal walked on its knees: smooth green body: lived on swallows and oysters.

OUTGRABE, past tense of the verb to Outgribe. (It is connected with the old verb to GRIKE or SHRIKE, from which are derived "shriek" and "creak.") "Squeaked."

Hence the literal English of the passage is: "It was evening, and the smooth active badgers were scratching and boring holes in the hill-side: all unhappy were the parrots; and the grave turtles squeaked out."

There were probably sun-dials on the top of the hill, and the "borogoves" were afraid that their nests would be undermined. The hill was probably full of the nests of "raths," which ran out, squeaking with fear, on hearing the "toves" scratching outside. This is an obscure, but yet deeply-affecting, relic of ancient Poetry. – Ed. [=LC]

Tommy's Dead

Written Dec. 31, 1857. There is a poem by Sydney Dobell with the same name, and something like this – but not very.

It's the last night of the year, boys,
You may bring out the bread and beer, boys,
We've nought else to do to-night, boys,
This crust is too hard to bite, boys,
Is the donkey all right in the stable, boys?
Set two or three chairs round the table, boys,
We must have some'at to eat afore we go, boys,
Stick another coal on the fire or so, boys,
For the night's very cold,
And I'm very old,

And Tommy's dead.
      Will somebody go and call t'owd wife, boys?
And just, while you're about it, fetch another knife, boys,
Get the loaf and cut me a slice, boys,
And how about the cheese, is it nice, boys?
I asked just now for a slice of bread, boys,
      I say – *did you hear what I said, boys?*
There's no end of crumbs, sweep up the floor, boys,
Mind you don't forget to bar the door, boys,
For the night's very cold, boys,   20
And I'm very old, boys,
And Tommy's dead.
      Come, cheer up your old daddy like men, boys,
Why, I declare it's nigh upon half-past ten, boys!
Bread's not much, I'd rather have had some tripe, boys,
D'ye think there's time for a quiet pipe, boys?
There'd be beer enough, if it hadn't been spilt, boys,
I wish I were snug under my quilt, boys
I does so like having a talk o' nights, boys!
Ah! boys, you're young, *I've* seen a pack o' sights, boys,   30
When you've lived as long as I, you'll know what it is, boys,
Lads like you think it's all to be done in a whiz, boys,
Well, you may carry me upstairs, it's so late, boys,
If it wasn't for the beer, I'm not much weight, boys,
My gout's not so well, so mind how you go, boys,
Some of you'll catch it, if you tread upon my toe, boys,
Gently now, don't trip up on the mat, boys,
There, I told you so, you stupids you, take *that*, boys!
It's good for you, and keeps my hands warm, boys,
I shan't apologise – quite an unnecessary form, boys,   40
For the night's very cold,
And I'm very old,
And Tommy's dead.

Additional Note. – The last three lines of each paragraph, and the second line of the poem, (perhaps the first as well,) are by Sydney Dobell. For the rest the Editor is responsible: he has taken a less melancholy view of the subject than the original writer did, in support of which theory he begs to record his firm conviction that "Tommy" was a cat. Recollections of its death cause a periodical gloom to come over the father's mind, accompanied always by the other two grounds of complaint which appear to have continually weighed upon him, cold and age: this gloom, we find, was only to be dispelled by one of three things, supper, the prospect of bed, and ill-temper.

There is something very instructive in the fact that the boys are never rude enough to interrupt, and probably never attend till he suggests going to bed, when they carry out his wishes with affectionate, almost unseemly, haste.

Ode to Damon
(From Chloe, who Understands His Meaning.)

Oh, do not forget the day when we met
      At the Lowther Arcade in the City:
When you *said* I was plain and excessively vain,
      But I knew that you *meant* I was pretty.

Oh forget not the hour when I purchased the flour
      (For the dumplings, you know) and the suet;
Whilst the apples I told my dear Damon to hold,
      (Just to see if you knew how to do it).

Likewise call to your mind how you left *me* behind,
      And went off in a bus with the pippins;
When you *said* you'd forgot, but I knew you had *not*;
      (It was merely to save the odd threepence!).

Then recall your delight in the dumplings that night,
      (Though you *said* they were tasteless and doughy,)
But you winked as you spoke, and I saw that the joke
      (*If it was one,*) was meant for your Chloe.

And remember the moment when my cousin Joe meant
    To show us the Great Exhibition;
You proposed a short cut, and we found the thing shut,
    (We were two hours too late for admission).   20

Your "short cut", dear, we found took us *seven miles round,*
    (And Joe said *exactly* what we did,)
Well, I helped you out then: (it was *just* like you men,
    Not an atom of sense when it's needed!)

You said "What's to be done?" and I thought you in fun
    (Never dreaming you were such a ninny).
"Home directly!" said I, and *you* paid for the fly,
    (And I *think* that you gave him a guinea).

Well! *that* notion, you said, had not entered your head,
    You proposed, "The best thing, as we're come, is"   30
(Since it opens again in the morning at ten,)
    "To wait," *oh you prince of all dummies!*

And when Joe asked you "Why, if a man were to die,
    Just as *you* ran a sword through his middle,
You'd be hung for the crime?" and you said, "give me time,"
    And brought to your Chloe the riddle,

Why, remember, you dunce, how I solved it at once,
    (The question which Joe had referred to you),
Why, I told you the cause, was "the force of the laws,"
    And you said *"it had never occurred to you!"*   40

"This instance will show that your brain is too slow,
    And, (though your exterior is showy,)
Yet so arrant a goose can be no sort of use
    To Society – *come to your Chloe!*

"You'll find *no one* like me, who can manage to see
        Your meaning, you talk so obscurely:
Why, if once I were gone, how *would* you get on?
        Come, you know what *I* mean, Damon, surely!"

[Riddle]

A monument – men all agree –
Am I in all sincerity,
        Half cat, half hindrance made.
If head and tail removed should be,
Then most of all you strengthen me;
Replace my head, the stand you see
        On which my tail is laid.

Other Early Verse

Prologue to "La Guida di Bragia"

Shall soldiers tread the murderous path of war,
Without a notion what they do it for?
Shall pallid mercers drive a roaring trade,
And sell the stuffs their hands have never made?
And shall not we, in this our mimic scene,
Be all that better actors e'er have been?
Awake again a Kemble's tragic tone,
And make a Liston's humour all our own?
Or vie with Mrs Siddons in the art
To rouse the feelings and to charm the heart?   10
While Shakespeare's self, with all his ancient fires,
Lights up the forms that tremble on our wires?
Why can't we have, in theatres ideal,
The good, without the evil of the real?
Why may not Marionettes be just as good
As larger actors made of flesh and blood?
Presumptuous thought! to you and your applause
In humbler confidence we trust our cause.

The Ligniad, in two Books

Book I

Of man in stature small yet deeds sublime,
Who, even from his tender toothless years,
Boldly essayed to swallow and digest
Whole tomes of massive learning, ostrich-like,
Sing, classic Muse! and speed my daring quill,
Whiles that in language all too poor and weak
For such high themes, I tremblingly recount
To listening world's an hero's history.

Nursed in a cradle framed of Doric reeds,
10 In a fly-leaf of Scapula enwrapped,
Fed on black-broth (oh classic privilege!)
Seasoned with Attic salt, the infant throve.
Small taste had he for toys of infancy;
The coral and the bells he put aside;
But in his cradle would soliloquise,
And hold high commune with his inner man
In Greek Iambics, aptly modified.
A smile sardonic wore he in his joy;
And in his sorrow shed no mawkish tear;
20 " 'ὤμοι, πέπληγμαι" was his only cry,
And with much "smiting of the breast," he wrestled,
And would have rent his hair, but that he had none.

A merry boy the infant hath become;
He leaps and dances in the light of life,
With his shrill laughter rings the ancient house,
The stairs re-echo to his tread, as light
As when beneath the solemn oaks at eve
The tricksy fairies in their revelry
Wheel in wild dance, nor mark the dewy grass.
30 Yet even now upon that chiselled brow,
Lately so bright and fair, a Shadow dwells;
It is the Ghost of Latin yet unlearnt,
And dark forebodings of the Greek-to-come!
What can his grief be? he has all he loves,
A Scapula, an "Ainsworth's Dictionary",
And "all the Greek, and all the Latin authors –"
Then wherefore, moody boy, that crystal tear?
"It is the thought," methinks *I* hear him moan,
Clasping with quivering hands his aching brow,
40 "That certain Plays Euripides hath written
Are lost, are lost, and *I* shall never see them!"
        "Homer may come, and Homer may go,
            And be shifted, like lumber, from shelf to shelf,
        But I will read no Greek, no Greek,
            Until the Lost Dramas I've found for myself!"

Thus, all unconscious, rhymed his agony,
Adapting to the anguish of the hour
A fragment from our Poet Laureate.

Book II

Sing ye, who list, the deeds of ancient might,
In tournament, or deadlier battle-fray: 50
Sing ye the havoc and the din of war,
A nobler and a gentler theme be mine!
Through twice nine years eventless passed his life,
Save that each day some large addition brought
To that vast mass of learning stored within.
But now bright Fancy thrilled his raptured mind,
And poised her wings for flight, yet ere she rose,
With ponderous Sense he loaded her to Earth;
And the full flood of Poesy within
He primly tortured into wooden verse: 60
            "Glory of the ancient time,
                Classic fount of other days!
            How shall I, in modern rhyme
                Fitly sing thy praise?
            It chanced, the other day,
A tattered beggar asked an alms of me:
'Bestow a trifle, sir, in charity!'
            I turned and said
                'Good man,
I have but sixpence in my purse   70
            Yet rather than
        In hunger you should pine,
            And so your misery grow worse,
            It shall be thine,
If you'll be only good enough to say
                That, in
                Latin.'
Was this encouragement to classic lore?
            Say rather, more!

80   So may my course for ever smoothly run,
              And onward swell
      In that smooth channel where it hath begun:
              Still climbing, climbing up the classic heights
                    Where Fame doth dwell
                    And still
                    I will
              From month to month, from week to week,
      Devote my drowsy days and wakeful nights
                    To Greek."

90   Such were the fancies of his lighter mood –
      His lighter mood, which very seldom came:
      But now my Muse, approaching higher themes,
      Shrinks from the task in trembling, for the field,
      Green and smooth-shaven, spreads before her sight;
      The wickets pitched, the players ranged around;
      And he, the hero, in his glory there;
      A sight to dream of, not to write about!
      Then fare thee well, greatest of little men,
      In Greek, in Latin, in the cricket-field:
100   Great as a bowler, greater as a bat,
      But as a "short slip" greater yet than that!

      CLD. MAY 23. 1853

*[From a letter to his younger sister and brother
Henrietta and Edwin, 31 January 1855]*

The questions are shouted from one to the other, and the answers
come back in the same way – it is rather confusing till you are
well used to it.
The lecture goes on something like this.

Tutor. "What is twice three?"
Scout. "What's a rice tree?"
Sub-Scout. "When is ice free?"

Sub-sub-Scout. "What's a nice fee?"
Pupil (timidly). "Half a guinea!"
Sub-sub-Scout. "Can't forge any!"
Sub-Scout. "Ho for Jinny!"
Scout. "Don't be a ninny!"
Tutor. (Looks offended, but tries another question). "Divide a
     hundred by twelve!"
Scout. "Provide wonderful bells!"   10
Sub-Scout. "Go ride under it yourself."
Sub-sub-Scout. "Deride the dunder-headed elf!"
Pupil (surprised). "Who do you mean?"
Sub-sub-Scout. "Doings between!"
Sub-Scout. "Blue is the screen!"
Scout. "Soup-tureen!"

And so the lecture proceeds.

Upon the Lonely Moor

I met an aged, aged man
     Upon the lonely moor:
I knew I was a gentleman,
     And he was but a boor.
So I stopped and roughly questioned him,
     "Come, tell me how you live!"
But his words impressed my ear no more
     Than if it were a sieve.

He said, "I look for soap-bubbles,
     That lie among the wheat,   10
And bake them into mutton-pies,
     And sell them in the street.
I sell them unto men", he said,
     "Who sail on stormy seas;
And that's the way I get my bread –
     A trifle, if you please."

But I was thinking of a way
    To multiply by ten,
And always, in the answer, get
    The question back again.
I did not hear a word he said,
    But kicked that old man calm,
And said, "Come, tell me how you live!"
    And pinched him in the arm.

His accents mild took up the tale:
    He said, "I go my ways,
And when I find a mountain-rill,
    I set it in a blaze.
And thence they make a stuff they call
    Rowland's Macassar Oil;
But fourpence-halfpenny is all
    They give me for my toil."

But I was thinking of a plan
    To paint one's gaiters green,
So much the colour of the grass
    That they could ne'er be seen.
I gave his ear a sudden box,
    And questioned him again,
And tweaked his grey and reverend locks,
    And put him into pain.

He said, "I hunt for haddocks' eyes
    Among the heather bright,
And work them into waistcoat-buttons
    In the silent night.
And these I do not sell for gold,
    Or coin of silver-mine,
But for a copper-halfpenny,
    And that will purchase nine.

"I sometimes dig for buttered rolls,
    Or set limed twigs for crabs;

I sometimes search the flowery knolls
   For wheels of hansom cabs.
And that's the way" (he gave a wink)
   "I get my living here,
And very gladly will I drink
   Your Honour's health in beer."

I heard him then, for I had just
   Completed my design
To keep the Menai bridge from rust
   By boiling it in wine.   60
I duly thanked him, ere I went,
   For all his stories queer,
But chiefly for his kind intent
   To drink my health in beer.

And now if e'er by chance I put
   My fingers into glue,
Or madly squeeze a right-hand foot
   Into a left-hand shoe;
Or if a statement I aver
   Of which I am not sure,   70
I think of that strange wanderer
   Upon the lonely moor.

From *"Novelty and Romancement:*
A broken spell"

[" 'When Desolation snatched her tearful prey"]

"When Desolation snatched her tearful prey
From the lorn empire of despairing day;
When all the light, by gemless fancy thrown,
Served but to animate the putrid stone;

When monarchs, lessening on the wildered sight,
Crumblingly vanished into utter night;
When murder stalked with thirstier strides abroad,
And redly flashed the never-sated sword;
In such an hour thy greatness had been seen –
That is, if such an hour had ever been –
In such an hour thy praises shall be sung,
If not by mine, by many a worthier tongue;
And thou be gazed upon by wondering men,
When such an hour arrives, but not till then!"

Alice, daughter of C. Murdoch, Esq

O child! O new-born denizen
Of life's great city! On thy head
The glory of the morn is shed,
Like a celestial benison!
Here at the portal thou dost stand,
And with thy little hand
Thou openest the mysterious gate
Into the future's undiscovered land,
I see its valves expand,
As at the touch of Fate!
Into those realms of love and hate,
Into that darkness blank and drear,
By some prophetic feeling taught,
I launch the bold, adventurous thought,
Freighted with hope and fear;
As upon subterranean streams,
In caverns unexplored and dark,
Men sometimes launch a fragile bark
Laden with flickering fire,
And watch its swift-receding beams,
Until at length they disappear,
And in the distant dark expire.

From *"The Legend of Scotland"*

["Lorenzo dwelt at Heighington"]

Lorenzo dwelt at Heighington,
(Hys cote was made of Dimity,)
Least-ways yf not exactly there,
Yet yn yts close proximity.
Hee called on mee – hee stayed to tee –
Yet not a word he ut-tered,
Untyl I sayd, "D'ye lyke your bread
Dry?" and hee answered "But-tered."
Noodle dumb
Has a noodle-head,   10
I hate such noodles, I do.

["Here I bee, and here I byde"]

Here I bee, and here I byde,
Till such tyme as yt betyde
That a Ladye of thys place,
Lyke to mee yn name and face,
(Though my name bee never known,
My initials shall bee shown,)
Shall be fotograffed aright –
Hedde and Feet bee both yn sight –
Then my face shall disappear,
Nor agayn affrite you heer.   10

[" 'Yn the Auckland Castell cellar"]

"Yn the Auckland Castell cellar,
Long, long ago,
I was shut – a brisk young feller –
Woe, woe, ah woe!
To take her at full-lengthe
I never hadde the strengthe
Tempore (and soe I tell her)
Praeterito!"
"She was hard – oh, she was cruel –
Long, long ago,
Starved mee here – not even gruel –
No, believe mee, no! –
Frae Scotland could I flee,
I'd gie my last bawbee, –
Arrah, bhoys, fair play's a jhewel,
Lave me, darlints, goe!"

*

["Into the wood – the dark, dark wood"]

Into the wood – the dark, dark wood –
    Forth went the happy Child;
And, in its stillest solitude,
    Talked to herself, and smiled:
And closer drew the scarlet Hood
    About her ringlets wild.

And now at last she treads the maze,
    And now she need not fear;
Frowning, she meets the sudden blaze
    Of noon light falling clear;
Nor trembles she, not turns, nor stays,
    Although the Wolf be near.

Disillusionised

I painted her a gushing thing –
      Her years perhaps a score;
I little thought to find them
      At least two dozen more!

My fancy gave her eyes of blue,
      A curly auburn head;
I came to find the blue a green,
      The auburn grown to red!

I painted her a lip and cheek
      In colour like the rose;   10
I little thought the selfsame hue
      Extended to her nose!

I dreamed of rounded features –
      A smile of ready glee –
But it was not fat I wanted,
      Nor a grin I hoped to see!

She boxed my ears this morning –
      They tingled very much –
I own that I could wish her
      A somewhat lighter touch;   20

And if you were to settle how
      Her charms might be improved,
I would not have them added to,
      But just a few removed!

She has the bear's ethereal grace,
      The bland hyena's laugh –
The footstep of the elephant,
      The neck of the giraffe;

I love her still – believe it –
30   Though my heart its passion hides;
She's all my fancy painted her,
           But oh! how much besides!

Those Horrid Hurdy-Gurdies!
A Monody, By a Victim

"My mother bids me bind my hair,"
           And not go about such a figure;
It's a bother, of course, but what do I care?
           I shall do as I please when I'm bigger.

"My lodging is on the cold, cold ground,"
           As the first-floor and attic were taken.
I tried the garret but once, and found
           That my wish for a change was mistaken.

"Ever of thee!" yes, "Ever of thee!"
10   They chatter more and more,
Till I groan aloud, "Oh! let me be!
           I have heard it all before!"

"Please remember the organ, sir,"
           What? hasn't he left me yet?
I promise, good man; for its tedious burr
           I never can forget.

[Prologue]

As when an anthem in full chorus-swell
Hath swept away, one solitary note,
Dreamy and low as chime of far-off-bell,
Through the deep silence tremblingly doth float –

As when the sun, in crimson clouds of even,
Hath sunk from sight, and all the hills are grey,
A feeble ray yet lingers in the heaven,
A smile upon the face of dying Day –

So, when the voices of the sons of song
Have rolled in thunder o'er a trancëd nation,   10
When silence falls upon that glorious throng,
And men are hushed in awful expectation,

Let Cam and Isis, with attunëd flow,
Through the dumb aching void prolong their strain,
Lest the vast music, that enchains us so,
With sudden pause the listening ear should pain.

The Majesty of Justice
An Oxford Idyll

They passed beneath the College gate;
And down the High went slowly on;
Then spake the Undergraduate
To that benign and portly Don:
"They say that Justice is a Queen –
A Queen of awful Majesty –
Yet in the papers I have seen
Some things that puzzle me.

"A Court obscure, so rumour states,
There is, called 'Vice-Cancellarii,'   10
Which keeps on Undergraduates,
Who do not pay their bills, a wary eye.
A case I'm told was lately brought
Into that tiniest of places,
And justice in that case was sought –
As in most other cases.

"Well! Justice as I hold, dear friend,
Is Justice, neither more than less:
I never dreamed it could depend
On ceremonial or dress.
I thought that her imperial sway
In Oxford surely would appear,
But all the papers seem to say
She's not majestic *here*."

The portly Don he made reply,
With the most roguish of his glances,
"Perhaps she drops her Majesty
Under peculiar circumstances."
"But that's the point!" the young man cried,
"The puzzle that I wish to pen you in –
How are the public to decide
Which article is genuine?

"Is't only when the Court is large
That we for 'Majesty' need hunt?
Would what is Justice in a barge
Be something different in a punt?"
"Nay, nay!" the Don replied, amused,
"You're talking nonsense, sir! You know it!
Such arguments were never used
By any friend of Jowett."

"Then is it in the men who trudge
(Beef-eaters I believe they call them)
Before each wigged and ermined judge,
For fear some mischief should befall them?
If I should recognise in one
(Through all disguise) my own domestic,
I fear 'twould shed a gleam of fun
Even on the 'Majestic'!"

The portly Don replied, "Ahem!
They can't exactly be its *essence*:   50
I scarcely think the want of them
The 'Majesty of Justice' lessens.
Besides, they always march awry;
Their gorgeous garments never fit:
Processions don't make Majesty –
I'm quite convinced of it."

"Then is it in the *wig* it lies,
Whose countless rows of rigid curls
Are gazed at with admiring eyes
By country lads and servant-girls?"   60
Out laughed that bland and courteous Don:
"Dear sir, I do not mean to flatter –
But surely you have hit upon
The essence of the matter.

"They will not own the Majesty
Of Justice, making Monarchs bow,
Unless as evidence they see
The horsehair wig upon her brow.
Yes, yes! That makes the silliest men
Seem wise; the meanest men look big: 70
The Majesty of Justice, then,
Is seated in the WIG."

R.W.G. Oxford March 1863

Miss Jones

'Tis a melancholy song, and it will not keep you long,
Tho I specs it will work upon your feelings very strong,
For the agonising moans of Miss Arabella Jones
Were warranted to melt the hearts of any paving stones.

Simon Smith was tall and slim, and she doted upon him,
But he always called her Miss Jones – he never got so far,
As to use her Christian name – it was too familiar.
When she called him "Simon dear" he pretended not to hear,
And she told her sister Susan he behaved extremely queer,
10 Who said, "Very right! very right! Shews his true affection.
If you'd prove your Simon's love follow my direction.
I'd certainly advise you just to write a simple letter,
And to tell him that the cold he kindly asked about is better.
And say that by the tanyard you will wait in loving hope,
At nine o'clock this evening if he's willing to elope
With his faithful Arabella."
So she wrote it, & signed it, & sealed it, & sent it, & dressed
       herself out in her holiday things.
With bracelets & brooches, & earrings, & necklace, a watch,
       & an eyeglass, & diamond rings,
For man is a creature weak and impressible, thinks such a
       deal of appearance, my dear.
20 So she waited for her Simon beside the tanyard gate,
       regardless of the pieman, who hinted it was late.
Waiting for Simon, she coughed in the chilly night, until the
       tanner found her,
And kindly brought a light old coat to wrap around her.
She felt her cold was getting worse,
Yet still she fondly whispered, "Oh, take your time, my
       Simon, although I've waited long.
I do not fear my Simon dear will fail to come at last,
Although I know that long ago the time I named is past.
My Simon! My Simon! Oh, charming man! Oh, charming
       man!
Dear Simon Smith, sweet Simon Smith.
Oh, there goes the church-clock, the town-clock, the station-
       clock and there go the other clocks, they are all striking
       twelve!
30 Oh, Simon, it is getting late, it's very dull to sit and wait.
And really I'm in such a state, I hope you'll come at any rate,
       quite early in the morning, quite early in the morning.

Then with prancing bays & yellow chaise, we'll away to
    Gretna Green.
For when I am with my Simon Smith – oh, that common
    name! Oh that vulgar name!
I shall never rest happy till he's changed that name, but when
    he has married me, maybe he'll love me to that degree,
    that he'll grant me my prayer
And will call himself 'Clare' –"
So she talked all alone, as she sat upon a stone,
Still hoping he would come and find her, and she started most
    unkimmon, when instead of darling "Simmon" 'twas a
    strange man that stood behind her,
Who civilly observed "Good evening, M'am,
I really am surprised to see that you're out here alone, for you
    must own from thieves you're not secure.
A watch, I see. Pray lend it me (I hope the gold is pure).   40
And all those rings, & other things – Don't scream, you know,
    for long ago
The policeman off from his beat has gone.
In the kitchen –" "Oh, you desperate villain! Oh, you
    treacherous thief!"
And these were the words of her anger and grief.
"When first to Simon Smith I gave my hand I never could
    have thought he would have acted half so mean as this,
And where's the new police? Oh, Simon, Simon! how could
    you treat your love so ill?"
They sit & chatter, they chatter with the cook, the guardians,
    so they're called, of public peace.
Through the tanyard was heard the dismal sound, "How on
    earth is it policemen never, never, never, can be found?"

*Alice's Adventures
in Wonderland*
(1865)

["All in the golden afternoon"]

All in the golden afternoon
   Full leisurely we glide;
For both our oars, with little skill,
   By little arms are plied,
While little hands make vain pretence
   Our wanderings to guide.

Ah, cruel Three! In such an hour,
   Beneath such dreamy weather,
To beg a tale of breath too weak
   To stir the tiniest feather!   10
Yet what can one poor voice avail
   Against three tongues together?

Imperious Prima flashes forth
   Her edict "to begin it":
In gentler tones Secunda hopes
   "There will be nonsense in it!"
While Tertia interrupts the tale
   Not *more* than once a minute.

Anon, to sudden silence won,
   In fancy they pursue   20
The dream-child moving through a land
   Of wonders wild and new,
In friendly chat with bird and beast –
   And half believe it true.

And ever, as the story drained
　　The wells of fancy dry,
And faintly strove that weary one
　　To put the subject by,
"The rest next time –" "It *is* next time!"
30　　The happy voices cry.

Thus grew the tale of Wonderland:
　　Thus slowly, one by one,
Its quaint events were hammered out –
　　And now the tale is done,
And home we steer, a merry crew,
　　Beneath the setting sun.

Alice! A childish story take,
　　And, with a gentle hand,
Lay it where Childhood's dreams are twined
40　　In Memory's mystic band,
Like pilgrim's wither'd wreath of flowers
　　Pluck'd in a far-off land.

["How doth the little crocodile"]

　　How doth the little crocodile
　　　　Improve his shining tail,
　　And pour the waters of the Nile
　　　　On every golden scale!

　　How cheerfully he seems to grin,
　　　　How neatly spreads his claws,
　　And welcomes little fishes in,
　　　　With gently smiling jaws!

[Mouse Tails]

["We lived beneath the mat"]

We lived beneath the mat
        Warm and snug and fat
                But one woe, & that
                        Was the cat!
                            To our joys
                            a clog, In
                            our eyes a
                            fog, On our
                            hearts a log
                        Was the dog!
            When the
        cat's away,
        Then
        the mice
        will
            play,
                But, alas!
                    one day, (So *they* say)
                            Came the dog and
                                    cat, Hunting
                                        for a
                                        rat,
                                    Crushed
                                    the mice
                                    all flat,
                                Each
                                one
                                as
                                he
                                sat

Underneath the mat, Warm & snug & fat – Think of that!

["Fury said to"]

"Fury said to
a mouse, That
he met in the
house, 'Let
us both go
to law: *I*
will prose-
cute *you.* –
Come, I'll
take no de-
nial: We
must have
the trial;
For really
this morn-
ing I've
nothing
to do.'
Said the
mouse to
the cur,
'Such a
trial, dear
sir, With
no jury
or judge,
would
be wast-
ing our
breath.'
'I'll be
judge,
I'll be
jury,'
said
cun-
ning
old
Fury:
'I'll
try
the
whole
cause,
and
con-
demn
you to
death'."

[" *'You are old, Father William,'*
the young man said"]

"You are old, Father William," the young man said,
    "And your hair has become very white;
And yet you incessantly stand on your head –
    Do you think, at your age, it is right?"

"In my youth," Father William replied to his son,
    "I feared it might injure the brain;
But, now that I'm perfectly sure I have none,
    Why, I do it again and again."

"You are old," said the youth, "as I mentioned before,
    And have grown most uncommonly fat;   10
Yet you turned a back-somersault in at the door –
    Pray, what is the reason for that?"

"In my youth," said the sage, as he shook his grey locks,
    "I kept all my limbs very supple
By the use of this ointment – one shilling the box –
    Allow me to sell you a couple?"

"You are old," said the youth, "and your jaws are too weak
    For anything tougher than suet;
Yet you finished the goose, with the bones and the beak –
    Pray, how did you manage to do it?"   20

"In my youth," said his father, "I took to the law,
    And argued each case with my wife;
And the muscular strength, which it gave to my jaw
    Has lasted the rest of my life."

"You are old," said the youth, "one would hardly suppose
    That your eye was as steady as ever;
Yet you balanced an eel on the end of your nose –
    What made you so awfully clever?"

"I have answered three questions, and that is enough,"
30   Said his father. "Don't give yourself airs!
Do you think I can listen all day to such stuff?
            Be off, or I'll kick you down-stairs!"

[The Duchess's Lullaby]

"Speak roughly to your little boy,
            And beat him when he sneezes:
He only does it to annoy,
            Because he knows it teases."

CHORUS

(in which the cook and the baby joined): –
"Wow! wow! wow!"

"I speak severely to my boy,
            I beat him when he sneezes;
For he can thoroughly enjoy
            The pepper when it pleases!"

CHORUS

"Wow! wow! wow!"

["Twinkle, twinkle, little bat"]

Twinkle, twinkle, little bat!
How I wonder what you're at!

Up above the world you fly,
Like a tea-tray in the sky.
                Twinkle, twinkle———

[The Mock Turtle's Song: I]

"Will you walk a little faster?" said a whiting to a snail,
"There's a porpoise close behind us, and he's treading on
      my tail.
See how eagerly the lobsters and the turtles all advance!
They are waiting on the shingle – will you come and join
      the dance?
      Will you, won't you, will you, won't you, will you
        join the dance?
      Will you, won't you, will you, won't you, won't you
        join the dance?

"You can really have no notion how delightful it will be
When they take us up and throw us, with the lobsters, out
      to sea!"
But the snail replied "Too far, too far!", and gave a look
      askance –
Said he thanked the whiting kindly, but he would not join
      the dance.   10
      Would not, could not, would not, could not, would
        not join the dance.
      Would not, could not, would not, could not, could
        not join the dance.

"What matters it how far we go?" his scaly friend replied.
"There is another shore, you know, upon the other side.
The further off from England the nearer is to France –
Then turn not pale, beloved snail, but come and join the
      dance.
      Will you, won't you, will you, won't you, will you
        join the dance?
      Will you, won't you, will you, won't you, won't you
        join the dance?"

[The Mock Turtle's Song in
"Alice's Adventures Under Ground"]

Beneath the waters of the sea,
Are lobsters thick as thick can be –
They love to dance with you and me,
My own, my gentle Salmon!

Chorus:

Salmon come up! Salmon go down!
Salmon come twist your tail around!
Of all the fishes of the sea
There's none so good as salmon!

[" 'Tis the voice of the Lobster: I heard him declare"]

'Tis the voice of the Lobster: I heard him declare
"You have baked me too brown, I must sugar my hair."
As a duck with his eyelids, so he with his nose
Trims his belt and his buttons, and turns out his toes.

When the sands are all dry, he is gay as a lark,
And will talk in contemptuous tones of the Shark:
But, when the tide rises and sharks are around,
His voice has a timid and tremulous sound.

[1886 completion of " 'Tis the
voice of the Lobster"]

I passed by his garden, and marked, with one eye,
How the Owl and the Panther were sharing a pie:
The panther took pie crust, and gravy, and meat,
While the Owl had the dish as its share of the treat.

When the pie was all finished, the Owl, as a boon,
Was kindly permitted to pocket the spoon:
While the Panther received knife and fork with a growl,
And concluded the banquet by————

[The Mock Turtle's Song: II]

"Beautiful soup, so rich and green,
Waiting in a hot tureen!
Who for such dainties would not stoop?
Soup of the evening, beautiful Soup!
Soup of the evening, beautiful Soup!
     Beau————ootiful Soo————oop!
     Beau————ootiful Soo————oop!
Soo————oop of the e————e————evening,
     Beautiful, beautiful Soup!

"Beautiful Soup! Who cares for fish,   10
Game, or any other dish?
Who would not give all else for two p
ennyworth only of beautiful Soup?
Pennyworth only of beautiful Soup?
     Beau————ootiful Soo————oop!
     Beau————ootiful Soo————oop!
Soo————oop of the e————e————evening,
     Beautiful, beauti————FUL SOUP!"

("Soo————oop of the e————e————evening,
     Beautiful, beautiful Soup!")   20

[The White Rabbit's Evidence]

    They told me you had been to her,
        And mentioned me to him:
    She gave me a good character,
        But said I could not swim.

He sent them word I had not gone
    (We know it to be true):
If she should push the matter on,
    What would become of you?

I gave her one, they gave him two,
    You gave us three or more;
They all returned from him to you,
    Though they were mine before.

If I or she should chance to be
    Involved in this affair,
He trusts to you to set them free,
    Exactly as we were.

My notion was that you had been
    (Before she had this fit)
An obstacle that came between
    Him, and ourselves, and it.

Don't let him know she liked them best,
    For this must ever be
A secret, kept from all the rest,
    Between yourself and me.

*Phantasmagoria and
Other Poems*
(1869)

Phantasmagoria

Canto I – The Trystyng

One winter night, at half-past nine,
    Cold, tired, and cross, and muddy,
I had come home, too late to dine,
And supper, with cigars and wine,
    Was waiting in the study.

There was a strangeness in the room,
    And something white and wavy
Was standing near me in the gloom –
I took it for the carpet-broom
    Left by that careless slavey.   10

But presently the thing began
    To shudder and to sneeze:
On which I said "Come, come, my man,
That's a most inconsiderate plan –
    Less noise there, if you please!"

"I've caught a cold," the thing replies,
    "Out there upon the landing –"
I turned to look in some surprise,
And there, before my very eyes,
    A little Ghost was standing!   20

He trembled when he caught my eye,
    And got behind a chair:
"How came you here," I said, "and why?
I never saw a thing so shy.
    Come out! Don't shiver there!"

He said "I'd gladly tell you how,
      And also tell you why,
But" (here he gave a little bow)
"You're in so bad a temper now,
      You'd think it all a lie.

"And as to being in a fright,
      Allow me to remark
That ghosts have just as good a right
In every way, to fear the light,
      As men to fear the dark."

"No plea," said I, "can well excuse
      Such cowardice in you:
For ghosts can visit when they choose,
Whereas we humans can't refuse
      To *grant* the interview."

He said "A flutter of alarm
      Is not unnatural, is it?
I really feared you meant some harm,
But, now I see that you are calm,
      Let me explain my visit.

"That last ghost left you on the third –
      Since then you've not been haunted:
But, as he never sent us word,
'Twas quite by accident we heard
      That any one was wanted.

"A Spectre has first choice, by right,
      In filling up a vacancy;
Then Phantom, Goblin, Elf, and Sprite –
If all these fail them, they invite
      The nicest Ghoul that they can see.

"The Spectres said the place was low,
        And that you kept bad wine:
So, as a Phantom had to go,
And I was first, of course, you know,
        I couldn't well decline."   60

"No doubt," said I, "they settled who
        Was fittest to be sent:
Yet still to choose a brat like you,
To haunt a man of forty-two,
        Was no great compliment."

"I'm not so young, Sir," he replied,
        "As you might think – the fact is,
In caverns by the water side,
And other places that I've tried,
        I've had a lot of practice: 70

"But I have never taken yet
        A strict domestic part,
And in my flurry I forget
The Five Good Rules of Etiquette
        We have to know by heart."

My sympathies were warming fast
        Towards the little fellow;
He was so *very* much aghast
At having found a man at last,
        And looked so scared and yellow.   80

"At least," I said, "I'm glad to find
        A ghost is not a *dumb* thing –
But pray sit down – you'll feel inclined
(If, like myself, you have not dined)
        To take a snack of something:

"(Though, certainly, you don't appear
         A thing to offer *food* to);
And then I shall be glad to hear
(If you will say them loud and clear)
         The rules that you allude to."

"Thanks! You shall hear them by and by –
         This *is* a piece of luck!"
"What may I offer you?" said I.
"Well, since you *are* so kind, I'll try
         A little bit of duck.

"*One* slice! And may I ask you for
         A little drop more gravy?"
I sat and looked at him in awe,
For certainly I never saw
         A thing so white and wavy.

And still he seemed to grow more white,
         More vapoury, and wavier –
Seen in the dim and flickering light,
As he proceeded to recite
         His "Maxims of Behaviour."

Canto II – Hys Fyve Rules

"My First – but don't suppose," he said,
         "I'm setting you a riddle –
Is – if your Victim be in bed,
Don't touch the curtains at his head,
         But take it in the middle,

"And wave it slowly to and fro,
         As if the wind was at it;
And in a minute's time or so
He'll be awake – and this you'll know
         By hearing him say '*Drat it*!'"

"(And here you must on no pretence
    Make the first observation:
Wait for the Victim to commence –
No ghost of any common sense
    Begins a conversation.) 120

"If he should say '*How came you here?*'
    (The way that *you* began, Sir),
In such a case your course is clear –
'*Just as you please, my little dear!*'
    Or any other answer.

"But if the wretch says nothing more,
    You'd best perhaps curtail your
Exertions – go and shake the door,
And then, if he begins to snore,
    You'll know the thing's a failure. 130

"By day, if he should be alone –
    At home or on a walk –
You merely give a hollow groan,
To indicate the kind of tone
    In which you mean to talk.

"But if you find him with his friends,
    The thing is rather harder.
In such a case success depends
On picking up some candle-ends,
    Or butter, in the larder. 140

"With this you make a kind of slide
    (It answers best with suet),
On which you must contrive to glide,
And swing yourself from side to side –
    One soon learns how to do it.

"The Second tells us what is right
          In ceremonious calls:
First burn a blue or crimson light,
(A thing I quite forgot to-night,)
          Then scratch the door or walls."

I said "You'll visit *here* no more,
          If you attempt the Guy:
I'll have no bonfires on *my* floor –
And, as for scratching at the door,
          I'd like to see you try!"

"The Third was written to protect
          The interests of the Victim,
And tells us, as I recollect,
To *treat him with a grave respect,*
          And not to contradict him."

"That's plain," said I, "as Tare and Tret,
          To any comprehension:
I only wish *some* ghosts I've met
Would not so *constantly* forget
          The maxim that you mention."

"Perhaps," he said, "*you* first transgressed
          The laws of hospitality:
You'll mostly come off second-best
When you omit to treat your guest
          With proper cordiality.

"If you address a ghost as 'thing,'
          Or strike him with a hatchet,
He is permitted by the king
To drop all *formal* parleying –
          And then you're *sure* to catch it!

"The Fourth prohibits trespassing
        Where other ghosts are quartered:
And those convicted of the thing
(Unless when pardoned by the king)
        Must instantly be slaughtered." 180

I said "That rule appears to me
        Wanting in common sense –"
" 'To slaughter' does not mean," said he,
" 'To kill' with us, and that, you see,
        Makes a *great* difference.

"In fact we're simply cut up small,
        (Ghosts soon unite anew;)
The process scarcely hurts at all,
Not more than when *you*'re what you call
        'Cut up' by a Review. 190

"The Fifth is one you may prefer
        That I should quote entire –
The king must be addressed as 'Sir':
This, from a simple courtier,
        Is all the laws require:

"But, should you wish to do the thing
        With out-and-out politeness,
Accost him as 'My Goblin-King!'
And always use, in answering,
        The phrase 'Your Royal Whiteness!' 200

"I'm getting rather hoarse, I fear,
        After so much reciting;
So, if you don't object, my dear,
We'll try a glass of bitter beer –
        I think it looks inviting."

Canto III – Scarmoges

"And did you really walk," said I,
　　　"On such a wretched night?
I always fancied ghosts could fly –
If not exactly in the sky,
　　　Yet at a fairish height."

"It's very well," he said, "for kings
　　　To fly above the earth:
But Phantoms often find that wings,
Like many other pleasant things,
　　　Cost more than they are worth.

"Spectres of course are rich, and so
　　　Can buy them from the Elves:
But *we* prefer to keep below –
They're stupid company, you know,
　　　For any but themselves.

"For, though they claim to be exempt
　　　From pride, they treat a Phantom
As something quite beneath contempt,
(Just as no turkey ever dreamt
　　　Of noticing a Bantam)."

"They seem too proud," said I, "to go
　　　To houses such as mine –
Pray how did they contrive to know
So quickly that 'the place was low,'
　　　And that I 'kept bad wine'?"

"Inspector Kobold called on you –"
　　　The little ghost began:
Here I broke in; "Inspector who?
Inspecting ghosts is something new:
　　　Explain yourself, my man!"

"His name is Kobold," said my guest,
      "One of the Spectre order:
You'll very often see him dressed
In a yellow gown, a crimson vest,
      And a night-cap with a border.   240

"He tried the Brocken business first,
      But caught a sort of chill;
So came to England to be nursed,
And here it took the form of *thirst*,
      Which he complains of still.

"The remedy, *he says*, is port,
      (Which he compares to nectar,)
And, as the inns where it is bought,
Have always been his chief resort,
      We call him the '*Inn-Spectre*.'"   250

I bear it as well as any man
      The washiest of witticisms;
And nothing could be sweeter than
My temper, till the ghost began
      Some most provoking criticisms.

"Cooks need not be indulged in waste,
      Yet still you'd better teach them
Dishes should have *some sort* of taste –
Pray, why are all the cruets placed
      Where nobody can reach them?   260

"That man of yours will never earn
      His living as a waiter –
Is that queer *thing* supposed to burn?
(It's far too dismal a concern
      To call a Moderator).

"The duck was tender, but the peas
      Were very much too old:
And just remember, if you please,
The *next* time you have toasted cheese,
      Don't let them send it cold.

"You'd find the bread improved, I think,
      By getting better flour:
And have you anything to drink
That looks a *little* less like ink,
      And isn't *quite* so sour?"

Then, peering round with curious eyes,
      He muttered "Goodness gracious!"
And so went on to criticise –
"Your room's an inconvenient size;
      It's neither snug nor spacious.

"That narrow window, I expect,
      Serves but to let the dusk in –"
I cried "But please to recollect
'Twas fashioned by an architect
      Who pinned his faith on Ruskin!"

"I don't care who he was, Sir, or
      On whom he pinned his faith!
Constructed by whatever law,
So poor a job I never saw,
      As I'm a living Wraith!

"What a re-markable cigar!
      How much are they a dozen?"
I growled "No matter what they are!
You're getting as familiar
      As if you were my cousin!

270

280

290

"Now that's a thing *I will not stand*,
　　And so I tell you flat –"
"Aha," said he, 'We're getting grand!"
(Taking a bottle in his hand,)
　　"I'll soon arrange for *that*!"   300

And here he took a careful aim,
　　And gaily cried "Here goes!"
I tried to dodge it as it came,
But somehow caught it, all the same,
　　Exactly on my nose.

And I remember nothing more
　　That I can clearly fix,
Till I was sitting on the floor,
Repeating "Two and five are four,
　　But *three and two* are six."   310

What really passed I never learned,
　　Nor guessed: I only know
That, when at last my sense returned,
The lamp, neglected, dimly burned –
　　The fire was getting low –

Through driving mists I seemed to see
　　A form of sheet and bone –
And found that he was telling me
The whole of his biography,
　　In a familiar tone.   320

Canto IV – Hys Nouryture

"Oh, when I was a little Ghost,
　　A merry time had we!
Each seated on his favourite post,
We chumped and chawed the buttered toast
　　They gave us for our tea."

"That story is in print!" I cried.
          "Don't say it's not, because
It's known as well as Bradshaw's Guide!"
(The ghost uneasily replied
          He hardly thought it was.)

"It's not in Nursery Rhymes? And yet
          I almost think it is –
'Three little ghostesses' were set
'On postesses,' you know, and ate
          Their 'buttered toastesses.'

"I have the book; so if you doubt it –"
          I turned to search the shelf –
"Don't stir!" he cried. "We'll do without it:
I now remember all about it;
          I wrote the thing myself.

"It came out in a 'Monthly,' or
          At least my agent said it did:
Some literary swell, who saw
It, thought it seemed adapted for
          The Magazine he edited.

"My father was a Brownie, Sir;
          My mother was a Fairy.
The notion had occurred to her,
The children would be happier,
          If they were taught to vary.

"The notion soon became a craze;
          And, when it once began, she
Brought us all out in different ways –
One was a Pixy, two were Fays,
          Another was a Banshee;

"The Fetch and Kelpie went to school
          And gave a lot of trouble;
Next came a Poltergeist and Ghoul,
And then two Trolls (which broke the rule),
          A Goblin, and a Double –   360

"(If that's a snuff-box on the shelf,"
          He added with a yawn,
"I'll take a pinch) – next came an Elf,
And then a Phantom (that's myself),
          And last, a Leprechaun.

"One day, some Spectres chanced to call,
          Dressed in the usual white:
I stood and watched them in the hall,
And couldn't make them out at all,
          They seemed so strange a sight: 370

"I wondered what on earth they were,
          That looked all head and sack;
But mother told me not to stare,
And then she twitched me by the hair,
          And punched me in the back.

"Since then I've often wished that I
          Had been a Spectre born:
But what's the use?" (He heaved a sigh.)
"*They* are the ghost-nobility,
          And look on *us* with scorn.   380

"My phantom-life was soon begun:
          When I was barely six,
I went out with an older one –
And just at first I thought it fun,
          And went at it like bricks.

"I've haunted dungeons, castles, towers –
    Wherever I was sent:
I've often sat and howled for hours,
Drenched to the skin with driving showers,
390   Upon a battlement.

"It's quite old-fashioned now to groan
    When you begin to speak:
This is the newest thing in tone –"
And here, (it chilled me to the bone)
    He gave an *awful* squeak.

"Perhaps," he added, "to *your* ear
    That sounds an easy thing?
Try it yourself, my little dear!
It took *me* something like a year,
400   With constant practising.

"And when you've learned to squeak, my man,
    And caught the double sob,
You're pretty much where you began –
Just try and gibber if you can!
    That's something *like* a job!

"*I've* tried it, and can only say
    I'm sure you couldn't do it, e-
ven if you practised night and day,
Unless you have a turn that way,
410   And natural ingenuity.

"Shakespeare I think it is who treats
    Of Ghosts, in days of old,
Who 'gibbered in the Roman streets,'
Dressed, if you recollect, in sheets –
    They must have found it cold.

"I've often spent ten pounds on stuff,
　　　In dressing as a Double,
But, though it answers as a puff,
It never has effect enough
　　　To make it worth the trouble.   420

"Long bills soon quenched the little thirst
　　　I had for being funny –
The setting-up is always worst:
Such heaps of things you want at first,
　　　One must be made of money!

"For instance, take a haunted tower,
　　　With skull, cross-bones, and sheet;
Blue lights to burn (say) two an hour,
Condensing lens of extra power,
　　　And set of chains, complete: 430

"What with the things you have to hire –
　　　The fitting on the robe –
And testing all the coloured fire –
The outfit of itself would tire
　　　The patience of a Job!

"And then they're so fastidious,
　　　The Haunted-House Committee:
I've often known them make a fuss
Because a ghost was French, or Russ,
　　　Or even from the City!   440

"Some dialects are objected to –
　　　For one, the *Irish* brogue is:
And then, for all you have to do,
One pound a week they offer you,
　　　And find yourself in Bogies!"

Canto V – Byckerment

"Don't they consult the 'Victims,' though?"
    I said. "They should, by rights,
Give them a chance – because, you know,
The tastes of people differ so,
    Especially in Sprites."

The Phantom shook his head and smiled:
    "Consult them? Not a bit!
'Twould be a job to drive one wild,
To satisfy one single child –
    There'd be no end to it!"

"Of course you can't leave *children* free,"
    Said I, "to pick and choose:
But, in the case of men like me,
I think 'Mine Host' might fairly be
    Allowed to state his views."

He said "It really wouldn't pay –
    Folk are so full of fancies.
We visit for a single day,
And whether then we go, or stay,
    Depends on circumstances.

"And, though we don't consult 'Mine Host'
    Before the thing's arranged,
Still, if the tenant quits his post,
Or is not a well-mannered ghost,
    Then you can have him changed.

"But if the host's a man like you –
    I mean a man of sense;
And if the house is not too new –"
"Why, what has *that*," said I, "to do
    With ghost's convenience?"

"A new house does not suit, you know –
        It's such a job to trim it:
But, after twenty years or so,
The wainscotings begin to go,
        So twenty is the limit."   480

"To trim" was not a phrase I could
        Remember having heard:
"Perhaps," I said, "you'll be so good
As tell me what is understood
        Exactly by that word?"

"It means the loosening all the doors,"
        The ghost replied, and laughed:
"It means the drilling holes by scores
In all the skirting-boards and floors,
        To make a thorough draught.   490

"You'll sometimes find that one or two
        Are all you really need
To let the wind come whistling through –
But *here* there'll be a lot to do!"
        I faintly gasped "Indeed!

"If I'd been rather later, I'll
        Be bound," I added, trying
(Most unsuccessfully) to smile,
"You'd have been busy all this while,
        Trimming and beautifying?"   500

"Why, no," said he; "perhaps I should
        Have stayed another minute –
But still no ghost, that's any good,
Without an introduction would
        Have ventured to begin it.

"The proper thing, as you were late,
        Was certainly to go:
But, with the roads in such a state,
I got the Knight-Mayor's leave to wait
510   For half an hour or so."

"Who's the Knight-Mayor?" I cried. Instead
        Of answering my question,
"Well! if you don't know *that*," he said,
"Either you never go to bed,
        Or you've a grand digestion!

"He goes about and sits on folk
        That eat too much at night:
His duties are to 'pinch, and poke,
And squeeze them till they nearly choke.'"
520   (I said "It serves them right!")

"And folk who sup on things like these –"
        He muttered, "eggs and bacon –
Lobster – and duck – and toasted cheese –
If they don't get an awful squeeze,
        I'm very much mistaken!

"He is immensely fat, and so
        Well suits the occupation:
In point of fact, if you must know,
We used to call him years ago,
530   '*The Mayor and Corporation*'!

"The day he was elected Mayor
        I *know* that every Sprite meant
To vote for *me*, but did not dare –
He was so frantic with despair
        And furious with excitement.

"When it was over, for a whim,
        He ran to tell the king;
And being the reverse of slim,
A two-mile trot was not for him
        A very easy thing.   540

"So, to reward him for his run,
        (As it was baking hot,
And he was over twenty stone,)
The king proceeded, half in fun,
        To knight him on the spot."

" 'Twas a great liberty to take!"
        (I fired up like a rocket.)
"He did it just for punning's sake –
'The man,' says Johnson, 'that would make
        A pun, would pick a pocket!' "   550

"A man," said he, "is not a king."
        I argued for a while,
And did my best to prove the thing –
The Phantom merely listening
        With a contemptuous smile.

At last, when, breath and patience spent,
        I had recourse to smoking –
"Your *aim*," he said, "is excellent:
But – when you call it *argument* –
        Of course you're only joking?"   560

Stung by his cold and snaky eye,
        I roused myself at length
To say "At least I do defy
The veriest sceptic to deny
        That union is strength!"

"That's true enough," said he, "yet stay –"
   I listened in all meekness –
"*Union* is strength, I'm bound to say;
In fact, the thing's as clear as day;
570   But *onions* – are a weakness."

Canto VI – Dyscomfyture

As one who strives a hill to climb,
   Who never climbed before:
Who finds it, in a little time,
Grow every moment less sublime,
   And votes the thing a bore:

Yet, having once begun to try,
   Dares not desert his quest,
But, climbing, ever keeps his eye
On one small hut against the sky,
580   Wherein he hopes to rest:

Who climbs till nerve and force be spent,
   With many a puff and pant:
Who still, as rises the ascent,
In language grows more violent,
   Although in breath more scant:

Who, climbing, gains at length the place
   That crowns the upward track;
And, entering with unsteady pace,
Receives a buffet in the face
590   That lands him on his back:

And feels himself, like one in sleep,
   Glide swiftly down again,
A helpless weight, from steep to steep,
Till, with a headlong giddy sweep,
   He drops upon the plain –

So I, that had resolved to bring
      Conviction to a ghost,
And found it quite a different thing
From any human arguing,
      Yet dared not quit my post: 600

But, keeping still the end in view
      To which I hoped to come,
I strove to prove the matter true
By putting everything I knew
      Into an axiom:

Commencing every single phrase
      With "therefore" or "because,"
I blindly reeled, a hundred ways,
About the syllogistic maze,
      Unconscious where I was.   610

Quoth he "That's regular clap-trap –
      Don't bluster any more.
Now *do* be cool and take a nap!
You're such a peppery old chap
      As never was before!

"You're like a man I used to meet,
      Who got one day so furious
In arguing, the simple heat
Scorched both his slippers off his feet!"
      I said *"That's very curious!"*   620

"Well, it *is* curious, I agree,
      And sounds perhaps like fibs:
But still it's true as true can be –
As sure as your name's Tibbs," said he.
      I said "My name's *not* Tibbs."

"*Not* Tibbs!" he cried – his tone became
        A shade or two less hearty –
"Why, no," said I: "my proper name
Is Tibbets –" "Tibbets?" "Aye, the same."
630   "Why, then YOU'RE NOT THE PARTY!"

With that he struck the board a blow
        That shivered half the glasses;
"Why couldn't you have told me so
Three quarters of an hour ago?
        You king of all the asses!

"To walk four miles through mud and rain,
        To spend the night in smoking,
And then to find that it's in vain –
And I've to do it all again –
640   It's really *too* provoking!

"Don't talk!" he cried, as I began
        To mutter some excuse.
"Who can have patience with a man
That's got no more discretion than
        An idiotic goose?

"To keep me waiting here, instead
        Of telling me at once
That this was not the house!" he said.
"There, that'll do – be off to bed!
650   Don't gape like that, you dunce!"

"It's very fine to throw the blame
        On *me* in such a fashion!
Why didn't you enquire my name
The very minute that you came?"
        I answered in a passion.

"Of course it worries you a bit
          To come so far on foot –
But how was *I* to blame for it?"
"Well, well!" said he, "I must admit
          That isn't badly put.   660

"And certainly you've given me
          The best of wine and victual –
Excuse my violence," said he,
"But accidents like this, you see,
          They put one out a little.

" 'Twas *my* fault after all, I find –
          Shake hands, old Turnip-top!"
The name was hardly to my mind,
But, as no doubt he meant it kind,
          I let the matter drop.   670

"Good-night, old Turnip-top, good-night!
          When I am gone, perhaps
They'll send you some inferior Sprite,
Who'll keep you in a constant fright
          And spoil your soundest naps.

"Tell him you'll stand no sort of trick;
          Then, if he leers and chuckles,
You just be handy with a stick,
(Mind that it's pretty hard and thick,)
          And rap him on the knuckles!   680

"Then carelessly remark 'Old coon!
          Perhaps you're not aware
That, if you don't behave, you'll soon
Be chuckling to another tune –
          And so you'd best take care!'

"That's the right way to cure a Sprite
          Of such-like goings-on –
But, gracious me! It's nearly light!
Good-night, old Turnip-top, good-night!"
690   A nod, and he was gone.

Canto VII – *Sad Souvenaunce*

"What's this?" I pondered. "Have I slept?
          Or can I have been drinking?"
But soon a gentler feeling crept
Upon me, and I sat and wept
          An hour or so, like winking.

Then, as my tears could never bring
          My favourite phantom back,
It seemed to me the proper thing
To mix another glass, and sing
700   The following Coronach.

Coronach

"And art thou gone, beloved ghost?
          Best of familiars!
Nay then, farewell, my duckling roast,
Farewell, farewell, my tea and toast,
          My meerschaum and cigars!

"The hues of life are dull and grey,
          The sweets of life insipid,
When thou, *my charmer, art away –*
Old brick, or rather, let me say,
710   *Old parallelepiped!"*

Instead of singing verse the third,
        I ceased; abruptly, rather –
But, after such a splendid word,
I felt that it would be absurd
        To try it any farther.

"No need for Bones to hurry so!"
        Thought I. "In fact, I doubt
If it was worth his while to go –
And who is Tibbs, I'd like to know,
        To make such work about?   720

"If Tibbs is anything like me,
        It's *possible*," I said,
"He won't be over-pleased to be
Dropped in upon at half-past three,
        After he's snug in bed.

"And if Bones plagues him anyhow –
        Squeaking and all the rest of it,
As he was doing here just now –
I prophesy there'll be a row,
        And Tibbs will have the best of it!"   730

So with a yawn I went my way
        To seek the welcome downy,
And slept, and dreamed till break of day
Of Poltergeist and Fetch and Fay
        And Leprechaun and Brownie!

And never since, by sea or land,
        On mountain or on plain,
'Mid Arctic snow, or Afric sand –
Not even "in the Strand, the Strand!"
        Has Bones appeared again.   740

A Quaker friend accosted me –
  Tall, stiff, as any column –
"Thee'rt out of sorts, I fear," said he;
"Verily I am grieved to see
  Thee go'st so grave and solemn."

"*The ghost's* not grave," I said, "but gay;
  Not solemn, but convivial:
I'm '*out of spirits*,' you should say,
Not '*out of sorts*' –" he turned away,
  Thinking the answer trivial.

For years I've not been visited
  By any kind of Sprite;
Yet still they echo in my head,
Those parting words, so kindly said,
  "Old Turnip-top, good-night!"

A Valentine
Feb. 13, 1860

To a friend at Radley College, who had complained "that I was glad enough to see him when he came, but did not seem to miss him if he stayed away."

And cannot pleasures, while they last,
Be actual, unless, when past,
They leave us shuddering and aghast,
  With anguish smarting?
And cannot friends be fond and fast,
  And yet bear parting?

And must I then, at Friendship's call,
Calmly resign the little all
(Trifling, I grant, it is, and small)
        I have of gladness,   10
And lend my being to the thrall
        Of gloom and sadness?

And think you that I should be dumb,
And full *dolorum omnium*
Excepting when *you* choose to come
        And share my dinner?
At other times be sour and glum,
        And daily thinner?

Must he then only live to weep,
Who'd prove his friendship true and deep,   20
By day a lonely shadow creep,
        At night rest badly,
Oft muttering in his broken sleep
        The name of Radley?

The lover, if, for certain days,
His fair one be denied his gaze,
Sinks not in grief and wild amaze,
        But, wiser wooer,
He spends the time in writing lays,
        And posts them to her.   30

And if he be an Oxford Don,
Or "Jonson's learned sock be on,"
A touching Valentine anon
        The post shall carry,
When thirteen days are come and gone
        Of February.

Farewell, dear friend, and when we meet
In desert waste or crowded street,
Perhaps before this week shall fleet,
          Perhaps to-morrow,
I trust to find *your* heart the seat
          Of wasting sorrow.

40

A Sea Dirge

There are certain things – as, a spider, a ghost,
          The income-tax, gout, an umbrella for three –
That I hate, but the thing that I hate the most
          Is a thing they call the Sea.

Pour some salt water over the floor –
          Ugly I'm sure you'll allow it to be:
Suppose it extended a mile or more,
          That's very like the Sea.

Beat a dog till it howls outright –
          Cruel, but all very well for a spree:
Suppose that he did so day and night,
          That would be like the Sea.

10

I had a vision of nursery-maids;
          Tens of thousands passed by me –
All leading children with wooden spades,
          And this was by the Sea.

Who invented those spades of wood?
          Who was it cut them out of the tree?
None, I think, but an idiot could –
          Or one that loved the Sea.

20

It is pleasant and dreamy, no doubt, to float
      With "thoughts as boundless, and souls as free"!
But, suppose you are very unwell in the boat,
      How do you like the Sea?

"But it makes the intellect clear and keen –"
      Prove it! Prove it! How can it be?
"Why, what does 'B sharp' (in music) mean.
      If not the 'natural C'?"

What, keen? With such questions as "When's high tide?
      Is shelling shrimps an improvement to tea?   30
Are donkeys adapted for Man to ride?"
      Such are our thoughts by the Sea.

There is an insect that people avoid
      (Whence is derived the verb "to flee");
Where have you been by it most annoyed?
      In lodgings by the Sea.

If you like coffee with sand for dregs,
      A decided hint of salt in your tea,
And a fishy taste in the very eggs –
      By all means choose the Sea.   40

And if, with these dainties to drink and eat,
      You prefer not a vestige of grass or tree,
And a chronic state of wet in your feet,
      Then – I recommend the Sea.

For *I* have friends who dwell by the coast –
      Pleasant friends they are to me!
It is when I am with them I wonder most
      That anyone likes the Sea.

They take me a walk: though tired and stiff,
50   To climb the heights I madly agree;
And, after a tumble or so from the cliff,
          They kindly suggest the Sea.

I try the rocks, and I think it cool
          That they laugh with such an excess of glee,
As I heavily slip into every pool
          That skirts the cold cold Sea.

Once I met a friend in the street,
          With wife, and nurse, and children three –
Never again such a sight may I meet
60   As that party from the Sea!

Their looks were sullen, their steps were slow,
          Convicted felons they seemed to be:
"Are you going to prison, dear friend?" "Oh no!
          We're returning – from the Sea!"

Ye Carpette Knyghte

I have a horse – a ryghte good horse –
          Ne doe I envie those
Who scoure ye plaine yn headie course,
          Tyll soddaine on theire nose
They lyghte wyth unexpected force –
          Yt ys – a horse of clothes.

I have a saddel – "Say'st thou soe?
          Wyth styrruppes, Knyghte, to boote?"
I sayde not that – I answere "Noe" –
10   Yt lacketh such, I woot –
It ys a mutton – saddel, loe!
          Parte of ye fleecie brute.

> I have a bytte – a ryghte good bytt –
>   As schall bee seene yn tyme.
> Ye jawe of horse yt wyll not fytte;
>   Yts use ys more sublyme.
> Fayre Syr, how deemest thou of yt?
>   Yt ys – thys bytte of rhyme.

Hiawatha's Photographing

In these days of imitation, I can claim no sort of merit for this slight attempt at doing what is known to be so easy. Any one who knows what verse is, with the slightest ear for rhythm, can throw off a composition in the easy running metre of "The Song of Hiawatha". Having, then, distinctly stated that I challenge no attention, in the following little poem, to its merely verbal jingle, I must beg the candid reader, to confine his criticism, to its treatment of the subject.

>   From his shoulder Hiawatha
> Took the camera of rosewood,
> Made of sliding, folding rosewood;
> Neatly put it all together.
> In its case it lay compactly,
> Folded into nearly nothing;
> But he opened out the hinges,
> Pushed and pulled the joints and hinges,
> Till it looked all squares and oblongs,
> Like a complicated figure   10
> In the Second Book of Euclid.
>   This he perched upon a tripod,
> And the family in order
> Sat before him for their pictures.
> Mystic, awful was the process.
>   First, a piece of glass he coated
> With Collodion, and plunged it
> In a bath of Lunar Caustic

Carefully dissolved in water:
20   There he left it certain minutes.
        Secondly, my Hiawatha
Made with cunning hand a mixture
Of the acid Pyro-gallic,
And of Glacial Acetic,
And of Alcohol and water:
This developed all the picture.
        Finally, he fixed each picture
With a saturate solution
Of a certain salt of Soda –
30   Chemists call it Hyposulphite.
(Very difficult the name is
For a metre like the present
But periphrasis has done it.)
        All the family in order
Sat before him for their pictures.
Each in turn, as he was taken,
Volunteered his own suggestions,
His invaluable suggestions.
        First, the Governor, the Father:
40   He suggested velvet curtains
Looped about a massy pillar;
And the corner of a table,
Of a rosewood dining-table.
He would hold a scroll of something,
Hold it firmly in his left-hand;
He would keep his right-hand buried
(Like Napoleon) in his waistcoat;
He would contemplate the distance
With a look of pensive meaning,
50   As of ducks that die in tempests.
He would gaze into the distance –
        Grand, heroic was the notion:
Yet the picture failed entirely:
Failed because he moved a little,
Moved because he couldn't help it.
        Next his better half took courage;

She would have her picture taken;
She came dressed beyond description,
Dressed in jewels and in satin,
Far too gorgeous for an empress.   60
Gracefully she sat down sideways,
With a simper scarcely human,
Holding in her hand a nosegay
Rather larger than a cabbage.
All the while that she was taking,
Still the lady chattered, chattered,
Like a monkey in the forest.
"Am I sitting still?" she asked him.
"Is my face enough in profile?
Shall I hold the nosegay higher?   70
Will it come into the picture?"
And the picture failed completely.

       Next the son, the Stunning-Cantab:
He suggested curves of beauty,
Curves pervading all his figure,
Which the eye might follow onward,
Till they centred in the breast-pin,
Centred in the golden breast-pin.
He had learnt it all from Ruskin,
(Author of The Stones of Venice,   80
"Seven Lamps of Architecture,
Modern Painters," and some others);
And perhaps he had not fully
Understood the author's meaning;
But, whatever was the reason,
All was fruitless, as the picture
Ended in a total failure.

       Next to him the eldest daughter:
She suggested very little;
Only asked if he would take her   90
With her look of "passive beauty."

       Her idea of passive beauty
Was a squinting of the left-eye,
Was a drooping of the right-eye,

Was a smile that went up sideways
To the corner of the nostrils.
    Hiawatha, when she asked him,
Took no notice of the question,
Looked as if he hadn't heard it;
But, when pointedly appealed to,
Smiled in a peculiar manner,
Coughed, and said it "didn't matter,"
Bit his lip and changed the subject.
    Nor in this was he mistaken,
As the picture failed completely.
    So, in turn, the other sisters.
Last, the youngest son was taken:
Very rough and thick his hair was,
Very dusty was his jacket,
Very fidgetty his manner,
And his overbearing sisters
Called him names he disapproved of:
Called him Johnny, "Daddy's Darling,"
Called him Jacky, "Scrubby School-boy."
And, so awful was the picture,
In comparison the others
Might be thought to have succeeded,
To have partially succeeded.
    Finally, my Hiawatha
Tumbled all the tribe together,
("Grouped" is not the right expression),
And, as happy chance would have it,
Did at last obtain a picture
Where the faces all succeeded:
Each came out a perfect likeness.
    Then they joined and all abused it,
Unrestrainedly abused it,
As "the worst and ugliest picture
They could possibly have dreamed of.
Giving one such strange expressions!
Sulkiness, conceit, and meanness!
Really any one would take us

(Any one who did not know us)
For the most unpleasant people!"
(Hiawatha seemed to think so,
Seemed to think it not unlikely).
All together rang their voices,
Angry, loud, discordant voices,
As of dogs that howl in concert,
As of cats that wail in chorus.   140
    But my Hiawatha's patience,
His politeness, and his patience,
Unaccountably had vanished,
And he left that happy party.
Neither did he leave them slowly,
With that calm deliberation,
That intense deliberation
Which photographers aspire to:
But he left them in a hurry,
Left them in a mighty hurry,   150
Vowing that he would not stand it.
    Hurriedly he packed his boxes,
Hurriedly the porter trundled
On a barrow all his boxes;
Hurriedly he took his ticket,
Hurriedly the train received him:
Thus departed Hiawatha.

The Lang Coortin'

The ladye she stood at her lattice high,
    Wi' her doggie at her feet;
Thorough the lattice she can spy
    The passers in the street.

"There's one that standeth at the door,
    And tirleth at the pin:
Now speak and say, my popinjay,*
    If I sall let him in."

Then up and spake the popinjay
That flew abune her head:
"Gae let him in that tirls the pin,
He cometh thee to wed."

O when he cam' the parlour in,
A woeful man was he!
"And dinna ye ken your lover again,
Sae well that loveth thee?"

"And how wad I ken ye loved me, Sir,
That have been sae lang away?
And how wad I ken ye loved me, Sir?
Ye never telled me sae."

Said – "ladye dear," and the salt salt tear
Cam' rinnin' doon his cheek,
"I have sent thee tokens of my love
This many and many a week.

"O didna ye get the rings, ladye,
The rings o' the gowd sae fine?
I wist that I have sent to thee
Four score, four score and nine."

"They cam' to me," said that fair ladye.
"Wow, they were flimsie things!"
Said – "that chain o' gowd, my doggie to houd,
It is made o' thae self-same rings."

"And didna ye get the locks, the locks,
The locks o' my ain black hair,
Whilk I sent by post, whilk I sent by box,
Whilk I sent by the carrier?"

"They cam' to me," said that fair ladye;
    "And I prithee send nae mair!"
Said – "that cushion sae red, for my doggie's head,
    It is stuffed wi' thae locks o' hair."   40

"And didna ye get the letter, ladye,
    Tied wi' a silken string,
Whilk I sent to thee frae the far countrie,
    A message of love to bring?"

"It cam' to me frae the far countrie
    Wi' its silken string and a';
But it wasna prepaid," said that high-born maid,
    "Sae I gar'd them tak' it awa'."

"O ever alack that ye sent it back,
    It was written sae clerkly and well!   50
Now the message it brought, and the boon that it sought,
    I must even say it mysel'."

Then up and spake the popinjay,
    Sae wisely counselled he:
"Now say it in the proper way,
    Gae doon upon thy knee!"

The lover he turned baith red and pale,
    Gaed doon upon his knee:
"O Ladye, hear the waesome tale
    That I have to tell to thee!   60

"For five lang years, and five lang years,
    I coorted thee by looks;
By nods and winks, by smiles and tears,
    As I had read in books.

"For ten lang years, O weary hours!
  I coorted thee by signs;
By sending game, by sending flowers,
  By sending Valentines.

"For five lang years, and five lang years,
70   I have dwelt in the far countrie,
Till that thy mind should be inclined
  Mair tenderly to me.

"Now thirty years are gane and past,
  I am come frae a foreign land:
I am come to tell thee my love at last;
  O Ladye, gie me thy hand!"

The ladye she turned not pale nor red,
  But she smiled a pitiful smile:
"Sic' a coortin' as yours, my man," she said
80   "Takes a lang and a weary while!"

And out and laughed the popinjay,
  A laugh of bitter scorn:
"A coortin' done in sic' a way,
  It ought not to be borne!"

Wi' that the doggie barked aloud,
  And up and doon he ran,
And tugged and strained his chain o' gowd,
  All for to bite the man.

"O hush thee, gentle popinjay!
90   O hush thee, doggie dear!
There is a word I fain wad say,
  It needeth he should hear!"

Aye louder screamed that ladye fair
     To still her doggie's bark;
Ever the lover shouted mair
     To make that ladye hark:

Shrill and more shrill the popinjay
     Kept up his angry squall:
I trow the doggie's voice that day
     Was louder than them all!   100

The serving-men and serving-maids
     Sat by the kitchen fire:
They heard sic' a din the parlour within
     As made them much admire.

Out spake the boy in buttons,
     (I ween he wasna thin,)
"Now wha will tae the parlour gae,
     And stay this deadlie din?"

And they have taen a kerchief,
     Casted their kevils** in,   110
For wha will tae the parlour gae,
     And stay that deadlie din.

When on that boy the kevil fell
     To stay the fearsome noise,
"Gae in," they cried, "whate'er betide,
     Thou prince of button-boys!"

Syne, he has taen a supple cane
     To beat that dog sae fat:
The doggie yowled, the doggie howled
     The louder aye for that.   120

Syne, he has taen a mutton-bane –
    The doggie hushed his noise,
And followed doon the kitchen stair
    That prince of button-boys!

Then sadly spake that ladye fair,
    Wi' a frown upon her brow:
"O dearer to me is my sma' doggie
    Than a dozen sic' as thou!

"Nae use, nae use for sighs and tears:
    Nae use at all to fret:
Sin' ye've bided sae well for thirty years,
    Ye may bide a wee langer yet!"

Sadly, sadly he crossed the floor
    And tirlèd at the pin:
Sadly went he through the door
    Where sadly he cam' in.

"O gin I had a popinjay,
    To fly abune my head,
To tell me what I ought to say,
    I had by this been wed.

"O gin I find anither ladye,"
    He said with sighs and tears,
"I wist my coortin' sall not be
    Anither thirty years.

"For gin I find a ladye gay,
    Exactly to my taste,
I'll pop the question, aye or nay,
    In twenty years at maist."

*Popinjay. This bird appears to have been a regular domestic
institution with our forefathers (see the "Minstrelsy of the Border"),

and to have volunteered advice and moral reflections on all possible occasions – much after the fashion of the Chorus in Greek Tragedy.

**Kevils*, lots. A method of deciding on a course of action, which was probably most popular with those who could not afford to keep a popinjay.

Melancholetta

With saddest music all day long
    She soothed her secret sorrow:
At night she sighed. "I fear 'twas wrong
    Such cheerful words to borrow;
Dearest, a sweeter, sadder song
    I'll sing to thee to-morrow."

I thanked her, but I could not say
    That I was glad to hear it:
I left the house at break of day,
    And did not venture near it   10
Till time, I hoped, had worn away
    Her grief, for naught could cheer it!

My dismal sister! Couldst thou know
    The wretched home thou keepest!
Thy brother, drowned in daily woe,
    Is thankful when thou sleepest;
For if I laugh, however low,
    When thou'rt awake, thou weepest!

I took my sister t'other day
    (Excuse the slang expression)   20
To Sadler's Wells to see the play,
    In hopes the new impression
Might in her thoughts, from grave to gay,
    Effect some slight digression.

I asked three friends of mine from town
          To join us in our folly,
Whose mirth, I thought, might serve to drown
          My sister's melancholy:
The lively Jones, the sportive Brown,
30   And Robinson the jolly.

I need not tell of soup and fish
          In solemn silence swallowed,
The sobs that ushered in each dish,
          And its departure followed,
Nor yet my suicidal wish
          To *be* the cheese I hollowed.

Some desperate attempts were made
          To start a conversation;
"Madam," the lively Jones essayed,
40   "Which kind of recreation,
Hunting or fishing, have you made
          Your special occupation?"

Her lips curved downwards instantly,
          As if of india-rubber.
"Hounds *in full cry* I like," said she,
          (Oh how I longed to snub her!)
"Of fish, a whale's the one for me,
          It is so full of blubber!"

The night's performance was "King John:"
50   "It's dull," she wept, "and so-so!"
Awhile I let her tears flow on,
          She said "they soothed her woe so!"
At length the curtain rose upon
          "Bombastes Furioso."

In vain we roared; in vain we tried
 To rouse her into laughter:
Her pensive glances wandered wide
 From orchestra to rafter –
"*Tier upon tier*!" she said, and sighed;
 And silence followed after.   60

The Three Voices

The First Voice

With hands tight clenched through matted hair,
He crouched in trance of dumb despair:
There came a breeze from out the air.

It passed athwart the glooming flat –
It fanned his forehead as he sat –
It lightly bore away his hat,

All to the feet of one who stood
Like maid enchanted in a wood,
Frowning as darkly as she could.

With huge umbrella, lank and brown, 10
Unerringly she pinned it down,
Right through the centre of the crown.

Then, with an aspect cold and grim,
Regardless of its battered rim,
She took it up and gave it him.

Awhile like one in dreams he stood,
Then faltered forth his gratitude,
In words just short of being rude:

For it had lost its shape and shine,
And it had cost him four-and-nine,
And he was going out to dine.

With grave indifference to his speech,
Fixing her eyes upon the beach,
She said "Each gives to more than each."

He could not answer yea or nay;
He faltered "Gifts may pass away."
Yet knew not what he meant to say.

"If that be so," she straight replied,
"Each heart with each doth coincide:
What boots it? For the world is wide."

And he, not wishing to appear
Less wise, said "This Material Sphere
Is but Attributive Idea."

But when she asked him "Wherefore so?"
He felt his very whiskers glow,
And frankly owned "I do not know."

While, like broad waves of golden grain,
Or sunlit hues on cloistered pane,
His colour came and went again.

Pitying his obvious distress,
Yet with a tinge of bitterness,
She said "The More exceeds the Less."

"A truth of such undoubted weight,"
He urged, "and so extreme in date,
It were superfluous to state."

Roused into sudden passion, she
In tone of cold malignity:
"To others, yes; but not to thee."

But when she saw him quail and quake,
And when he urged "For pity's sake!"   50
Once more in gentle tones she spake:

"Thought in the mind doth still abide;
That is by Intellect supplied,
And within that Idea doth hide.

"And he, that yearns the truth to know,
Still further inwardly may go,
And find Idea from Notion flow.

"And thus the chain, that sages sought,
Is to a glorious circle wrought,
For Notion hath its source in Thought."   60

When he, with racked and whirling brain,
Feebly implored her to explain,
She simply said it all again.

Wrenched with an agony intense,
He spake, neglecting Sound and Sense
And careless of all consequence:

"Mind – I believe – is Essence – Ent –
Abstract – that is – an Accident –
Which we – that is to say – I meant –"

When, with quick breath and cheeks flushed,   70
At length his speech was somewhat hushed,
She looked at him, and he was crushed.

It needed not her calm reply;
She fixed him with a stony eye,
And he could neither fight nor fly,

While she dissected, word by word,
His speech, half guessed at and half heard,
As might a cat a little bird.

Then, having wholly overthrown
His views, and stripped them to the bone,
Proceeded to unfold her own.

So passed they on with even pace,
Yet gradually one might trace
A shadow growing on his face.

The Second Voice

They walked beside the wave-worn beach,
Her tongue was very apt to teach,
And now and then he did beseech

She would abate her dulcet tone,
Because the talk was all her own,
And he was dull as any drone.

She urged "No cheese is made of chalk:"
And ceaseless flowed her dreary talk,
Tuned to the footfall of a walk.

Her voice was very full and rich,
And, when at length she asked him "Which?"
It mounted to its highest pitch.

He a bewildered answer gave,
Drowned in the sullen moaning wave,
Lost in the echoes of the cave.

He answered her he knew not what;   100
Like shaft from bow at random shot:
He spoke, but she regarded not.

She waited not for his reply,
But with a downward leaden eye
Went on as if he were not by.

Sound argument and grave defence,
Strange questions raised on "Why?" and "Whence?"
And weighted down with common sense.

"Shall Man be Man? and shall he miss
Of other thoughts no thought but this,   110
Harmonious dews of sober bliss?

"What boots it? Shall his fevered eye
Through towering nothingness descry
This grisly phantom hurry by?

"And hear dumb shrieks that fill the air;
See mouths that gape, and eyes that stare
And redden in the dusky glare?

"The meadows breathing amber light,
The darkness toppling from the height,
The feathery train of granite Night?   120

"Shall he, grown grey among his peers,
Through the thick curtain of his tears
Catch glimpses of his earlier years,

"And hear the sounds he knew of yore,
Old shuffling on the sanded floor,
Old knuckles tapping at the door?

"Yet still before him as he flies
One pallid form shall ever rise,
And, bodying forth in glassy eyes

130

"A vision of a vanished good,
Low peering through the tangled wood,
Shall freeze the current of his blood."

Still from each fact, with skill uncouth
And savage rapture, like a tooth
She wrenched some slow reluctant truth.

Till, like some silent water-mill
When summer suns have dried the rill,
She reached a full stop, and was still.

Dead calm succeeded to the fuss,

140

As when the loaded omnibus
Has reached the railway terminus;

When for the tumult of the street
Is heard the engine's stifled beat,
The wary tread of porters' feet.

With glance that ever sought the ground,
She moved her lips without a sound,
And every now and then she frowned.

He gazed upon the sleeping sea,
And joyed in its tranquillity,

150

And in that silence dead, but she

To muse a little space did seem,
Then, like the echo of a dream,
Harped back upon her threadbare theme.

Still an attentive ear he lent,
But could not fathom what she meant:
She was not deep, nor eloquent.

He marked the ripple on the sand:
The even swaying of her hand
Was all that he could understand.

He left her, and he turned aside: 160
He sat and watched the coming tide
Across the shores so newly dried.

He wondered at the waters clear,
The breeze that whispered in his ear,
The billows heaving far and near;

And why he had so long preferred
To hang upon her every word;
"In truth," he said, "it was absurd."

The Third Voice

Not long this transport held its place:
Within a little moment's space   170
Quick tears were raining down his face.

His heart stood still, aghast with fear;
A wordless voice, nor far nor near,
He seemed to hear and not to hear.

"Tears kindle not the doubtful spark:
If so, why not? Of this remark
The bearings are profoundly dark."

"Her speech," he said, "hath caused this pain;
Easier I count it to explain
The jargon of the howling main,   180

"Or, stretched beside some sedgy brook,
To con, with inexpressive look,
An unintelligible book."

Low spake the voice within his head,
In words imagined more than said,
Soundless as ghost's intended tread:

"If thou art duller than before,
Why quittedst thou the voice of lore?
Why not endure, expecting more?"

190   "Rather than that," he groaned aghast,
"I'd writhe in depths of cavern vast,
Some loathly vampire's rich repast."

" 'Twere hard," it answered, "themes immense
To coop within the narrow fence
That rings *thy* scant intelligence."

"Not so," he urged, "nor once alone:
But there was that within her tone
That chilled me to the very bone.

"Her style was anything but clear
200   And most unpleasantly severe;
Her epithets were very queer.

"And yet, so grand were her replies,
I could not choose but deem her wise;
I did not dare to criticise;

"Nor did I leave her, till she went
So deep in tangled argument
That all my powers of thought were spent."

A little whisper inly slid;
"Yet truth is truth: you know you did –"
210   A little wink beneath the lid.

And, sickened with excess of dread,
Prone to the dust he bent his head,
And lay like one three-quarters dead.

Forth went the whisper like a breeze;
Left him amid the wondering trees,
Left him by no means at his ease.

Once more he weltered in despair,
With hands, through denser-matted hair,
More tightly clenched than then they were.

When, bathed in dawn of living red,   220
Majestic frowned the mountain head,
"Tell me my fault," was all he said.

When, at high noon, the blazing sky
Scorched in his head each haggard eye,
Then keenest rose his weary cry.

And when at eve the unpitying sun
Smiled grimly on the solemn fun,
"Alack," he sighed, "what *have* I done?"

But saddest, darkest was the sight,
When the cold grasp of leaden Night   230
Dashed him to earth and held him tight.

Tortured, unaided, and alone,
Thunders were silence to his groan,
Bagpipes sweet music to its tone:

"What? Ever thus, in dismal round,
Shall Pain and Mystery profound
Pursue me like a sleepless hound,

"With crimson-dashed and eager jaws,
Me, still in ignorance of the cause,
240   Unknowing what I brake of laws?"

The whisper to his ear did seem
Like echoed flow of silent stream,
Or shadow of forgotten dream;

The whisper, trembling in the wind:
"Her fate with thine was intertwined,"
So spake it in his inner mind;

"Each orbed on each a baleful star,
Each proved the other's blight and bar,
Each unto each were best, most far:

250   "Yea, each to each was worse than foe,
Thou, a scared dullard, gibbering low,
And she, an avalanche of woe."

A Double Acrostic

The Double Acrostic, a form of puzzle which has lately
become fashionable, is constructed thus: – Two words are
selected having the same number of letters: these are sup-
posed to be written in two parallel columns, and a series
of words is then found (their length is immaterial) such
that the first column may consist of their initial letters, and
the second of their final letters. For instance, if the
column-words selected were "rose" and "ring" we might
fill up thus: –

r i v e r
o b i
s e v e n
e g g

The two column-words, and the horizontal words, are
then described in a series of lines or verses, and the puzzle
is complete.

The innumerable specimens of this form of puzzle
already published are in every way (if we except the stud-
ied insipidity of the separate verses, and their total want
of connexion one with another) to be commended. The
following attempt made at the request of some friends
who had gone to a ball at an Oxford Commemoration, is
printed in the hope of suggesting a possible improvement
in the treatment of the subject.

There was an ancient city, stricken down
       With a strange frenzy, and for many a day
They paced from morn to eve the noisy town,
       And danced the night away.

I asked the cause: the aged man grew sad –
       They pointed to a building grey and tall,
And hoarsely answered "Step inside, my lad,
       And then you'll see it all."

Yet what are all such gaieties to me
       Whose thoughts are full of indices and surds?   10

$$X^2 + 7X + 53$$
$$= \frac{11}{3} \ .$$

But something whispered "It will soon be done –
       Bands cannot always play, or ladies smile:
Endure with patience the distasteful fun
       For just a little while!"

A change came o'er my Vision – it was night:
       We clove a pathway through a frantic throng;
The steeds, wild-plunging, filled us with affright;
       The chariots whirled along.   20

Within a marble hall a river ran –
    A living tide, half muslin and half cloth:
And here one mourned a broken wreath or fan,
    Yet swallowed down her wrath;

And here one offered to a thirsty fair
    (His words half-drowned amid those
        thunders tuneful)
Some frozen viand (there were many there),
    A tooth-ache in each spoonful.

There comes a happy pause, for human strength
30   Will not endure to dance without cessation;
And every one must reach the point at length
    Of absolute prostration.

At such a moment ladies learn to give
    To partners, who would urge them over-much,
A flat and yet decided negative –
    Photographers love such.

There comes a welcome summons – hope revives,
    And fading eyes grow bright, and pulses quicken;
Incessant pop the corks, and busy knives
40   Dispense the tongue and chicken.

Flushed with new life, the crowd flows back again:
    And all is tangled talk and mazy motion –
Much like a waving field of golden grain,
    Or a tempestuous ocean.

And thus they give the time that Nature meant
    For peaceful sleep and meditative snores,
To thoughtless din, and mindless merriment,
    And waste of shoes and floors.

And one (we name him not) that flies the flowers,
    That dreads the dances, and that shuns the salads,   50
They doom to pass in solitude the hours,
    Writing acrostic-ballads.

How late it grows! Long since the hour is past
    That should have warned us with its double knock;
The twilight wanes, and morning comes at last –
    "Oh, Uncle! what's o'clock?"

The Uncle gravely nods, and wisely winks –
    It *may* mean much; but how is one to know?
He opes his mouth – yet out of it, methinks,
    No words of wisdom flow.   60

Size and Tears

    When on the sandy shore I sit,
        Beside the salt sea-wave,
    And fall into a weeping fit
        Because I dare not shave –
    A little whisper at my ear
    Enquires the reason of my fear.

    I answer "If that ruffian Jones,
        Should recognise me here,
    He'd bellow out my name in tones
        Offensive to the ear: 10
    He chaffs me so on being stout
    (A thing that always puts me out)."

    Ah me! I see him on the cliff!
        Farewell, farewell to hope,
    If he should look this way, and if
        He's got his telescope!
    To whatsoever place I flee,
    My odious rival follows me!

For every night, and everywhere,
      I meet him out at dinner;
And when I've found some charming fair,
      And vowed to die or win her,
The wretch (he's thin and I am stout)
Is sure to come and cut me out!

The girls (just like them!) all agree
      To praise J. Jones, Esquire:
I ask them what on earth they see
      About him to admire?
They cry "He is so sleek and slim,
It's quite a treat to look at him!"

They vanish in tobacco smoke,
      Those visionary maids –
I feel a sharp and sudden poke
      Between the shoulder-blades –
"Why, Brown, my boy! You're growing stout!"
(I told you he would find me out!)

"My growth is not *your* business, Sir!"
      "No more it is, my boy!
But if it's *yours*, as I infer,
      Why, Brown, I give you joy!"
A man, whose business prospers so,
Is just the sort of man to know!

"It's hardly safe, though, talking here –
      I'd best get out of reach:
For such a weight as yours, I fear,
      Must shortly sink the beach!' –
Insult me thus because I'm stout!
I vow I'll go and call him out!

Poeta Fit Non Nascitur

"How shall I be a poet?
        How shall I write in rhyme?
You told me once 'the very wish
        Partook of the sublime:'
Then tell me how! Don't put me off
        With your 'another time'!"

The old man smiled to see him,
        To hear his sudden sally;
He liked the lad to speak his mind
        Enthusiastically: 10
And thought "There's no hum-drum in him,
        Nor any shilly-shally."

"And would you be a poet
        Before you've been to school?
Ah, well! I hardly thought you
        So absolute a fool.
First learn to be spasmodic –
        A very simple rule.

"For first you write a sentence,
        And then you chop it small;   20
Then mix the bits, and sort them out
        Just as they chance to fall:
The order of the phrases makes
        No difference at all.

"Then, if you'd be impressive,
        Remember what I say,
That abstract qualities begin
        With capitals alway:
The True, the Good, the Beautiful –
        Those are the things that pay!   30

"Next, when you are describing
          A shape, or sound, or tint;
Don't state the matter plainly,
          But put it in a hint;
And learn to look at all things
          With a sort of mental squint."

"For instance, if I wished, Sir,
          Of mutton-pies to tell,
Should I say 'dreams of fleecy flocks
          Pent in a wheaten cell'?"
"Why, yes," the old man said; "that phrase
          Would answer very well.

"Then fourthly, there are epithets
          That suit with any word –
As well as Harvey's Reading Sauce
          With fish, or flesh, or bird –
Of these, 'wild,' 'lonely,' 'weary,' 'strange,'
          Are much to be preferred."

"And will it do, O will it do
          To take them in a lump –
As 'the wild man went his weary way
          To a strange and lonely pump'?"
"Nay, nay! You must not hastily
          To such conclusions jump.

"Such epithets, like pepper,
          Give zest to what you write;
And, if you strew them sparely,
          They whet the appetite:
But if you lay them on too thick,
          You spoil the matter quite.

"Last, as to the arrangement:
          Your reader, you should show him,
Must take what information he
          Can get, and look for no im-
mature disclosure of the drift
          And purpose of your poem.

"Therefore, to test his patience –
          How much he can endure –
Mention no places, names, or dates,
          And evermore be sure   70
Throughout the poem to be found
          Consistently obscure.

"First fix upon the limit
          To which it shall extend:
Then fill it up with 'Padding' –
          (Beg some of any friend):
Your great SENSATION-STANZA
          You place towards the end."

"And what is a Sensation,
          Grandfather, tell me, pray?   80
I think I never heard the word
          So used before to-day:
Be kind enough to mention one
          'Exempli gratiâ.' "

And the old man, looking sadly
          Across the garden-lawn,
Where here and there a dew-drop
          Yet glittered in the dawn,
Said "Go to the Adelphi,
          And see the 'Colleen Bawn.'   90

"The word is due to Boucicault –
      The theory is his,
Where Life becomes a spasm,
      And History a whiz:
If that is not Sensation,
      I don't know what it is.

"Now try your hand, ere Fancy
      Have lost its present glow –"
"And then," his grandson added,
      "We'll publish it, you know:
Green cloth – gold-lettered at the back –
      In duodecimo!"

Then proudly smiled that old man
      To see the eager lad
Rush madly for his pen and ink
      And for his blotting-pad –
But, when he thought of *publishing*,
      His face grew stern and sad.

Atalanta in Camden Town

Ay, 'twas here, on this spot,
      In that summer of yore,
Atalanta did not
      Vote my presence a bore,
Nor reply, to my tenderest talk, she had "heard all that
      nonsense before."

She'd the brooch I had bought
      And the necklace and sash on,
And her heart, as I thought,
      Was alive to my passion;
And she'd done up her hair in the style that the Empress
      had brought into fashion.

I had been to the play
        With my pearl of a Peri –
But, for all I could say,
        She declared she was weary,
That "the place was so crowded and hot", and she "couldn't
    abide that Dundreary."

Then I thought " 'Tis for me
        That she whines and she whimpers!"
And it soothed me to see
        Those sensational simpers,
And I said "This is scrumptious!" – a phrase I had learned
    from the Devonshire shrimpers.   20

And I vowed " 'Twill be said
        I'm a fortunate fellow,
When the breakfast is spread,
        When the topers are mellow,
When the foam of the bride-cake is white, and the fierce
    orange-blossoms are yellow."

O that languishing yawn!
        O those eloquent eyes!
I was drunk with the dawn
        Of a splendid surmise –
I was stung by a look, I was slain by a tear, by a tempest
    of sighs.   30

And I whispered "I guess
        The sweet secret thou keepest,
And the dainty distress
        That thou wistfully weepest;
And the question is 'License or banns?', though undoubtedly
    banns are the cheapest."

> Then her white hand I clasped,
>   And with kisses I crowned it:
> But she glared and she gasped,
>   And she muttered "Confound it!" –
> 40   Or at least it was something like that, but the noise
>   Of the omnibus drowned it.

The Elections to The Hebdomadal Council

In the year 1866, a Letter with the above title was pub-
lished in Oxford, addressed by Mr. Goldwin Smith to the
Senior Censor of Christ Church, with the two-fold object
of revealing to the University a vast political misfortune
which it had unwittingly encountered, and of suggesting a
remedy which should at once alleviate the bitterness of the
calamity and secure the sufferers from its recurrence. The
misfortune thus revealed was no less than the fact that,
at a recent election of Members to the Hebdomadal Coun-
cil, two Conservatives had been chosen, thus giving a
Conservative majority in the Council; and the remedy sug-
gested was a sufficiently sweeping one, embracing, as it
did, the following details: –

1. "The exclusion" (from Congregation) "of the non-
academical elements which form a main part of the strength
of this party domination." These "elements" are afterwards
enumerated as "the parish clergy and the professional
men of the city, and chaplains who are without any aca-
demical occupation."

2. The abolition of the Hebdomadal Council.

3. The abolition of the legislative functions of Convocation.
These are all the main features of this remarkable scheme
of Reform, unless it be necessary to add –

4. "To preside over a Congregation with full legislative

powers, the Vice-Chancellor ought no doubt to be a man of real capacity."

But it would be invidious to suppose that there was any intention of suggesting this as a novelty.

The following rhythmical version of the Letter develops its principles to an extent which possibly the writer had never contemplated.

The Hebdomadal Council

"Now is the *Winter* of our discontent."[1]

"Heard ye the arrow hurtle in the sky?
Heard ye the dragon-monster's dreadful cry?" –
Excuse this sudden burst of the Heroic;
The present state of things would vex a Stoic!
And just as Sairey Gamp, for pains within,
Administered a modicum of gin,
So does my mind, when vexed and ill at ease,
Console itself with soothing similes,
The "dragon-monster" (pestilential schism!)
I need not tell you is Conservatism;   10
The "hurtling arrow" (till we find a better)
Is represented by the present Letter.

    'Twas, I remember, but the other day,
Dear Senior Censor, that you chanced to say
You thought these party-combinations would
Be found, "though needful, no unmingled good."
Unmingled good? They are unmingled ill![2]
I never took to them, and never will[3] –
What am I saying? Heed it not, my friend:
On the next page I mean to recommend   20
The very dodges that I now condemn
In the Conservatives! Don't hint to them ⎫
A word of this! (In confidence. Ahem!) ⎭

Need I rehearse the history of Jowett?
I need not, Senior Censor, for you know it.[4]
That was the Board Hebdomadal, and oh!
Who would be free, themselves must strike the blow!
Let each that wears a beard, and each that shaves,
Join in the cry "We never will be slaves!"

30   "But can the University afford
To be a slave to any kind of board?
A *slave*?" you shuddering ask. "Think you it can, Sir?"
"*Not at the present moment*," is my answer.[5]
I've thought the matter o'er and o'er again
And given to it all my powers of brain;
I've thought it out, and this is what I make it,
(And I don't care a Tory how you take it:)
It may be right to go ahead, I guess:
It may be right to stop, I do confess: ⎤
40   Also, it may be right to retrogress.[6] ⎦
So says the oracle, and, for myself, I
Must say it beats to fits the one at Delphi!

         To save beloved Oxford from the yoke,
(For this majority's beyond a joke,)
We must combine,[7] aye! hold a *caucus*-meeting,[8]
Unless we want to get another beating.
That they should "bottle" us is nothing new –
But shall they bottle us and *caucus* too?
See the "fell unity of purpose" now
50   With which Obstructives plunge into the row![9]
"Factious Minorities," we used to sigh –
"Factious Majorities" is now the cry.
"Votes – ninety-two" – no combination here:
"Votes – ninety-three" – conspiracy, 'tis clear![10]
You urge " 'Tis but a unit." I reply
That in that unit lurks their "unity."
Our voters often bolt, and often baulk us,
But then, they never, never go to *caucus!*
Our voters can't forget the maxim famous
60   "*Semel electum semper eligamus*;"

They never can be worked into a ferment
By visionary promise of preferment,
Nor taught, by hints of "Paradise"[11] beguiled,
To whisper "C for Chairman" like a child![12]
And thus the friends that we have tempted down
Oft take the two-o'clock Express for town.[13]
     This is our danger: this the secret foe
That aims at Oxford such a deadly blow.
What champion can we find to save the State,
To crush the plot? We darkly whisper "Wait!"[14]   70
     My scheme is this: remove the votes of all
The residents that are not Liberal[15] –
Leave the young Tutors uncontrolled and free,
And Oxford then shall see – what it shall see.
What next? Why then, I say, let Convocation
Be shorn of all her powers of legislation.[16]
But why stop there? Let us go boldly on –
Sweep everything beginning with a "Con"
Into oblivion! Convocation first,
Conservatism next, and, last and worst,   80
"*Concilium Hebdomadale*" must,
Consumed and conquered, be consigned to dust![17]
     And here I must relate a little fable
I heard last Saturday at our high table: –
The cats, it seems, were masters of the house,
And held their own against the rat and mouse:
Of course the others couldn't stand it long,
So held a *caucus* (not, in their case, wrong:)
And, when they were assembled to a man,
Uprose an aged rat, and thus began: –   90
     "Brothers in bondage! Shall we bear to be
For ever left in a minority?
With what 'fell unity of purpose' cats
Oppress the trusting innocence of rats!
So unsuspicious are we of disguise,
Their machinations take us by surprise[18] –
Insulting and tyrannical absurdities![19]
It is too bad by half – upon my word it is!

For, now that these Con—, cats, I should say (frizzle 'em!),
100　Are masters, they exterminate like Islam![20]
How shall we deal with them? I'll tell you how: –
Let none but kittens be allowed to miaow!
The Liberal kittens seize us but in play,
And, while they frolic, we can run away:
But older cats are not so generous,
Their claws are too Conservative for us!
Then let *them* keep the stable and the oats,
While kittens, rats, and mice have all the votes.
　　　"Yes; banish cats! The kittens would not use
110　Their powers for blind obstruction,[21] nor refuse
To let us sip the cream and gnaw the cheese –
How glorious then would be our destinies![22]
Kittens and rats would occupy the throne,
And rule the larder for itself alone!"[23]

　　　　　So rhymed my friend, and asked me what I thought
　　　　　　　of it.
I told him that so much as I had caught of it
Appeared to me (as I need hardly mention)
Entirely undeserving of attention.
But now, to guide the Congregation, when
120　It numbers none but really "able" men,
A "Vice-Cancellarius" will be needed
Of every kind of human weakness weeded!
Is such the president that we have got?
He ought no doubt to be; why should he not?[24]

　　　　　I do not hint that Liberals should dare
To oust the present holder of the chair –
But surely he would not object to be
Gently examined by a Board of three?
Their duty being just to ascertain
130　That he's "all there" (I mean, of course, in brain),
And that his mind, from "petty details" clear,
Is fitted for the duties of his sphere.

　　　　　All this is merely moonshine, till we get
The seal of Parliament upon it set.

A word then, Senior Censor, in your ear:
The Government is in a state of fear –
Like some old gentleman, abroad at night,
Seized with a sudden shiver of affright,
Who offers money, on his bended knees,
To the first skulking vagabond he sees –   140
Now is the lucky moment for our task;
They daren't refuse us anything we ask![25]
          And then our Fellowships shall open be
To Intellect, no meaner quality!
No moral excellence, no social fitness
Shall ever be admissible as witness.
"Avaunt, dull Virtue!" is Oxonia's cry:
"Come to my arms, ingenious Villainy!"
          For Classic Fellowships, an honour high,
Simonides and Co. will then apply –   150
Our Mathematics will to Oxford bring
The 'cutest members of the betting-ring –
Law Fellowships will start upon their journeys
A myriad of unscrupulous attorneys –
While prisoners, doomed till now to toil unknown,
Shall mount the Physical Professor's throne!
          To what a varied feast of learning then
Should we invite our intellectual men!
Professor Caseley should instruct our flock
To analyse the mysteries of Locke –   160
Barnum should lecture them on Rhetoric –
The Davenports upon the cupboard-trick –
Robson and Redpath, Strahan and Paul and Bates
Should store the minds of undergraduates –
From Fagin's lecture-room a class should come
Versed in all arts of finger and of thumb,
To illustrate in practice (though by stealth)
The transitory character of wealth.
And thus would Oxford educate, indeed,
Men far beyond a merely local need –   170

With no career before them, I may say,[26]
Unless they're wise enough to go away,
And seek, far West, or in the distant East,
Another flock of pigeons to be fleeced.

    I might go on, and trace the destiny
Of Oxford in an age which, though it be
Thus breaking with tradition, owns a new
Allegiance to the intellectual few –
(I mean, of course, the – pshaw! no matter who!)
But, were I to pursue the boundless theme,   180
I fear that I should seem to you to dream.[27]
This to fulfil, or even – humbler far –
To shun Conservatism's noxious star
And all the evils that it brings behind,
These pestilential coils must be untwined – ⎫
The party-coils, that clog the march of Mind – ⎭
Choked in whose meshes Oxford, slowly wise,
Has lain for three disastrous centuries.[28]
Away with them! (It is for this I yearn.)
Each twist untwist, each Turner overturn!   190
Disfranchise each Conservative, and cancel
The votes of Michell, Liddon, Wall, and Mansel!
Then, then shall Oxford be herself again,
Neglect the heart, and cultivate the brain –
Then this shall be the burden of our song,
"All change is good – whatever is, is wrong" –
Then Intellect's proud flag shall be unfurled,
And Brain, and Brain alone, shall rule the world!

1. Dr. Wynter, President of St. John's, one of the recently elected Conservative members of Council.

2. "In a letter on a point connected with the late elections to the Hebdomadal Council you incidentally remarked to me that our combinations for these elections, 'though necessary, were not an unmixed good.' They are an unmixed evil."

3. "I never go to a *caucus* without reluctance: I never write a canvassing letter without a feeling of repugnance to my task."

4. "I need not rehearse the history of the Regius Professorship of Greek."

5. "The University cannot afford at the present moment to be delivered over as a slave to any non-academical interest whatever."

6. "It may be right to go on, it may be right to stand still, or it may be right to go back."

7. "To save the University from going completely under the yoke . . . we shall still be obliged to combine."

8. "Caucus-holding and wire-pulling would still be almost inevitably carried on to some extent."

9. "But what are we to do? Here is a great political and theological party . . . labouring under perfect discipline and with fell unity of purpose, to hold the University in subjection, and fill her government with its nominees."

10. At a recent election to Council, the Liberals mustered ninety-two votes, and the Conservatives ninety-three; whereupon the latter were charged with having obtained their victory by a conspiracy.

11. "Not to mention that, as we cannot promise Paradise to our supporters, they are very apt to take the train for London just before the election."

12. It is not known to what the word "Paradise" was intended to allude, and therefore the hint, here thrown out, that the writer meant to recall the case of the late Chairman of Mr. Gathorne Hardy's committee, who had been recently collated to the See of Chester, is wholly wanton and gratuitous.

13. A case of this had actually occurred on the occasion of the division just alluded to.

14. Mr. Wayte, now President of Trinity, then put forward as the Liberal candidate for election to Council.

15. "You and others suggest, as the only effective remedy, that the Constituency should be reformed, by the exclusion of the non-academical elements which form a main part of the strength of this party domination."

16. "I confess that, having included all the really academical elements in Congregation, I would go boldly on, and put an end to the legislative functions of Convocation."

17. "This conviction, that while we have Elections to Council we shall not entirely get rid of party organisation and its evils, leads me to venture a step further, and to raise the question whether it is really necessary that we should have an Elective Council for legislative purposes at all."

18. "Sometimes, indeed, not being informed that the wires are at work, we are completely taken by surprise."

19. "We are without protection against this most insulting and tyrannical absurdity."

20. "It is as exterminating as Islam."

21. "Their powers would scarcely be exercised for the purposes of fanaticism, or in a spirit of blind obstruction."

22. "These narrow local bounds, within which our thoughts and schemes have hitherto been pent, will begin to disappear, and a far wider sphere of action will open on the view."

23. "Those councils must be freely opened to all who can serve her well and who will serve her for herself."

24. "To preside over a Congregation with full legislative powers, the Vice-chancellor ought no doubt to be a man of real capacity; but why should he not? His mind ought also, for this as well as for his other high functions, to be clear of petty details, and devoted to the great matters of University business; but why should not this condition also be fulfilled?"

25. "If you apply now to Parliament for this or any other University reform, you will find the House of Commons in a propitious mood . . . Even the Conservative Government, as it looks for the support of moderate Liberals on the one great subject, is very unwilling to present itself in such an aspect that these men may not be able decently to give it their support."

26. "With open Fellowships, Oxford will soon produce a supply of men fit for the work of high education far beyond her own local demands, and in fact with no career for them unless a career can be opened elsewhere."

27. "I should seem to you to dream if I were to say what I think the destiny of the University may be in an age which, though it is breaking with tradition, is, from the same causes, owning a new allegiance to intellectual authority."

28. "But to fulfil this, or even a far humbler destiny – to escape the opposite lot – the pestilential coils of party, in which the University has lain for three disastrous centuries choked, must be untwined."

Phantasmagoria: Part 2

The Valley of the Shadow of Death

Hark, said the dying man, and sighed,
    To that complaining tone –
Like sprite condemned, each eventide,
    To walk the world alone:
At sunset, when the air is still,
I hear it creep from yonder hill;
It breathes upon me, dead and chill,
    A moment, and is gone.

My son, it minds me of a day
    Left half a life behind,   10
That I have prayed to put away
    For ever from my mind.
But bitter memory will not die:
It haunts my soul when none is nigh:
I hear its whisper in the sigh
    Of that complaining wind.

And now in death my soul is fain
    To tell the tale of fear
That hidden in my breast hath lain
    Through many a weary year: 20

Yet time would fail to utter all –
The evil spells that held me thrall,
And thrust my life from fall to fall,
    Thou needest not to hear.

The spells that bound me with a chain,
    Sin's stern behests to do,
Till Pleasure's self, invoked in vain,
    A heavy burden grew –
Till from my spirit's fevered eye,
30   A hunted thing, I seemed to fly
Through the dark woods that underlie
    Yon mountain-range of blue.

Deep in those woods I found a vale
    No sunlight visiteth,
Nor star, nor wandering moonbeam pale;
    Where never comes the breath
Of summer-breeze – there in mine ear,
Even as I lingered half in fear,
I heard a whisper, cold and clear,
40   "This is the gate of Death.

"O bitter is it to abide
    In weariness alway;
At dawn to sigh for eventide,
    At eventide for day.
Thy noon hath fled: thy sun hath shone:
The brightness of thy day is gone –
What need to lag and linger on
    Till life be cold and grey?

"O well," it said, "beneath yon pool,
50   In some still cavern deep,
The fevered brain might slumber cool,
    The eyes forget to weep:

Within that goblet's mystic rim
Are draughts of healing, stored for him
Whose heart is sick, whose sight is dim,
    Who prayeth but to sleep!"

The evening-breeze went moaning by,
    Like mourner for the dead,
And stirred, with shrill complaining sigh,
    The tree-tops overhead –   60
My guardian-angel seemed to stand
And mutely wave a warning hand –
With sudden terror all unmanned,
    I turned myself and fled!

A cottage-gate stood open wide:
    Soft fell the dying ray
On two fair children, side by side,
    That rested from their play –
Together bent the earnest head,
As ever and anon they read   70
From one dear Book: the words they said
    Come back to me to-day.

Like twin cascades on mountain-stair
    Together wandered down
The ripples of the golden hair,
    The ripples of the brown:
While, through the tangled silken haze,
Blue eyes looked forth in eager gaze,
More starlike than the gems that blaze
    About a monarch's crown.   80

My son, there comes to each an hour
    When sinks the spirit's pride –
When weary hands forget their power
    The strokes of death to guide:

In such a moment, warriors say,
A word the panic-rout may stay,
A sudden charge redeem the day
    And turn the living tide.

I could not see, for blinding tears,
    The glories of the west:
A heavenly music filled mine ears,
    A heavenly peace my breast.
"Come unto Me, come unto Me –
All ye that labour, unto Me –
Ye heavy-laden, come to Me –
    And I will give you rest."

The night drew onwards: thin and blue
    The evening mists arise
To bathe the thirsty land in dew,
    As erst in Paradise –
While over silent field and town
The deep blue vault of heaven looked down;
Not, as of old, in angry frown,
    But bright with angels' eyes.

Blest day! Then first I heard the voice
    That since hath oft beguiled
These eyes from tears, and bid rejoice
    This heart with anguish wild –
Thy mother, boy, thou hast not known,
So soon she left me here to moan –
Left me to weep and watch, alone,
    Our one beloved child.

Though, parted from my aching sight,
    Like homeward-speeding dove,
She passed into the perfect light
    That floods the world above;

Yet our twin spirits, well I know –
Though one abide in pain below –
Love, as in summers long ago,
    And evermore shall love.   120

So with a glad and patient heart
    I move toward mine end:
The streams, that flow awhile apart,
    Shall both in ocean blend.
I dare not weep: I can but bless
The Love that pitied my distress,
And lent me, in Life's wilderness,
    So sweet and true a friend.

But if there be – O if there be
    A truth in what they say,   130
That angel-forms we cannot see
    Go with us on our way;
Then surely she is with me here,
I dimly feel her spirit near –
The morning-mists grow thin and clear,
    And Death brings in the Day.

Beatrice

In her eyes is the living light
    Of a wanderer to earth
From a far celestial height:
    Summers five are all the span –
    Summers five since Time began
To veil in mists of human night
    A shining angel-birth.

Does an angel look from her eyes?
　　Will she suddenly spring away,
And soar to her home in the skies?
　　　　Beatrice! Blessing and blessed to be!
　　　　Beatrice! Still, as I gaze on thee,
Visions of two sweet maids arise,
　　　　Whose life was of yesterday:

Of a Beatrice pale and stern,
　　With the lips of a dumb despair,
With the innocent eyes that yearn –
　　　　Yearn for the young sweet hours of life,
　　　　Far from sorrow and far from strife,
For the happy summers, that never return,
　　　　When the world seemed good and fair:

Of a Beatrice glorious, bright –
　　Of a sainted, ethereal maid,
Whose blue eyes are deep fountains of light,
　　　　Cheering the poet that broodeth apart,
　　　　Filling with gladness his desolate heart,
Like the moon when she shines thro' a cloudless night
　　　　On a world of silence and shade.

And the visions waver and faint,
　　And the visions vanish away
That my fancy delighted to paint –
　　　　She is here at my side, a living child,
　　　　With the glowing cheek and the tresses wild,
Nor death-pale martyr, nor radiant saint,
　　　　Yet stainless and bright as they.

For I think, if a grim wild beast
　　Were to come from his charnel-cave,
From his jungle-home in the East –
　　　　Stealthily creeping with bated breath,
　　　　Stealthily creeping with eyes of death –
He would all forget his dream of the feast,
　　　　And crouch at her feet a slave.

She would twine her hand in his mane,
    She would prattle in silvery tone,
Like the tinkle of summer rain –
    Questioning him with her laughing eyes,
    Questioning him with a glad surprise,
Till she caught from those fierce eyes again
    The love that lit her own.

And be sure, if a savage heart,   50
    In a mask of human guise,
Were to come on her here apart –
    Bound for a dark and a deadly deed,
    Hurrying past with pitiless speed –
He would suddenly falter and guiltily start
    At the glance of her pure blue eyes.

Nay, be sure, if an angel fair,
    A bright seraph undefiled,
Were to stoop from the trackless air,
    Fain would she linger in glad amaze –   60
    Lovingly linger to ponder and gaze,
With a sister's love and a sister's care,
    On the happy, innocent child.

[Acrostic Lines to Lorina, Alice and Edith]

    Little maidens, when you look
    On this little story-book,
    Reading with attentive eye
    Its enticing history;
    Never think that hours of play
    Are your only holiday,
    And that, in a time of joy,
    Lessons serve but to annoy.
    If in any HOUSE you find
    Children of a gentle mind,   10

Each the others helping ever,
Each the others vexing never,
Daily task and pastime daily
In their order taking gaily –
Then be very sure that they
Have a *life* of HOLIDAY.

The Path of Roses

In the dark silence of an ancient room,
Whose one tall window fronted to the West,
Where, through laced tendrils of a hanging vine,
The sunset glow was fading into night,
Sat a pale Lady, resting weary hands
Upon a great clasped volume, and her face
Within her hands. Not as in rest she bowed,
But large hot tears went coursing down her cheek,
And her low-panted sobs broke awfully
Upon the sleeping echoes of the night.
Soon she unclasped the volume once again,
And read the words in tone of agony,
As in self-torture, weeping as she read:

"He crowns the glory of his race;
He prayeth but in some fair place
To meet his foeman face to face;

"And battling for the true, the right,
From ruddy dawn to purple night,
To perish in the midmost fight;

"Where foes are fierce, and weapons strong
Where roars the battle loud and long,
Where blood is dropping in the throng.

"Still, with a dim and glazing eye
To watch the tide of victory,
To hear in death the battle-cry.

"Then, gathered grandly to his grave,
To rest among the true and brave,
In holy ground, where yew-trees wave;

"Where, from church-windows sculptured fair,
Float out upon the evening air   30
The note of praise, the voice of prayer;

"Where no vain marble mockery
Insults with loud and boastful lie
The simple soldier's memory;

"Where sometimes little children go,
And read, in whispered accent slow,
The name of him who sleeps below."

Her voice died out; like one in dreams she sat.
"Alas!" she sighed, "for what can woman do?
Her life is aimless, and her death unknown;   40
Hemmed in by social forms she pines in vain:
Man has his work, but what can woman do?"
        And answer came there from the creeping gloom,
The creeping gloom that settled into night:
"Peace, for thy lot is other than a man's:
His is a path of thorns; he beats them down –
He faces death – he wrestles with despair:
Thine is of roses; to adorn and cheer
His barren lot, and hide the thorns in flowers."
        She spake again: in bitter tone she spake: 50
"Aye, as a toy, the puppet of an hour;
Or a fair posy, newly plucked at morn,
But flung aside and withered ere the night."
        And answer came there from the creeping gloom,
The creeping gloom, that blackened into night:
"So shalt thou be the lamp to light his path,
What time the shades of sorrow close around."
        And, so it seemed to her, an awful light

Pierced slowly through the darkness, orbed, and grew,
60 Until all passed away – the ancient room –
The sunlight dying through the trellised vine –
The one tall window – all had passed away,
And she was standing on the mighty hills.

    Beneath, around, and far as eye could see,
Squadron on squadron, stretched opposing hosts,
Ranked as for battle, mute and motionless.
Anon a distant thunder shook the ground,
The tramp of horses, and a troop shot by –
Plunged headlong in that living sea of men –
70 Plunged to their death: back from that fatal field
A scattered handful, fighting hard for life,
Broke through the serried lines; but, as she gazed
They shrank and melted, and their forms grew thin –
Grew pale as ghosts when the first morning ray
Dawns from the East – the trumpet's brazen blare
Died into silence – and the vision passed; –

    Passed to a room where sick and dying lay,
In long, sad line – there brooded Fear and Pain –
Darkness was there, the shade of Azrael's wing.
80 But there was one that ever, to and fro,
Moved with light footfall: purely calm her face,
And those deep steadfast eyes that starred the gloom:
Still, as she went, she ministered to each
Comfort and counsel; cooled the fevered brow
With softest touch, and in the listening ear
Of the pale sufferer whispered words of peace.
The dying warrior, gazing as she passed,
Clasped his thin hands and blessed her. Bless her too,
THOU who didst bless the merciful of old!
90   So prayed the Lady, watching tearfully
Her gentle moving onward, till the night
Had veiled her wholly, and the vision passed.

    Then once again the awful whisper came:
"So in the darkest path of man's despair,

Where War and Terror shake the troubled earth,
Lies woman's mission; with unblenching brow
To pass through scenes of anguish and affright
Where men grow sick and tremble; unto her
All things are sanctified, for all are good.
Nothing so mean, but shall deserve her care;   100
Nothing so great, but she may bear her part.
No life is vain: each hath his place assigned:
Do thou thy task, and leave the rest to heaven."
And there was silence, but the Lady made
No answer, save one deeply-breathed "Amen."

      And she arose, and in that darkening room
Stood lonely as a spirit of the night –
Stood calm and fearless in the gathered night –
And raised her eyes to heaven. There were tears
Upon her face, but in her heart was peace,   110
Peace that the world nor gives nor takes away!

The Sailor's Wife

See! There are tears upon her face –
    Tears newly shed, and scarcely dried:
Close, in an agonised embrace,
    She clasps the infant at her side.

Peace dwells in those soft-lidded eyes,
    Those parted lips that faintly smile –
Peace, the foretaste of Paradise,
    In heart too young for care or guile.

No peace that mother's features wear;
    But quivering lip, and knotted brow,   10
And broken mutterings, all declare
    The fearful dream that haunts her now.

The storm-wind, rushing through the sky,
      Wails from the depths of cloudy space;
Shrill, piercing as the seaman's cry
      When Death and he are face to face.

Familiar tones are in the gale;
      They ring upon her startled ear:
And quick and low she pants the tale
20   That tells of agony and fear:

"Still that phantom-ship is nigh –
      With a vexed and life-like motion,
All beneath an angry sky,
      Rocking on an angry ocean.

"Round the straining mast and shrouds
      Throng the spirits of the storm;
Darkly seen through driving clouds,
      Bends each gaunt and ghastly form.

"See! The good ship yields at last!
30   Dumbly yields, and fights no more;
Driving, in the frantic blast,
      Headlong on the fatal shore.

"Hark! I hear her battered side,
      With a low and sullen shock,
Dashed, amid the foaming tide,
      Full upon a sunken rock.

"His face shines out against the sky,
      Like a ghost, so cold and white;
With a dead despairing eye
40   Gazing through the gathered night.

"Is he watching, through the dark,
      Where a mocking ghostly hand
Points to yonder feeble spark
      Glimmering from the distant land?

"Sees he, in this hour of dread,
      Hearth and home, and wife and child?
Loved ones who, in summers fled,
      Clung to him and wept and smiled?

"Reeling sinks the fated bark
      To her tomb beneath the wave;   50
Must he perish in the dark –
      Not a hand stretched out to save?

"See the spirits, how they crowd!
      Watching death with eyes that burn!
Waves rush in –" she shrieks aloud,
      Ere her waking sense return.

The storm is gone: the skies are clear:
      Hush'd is that bitter cry of pain:
The only sound that meets her ear
      The heaving of the sullen main.   60

Though heaviness endure the night,
      But joy shall come with break of day;
She shudders with a strange delight –
      The fearful dream is pass'd away.

She wakes; the grey dawn streaks the dark;
      With early song the copses ring:
Far off she hears the watch-dog bark
      A joyful bark of welcoming!

Stolen Waters

The light was faint, and soft the air
      That breathed around the place;
And she was lithe, and tall, and fair,
      And with a wayward grace
      Her queenly head she bare.

With glowing cheek, with gleaming eye,
    She met me on the way:
My spirit owned the witchery
    Within her smile that lay:
10 I followed her, I know not why.

The trees were thick with many a fruit,
    The grass with many a flower:
My soul was dead, my tongue was mute,
    In that accursëd hour.

And, in my dream, with silvery voice,
    She said, or seemed to say,
"Youth is the season to rejoice –"
    I could not choose but stay;
    I could not say her nay.

20 She plucked a branch above her head,
    With rarest fruitage laden:
"Drink of the juice, Sir Knight," she said,
    " 'Tis good for knight and maiden."

Oh, blind mine eye that would not trace –
    And deaf mine ear that would not heed –
The mocking smile upon her face,
    The mocking voice of greed!

I drank the juice, and straightway felt
    A fire within my brain;
30 My soul within me seemed to melt
    In sweet delirious pain.

"Sweet is the stolen draught," she said;
    "Hath sweetness stint or measure?
Pleasant the secret hoard of bread;
    What bars us from our pleasure?"

"Yea, take we pleasure while we may,"
  I heard myself replying.
In the red sunset, far away,
  My happier life was dying:
My heart was sad, my voice was gay.   40

And unawares, I knew not how,
  I kissed her dainty finger-tips,
I kissed her on the lily brow,
  I kissed her on the false, false lips –
That burning kiss, I feel it now!

"True love gives true love of the best:
  Then take," I cried, "my heart to thee!"
The very heart from out my breast
  I plucked, I gave it willingly:
    Her very heart she gave to me – 50
Then died the glory from the west.

In the grey light I saw her face,
  And it was withered, old, and grey;
The flowers were fading in their place,
  Were fading with the fading day.

Forth from her, like a hunted deer,
  Through all that ghastly night I fled,
And still behind me seemed to hear
  Her fierce unflagging tread;
And scarce drew breath for fear.   60

Yet marked I well how strangely seemed
  The heart within my breast to sleep:
Silent it lay, or so I dreamed,
  With never a throb or leap.

For hers was now my heart, she said,
      The heart that once had been mine own:
And in my breast I bore instead
      A cold, cold heart of stone.
So grew the morning overhead.

70   The sun shot downward through the trees
      His old familiar flame;
All ancient sounds upon the breeze
      From copse and meadow came –
      But I was not the same.

They call me mad: I smile, I weep,
      Uncaring how or why:
Yea, when one's heart is laid asleep,
      What better than to die?
So that the grave be dark and deep.

80   To die! To die? And yet, methinks,
      I drink of life, to-day,
Deep as the thirsty traveller drinks
      Of fountain by the way:
      My voice is sad, my heart is gay.

When yestereve was on the wane,
      I heard a clear voice singing;
And suddenly, like summer-rain,
      My happy tears came springing:
My human heart returned again.

90   *"A rosy child –*
Sitting and singing, in a garden fair,
    The joy of hearing, seeing,
    The simple joy of being –
Or twining rosebuds in the golden hair
    That ripples free and wild.

"*A sweet pale child –*
Wearily looking to the purple West –
Waiting the great For-ever
That suddenly shall sever
The cruel chains that hold her from her rest –   100
By earth-joys unbeguiled.

"*An angel-child –*
Gazing with living eyes on a dead face:
The mortal form forsaken,
That none may now awaken,
That lieth painless, moveless in her place,
As though in death she smiled!

"*Be as a child –*
So shalt thou sing for very joy of breath –
So shalt thou wait thy dying,   110
In holy transport lying –
So pass rejoicing through the gate of death,
In garment undefiled."

Then call me what they will, I know
        That now my soul is glad:
If this be madness, better so,
        Far better to be mad,
Weeping or smiling as I go.

For if I weep, it is that now
        I see how deep a loss is mine,   120
And feel how brightly round my brow
        The coronal might shine,
Had I but kept mine early vow:

And if I smile, it is that now
        I see the promise of the years –
The garland waiting for my brow,
        That must be won with tears,
With pain – with death – I care not how.

Stanzas for Music

The morn was bright, the steeds were light,
        The wedding guests were gay;
Young Ellen stood within the wood
        And watched them pass away.
She scarcely saw the gallant train,
        The tear-drop dimmed her ee;
Unheard the maiden did complain
        Beneath the Willow tree.

"O Robin, thou didst love me well,
        Till on a bitter day
She came, the Lady Isabel,
        And stole my Love away.
My tears are vain, I live again
        In days that used to be,
When I could meet thy welcome feet
        Beneath the Willow tree.

"O Willow grey, I may not stay
        Till Spring renew thy leaf,
But I will hide myself away,
        And nurse a hopeless grief.
It shall not dim life's joy for him,
        My tears he shall not see;
While he is by, I'll come not nigh
        My weeping Willow tree.

"But when I die, O let me lie
        Beneath thy loving shade,
That he may loiter careless by
        Where I am lowly laid.
And let the white white marble tell,
        If he should stoop to see,
'Here lies a maid that loved thee well,
        Beneath the Willow tree.'"

Solitude

I love the stillness of the wood,
    I love the music of the rill,
I love to couch in pensive mood
    Upon some silent hill.

Scarce heard, beneath yon arching trees,
    The silver-crested ripples pass;
And, like a mimic brook, the breeze
    Whispers among the grass.

Here from the world I win release,
    Nor scorn of men, nor footsteps rude,   10
Break in to mar the holy peace
    Of this great solitude.

Here may the silent tears I weep
    Lull the vexed spirit into rest,
As infants sob themselves to sleep
    Upon a mother's breast.

But when the bitter hour is gone,
    And the keen throbbing pangs are still,
Oh, sweetest then to couch alone
    Upon some silent hill!   20

To live in joys that once have been,
    To put the cold world out of sight,
And deck life's drear and barren scene
    With hues of rainbow light.

For what to man the gift of breath,
    If sorrow be his lot below;
If all the day that ends in death
    Be dark with clouds of woe?

Shall the poor transport of an hour
    Repay long years of sore distress –
The fragrance of a lonely flower
    Make glad the wilderness?

Ye golden hours of life's young spring,
    Of innocence, of love and truth!
Bright, beyond all imagining,
    Thou fairy dream of youth!

I'd give all wealth that years hath piled,
    The slow result of life's decay,
To be once more a little child
    For one bright summer day.

Only a Woman's Hair

After the death of Dean Swift, there was found among his
papers a small packet containing a single lock of hair and
inscribed with the above words.

"Only a woman's hair"! Fling it aside!
    A bubble on Life's mighty stream:
Heed it not, man, but watch the broadening tide
    Bright with the western beam.

Nay! In those words there rings from other years
    The echo of a long low cry,
Where a proud spirit wrestles with its tears
    In loneliest agony.

And, as I touch that lock, strange visions rise
    Before me in a shadowy throng –
Of woman's hair, the joy of lovers' eyes,
    The theme of poet's song.

A child's bright tresses, by the breezes kissed
        To sweet disorder as she flies,
Veiling, beneath a cloud of golden mist,
        Flushed cheek and laughing eyes –

Or fringing like a shadow, raven-black,
        The glory of a queen-like face –
Or from a gipsy's sunny brow tossed back
        In wild and wanton grace –   20

Or crown-like on the hoary head of Age,
        Whose tale of life is well-nigh told –
Or, last, in dreams I make my pilgrimage
        To Bethany of old.

I see the feast – the purple and the gold –
        The gathering crowd of Pharisees,
Whose scornful eyes are centred to behold
        Yon woman on her knees.

The stifled sob rings strangely on mine ears,
        Wrung from the depth of sin's despair: 30
And still she bathes the sacred feet with tears,
        And wipes them with her hair.

He scorned not then the simple loving deed
        Of her, the lowest and the last;
Then scorn not thou, but use with earnest heed
        This relic of the past.

The eyes that loved it once no longer wake:
        So lay it by with reverent care –
Touching it tenderly for sorrow's sake –
        It is a woman's hair.   40

Three Sunsets

He saw her once, and in the glance,
 A moment's glance of meeting eyes,
His heart stood still in sudden trance:
 He trembled with a sweet surprise –
All in the waning light she stood,
The star of perfect womanhood.

That summer-eve his heart was light,
 With lighter step he trod the ground,
And life was fairer in his sight,
 And music was in every sound;
He blessed the world where there could be
So beautiful a thing as she.

There once again, as evening fell
 And stars were peering overhead,
Two lovers met to bid farewell:
 The western sun gleamed faint and red,
Lost in a drift of purple cloud
That wrapped him like a funeral-shroud.

Long time the memory of that night –
 The hand that clasped, the lips that kissed,
The form that faded from his sight
 Slow sinking through the tearful mist –
In dreamy music seemed to roll
Through the dark chambers of his soul.

So after many years he came
 A wanderer from a distant shore;
The street, the house, were still the same,
 But those he sought were there no more:
His burning words, his hopes and fears,
Unheeded fell on alien ears.

Only the children from their play
      Would pause the mournful tale to hear,
Shrinking in half-alarm away,
      Or, step by step, would venture near
To touch with timid curious hands
That strange wild man from other lands.

He sat beside the busy street,
      There, where he last had seen her face;
And thronging memories, bitter-sweet,
      Seemed yet to haunt the ancient place: 40
Her footfall ever floated near,
Her voice was ever in his ear.

He sometimes, as the daylight waned
      And evening mists began to roll,
In half-soliloquy complained
      Of that black shadow on his soul,
And blindly fanned, with cruel care,
The ashes of a vain despair.

The summer fled: the lonely man
      Still lingered out the lessening days: 50
Still, as the night drew on, would scan
      Each passing face with closer gaze –
Till, sick at heart, he turned away,
And sighed "She will not come to-day."

So by degrees his spirit bent
      To mock its own despairing cry,
In stern self-torture to invent
      New luxuries of agony,
And people all the vacant space
With visions of her perfect face: 60

Till for a moment she was nigh,
          He heard no step, but she was there;
As if an angel suddenly
          Were bodied from the viewless air,
And all her fine ethereal frame
Should fade as swiftly as it came.

So, half in fancy's sunny trance,
          And half in misery's aching void,
With set and stony countenance
70   His bitter being he enjoyed,
And thrust for ever from his mind
The happiness he could not find.

As when the wretch, in lonely room,
          To selfish death is madly hurled,
The glamour of that fatal fume
          Shuts out the wholesome living world –
So all his manhood's strength and pride
One sickly dream had swept aside.

Yea, brother, and we passed him there,
80   But yesterday, in merry mood,
And marvelled at the lordly air
          That shamed his beggar's attitude,
Nor heeded that ourselves might be
Wretches as desperate as he;

Who let the thought of bliss denied
          Make havoc of our life and powers,
And pine, in solitary pride,
          For peace that never shall be ours,
Because we will not work and wait
90   In trustful patience for our fate.

And so it chanced once more that she
    Came by the old familiar spot;
The face he would have died to see
    Bent o'er him, and he knew it not;
Too rapt in selfish grief to hear,
Even when happiness was near.

And pity filled her gentle breast
    For him that would not stir nor speak;
The dying crimson of the west,
    That faintly tinged his haggard cheek,   100
Fell on her as she stood, and shed
A glory round the patient head.

Awake, awake! The moments fly;
    This awful tryst may be the last.
And see! The tear, that dimmed her eye,
    Had fallen on him ere she passed –
She passed: the crimson paled to grey:
And hope departed with the day.

The heavy hours of night went by,
    And silence quickened into sound,   110
And light slid up the eastern sky,
    And life began its daily round –
But light and life for him were fled:
His name was numbered with the dead.

Christmas Greetings

[From a Fairy to a Child.]

Lady dear, if fairies may
    For a moment lay aside
Cunning tricks and elfish play –
    'Tis at happy Christmas-tide.

We have heard the children say –
    Gentle children, whom we love –
Long ago, on Christmas Day
    Came a message from above.

Still, as Christmas time comes round,
    They remember it again –
Echo still the joyful sound
    "Peace on earth, good will to men!"

Yet the hearts must child-like be
    Where such heavenly guests abide:
Unto children in their glee
    All the year is Christmas-tide!

So, forgetting tricks and play
    For a moment, lady dear,
We would wish you, if we may,
    Merry Christmas, glad New Year!

After Three Days

Written after seeing Holman Hunt's picture of "Christ in
the Temple."

    I stood within the gate
Of a great temple, 'mid the living stream
Of worshippers that thronged its regal state
    Fair pictured in my dream.

    Jewels and gold were there;
And floors of marble lent a crystal sheen
To body forth, as in a lower air,
    The wonders of the scene.

Such wild and lavish grace
Had whispers in it of a coming doom;   10
As richest flowers lie strown about the face
    Of her that waits the tomb.

The wisest of the land
Had gathered there, three solemn trysting-days,
For high debate: men stood on either hand
    To listen and to gaze.

The aged brows were bent,
Bent to a frown, half thought, and half annoy,
That all their stores of subtlest argument
    Were baffled by a boy.   20

In each averted face
I marked but scorn and loathing, till mine eyes
Fell upon one that stirred not in his place,
    Tranced in a dumb surprise.

Surely within his mind
Strange thoughts are born, until he doubts the lore
Of those old men, blind leaders of the blind,
    Whose kingdom is no more.

Surely he sees afar
A day of death the stormy future brings;   30
The crimson setting of the herald-star
    That led the Eastern kings.

Thus, as a sunless deep
Mirrors the shining heights that crown the bay,
So did my soul create anew in sleep
    The picture seen by day.

Gazers came and went –
A restless hum of voices marked the spot –
In varying shades of critic discontent
40   Prating they knew not what.

"Where is the comely limb,
The form attuned in every perfect part,
The beauty that we should desire in him?"
         Ah! Fools and slow of heart!

Look into those deep eyes,
Deep as the grave, and strong with love divine;
Those tender, pure, and fathomless mysteries,
         That seem to pierce through thine.

Look into those deep eyes,
50   Stirred to unrest by breath of coming strife,
Until a longing in thy soul arise
         That this indeed were life:

That thou couldst find Him there,
Bend at His sacred feet thy willing knee,
And from thy heart pour out the passionate prayer
         "Lord, let me follow Thee!"

But see the crowd divide;
Mother and sire have found their lost one now:
The gentle voice, that fain would seem to chide
60   Whispers, "Son, why hast thou" –

In tone of sad amaze –
"Thus dealt with us, that art our dearest thing?
Behold, thy sire and I, three weary days,
         Have sought thee sorrowing."

And I had stayed to hear
The loving words, "How is it that ye sought?" –
But that the sudden lark, with matins clear,
    Severed the links of thought.

    Then over all there fell
Shadow and silence; and my dream was fled,   70
As fade the phantoms of a wizard's cell
    When the dark charm is said.

    Yet, in the gathering light
I lay with half-shut eyes that would not wake,
Lovingly clinging to the skirts of night
    For that sweet vision's sake.

Faces in the Fire

The night creeps onward, sad and slow:
In these red embers' dying glow
The forms of Fancy come and go.

An island-farm – broad seas of corn
Swayed by the wandering breath of morn –
The happy spot where I was born.

The picture fadeth in its place:
Amid the glow I seem to trace
The shifting semblance of a face.

'Tis now a little childish form –   10
Red lips for kisses pouted warm –
And elf-locks tangled in the storm.

'Tis now a grave and gentle maid,
At her own beauty half afraid,
Shrinking, and willing to be stayed.

Oh, time was young, and life was warm,
When first I saw that fairy form,
Her dark hair fluttering in the storm;

And fast and free these pulses played,
When last I met that gentle maid –
When last her hand in mine was laid.

Those locks of jet are turned to grey,
And she is strange and far away
That might have been mine own to-day –

That might have been mine own, my dear,
Through many and many a happy year –
That might have sat beside me here.

Aye, changeless through the changing scene,
The ghostly whisper rings between,
The dark refrain of "might have been."

The race is o'er I might have run,
The deeds are past I might have done,
And sere the wreath I might have won.

Sunk is the last faint, flickering blaze;
The vision of departed days
Is vanished even as I gaze.

The pictures with their ruddy light
Are changed to dust and ashes white,
And I am left alone with night.

Puzzles from Wonderland
(1870)

I

Dreaming of apples on a wall,
And dreaming often, dear,
I dreamed that, if I counted all,
– How many would appear?

II

A stick I found that weighed two pound:
I sawed it up one day
In pieces eight of equal weight!
How much did each piece weigh?

III

John gave his brother James a box:
About it there were many locks.

James woke and said it gave him pain;
So gave it back to John again.

The box was not with lid supplied,
Yet caused two lids to open wide:

And all these locks had never a key –
What kind of a box, then, could it be?

IV

What is most like a bee in May?
"Well, let me think: perhaps –" you say.
Bravo! You're guessing well to-day!

V

Three sisters at breakfast were feeding the cat,
The first gave it sole – Puss was grateful for that:
The next gave it salmon – which Puss thought a treat:
The third gave it herring – which Puss wouldn't eat.
(Explain the conduct of the cat.)

VI

Said the Moon to the Sun,
"Is the daylight begun?"
Said the Sun to the Moon,
"Not a minute too soon."
"You're a Full Moon," said he.
She replied with a frown,
"Well! I never did see
So uncivil a clown!"
(Query. Why was the moon so angry?)

VII

When the King found that his money was nearly all gone,
and that he really must live more economically, he decided
on sending away most of his Wise Men. There were some
hundreds of them – very fine old men, and magnificently
dressed in green velvet gowns with gold buttons: if they
had a fault, it was that they always contradicted one

another when he asked for their advice – and they certainly ate and drank enormously. So, on the whole, he was rather glad to get rid of them. But there was an old law, which he did not dare to disobey, which said that there must always be

> *"Seven blind of both eyes:*
> *Two blind of one eye:*
> *Five that see with both eyes:*
> *Nine that see with one eye."*
> *(Query. How many did he keep?)*

*Through the Looking-Glass,
and What Alice Found There*
(1872)

[Prologue to "Through the Looking-Glass"]

Child of the pure unclouded brow
　　And dreaming eyes of wonder!
Though time be fleet, and I and thou
　　Are half a life asunder,
Thy loving smile will surely hail
The love-gift of a fairy-tale.

I have not seen thy sunny face,
　　Nor heard thy silver laughter:
No thought of me shall find a place
　　In thy young life's hereafter –　　　　10
Enough that now thou wilt not fail
To listen to my fairy-tale.

A tale begun in other days,
　　When summer suns were glowing –
A simple chime, that served to time
　　The rhythm of our rowing –
Whose echoes live in memory yet,
Though envious years would say "forget."

Come, hearken then, ere voice of dread,
　　With bitter tidings laden,　　　　　　20
Shall summon to unwelcome bed
　　A melancholy maiden!
We are but older children, dear,
Who fret to find our bedtime near.

Without, the frost, the blinding snow,
　　The storm-wind's moody madness –
Within, the firelight's ruddy glow,
　　And childhood's nest of gladness.

The magic words shall hold thee fast:
Thou shalt not heed the raving blast.

And though the shadow of a sigh
    May tremble through the story,
For "happy summer days" gone by,
    And vanish'd summer glory –
It shall not touch with breath of bale
The pleasance of our fairy-tale.

Jabberwocky

Jabberwocky

'Twas brillig, and the slithy toves
Did gyre and gimble in the wabe:
All mimsy were the borogoves,
And the mome raths outgrabe.

'Twas brillig, and the slithy toves
        Did gyre and gimble in the wabe:
All mimsy were the borogoves,
        And the mome raths outgrabe.

"Beware the Jabberwock, my son!
        The jaws that bite, the claws that catch!
Beware the Jubjub bird, and shun
        The frumious Bandersnatch!"

He took his vorpal sword in hand:
        Long time the manxome foe he sought –
So rested he by the Tumtum tree,
        And stood awhile in thought.

And, as in uffish thought he stood,
        The Jabberwock, with eyes of flame,
Came whiffling through the tulgey wood,
        And burbled as it came!

One, two! One, two! And through and through
    The vorpal blade went snicker-snack!
He left it dead, and with its head
    He went galumphing back.   20

"And, hast thou slain the Jabberwock?
    Come to my arms, my beamish boy!
O frabjous day! Callooh! Callay!"
    He chortled in his joy.

'Twas brillig, and the slithy toves
    Did gyre and gimble in the wabe:
All mimsy were the borogoves,
    And the mome raths outgrabe.

[*"Tweedledum and Tweedledee"*]

Tweedledum and Tweedledee
    Agreed to have a battle;
For Tweedledum said Tweedledee
    Had spoiled his nice new rattle.

Just then flew down a monstrous crow,
    As black as a tar-barrel;
Which frightened both the heroes so,
    They quite forgot their quarrel.

The Walrus and the Carpenter

The sun was shining on the sea,
    Shining with all his might:
He did his very best to make
    The billows smooth and bright –
And this was odd, because it was
    The middle of the night.

The moon was shining sulkily,
  Because she thought the sun
Had got no business to be there
  After the day was done –
"It's very rude of him," she said,
  "To come and spoil the fun."

The sea was wet as wet could be,
  The sands were dry as dry.
You could not see a cloud, because
  No cloud was in the sky:
No birds were flying overhead –
  There were no birds to fly.

The Walrus and the Carpenter
  Were walking close at hand.
They wept like anything to see
  Such quantities of sand:
"If this were only cleared away,"
  They said, "it *would* be grand!"

"If seven maids with seven mops
  Swept it for half a year,
Do you suppose," the Walrus said,
  "That they could get it clear?"
"I doubt it," said the Carpenter,
  And shed a bitter tear.

"O Oysters, come and walk with us!"
  The Walrus did beseech.
"A pleasant walk, a pleasant talk,
  Along the briny beach:
We cannot do with more than four,
  To give a hand to each."

The eldest Oyster looked at him,
 But never a word he said:
The eldest Oyster winked his eye,
 And shook his heavy head –   40
Meaning to say he did not choose
 To leave the oyster-bed.

But four young Oysters hurried up,
 All eager for the treat:
Their coats were brushed, their faces washed,
 Their shoes were clean and neat –
And this was odd, because, you know,
 They hadn't any feet.

Four other Oysters followed them,
 And yet another four;   50
And thick and fast they came at last,
 And more, and more, and more –
All hopping through the frothy waves,
 And scrambling to the shore.

The Walrus and the Carpenter
 Walked on a mile or so,
And then they rested on a rock
 Conveniently low:
And all the little Oysters stood
 And waited in a row.   60

"The time has come," the Walrus said,
 "To talk of many things:
Of shoes – and ships – and sealing-wax –
 Of cabbages – and kings –
And why the sea is boiling hot –
 And whether pigs have wings."

"But wait a bit," the Oysters cried,
    "Before we have our chat:
For some of us are out of breath,
    And all of us are fat!"
"No hurry!" said the Carpenter.
    They thanked him much for that.

"A loaf of bread," the Walrus said,
    "Is what we chiefly need:
Pepper and vinegar besides
    Are very good indeed –
Now if you're ready, Oysters dear,
    We can begin to feed."

"But not on us!" the Oysters cried,
    Turning a little blue.
"After such kindness, that would be
    A dismal thing to do!"
"The night is fine," the Walrus said.
    "Do you admire the view?

"It was so kind of you to come!
    And you are very nice!"
The Carpenter said nothing but
    "Cut us another slice,
I wish you were not quite so deaf –
    I've had to ask you twice!"

"It seems a shame," the Walrus said,
    "To play them such a trick,
After we've brought them out so far,
    And made them trot so quick!"
The Carpenter said nothing but
    "The butter's spread too thick!"

"I weep for you," the Walrus said:
    "I deeply sympathise."
With sobs and tears he sorted out
    Those of the largest size,   100
Holding his pocket-handkerchief
    Before his streaming eyes.

"O Oysters," said the Carpenter,
    "You've had a pleasant run!
Shall we be trotting home again?"
    But answer came there none –
And this was scarcely odd, because
    They'd eaten every one.

        [*Humpty Dumpty's Song*
"written entirely for Alice's amusement"]

In winter, when the fields are white,
I sing this song for your delight———

In spring, when woods are getting green,
I'll try and tell you what I mean:

In summer, when the days are long,
Perhaps you'll understand the song:

In autumn, when the leaves are brown,
Take pen and ink, and write it down.

I sent a message to the fish:
I told them "This is what I wish."   10

The little fishes of the sea
They sent an answer back to me.

The little fishes' answer was
"We cannot do it, Sir, because———"

I sent to them again to say
"It will be better to obey."

The fishes answered with a grin
"Why, what a temper you are in!"

I told them once, I told them twice:
They would not listen to advice.

I took a kettle large and new,
Fit for the deed I had to do.

My heart went hop, my heart went thump:
I filled the kettle at the pump.

Then some one came to me and said,
"The little fishes are in bed."

I said to him, I said it plain,
"Then you must wake them up again."

I said it very loud and clear;
I went and shouted in his ear.

But he was very stiff and proud;
He said "You needn't shout so loud!"

And he was very proud and stiff;
He said "I'd go and wake them, if——"

I took a corkscrew from the shelf:
I went to wake them up myself.

And when I found the door was locked,
I pulled and pushed and kicked and knocked.

And when I found the door was shut.
I tried to turn the handle, but——

[The White Knight's Song]

I'll tell thee everything I can:
    There's little to relate.
I saw an aged, aged man,
    A-sitting on a gate.
"Who are you, aged man?" I said.
    "And how is it you live?"
And his answer trickled through my head,
    Like water through a sieve.

He said, "I look for butterflies
    That sleep among the wheat;   10
I make them into mutton-pies,
    And sell them in the street.
I sell them unto men," he said,
    "Who sail on stormy seas;
And that's the way I get my bread –
    A trifle, if you please."

But I was thinking of a plan
    To dye one's whiskers green,
And always use so large a fan
    That they could not be seen.   20
So, having no reply to give
    To what the old man said,
I cried, "Come, tell me how you live!"
    And thumped him on the head.

His accents mild took up the tale:
    He said, "I go my ways,
And when I find a mountain-rill,
    I set it in a blaze;
And thence they make a stuff they call
    Rowland's Macassar-Oil –   30
Yet twopence-halfpenny is all
    They give me for my toil."

But I was thinking of a way
        To feed oneself on batter,
And so go on from day to day
        Getting a little fatter.
I shook him well from side to side,
        Until his face was blue,
"Come, tell me how you live," I cried,
40   "And what it is you do!"

He said, "I hunt for haddocks' eyes
        Among the heather bright,
And work them into waistcoat-buttons
        In the silent night.
And these I do not sell for gold
        Or coin of silvery shine,
But for a copper halfpenny,
        And that will purchase nine.

"I sometimes dig for buttered rolls,
50   Or set limed twigs for crabs;
I sometimes search the grassy knolls
        For wheels of hansom-cabs.
And that's the way" (he gave a wink)
        "By which I get my wealth –
And very gladly will I drink
        Your Honour's noble health."

I heard him then, for I had just
        Completed my design
To keep the Menai bridge from rust
60   By boiling it in wine.
I thanked him much for telling me
        The way he got his wealth,
But chiefly for his wish that he
        Might drink my noble health.

And now, if e'er by chance I put
    My fingers into glue,
Or madly squeeze a right-hand foot
    Into a left-hand shoe,
Or if I drop upon my toe
    A very heavy weight,   70
I weep, for it reminds me so
Of that old man I used to know –
Whose look was mild, whose speech was slow,
Whose hair was whiter than the snow,
Whose face was very like a crow,
With eyes, like cinders, all aglow,
Who seemed distracted with his woe,
Who rocked his body to and fro,
And muttered mumblingly and low,
As if his mouth were full of dough,   80
Who snorted like a buffalo –
That summer evening long ago,
    A-sitting on a gate.

[The Red Queen's Lullaby]

Hush-a-by lady, in Alice's lap!
Till the feast's ready, we've time for a nap.
When the feast's over, we'll go to the ball –
Red Queen, and White Queen, and Alice, and all!

["To the Looking-Glass world it was Alice that said"]

To the Looking-Glass world it was Alice that said
"I've a sceptre in hand, I've a crown on my head.
Let the Looking-Glass creatures, whatever they be
Come and dine with the Red Queen, the White Queen,
    and me!"

Then fill up the glasses as quick as you can,
And sprinkle the table with buttons and bran:
Put cats in the coffee, and mice in the tea –
And welcome Queen Alice with thirty-times-three!

"O Looking-Glass creatures," quoth Alice, "draw near!
'Tis an honour to see me, a favour to hear:
'Tis a privilege high to have dinner and tea
Along with the Red Queen, the White Queen, and me!"

Then fill up the glasses with treacle and ink,
Or anything else that is pleasant to drink:
Mix sand with the cider, and wool with the wine –
And welcome Queen Alice with ninety-times-nine!

[The White Queen's Riddle]

"First, the fish must be caught."
That is easy: a baby, I think, could have caught it.
"Next, the fish must be bought."
That is easy: a penny, I think, would have bought it.

"Now cook me the fish!"
That is easy, and will not take more than a minute.
"Let it lie in a dish!"
That is easy, because it already is in it.

"Bring it here! Let me sup!"
It is easy to set such a dish on the table.
"Take the dish-cover up!"
Ah, *that* is so hard that I fear I'm unable!

For it holds it like glue –
Holds the lid to the dish, while it lies in the middle:
Which is easiest to do,
Un-dish-cover the fish, or dishcover the riddle?

Wasp in a Wig

When I was young, my ringlets waved
    And curled and crinkled on my head:
And then they said "You have been shaved,
    And wear a yellow wig instead."

But when I followed their advice,
    And they had noticed the effect,
They said I did not look so nice
    As they had ventured to expect.

They said it did not fit, and so
    It made me look extremely plain: 10
But what was I to do, you know?
    My ringlets would not grow again.

So now that I am old and grey,
    And all my hair is nearly gone,
They take my wig from me and say
    "How can you put such rubbish on?"

And still, whenever I appear,
    They hoot at me and call me "Pig!"
And that is why they do it, dear,
    Because I wear a yellow wig.   20

["A boat beneath a sunny sky"]

A boat beneath a sunny sky,
Lingering onward dreamily
In an evening of July –

Children three that nestle near,
Eager eye and willing ear,
Pleased a simple tale to hear –

Long has paled that sunny sky:
Echoes fade and memories die:
Autumn frosts have slain July.

10   Still she haunts me, phantomwise,
Alice moving under skies
Never seen by waking eyes.

Children yet, the tale to hear,
Eager eye and willing ear,
Lovingly shall nestle near.

In a Wonderland they lie,
Dreaming as the days go by,
Dreaming as the summers die:

Ever drifting down the stream—
20   Lingering in the golden gleam—
Life, what is it but a dream?

Oxford Poems, with some
Memoria Technica

Examination Statute

A is for A[cland], who'd physic the Masses,
B is for B[rodie], who swears by the gases.
C is for C[onington], constant to Horace.
D is for D[onkin], who integrates for us.
E is for E[vans], with rifle well steadied.
F is for F[reeman], Examiner dreaded!
G's G[oldwin Smith], by the "Saturday" quoted.
H is for H[eurtley], to "Margaret" devoted.
I am the Author, a rhymer erratic –
J is for J[owett], who lectures in Attic: 10
K is for K[itchin], than attic much warmer.
L is for L[iddell], relentless reformer!
M is for M[ansel], our Logic-provider,
And N[orris] is N, once a famous rough-rider.
O[gilvie]'s O, Orthodoxy's Mendoza!
And P[arker] is P, the amendment-proposer.
Q is the Quad, where the Dons are collecting.
R is for R[olleston], who lives for dissecting:
S is for S[tanley], sworn foe to formality.
T's T[ravers Twiss], full of Civil Legality.   20
U's U[niversity], factiously splitting,
V's the V[ice-Chancellor], ceaselessly sitting.
W's W[all], by Museum made frantic,
X the Xpenditure, grown quite gigantic.
Y are the Young men, whom nobody thought about –
Z is the Zeal that this victory brought about.

The Deserted Parks

"Solitudinem faciunt: *Parcum* appellant."

Museum! loveliest building of the plain
Where Cherwell winds towards the distant main;
How often have I loitered o'er thy green,
Where humble happiness endeared the scene!
How often have I paused on every charm,
The rustic couple walking arm in arm –
The groups of trees, with seats beneath the shade
For prattling babes and whisp'ring lovers made –
The never-failing brawl, the busy mill
Where tiny urchins vied in fistic skill –
(Two phrases only have that dusky race
Caught from the learned influence of the place;
Phrases in their simplicity sublime,
"Scramble a copper!" "Please, Sir, what's the time?")
These round thy walks their cheerful influence shed;
There were thy charms – but all these charms are fled.
Amidst thy bowers the tyrant's hand is seen,
And rude pavilions sadden all thy green;
One selfish pastime grasps the whole domain,
And half a faction swallows up the plain;
Adown thy glades, all sacrificed to cricket,
The hollow-sounding bat now guards the wicket;
Sunk are thy mounds in shapeless level all,
Lest aught impede the swiftly rolling ball;
And trembling, shrinking from the fatal blow,
Far, far away thy hapless children go.
Ill fares the place, to luxury a prey,
Where wealth accumulates, and minds decay;
Athletic sports may flourish or may fade,
Fashion may make them, even as it has made;
But the broad parks, the city's joy and pride,
When once destroyed can never be supplied!

Ye friends to truth, ye statesmen, who survey
The rich man's joys increase, the poor's decay,
'Tis yours to judge, how wide the limits stand
Between a splendid and a happy land.
Proud swells go by with laugh of hollow joy,
And shouting Folly hails them with "Ahoy!"
Funds even beyond the miser's wish abound,
And rich men flock from all the world around.   40
Yet count our gains. This wealth is but a name,
That leaves our useful products still the same.
Not so the loss. The man of wealth and pride
Takes up a space that many poor supplied;
Space for the game, and all its instruments,
Space for pavilions and for scorers' tents;
The ball, that raps his shins in padding cased,
Has wore the verdure to an arid waste;
His Park, where these exclusive sports are seen,
Indignant spurns the rustic from the green;   50
While through the plain, consigned to silence all,
In barren splendour flits the russet ball.
In peaceful converse with his brother Don,
Here oft the calm Professor wandered on;
Strange words he used – men drank with wondering ears
The languages called "dead," the tongues of other years.
(Enough of Heber! Let me once again
Attune my verse to Goldsmith's liquid strain.)
A man he was to undergraduates dear,
And passing rich with forty pounds a year.   60
And so, I ween, he would have been till now,
Had not his friends ('twere long to tell you how)
Prevailed on him, Jack-Horner-like, to try
Some method to evaluate his pie,
And win from those dark depths, with skilful thumb,
Five times a hundredweight of luscious plum –
Yet for no thirst of wealth, no love of praise,
In learned labour he consumed his days!
O Luxury! thou cursed by Heaven's decree,
How ill exchanged are things like these for thee!   70

How do thy potions, with insidious joy,
Diffuse their pleasures only to destroy;
Iced cobbler, Badminton, and shandy-gaff,
Rouse the loud jest and idiotic laugh;
Inspired by them, to tipsy greatness grown,
Men boast a florid vigour not their own;
At every draught more wild and wild they grow;
While pitying friends observe "I told you so!"
Till, summoned to their post, at the first ball,
A feeble under-hand, their wickets fall.
Even now the devastation is begun,
And half the business of destruction done;
Even now, methinks while pondering here in pity,
I see the rural Virtues leave the city.
Contented Toil, and calm scholastic Care,
And frugal Moderation, all are there;
Resolute Industry that scorns the lure
Of careless mirth – that dwells apart secure –
To science gives her days, her midnight oil,
Cheered by the sympathy of others' toil –
Courtly Refinement, and that Taste in dress
That brooks no meanness, yet avoids excess –
All these I see, with slow reluctant pace
Desert the long-beloved and honoured place!
While yet 'tis time, Oxonia, rise and fling
The spoiler from thee: grant no parleying!
Teach him that eloquence, against the wrong,
Though very poor, may still be very strong;
That party-interests we must forgo,
When hostile to "pro bono publico";
That faction's empire hastens to its end,
When once mankind to common sense attend;
While independent votes may win the day
Even against the potent spell of "Play!"

May 1867.

The New Belfry of Christ Church, Oxford

"If thou wouldst view the Belfry aright,
Go visit it at the mirk midnight–
For the least hint of open day
Scares the beholder quite away.
When wall and window are black as pitch,
And there's no deciding which is which;
When the dark Hall's uncertain roof
In horror seems to stand aloof;
When corner and corner, alternately,
Is wrought to an odious symmetry;   10
When distant Thames is heard to sigh
And shudder as he hurries by;
Then go, if it be worth the while,
Then view the Belfry's monstrous pile,
And, home returning, soothly swear
''Tis more than Job himself could bear !'

"Is it the glow of conscious pride –
Of pure ambition gratified –
That seeks to read in other eye
Something of its own ecstasy?   20
Or wrath, that worldlings should make fun
Of anything 'the House' has done?
Or puzzlement, that seeks in vain
The rigid mystery to explain?
Or is it shame that, knowing not
How to defend or cloak the blot –
The foulest blot on fairest face
That ever marred a noble place –
Burns with the pangs it will not own,
Pangs felt by loyal sons alone?"   30

Song and Chorus

Five fathoms square the Belfry frowns;
         All its sides of timber made;
Painted all in greys and browns;
         Nothing of it that will fade.
Christ Church may admire the change –
Oxford thinks it sad and strange.
Beauty's dead! Let's ring her knell.
Hark! now I hear them – ding-dong, bell.

From *The Vision of the Three T's: A Threnody by the
Author of "The New Belfry"* (1873)

The Wandering Burgess

Our Willie had been sae lang awa'
         Frae bonnie Oxford toon,
The townsfolk they were greeting a'
         As they went up and doon.

He hadna been gane a year, a year,
         A year but barely ten,
When word came unto Oxford toon,
         Our Willie wad come agen.

Willie he stude at Thomas his Gate,
         And made a lustie din;
And who so blithe as the gate-porter
         To rise and let him in?

10

"Now enter Willie, now enter Willie,
  And look around the place,
And see the pain that we have ta'en
  Thomas his Quad to grace."

The first look that our Willie cast,
  He leuch loud laughters three,
The neist look that our Willie cast,
  The tear blindit his e'e.   20

Sae square and stark the Tea-chest frowned
  Athwart the upper air,
But when the Trench our Willie saw,
  He thocht the Tea-chest fair.

Sae murderous-deep the Trench did gape
  The parapet aboon,
But when the Tunnel Willie saw
  He loved the Trench eftsoon.

'Twas mirk beneath the tane archway,
  'Twas mirk beneath the tither;   30
Ye wadna ken a man therein,
  Though it were your ain dear brither.

He turned him round and round about,
  And looked upon the Three;
And dismal grew his countenance,
  And drumlie grew his e'e.

"What cheer, what cheer, my gallant knight?"
  The gate-porter 'gan say.
"Saw ever ye sae fair a sight
  As ye have seen this day?"   40

"Now haud your tongue of your prating, man:
  Of your prating now let me be.
For, as I'm a true knight, a fouler sight
  I'll never live to see.

"Before I'd be the ruffian dark
    Who planned this ghastly show,
I'd serve as secretary's clerk
    To Ayrton or to Lowe.

"Before I'd own the loathly thing
    That Christ Church Quad reveals,
I'd serve as shoeblack's underling
    To Odger and to Beales!"

A Bachanalian Ode

Here's to the Freshman of bashful eighteen!
    Here's to the Senior of twenty!
Here's to the youth whose moustache can't be seen!
    And here's to the man who has plenty!
        Let the men Pass!
        Out of the mass
I'll warrant we'll find you some fit for a Class!

Here's to the Censors, who symbolise Sense,
    Just as Mitres incorporate Might, Sir!
To the Bursar, who never expands the expense!
    And the Readers, who always do right, Sir!
        Tutor and Don,
        Let them jog on!
I warrant they'll rival the centuries gone!

Here's to the Chapter, melodious crew!
    Whose harmony surely *intends* well:
For, though it commences with "harm," it is true,
    Yet its motto is "All's well that ends well!"
        'Tis love, I'll be bound,
        That makes it go round!
For "In for a penny is in for a pound"!

Here's to the Governing Body, whose Art
   (For they're Masters of Arts to a man, Sir!)
Seeks to beautify Christ Church in every part,
   Though the method seems hardly to answer!
    With three T's it is graced –
    Which letters are placed
To stand for the names of Tact, Talent, and Taste!

[The Wine Committee]

"Four frantic Members of a chosen Committee!
One of them resigned – then there were Three.

"Three thoughtful Members: that may pull us through!
One was invalided – then there were Two.

"Two tranquil Members: much may yet be done!
But they never came together, so I had to work with One."

["I love my love with a T"]

"I love my love with a T,
   Because he is Tethered and Tied:
I hate him with a T,
Because, in spite of me,
   He is not Terrified!"

["He took a second-story flat"]

"He took a second-story flat
In which you could not swing a cat.
But such was never his intent:
His only object was low rent:
And to swing cats he never meant, etc."

MEMORIA TECHNICA.
for Numbers.

1	2	3	4	5	6	7	8	9	0
b	d	t	f	l	s	p	h	n	z
c	w	j	qu	v	x	m	k	g	r

Each digit is represented by one or other of two consonants, according to the above table: vowels are then inserted *ad libitum* to form words, the significant consonants being always at the *end* of a line: the object of this is to give the important words the best chance of being, by means of the rhyme, remembered accurately.

The consonants have been chosen for the following reasons.

(1) *b, c,* first two consonants.
(2) *d* from "*deux*"; *w* from "*two*"
(3) *t* from "*trois*"; *j* was the last consonant left unappropriated.
(4) *f* from "*four*"; *qu* from "*quatre*."
(5) *l* = 50; *v* = 5.
(6) *s, x,* from "*six*."
(7) *p, m,* from "*septem*."
(8) *h* from "*huit*"; *k* from ὀκτώ.
(9) *n* from "*nine*"; *g* from its shape.
(0) *z, r,* from "*zero*."

They were also assigned in accordance, as far as possible, with the rule of giving to each digit one consonant in common use, and one rare one.

Since *y* is reckoned as a vowel, many whole words, (such as "ye", "you", "eye"), may be put in to make sense, without interfering with the significant letters.

Take as an example of this system the two dates of "Israelites leave Egypt — 1495," and "Israelites enter Canaan — 1455" :—

> "Shout again! We are free!"
> Says the loud voice of glee.
> "Nestle home like a dove,"
> Says the low voice of love.

Ch. Ch.
June 27/77

The First Crusade.

The First Crusaders all
Deserved a *coronal.*   [date: 1095]

Wycliffe's Bible completed.

The Bible to translate
Brought Wycliffe nought but hate.   [date: 1383]

French Revolution.

I loathe your cry of "Liberty!
"Equality, Fraternity!"
A miserable orphan I.   [date: 1789]

The Hunting of the Snark
(1876)

[Acrostic dedication to Gertrude Chataway]

Inscribed to a dear Child:
In memory of golden summer hours
and whispers of a summer sea

Girt with a boyish garb for boyish task,
      Eager she wields her spade: yet loves as well
Rest on a friendly knee, intent to ask
        The tale he loves to tell.

Rude spirits of the seething outer strife,
      Unmeet to read her pure and simple spright,
Deem, if you list, such hours a waste of life,
        Empty of all delight!

Chat on, sweet Maid, and rescue from annoy
      Hearts that by wiser talk are unbeguiled.   10
Ah, happy he who owns that tenderest joy,
        The heart-love of a child!

Away, fond thoughts, and vex my soul no more
      Work claims my wakeful nights, my busy days –
Albeit bright memories of that sunlit shore
        Yet haunt my dreaming gaze!

Fit the First
The Landing

"Just the place for a Snark!" the Bellman cried,
    As he landed his crew with care;
Supporting each man on the top of the tide
    By a finger entwined in his hair.

"Just the place for a Snark! I have said it twice:
    That alone should encourage the crew.
Just the place for a Snark! I have said it thrice:
    What I tell you three times is true."

The crew was complete: it included a Boots –
10   A maker of Bonnets and Hoods –
A Barrister, brought to arrange their disputes –
    And a Broker, to value their goods.

A Billiard-marker, whose skill was immense,
    Might perhaps have won more than his share –
But a Banker, engaged at enormous expense,
    Had the whole of their cash in his care.

There was also a Beaver, that paced on the deck,
    Or would sit making lace in the bow:
And had often (the Bellman said) saved them from wreck
20   Though none of the sailors knew how.

There was one who was famed for the number of things
    He forgot when he entered the ship:
His umbrella, his watch, all his jewels and rings,
    And the clothes he had bought for the trip.

He had forty-two boxes, all carefully packed,
    With his name painted clearly on each:
But, since he omitted to mention the fact,
    They were all left behind on the beach.

The loss of his clothes hardly mattered, because
30   He had seven coats on when he came,
With three pairs of boots – but the worst of it was,
    He had wholly forgotten his name.

He would answer to "Hi!" or to any loud cry,
    Such as "Fry me!" or "Fritter my wig!"
To "What-you-may-call-um!" or "What-was-his-name!"
    But especially "Thing-um-a-jig!"

While, for those who preferred a more forcible word,
    He had different names from these:
His intimate friends called him "Candle-ends,"
    And his enemies "Toasted-cheese."   40

"His form is ungainly – his intellect small –"
    (So the Bellman would often remark) –
"But his courage is perfect! And that, after all,
    Is the thing that one needs with a Snark."

He would joke with hyaenas, returning their stare
    With an impudent wag of the head:
And he once went a walk, paw-in-paw, with a bear,
    "Just to keep up its spirits," he said.

He came as a Baker: but owned, when too late –
    And it drove the poor Bellman half-mad –   50
He could only bake Bridecake – for which, I may state,
    No materials were to be had.

The last of the crew needs especial remark,
    Though he looked an incredible dunce:
He had just one idea – but, that one being "Snark,"
    The good Bellman engaged him at once.

He came as a Butcher: but gravely declared,
    When the ship had been sailing a week,
He could only kill Beavers. The Bellman looked scared,
    And was almost too frightened to speak: 60

But at length he explained, in a tremulous tone,
    There was only one Beaver on board;
And that was a tame one he had of his own,
    Whose death would be deeply deplored.

The Beaver, who happened to hear the remark,
    Protested, with tears in its eyes,
That not even the rapture of hunting the Snark
    Could atone for that dismal surprise!

It strongly advised that the Butcher should be
70   Conveyed in a separate ship:
But the Bellman declared that would never agree
    With the plans he had made for the trip:

Navigation was always a difficult art,
    Though with only one ship and one bell:
And he feared he must really decline, for his part,
    Undertaking another as well.

The Beaver's best course was, no doubt, to procure
    A second-hand dagger-proof coat –
So the Baker advised it – and next, to insure
80   Its life in some Office of note:

This the Banker suggested, and offered for hire
    (On moderate terms), or for sale,
Two excellent Policies, one Against Fire,
    And one Against Damage From Hail.

Yet still, ever after that sorrowful day,
    Whenever the Butcher was by,
The Beaver kept looking the opposite way,
    And appeared unaccountably shy.

Fit the Second
The Bellman's Speech

The Bellman himself they all praised to the skies –
  Such a carriage, such ease and such grace!
Such solemnity, too! One could see he was wise,
  The moment one looked in his face!

He had bought a large map representing the sea,
  Without the least vestige of land:
And the crew were much pleased when they found it to be
  A map they could all understand.

"What's the good of Mercator's North Poles and Equators,
  Tropics, Zones, and Meridian Lines?"   10
So the Bellman would cry: and the crew would reply
  "They are merely conventional signs!

"Other maps are such shapes, with their islands and capes!
  But we've got our brave Captain to thank"
(So the crew would protest) "that he's bought *us* the best –
  A perfect and absolute blank!"

This was charming, no doubt: but they shortly found out
  That the Captain they trusted so well
Had only one notion for crossing the ocean,
  And that was to tingle his bell.   20

He was thoughtful and grave – but the orders he gave
  Were enough to bewilder a crew.
When he cried "Steer to starboard, but keep her head larboard!"
  What on earth was the helmsman to do?

Then the bowsprit got mixed with the rudder sometimes:
  A thing, as the Bellman remarked,
That frequently happens in tropical climes,
  When a vessel is, so to speak, "snarked."

But the principal failing occurred in the sailing,
30   And the Bellman, perplexed and distressed,
Said he *had* hoped, at least, when the wind blew due East,
    That the ship would *not* travel due West!

But the danger was past – they had landed at last,
    With their boxes, portmanteaus, and bags:
Yet at first sight the crew were not pleased with the view
    Which consisted of chasms and crags.

The Bellman perceived that their spirits were low,
    And repeated in musical tone
Some jokes he had kept for a season of woe –
40   But the crew would do nothing but groan.

He served out some grog with a liberal hand,
    And bade them sit down on the beach:
And they could not but own that their Captain looked
        grand,
    As he stood and delivered his speech.

"Friends, Romans, and countrymen, lend me your ears!"
    (They were all of them fond of quotations:
So they drank to his health, and they gave him three cheers,
    While he served out additional rations).

"We have sailed many months, we have sailed many weeks,
50   (Four weeks to the month you may mark),
But never as yet ('tis your Captain who speaks)
    Have we caught the least glimpse of a Snark!

"We have sailed many weeks, we have sailed many days,
    (Seven days to the week I allow),
But a Snark, on the which we might lovingly gaze,
    We have never beheld till now!

"Come, listen, my men, while I tell you again
   The five unmistakable marks
By which you may know, wheresoever you go,
   The warranted genuine Snarks.   60

"Let us take them in order. The first is the taste,
   Which is meagre and hollow, but crisp:
Like a coat that is rather too tight in the waist,
   With a flavour of Will-o'-the-Wisp.

"Its habit of getting up late you'll agree
   That it carries too far, when I say
That it frequently breakfasts at five-o'clock tea,
   And dines on the following day.

"The third is its slowness in taking a jest.
   Should you happen to venture on one,   70
It will sigh like a thing that is deeply distressed:
   And it always looks grave at a pun.

"The fourth is its fondness for bathing-machines,
   Which it constantly carries about,
And believes that they add to the beauty of scenes –
   A sentiment open to doubt.

"The fifth is ambition. It next will be right
   To describe each particular batch:
Distinguishing those that have feathers, and bite,
   And those that have whiskers, and scratch.   80

"For, although common Snarks do no manner of harm,
   Yet, I feel it my duty to say,
Some are Boojums –" The Bellman broke off in alarm,
   For the Baker had fainted away.

Fit the Third
The Baker's Tale

They roused him with muffins – they roused him with ice –
  They roused him with mustard and cress –
They roused him with jam and judicious advice –
  They set him conundrums to guess.

When at length he sat up and was able to speak,
  His sad story he offered to tell;
And the Bellman cried "Silence! Not even a shriek!"
  And excitedly tingled his bell.

There was silence supreme! Not a shriek, not a scream,
10   Scarcely even a howl or a groan,
As the man they called "Ho!" told his story of woe
  In an antediluvian tone.

"My father and mother were honest, though poor –"
  "Skip all that!" cried the Bellman in haste.
"If it once becomes dark, there's no chance of a Snark –
  We have hardly a minute to waste!"

"I skip forty years," said the Baker in tears,
  "And proceed without further remark
To the day when you took me aboard of your ship
20   To help you in hunting the Snark.

"A dear uncle of mine (after whom I was named)
  Remarked, when I bade him farewell –"
"Oh, skip your dear uncle!" the Bellman exclaimed,
  As he angrily tingled his bell.

"He remarked to me then," said that mildest of men,
  " 'If your Snark be a Snark, that is right:
Fetch it home by all means – you may serve it with greens
  And it's handy for striking a light.

" 'You may seek it with thimbles – and seek it with care –
  You may hunt it with forks and hope;   30
You may threaten its life with a railway-share;
  You may charm it with smiles and soap –' "

("That's exactly the method," the Bellman bold
  In a hasty parenthesis cried,
"That's exactly the way I have always been told
  That the capture of Snarks should be tried!")

" 'But oh, beamish nephew, beware of the day,
  If your Snark be a Boojum! For then
You will softly and suddenly vanish away,
  And never be met with again!'   40

"It is this, it is this that oppresses my soul,
  When I think of my uncle's last words:
And my heart is like nothing so much as a bowl
  Brimming over with quivering curds!

"It is this, it is this –" "We have had that before!"
  The Bellman indignantly said.
And the Baker replied "Let me say it once more.
  It is this, it is this that I dread!

"I engage with the Snark – every night after dark –
  In a dreamy delirious fight: 50
I serve it with greens in those shadowy scenes,
  And I use it for striking a light:

"But if ever I meet with a Boojum, that day,
  In a moment (of this I am sure),
I shall softly and suddenly vanish away –
  And the notion I cannot endure!"

Fit the Fourth
The Hunting

The Bellman looked uffish, and wrinkled his brow.
    "If only you'd spoken before!
It's excessively awkward to mention it now,
    With the Snark, so to speak, at the door!

"We should all of us grieve, as you well may believe,
    If you never were met with again –
But surely, my man, when the voyage began,
    You might have suggested it then?

"It's excessively awkward to mention it now –
10   As I think I've already remarked."
And the man they called "Hi!" replied, with a sigh,
    "I informed you the day we embarked.

"You may charge me with murder – or want of sense –
    (We are all of us weak at times):
But the slightest approach to a false pretence
    Was never among my crimes!

"I said it in Hebrew – I said it in Dutch –
    I said it in German and Greek:
But I wholly forgot (and it vexes me much)
20   That English is what you speak!"

" 'Tis a pitiful tale," said the Bellman, whose face
    Had grown longer at every word:
"But, now that you've stated the whole of your case,
    More debate would be simply absurd.

"The rest of my speech" (he explained to his men)
    "You shall hear when I've leisure to speak it.
But the Snark is at hand, let me tell you again!
    'Tis your glorious duty to seek it!

"To seek it with thimbles, to seek it with care;
　　To pursue it with forks and hope;　　　　　　　30
To threaten its life with a railway-share;
　　To charm it with smiles and soap!

"For the Snark's a peculiar creature, that won't
　　Be caught in a commonplace way.
Do all that you know, and try all that you don't:
　　Not a chance must be wasted to-day!

"For England expects – I forbear to proceed:
　　'Tis a maxim tremendous, but trite:
And you'd best be unpacking the things that you need
　　To rig yourselves out for the fight."　　　　　　40

Then the Banker endorsed a blank cheque (which he
　　　crossed),
　　And changed his loose silver for notes:
The Baker with care combed his whiskers and hair,
　　And shook the dust out of his coats:

The Boots and the Broker were sharpening a spade –
　　Each working the grindstone in turn:
But the Beaver went on making lace, and displayed
　　No interest in the concern:

Though the Barrister tried to appeal to its pride,
　　And vainly proceeded to cite　　　　　　　　　50
A number of cases, in which making laces
　　Had been proved an infringement of right.

The maker of Bonnets ferociously planned
　　A novel arrangement of bows:
While the Billiard-marker with quivering hand
　　Was chalking the tip of his nose.

But the Butcher turned nervous, and dressed himself fine,
  With yellow kid gloves and a ruff –
Said he felt it exactly like going to dine,
60   Which the Bellman declared was all "stuff."

"Introduce me, now there's a good fellow," he said,
  "If we happen to meet it together!"
And the Bellman, sagaciously nodding his head,
  Said "That must depend on the weather."

The Beaver went simply galumphing about,
  At seeing the Butcher so shy:
And even the Baker, though stupid and stout,
  Made an effort to wink with one eye.

"Be a man!" said the Bellman in wrath, as he heard
70   The Butcher beginning to sob.
"Should we meet with a Jubjub, that desperate bird,
  We shall need all our strength for the job!"

Fit the Fifth
The Beaver's Lesson

They sought it with thimbles, they sought it with care;
  They pursued it with forks and hope;
They threatened its life with a railway-share;
  They charmed it with smiles and soap.

Then the Butcher contrived an ingenious plan
  For making a separate sally;
And had fixed on a spot unfrequented by man,
  A dismal and desolate valley.

But the very same plan to the Beaver occurred:
10   It had chosen the very same place:
Yet neither betrayed, by a sign or a word,
  The disgust that appeared in his face.

Each thought he was thinking of nothing but "Snark"
    And the glorious work of the day;
And each tried to pretend that he did not remark
    That the other was going that way.

But the valley grew narrow and narrower still,
    And the evening got darker and colder,
Till (merely from nervousness, not from goodwill)
    They marched along shoulder to shoulder.   20

Then a scream, shrill and high, rent the shuddering sky,
    And they knew that some danger was near:
The Beaver turned pale to the tip of its tail,
    And even the Butcher felt queer.

He thought of his childhood, left far far behind –
    That blissful and innocent state –
The sound so exactly recalled to his mind
    A pencil that squeaks on a slate!

" 'Tis the voice of the Jubjub!" he suddenly cried.
    (This man, that they used to call "Dunce.")   30
"As the Bellman would tell you," he added with pride,
    "I have uttered that sentiment once.

" 'Tis the note of the Jubjub! Keep count, I entreat.
    You will find I have told it you twice.
'Tis the song of the Jubjub! The proof is complete.
    If only I've stated it thrice."

The Beaver had counted with scrupulous care,
    Attending to every word:
But it fairly lost heart, and outgrabe in despair,
    When the third repetition occurred.   40

It felt that, in spite of all possible pains,
    It had somehow contrived to lose count,
And the only thing now was to rack its poor brains
    By reckoning up the amount.

"Two added to one – if that could but be done,"
    It said, "with one's fingers and thumbs!"
Recollecting with tears how, in earlier years,
    It had taken no pains with its sums.

"The thing can be done," said the Butcher, "I think.
50   The thing must be done, I am sure.
The thing shall be done! Bring me paper and ink,
    The best there is time to procure."

The Beaver brought paper, portfolio, pens,
    And ink in unfailing supplies:
While strange creepy creatures came out of their dens,
    And watched them with wondering eyes.

So engrossed was the Butcher, he heeded them not,
    As he wrote with a pen in each hand,
And explained all the while in a popular style
60   Which the Beaver could well understand.

"Taking Three as the subject to reason about –
    A convenient number to state –
We add Seven, and Ten, and then multiply out
    By One Thousand diminished by Eight.

"The result we proceed to divide, as you see,
    By Nine Hundred and Ninety and Two:
Then subtract Seventeen, and the answer must be
    Exactly and perfectly true.

"The method employed I would gladly explain,
    While I have it so clear in my head,   70
If I had but the time and you had but the brain –
    But much yet remains to be said.

"In one moment I've seen what has hitherto been
    Enveloped in absolute mystery,
And without extra charge I will give you at large
    A Lesson in Natural History."

In his genial way he proceeded to say
    (Forgetting all laws of propriety,
And that giving instruction, without introduction,
    Would have caused quite a thrill in Society),   80

"As to temper the Jubjub's a desperate bird,
    Since it lives in perpetual passion:
Its taste in costume is entirely absurd –
    It is ages ahead of the fashion:

"But it knows any friend it has met once before:
    It never will look at a bribe:
And in charity-meetings it stands at the door,
    And collects – though it does not subscribe.

"Its flavour when cooked is more exquisite far
    Than mutton, or oysters, or eggs: 90
(Some think it keeps best in an ivory jar,
    And some, in mahogany kegs:)

"You boil it in sawdust: you salt it in glue:
    You condense it with locusts and tape:
Still keeping one principal object in view –
    To preserve its symmetrical shape."

The Butcher would gladly have talked till next day,
    But he felt that the lesson must end,
And he wept with delight in attempting to say
100   He considered the Beaver his friend:

While the Beaver confessed, with affectionate looks
    More eloquent even than tears,
It had learned in ten minutes far more than all books
    Would have taught it in seventy years.

They returned hand-in-hand, and the Bellman, unmanned
    (For a moment) with noble emotion,
Said "This amply repays all the wearisome days
    We have spent on the billowy ocean!"

Such friends, as the Beaver and Butcher became,
110   Have seldom if ever been known;
In winter or summer, 'twas always the same –
    You could never meet either alone.

And when quarrels arose – as one frequently finds
    Quarrels will, spite of every endeavour –
The song of the Jubjub recurred to their minds,
    And cemented their friendship for ever!

Fit the Sixth
The Barrister's Dream

They sought it with thimbles, they sought it with care;
    They pursued it with forks and hope;
They threatened its life with a railway-share;
    They charmed it with smiles and soap.

But the Barrister, weary of proving in vain
    That the Beaver's lace-making was wrong,
Fell asleep, and in dreams saw the creature quite plain
    That his fancy had dwelt on so long.

He dreamed that he stood in a shadowy Court,
   Where the Snark, with a glass in its eye,   10
Dressed in gown, bands, and wig, was defending a pig
   On the charge of deserting its sty.

The Witnesses proved, without error or flaw,
   That the sty was deserted when found:
And the Judge kept explaining the state of the law
   In a soft under-current of sound.

The indictment had never been clearly expressed,
   And it seemed that the Snark had begun,
And had spoken three hours, before any one guessed
   What the pig was supposed to have done.   20

The Jury had each formed a different view
   (Long before the indictment was read),
And they all spoke at once, so that none of them knew
   One word that the others had said.

"You must know ——" said the Judge: but the Snark
      exclaimed "Fudge!
   That statute is obsolete quite!
Let me tell you, my friends, the whole question depends
   On an ancient manorial right.

"In the matter of Treason the pig would appear
   To have aided, but scarcely abetted: 30
While the charge of Insolvency fails, it is clear,
   If you grant the plea 'never indebted.'

"The fact of Desertion I will not dispute;
   But its guilt, as I trust, is removed
(So far as relates to the costs of this suit)
   By the Alibi which has been proved.

"My poor client's fate now depends on your votes."
　　Here the speaker sat down in his place,
And directed the Judge to refer to his notes
40　　And briefly to sum up the case.

But the Judge said he never had summed up before;
　　So the Snark undertook it instead,
And summed it so well that it came to far more
　　Than the Witnesses ever had said!

When the verdict was called for, the Jury declined,
　　As the word was so puzzling to spell;
But they ventured to hope that the Snark wouldn't mind
　　Undertaking that duty as well.

So the Snark found the verdict, although, as it owned,
50　　It was spent with the toils of the day:
When it said the word "GUILTY!" the Jury all groaned,
　　And some of them fainted away.

Then the Snark pronounced sentence, the Judge being quite
　　Too nervous to utter a word:
When it rose to its feet, there was silence like night,
　　And the fall of a pin might be heard.

"Transportation for life" was the sentence it gave,
　　"And *then* to be fined forty pound."
The Jury all cheered, though the Judge said he feared
60　　That the phrase was not legally sound.

But their wild exultation was suddenly checked
　　When the jailer informed them, with tears,
Such a sentence would have not the slightest effect,
　　As the pig had been dead for some years.

The Judge left the Court, looking deeply disgusted
   But the Snark, though a little aghast,
As the lawyer to whom the defence was intrusted,
   Went bellowing on to the last.

Thus the Barrister dreamed, while the bellowing seemed
   To grow every moment more clear: 70
Till he woke to the knell of a furious bell,
   Which the Bellman rang close at his ear.

Fit the Seventh
The Banker's Fate

They sought it with thimbles, they sought it with care;
   They pursued it with forks and hope;
They threatened its life with a railway-share;
   They charmed it with smiles and soap.

And the Banker, inspired with a courage so new
   It was matter for general remark,
Rushed madly ahead and was lost to their view
   In his zeal to discover the Snark.

But while he was seeking with thimbles and care,
   A Bandersnatch swiftly drew nigh   10
And grabbed at the Banker, who shrieked in despair,
   For he knew it was useless to fly.

He offered large discount – he offered a cheque
   (Drawn "to bearer") for seven-pounds-ten:
But the Bandersnatch merely extended its neck
   And grabbed at the Banker again.

Without rest or pause – while those frumious jaws
   Went savagely snapping around –
He skipped and he hopped, and he floundered and flopped,
   Till fainting he fell to the ground.   20

The Bandersnatch fled as the others appeared
    Led on by that fear-stricken yell:
And the Bellman remarked "It is just as I feared!"
    And solemnly tolled on his bell.

He was black in the face, and they scarcely could trace
    The least likeness to what he had been:
While so great was his fright that his waistcoat turned white –
    A wonderful thing to be seen!

To the horror of all who were present that day,
30   He uprose in full evening dress,
And with senseless grimaces endeavoured to say
    What his tongue could no longer express.

Down he sank in a chair – ran his hands through his hair –
    And chanted in mimsiest tones
Words whose utter inanity proved his insanity,
    While he rattled a couple of bones.

"Leave him here to his fate – it is getting so late!"
    The Bellman exclaimed in a fright.
"We have lost half the day. Any further delay,
40   And we shan't catch a Snark before night!"

Fit the Eighth
The Vanishing

They sought it with thimbles, they sought it with care;
    They pursued it with forks and hope;
They threatened its life with a railway-share;
    They charmed it with smiles and soap.

They shuddered to think that the chase might fail,
    And the Beaver, excited at last,
Went bounding along on the tip of its tail,
    For the daylight was nearly past.

"There is Thingumbob shouting!" the Bellman said,
  "He is shouting like mad, only hark!   10
He is waving his hands, he is wagging his head,
  He has certainly found a Snark!"

They gazed in delight, while the Butcher exclaimed
  "He was always a desperate wag!"
They beheld him – their Baker – their hero unnamed –
  On the top of a neighbouring crag,

Erect and sublime, for one moment of time,
  In the next, that wild figure they saw
(As if stung by a spasm) plunge into a chasm,
  While they waited and listened in awe.   20

"It's a Snark!" was the sound that first came to their ears,
  And seemed almost too good to be true.
Then followed a torrent of laughter and cheers:
  Then the ominous words "It's a Boo–"

Then, silence. Some fancied they heard in the air
  A weary and wandering sigh
That sounded like "–jum!" but the others declare
  It was only a breeze that went by.

They hunted till darkness came on, but they found
  Not a button, or feather, or mark,   30
By which they could tell that they stood on the ground
  Where the Baker had met with the Snark.

In the midst of the word he was trying to say,
  In the midst of his laughter and glee,
He had softly and suddenly vanished away –
  For the Snark *was* a Boojum, you see.

*Poems for Friends, including
acrostics, riddles, "charades"
and a cipher-poem*

(Solutions to riddles and hidden
names will be found in the Notes!)

[Two Prologues]

[Prologue to "The Loan of a Lover"]

Curtain rises and discovers the Speaker, who comes forward, thinking aloud,
[*Speaker.*]
"Ladies and Gentlemen" seems stiff and cold.
There's something personal in "Young and Old";
I'll try "Dear Friends" *(addresses audience)*

Oh! let me call you so.
Dear friends, look kindly on our little show.
Contrast us not with giants in the Art,
Nor say "You should see Sothern in that part";
Nor yet, unkindest cut of all, in fact,
Condemn the actors, while you praise the Act.
Having by coming proved you find a charm in it,   10
Don't go away, and hint there may be harm in it.

Miss Crabb.
My dear Miss Verjuice, can it really be?
You're just in time, love, for a cup of tea;
And so, you went to see those people play.

Miss Verjuice.
Well! yes, Miss Crabb, and I may truly say
You showed your wisdom when you stayed *away*.

Miss C.
Doubtless! Theatricals in *our* quiet town!
I've always said, "The law should put them down,"
They mean no harm, tho' I begin to doubt it –
But now sit down and tell me all about it.   20

Miss V.
> Well then, Miss Crabb, I won't deceive you, dear;
> I heard some things I – didn't like to hear:

Miss C.
> But don't omit them now.

Miss V.
> Well! No! I'll try
> To tell you *all* the painful history.
>   (*They whisper alternately behind a small fan.*)

Miss V.
> And then, my dear, Miss Asterisk and he
> Pretended they were lovers!!

Miss C.
> Gracious me!!

>   (*More whispering behind fan.*)

Speaker.
> What! *Acting* love!! And has that ne'er been seen
> 30 Save with a row of footlights placed between?
> My gentle censors, let me roundly ask,
> Do none but actors ever wear a mask?
> Or have we reached at last that golden age
> That finds deception only on the Stage?
> Come, let's confess all round before we budge,
> When all are guilty, none should play the Judge.
> We're actors all, a motley company,
> Some on the Stage, and others – on the sly –
> And guiltiest he who paints so well his phiz
> 40 His brother actors scarce know what he is.
> A truce to moralising; we invite
> The goodly company we see to-night
> To have the little banquet we have got,
> Well dressed, we hope, and served up *hot & hot.*
> "Loan of a Lover" is the leading dish,
> Concluding with a dainty course of fish;

"Whitebait at Greenwich" in the best condition
(By Mr Gladstone's very kind permission).
Before the courses will be handed round
An *Entrée* made of Children, nicely browned.   *Bell rings.*   50

But hark! The bell to summon me away;
They're anxious to begin their little Play.
One word before I go – We'll do our best,
And crave your kind indulgence for the rest;
Own that at least we've striven to succeed,
And take the good intention for the deed.

[Prologue to "Checkmate"]

*Enter Beatrice, leading Wilfred. She leaves him at centre
(front), and after going round on tip-toe, to make sure they
are not overheard, returns and takes his arm.*

B.
"Wiffie! I'm *sure* that something *is* the matter,
All day there's been – oh, *such* a fuss and clatter!
Mamma's been trying on a funny dress –
I never *saw* the house in such a mess! *(puts her arm round
his neck)*

Is there a secret, Wiffie?"

W.
(shaking her off)
"Yes, of course!"

B.
"And you won't tell it? *(whimpers)*
Then you're very cross! *(turns away from him and clasps
her hands, looking up ecstatically)*

I'm sure of *this*! It's something *quite* uncommon!"

W.

(stretching up his arms, with a mock-heroic air)
"Oh, Curiosity! Thy name is Woman! *(puts his arm round*
10   *her coaxingly)*

Well, Birdie, then I'll tell! *(mysteriously)*
What should you say
If they were going to act – a little play?"

B.

(jumping and clapping her hands)
"I'd say 'HOW NICE!' "

W.

(pointing to audience)
"But will it please the rest?"

B.

"Oh *yes*! Because, you know, they'll do their best! *(turns*
to audience)

You'll praise them, won't you, when you've seen the play?
Just say 'HOW NICE!' before you go away!"
                                    (They run away hand in hand.)

[*Some poems to Colleagues and Friends*]

[*A Request*]

O come to me at two today,
Harcourt, come to me!
And show me how my dark room may
Illuminated be.

Though gondolas may lightly glide,
For me, unless you come,
No friend remains but cyanide
Of pale potassium!

Though maidens sing sweet barcaroles
(Whatever they may be)   10
To captivate Lee's-Readers' souls,
Yet, Harcourt, come to me!
Yes, come to me at two today,
Or else at two tomorrow,
Nor leave thy friend to pine away
In photographic sorrow!

[Winter Birthday]

"The year when boilers froze and ket-
tles crystallised the fender
The natal day of Bosanquet
Dawned on us in its splendour.

For those who wear wool hosen cat-
ching colds a thing unheard of
But this great maxim Bosanquet
Would not believe a word of.

When Frenchmen say 'sare, no zank' et-
iquette suggests the answer   10
'A zoughtless, zankless Bosanquet
Would be more zief zan man Sir.'

Dear Bosanquet I've here expressed
The grateful feeling that is
But due to one who treats his guest
To genuine oyster patties."

C.L.D.

Dreamland

When midnight mists are creeping,
    And all the land is sleeping,
Around me tread the mighty dead,
    And slowly pass away.

Lo, warriors, saints, and sages,
    From out the vanished ages,
With solemn pace and reverend face
    Appear and pass away.

The blaze of noonday splendour,
    The twilight soft and tender,
May charm the eye: yet they shall die,
    Shall die and pass away.

But here, in Dreamland's centre,
    No spoiler's hand may enter,
These visions fair, this radiance rare,
    Shall never pass away.

I see the shadows falling,
    The forms of old recalling;
Around me tread the mighty dead,
    And slowly pass away.

To "Hallie"

Oh Caledonian Maiden!
    Oh Hallie shy and still!
When'ere I hear sweet music,
    Of you my thoughts will fill.

I shall think of those "half hours"
   In Ripon spent with you;
I shall dream of great Beethoven
   And of Mendelssohn so true.

If "sleepless nights" assail me,
   And I toss about in vain,   10
The memory of Heller
   Will make me rest again.

A chord of "Caller Herrin",
   A note of "Home sweet Home;"
A bar of Scotland's "Blue Bells;"
   Will make my spirit roam

To a Drawing-room in the Crescent
   Where those sweet sounds I heard,
And where I fain would follow
   If I were *but* a bird.   20

Then Hallie! Dear Childe Hallie!
   Be to your "talent" *true*;
And sometimes when you're playing
   Think *I* am watching you. –

Think how I loved your Music,
   Not for itself alone,
But for the hands that played it
   The mind that felt its tone.

And now farewell "Childe Hallie"!
   Though *I* am growing old,   30
Fond mem'ry still will charm me,
   To *you* I'll ne'er grow cold.

["My dear Christie"]

My dear Christie,
I greatly fear
I'm wanted here,
Which makes it clear
I can't appear
At your "pour rire" –
Would I were freer!
So, with a tear
(At which don't sneer)
10   I am, my dear,
Your most sincere
        C.L.Dodgson

[Letter to Maggie Cunnynghame]

Dear Maggie, I found that the *"friend"*,
That the little girl asked me to write to,
Lived at Ripon, and *not* at Land's End –
A nice sort of place to invite to!
It looked rather suspicious to me –
And soon after, by dint of incessant
Enquiries, I found out that she
Was called "Maggie", and lived in a Crescent!
Of course I declared, "after *that*"
10   (The language I used doesn't matter),
"I will *not* address her, that's flat!
So do not expect me to flatter."

Well, I hope you will soon see
Your beloved Pa come back –
For consider, should you be
Quite content with only Jack?

Just suppose they made a blunder!
(Such things happen now and then)
Really, now, I shouldn't wonder
If your "John" came home again,   20
And your father stayed at school!

A most awkward thing, no doubt.
How would you receive him? You'll
Say, perhaps, "you'd turn him out."
That would answer well, so far
As concerns the boy, you know –
But consider your Papa,
Learning lessons in a row
Of great inky schoolboys! This
(Though unlikely) *might* occur: 30
"Haly" would be grieved to miss
Him (don't mention it to her).

No *carte* has yet been done of me
that does real justice to my *smile*;
And so I hardly like, you see,
To send you one – however, I'll
Consider if I will or not –
Meanwhile, I send a little thing
To give you an idea of what
I look like when I'm lecturing.   40
The merest sketch, you will allow –
Yet still I think there's something grand
In the expression of the brow
And in the action of the hand.

Have you read my fairy tale
In *Aunt Judy's Magazine*?
If you have you will not fail
To discover what I mean
When I say "Bruno yesterday came

50   To remind me that he was my godson
     On the ground that I gave him a name"!

     Your affectionate friend,
     C.L. Dodgson.

     P.S.
     I would send, if I were not too shy,
     The same message to "Hally" that she
     (Though I do not deserve it, not I!)
     Has sent through her sister to me.
     My best love to yourself – to your Mother
     My kindest regards – to your small,
60   Fat, impertinent, ignorant brother
     My hatred – I think that is all.

To *Three Puzzled Little Girls, From the Author*

[To the three Misses Drury 1]

Three little maidens weary of the rail,
Three pairs of little ears listening to a tale,
Three little hands held out in readiness,
For three little puzzles very hard to guess.
Three pairs of little eyes, open wonder-wide,
At three little scissors lying side by side.
Three little mouths that thanked an unknown Friend,
For one little book, he undertook to send.
   Though whether they'll remember a friend, or book, or day –
10 In three little weeks is very hard to say.

August 1869.

[To the three Misses Drury 2]

Three little maids, one winter day,
While others went to feed,
To sing, to laugh, to dance, to play,
More wisely went to – Reed.

Others, when lesson-time's begun,
Go, half inclined to cry,
Some in a walk, some in a run;
But *these* went in a – Fly.

I give to other little maids
A smile, a kiss, a look,   10
Presents whose memory quickly fades;
I give to these – a Book.

Happy Arcadia may blind,
While *all abroad*, their eyes;
At home, this book (I trust) they'll find
A *very catching* prize.

[To the three Misses Drury 3]

Two thieves went out to steal one day
Thinking that no one knew it:
Three little maids, I grieve to say,
Encouraged them to do it.
'Tis sad that little children should
Encourage men in stealing!
But these, I've always understood,
Have got no proper feeling.

An aged friend, who chanced to pass
10   Exactly at the minute,
         Said "Children! Take this Looking-glass,
         And see your badness in it."

Jan. 11. 1872.

[" 'No mind!' the little maiden cried"]

"No mind!" the little maiden cried
     In half-indignant tone,
"To think that I should be denied
     A mind to call my own!"
And echo heard, and softly sighed (or seemed to sigh)
         "My own!"

"No mind!" the little maiden said,
     "You'd think it, I suppose!
And yet you know I've got a head
     With chin, cheek, mouth, eye, nose –"
And echo heard, and sweetly said (or seemed to say)
10   "I knows!"

"You have no mind to be unkind,"
     Said echo in her ear:
"No mind to bring a living thing
     To suffering or fear.
For all that's bad, or mean, or sad, you have no mind,
         my dear."

Then if the friend whom you deride,
     To all your merits blind,
Should say that, though he's tried and tried,
     Your mind he *cannot* find . . .
20   'Tis but a jest for Christmas-tide, so, Janet, *never mind*!

To Miss Mary Watson

Three children (their names were so fearful
You'll excuse me for leaving them out)
Sat silent, with faces all tearful –
What *was* it about?

They were sewing, but needles are prickly,
And fingers were cold as could be –
So they didn't get on very quickly,
And they wept, silly Three!

"O Mother!" said they, "Guildford's not a
Nice place for the winter, that's flat.   10
If you know any country that's hotter,
Please take us to that!"

"Cease crying," said she, "little daughter!
And when summer comes back with the flowers,
You shall roam by the edge of the water,
In sunshiny hours."

"And in summer," said sorrowful Mary,
"We shall hear the shrill scream of the train
That will bring that dear writer of fairy-
tales hither again."   20

(Now the person she meant to allude to
Was – well! it is best to forget.
It was some one she *always* was rude to,
Whenever they met.)

"It's my duty," their Mother continued,
"To fill with things useful and right
Your small minds: if I put nothing in, you'd
Be ignorant quite.

30

"But enough now of lessons and thinking:
Your meal is quite ready, I see –
So attend to your eating and drinking,
You thirsty young Three!"

Apr. 10, 1871.

[*Two Poems to Rachel Daniel*]

I

[*"Oh pudgy podgy pup"*]

"Oh pudgy podgy pup!
Why *did* they wake you up?
Those crude nocturnal yells
Are *not* like silver bells:
Nor ever would recall
Sweet Music's "dying fall".
They rather bring to mind
The bitter winter wind
Through keyholes shrieking shrilly
When nights are dark and chilly:
Or like some dire duett,
Or quarrelsome quartette,
Of cats who chant their joys
With execrable noise,
And murder Time and Tune
To vex the patient Moon!"

10

Nov. 1880.

II

["What hand may wreathe thy natal crown"]

What hand may wreathe thy natal crown,
O tiny tender Spirit-blossom,
That out of Heaven hast fluttered down
Into this Earth's cold bosom?

And how shall mortal bard aspire
All sin-begrimed and sorrow-laden
To welcome, with the Seraph-choir,
A pure and perfect Maiden?

Are not God's minstrels ever near,
Flooding with joy the woodland mazes?   10
Which shall we summon,
Baby dear, to carol forth thy praises?

With sweet sad song the Nightingale
May soothe the broken hearts that languish
Where graves are green – the orphans' wail,
The widow's lonely anguish:

The Turtle-dove with amorous coo
May chide the blushing maid that lingers
To twine her bridal wreath anew
With weak and trembling fingers: 20

But human loves and human woes
Would dim the radiance of thy glory
Only the Lark such music knows
As fits thy stainless story.

The world may listen as it will
She recks not, to the skies up-springing:
Beyond our ken she singeth still
For very joy of singing.

The Lyceum

It is the lawyer's daughter,
And she is grown so dear, so dear,
She costs me, in one evening,
The income of a year!

"You can't have children's love," she cried,
"Unless you choose to fee 'em!"
"And what's your fee, child?" I replied.
She simply said ——

We saw "The Cup." I *hoped* she'd say,
"I'm grateful to you, very."
She murmured, as she turned away,
"That lovely ——"

"Compared with her, the rest," she cried,
"Are just like two or three um-
"berellas standing side by side!
Oh, gem of ——"

We saw Two Brothers. I confess
To *me* they seemed one man.
"Now which is which, child? Can you guess?"
She cried, "A-course I can!"

Bad puns like this I *always* dread,
And am resolved to flee 'em.
And so I left her there, and fled;
She *lives* at ——

["Something fails"]

Something fails –
Perhaps the gales –
Still, there *are* scales
On the rails,
Packed in bales
With the mails,
Coming to a writer who regales
Little friends of his with fairy-tales.

[Letter to Violet Dodgson]

Dear Violet, I'm glad to hear
You children like the magazine
I ordered for you for a year:
And if you happen to have seen
The book about "Lord Fauntleroy,"
You'll find an interesting bit
About the child that acts a Boy
(Now they have made a Play of it)
In Number Six. She seems to be
A child without one bit of pride: 10
A pretty name too, hasn't she?
The little "Elsie Leslie Lyde."

I grieve to hear your bantam-hen
Is fond of rolling eggs away
You should remind it, now and then,
Of "Waste not, want not." You should say
"A bantam-hen that wastes an egg,
Is sure to get extremely poor
And to be forced at last to beg
For hard-boiled eggs from door to door.   20

How would you like it, Bantam-hen,"
You should go on, "if all your brood
Were hard-boiled chickens, you would then
Be sorry you had been so rude!"
Tell it all this and don't forget!
And now I think it's time for me
To sign myself, dear Violet,

Your loving Uncle,
C.L.D.

[*Acrostics, riddles and a cipher-poem*]

[*Cipher-poem and translation*]

Key word "fox"
"Jgmu qjl vgrv x ugemdt pupdeto?" wxxl x ugmh vj f jji.
"Ge'n ijsk tukcbb qfds fb qrug eq xud eyk cxdmfit ddjdef:
Fbu cgkskg mglb gf mstutt, had ubj, okc Ljudz *jgmu* nt
    jxxmh,
Pa st'ok krv eykgb vj dogoq gruke vqb zmfvtn as tuemak
    exjmh."
Wrs-brs, brs-brs, wrs-brs, brs-brs: "Vrct fdjsi!" fgu, Ugmh.
Njj-sjj, sjj-sjj, njj-sjj, sjj-sjj; Jji wxxl "Urbe ek fxdmh."
"Ljsv efdn ma lb as zapsi hlgvv," wxxl Srr, "zru qrsmxbr yadsl!
Lh jtbv xok urbt jgey zxmkkm imlk, eyce nypdef mhtt vj mht
    zxjlbu.
Xv pn cz rsk xbcbbexak – na Urdmh btblk'm wvrdu:
Nht dok'm gkkkkm o ifvtsu ruut mhkm'w brxey genstxiqmgk
10   zamc!"
Njj-sjj, sjj-sjj, njj-sjj, sjj-sjj: "G urbe dogb jjo Ljudz!"
Eab-jab, jab-jab, eab-jab, jab-jab: Umgh wxxl "Eyoe'n jjudz."

[*translation*]

"Will you trot a little quicker?" said a Lily to a Fox.
"It's gone eleven half an hour, by all the village clocks:
And dinner-time is twelve, you know, and Dolly *will* be
        wroth.
If we're not there to carry round the plates of mutton-broth."
Bow-wow, bow-wow, bow-wow, bow, wow: "Come along!"
        said Lily.
Bow-wow, wow-wow, bow-wow, wow-wow: Fox said "Don't
        be silly."

"Don't talk to me of going quick," said Fox, "you howling
        Hound!
My feet are done with patent glue, that sticks them to the
        ground.
It is my own invention – so Dolly needn't scold:
She can't invent a patent glue that's worth its weight in
        gold!"   10
Bow-wow, wow-wow, bow-wow, wow-wow: "I don't care
        for Dolly!"
Bow-wow, wow-wow, bow-wow, wow-wow; Lily said
        "That's folly."

A Riddle

Tell me truly, Maidens three,
Where can all these wonders be?
Where tooth of lion, eye of ox,
And foot of cat and tail of fox,
With ear of mouse and tongue of hound
And beard of goat, together bound
With hair of Maiden, strew the ground.

[*Puzzle*]
(To Mary, Ina, and Harriet or 'Hartie' Watson.)

When . a . y and I . a told . a .. ie they'd seen a
Small .. ea . u . e with . i ..., dressed in crimson and blue,
. a .. ie cried " 'Twas a . ai . y! Why, I . a and . a .y,
I *should* have been happy if I had been you!"

Said . a . y "You wouldn't." Said I . a 'You shouldn't –
Since *you* can't be *us*, and *we* couldn't be *you*.
You are *one*, my dear . a .. ie, but *we* are a . a .. y,
And a . i ... e . i . tells us that *one* isn't *two*."

[*Acrostic for Ruth Dymes*]

Round the wondrous globe I wander wild,
Up and down-hill – Age succeeds to youth –
Toiling all in vain to find a child
Half so loving, half so dear as Ruth.

To Miss Margaret Dymes

Maidens, if a maid you meet
Always free from pout and pet,
Ready smile and temper sweet,
Greet my little Margaret.
And if loved by all she be
Rightly, not a pampered pet,
Easily you then may see
'Tis my little Margaret.

[*"No, no! I cannot write a line"*]

No, no! I cannot write a line,
    I cannot write a word:
The thoughts I think appear in ink
    So shockingly absurd.

To wander in an empty cave
    Is fruitless work, 'tis said:
What must it be for one like me
    To *wander in his head*?

You say that I'm "to write a verse" –
    O Maggie, put it quite   10
The other way, and kindly say
    That I'm "averse to write"!

[*" 'Are you deaf, Father William?'*
the young man said"]

"Are you deaf, Father William?" the young man said,
"Did you hear what I told you just now?
Excuse me for shouting! Don't waggle your head
Like a blundering, sleepy old cow!

"A little maid dwelling in Wallington Town,
Is my friend, so I beg to remark:
Do you think she'd be pleased if a book were sent down
Entitled 'The Hunt of the Snark?' "

"Pack it up in brown paper!" the old man cried,
And seal it with olive-and-dove.   10
"I command you to do it!" he added with pride,
"Nor forget, my good fellow, to send her beside
Easter Greetings, and give her my love."

To the Misses Drury

"Maidens! if you love the tale,
If you love the Snark,
Need I urge you, spread the sail,
Now, while freshly blows the gale,
In your ocean-barque!

"English Maidens love renown,
Enterprise, and fuss!"
Laughingly those Maidens frown;
Laughingly, with eyes cast down;
10   And they answer thus:

"English Maidens fear to roam.
Much we dread the dark;
Much we dread what ills might come,
If we left our English home,
Even for a Snark!"

["Alice dear, will you join me in hunting the Snark"]

Alice dear, will you join me in hunting the Snark?
        Let us go to the chase hand-in-hand:
If we only can find one before it gets dark,
        Could anything happen more grand?

Ever ready to share in the Beaver's despair,
        Count your poor little fingers and thumbs;
Recollecting with tears all the smudges and smears
        On the page where you work at your sums!

May I help you to seek it with thimbles and care?
    Pursuing with forks and hope?   10
To threaten its life with a railway-share?
Or to charm it with smiles – but a maiden so fair
    Need not trouble herself about soap!

["Alice dreamed one night that she"]

Alice dreamed one night that she
Left her home in Wonderland:
In a house called "Number Three
Carleton Road" she seemed to be,
Empress of a Bellman's band.

Patiently the chase she led,
Running over Tufnell Park –
All because a book she read,
That was running in her head;
'Twas "The Hunting of the Snark"!   10

["From the air do they come"]

From the air do they come?
Little voices that tell
Of "boo" and of "jum,"
Ringing clear like a bell –

"Even here," they repeat,
Now and then, when it's dark,
Chance will aid you to meet,
Even here, with a Snark!

Sep. 2, 1876

[*"Love-lighted eyes, that will not start"*]

Love-lighted eyes, that will not start
At frown of rage or malice!
Uplifted brow, undaunted heart
Ready to dine on raspberry-tart
Along with fairy Alice!
In scenes as wonderful as if
She'd flitted in a magic skiff
Across the sea to Calais:
Be sure this night, in Fancy's feast,
Even till Morning gilds the east,
Laura will dream of Alice!

Perchance, as long years onward haste,
Laura will weary of the taste
Of Life's embittered chalice:
May she, in such a woeful hour,
Endued with Memory's mystic power,
Recall the dreams of Alice!

June 17, 1876.

Madrigal

He shouts amain, he shouts again,
        (Her brother, fierce, as bluff King Hal),
"I tell you flat, I shall do that!"
        She softly whispers " 'May' for 'shall'!"

He wistful sighed one eventide
        (Her friend, that made this Madrigal),
"And shall I kiss you, pretty Miss!"
        She softly whispers " 'May' for 'shall'."

With eager eyes my reader cries,
     "Your friend must be indeed a val-   10
-uable child, so sweet, so mild!
     What do you call her?" "May For shall."

[Anagrammatic Sonnet]

As to the war, try elm. I tried.
The wig cast in, I went to ride
"Ring? Yes." We rang. "Let's rap." We don't.
"O shew her wit!" As yet she won't.
Saw eel in Rome. Dry one: he's wet.
I am dry. O forge! Th'rogue. Why a net?

["They both make a roaring – a roaring all night"]

They both make a roaring – a roaring all night:
They both are a fisherman-father's delight:
They are both, when in fury, a terrible sight!

The First nurses tenderly three little hulls,
To the lullaby-music of shrill-screaming gulls,
And laughs when they dimple his face with their skulls.

The Second's a tidyish sort of a lad,
Who behaves pretty well to a man he calls "Dad,"
And earns the remark "Well, he isn't so bad!"

Of the two put together, oh what shall I say?   10
'Tis a time when "to live" means the same as "to play":
When the busiest person does nothing all day:

When the grave College Don, full of lore inexpressi-
ble, puts it all by, and is forced to confess he
Can think but of Agnes and Evey [and Jessie.]

Love Among the Roses

"Seek ye Love, ye fairy-sprites?
        Ask where reddest roses grow.
Rosy fancies he invites,
And in roses he delights,
        Have ye found him?" "No!"

"Seek again, and find the boy
        In Childhood's heart, so pure and clear."
Now the fairies leap for joy,
        Crying, "Love is here!"

10 "Love has found his proper nest;
        And we guard him while he dozes
In a dream of peace and rest
        Rosier than roses."

Jan. 3, 1878.

["Around my lonely hearth to-night"]

Around my lonely hearth to-night,
Ghostlike the shadows wander:
Now here, now there, a childish sprite,
Earthborn and yet as angel bright,
Seems near me as I ponder.

Gaily she shouts: the laughing air
Echoes her note of gladness –
Or bends herself with earnest care
Round fairy-fortress to prepare
10 Grim battlement or turret-stair –
In childhood's merry madness!

New raptures still hath youth in store.
Age may but fondly cherish
Half-faded memories of yore –
Up, craven heart! repine no more!
Love stretches hands from shore to shore:
Love is, and shall not perish!

[Poem for Dolly Draper]

Dear Dolly, since I do not know
Of any grander name than "Dolly"
Let me for once address you so,
Leaving "Miss Draper" out, although
You *may* be startled at my folly!
Day, "twenty-seventh"; month, "the first";
Rejoice that now you know the worst!
And, though you may be tall and stately,
Putting your pride in a moment by,
Excuse my telling you that I   10
Remain yours most affectionately,

Lewis Carroll

To M. A. B.

(To Miss Marion Terry, "Mary Ann Bessie Terry.")

The royal MAB, dethroned, discrowned
By fairy rebels wild,
Has found a home on English ground,
And lives an English child.
I know it, Maiden, when I see
A fairy-tale upon your knee –
And note the page that idly lingers
Beneath those still and listless fingers –

And mark those dreamy looks that stray
10   To some bright vision far away,
Still seeking, in the pictured story,
The memory of a vanished glory.

[This is a response to her reply]

Maiden, though thy heart may quail
And thy quivering lip grow pale,
Read the Bellman's tragic tale!

Is it Life of which it tells?
Of a pulse that sinks and swells,
Never lacking chime of bells?

Bells of sorrow, bells of cheer,
Easter, Christmas, glad New Year,
Still they sound, afar, anear.

10   So may Life's sweet bells for thee,
In the summers yet to be,
Evermore make melody!

To Miss Gaynor Simpson

My first tends his aid when you plunge into trade:
My second in jollifications:
My whole, laid on thinnish, imparts a neat finish
To pictorial representations.

For Alexandra Kitchin

My First's a drink resembling wine:
My Second closely follows nine:
My Third doth sentences combine:
My Fourth is hung upon "the line":

My Whole's a victim I design
To photograph when days are fine.

Feb. 23. 1880

A Charade

My First heads all atrocity heartrending:
My Next to finish it is ever tending:
My Third in Town its merry life is spending:
My fourth is the beginning of an ending.
My Whole is one of those perplexing misses,
Where looks of Youth encourage friendly kisses,
And yet where Age is sober fact, and this is
Destruction to such transitory blisses!

Dedicated to a tea-tea. Why? Oh, when?

_____

"Te veniente die, te decedente canemus"
"From dawn to decline of day of tea we will utter thy praises".

_____

Give tea to my first: 'tis as round as a ball
        And when stunted & small,
        I can't spare it at all.

Give tea to my second: 'tis quite the best way
        For concluding delay
        When you don't want to stay.

Give tea to my Third: it's a name I assign
        To plate, pictures, or wine,
        Which is yours and not mine.

10   Give no tea to my Whole: it will keep her awake,
                         And her small head will ache,
                         And a riot she'll make,
                         Till, for quietness's sake,
                         You supply her with cake.

To my Pupil

          Beloved Pupil! Tamed by thee,
          Addish-, Subtrac-, Multiplica-tion,
          Division, Fractions, Rule of Three,
          Attest thy deft manipulation!
          Then onward! Let the voice of Fame
          From Age to Age repeat thy story,
          Till thou hast won thyself a name
          Exceeding even Euclid's glory.

To My Child-Friend
Dedication to "The Game Of Logic"

          I charm in vain: for never again,
          All keenly as my glance I bend,
          Will Memory, goddess coy,
          Embody for my joy
          Departed days, nor let me gaze
          On thee, my Fairy Friend!

          Yet could thy face, in mystic grace,
          A moment smile on me, 'twould send
          Far-darting rays of light
10   From Heaven athwart the night,
          By which to read in very deed
          Thy spirit, sweetest Friend!

So may the stream of Life's long dream
Flow gently onward to its end,
With many a floweret gay,
A-down its willowy way:
May no sigh vex, no care perplex,
My loving little Friend!

1886.

To Miss Emmie Drury

"I'm EMInent in RHYME!" she said.
"I make WRY Mouths of RYE-Meal gruel!"
The Poet smiled, and shook his head:
"Is REASON, then, the missing jewel?"

A Nursery Darling
Dedication to the Nursery "Alice," 1889

A Mother's breast:
Safe refuge from her childish fears,
From childish troubles, childish tears,
Mists that enshroud her dawning years!
See how in sleep she seems to sing
A voiceless psalm – an offering
Raised, to the glory of her King,
In Love: for Love is Rest.

A Darling's kiss:
Dearest of all the signs that fleet   10
From lips that lovingly repeat
Again, again, their message sweet!
Full to the brim with girlish glee,
A child, a very child is she,
Whose dream of Heaven is still to be
At Home: for Home is Bliss.

[*"Girlie to whom in perennial bloom"*]

Girlie to whom in perennial bloom
Life is all "Os" and no crosses:
Artists may take other themes for their skill,
Dreaming of fairyland just as they will;
You desire nothing but horses.

Sunbeams may glance, happy midges may dance,
Brooks prattle on in their courses;
Artists may paint just whatever they please,
Landscapes and Seascapes and Mountains and Trees;
10 *You* are content with your horses.

[*Double Acrostics*]

(To Miss E. M. Argles.)

I sing a place wherein agree
All things on land that fairest be,
All that is sweetest of the sea.

Nor can I break the silken knot
That binds my memory to the spot
And friends too dear to be forgot.

On rocky brow we loved to stand
And watch in silence, hand in hand,
The shadows veiling sea and land.

Then dropped the breeze; no vessel passed: 10
So silent stood each taper mast,
You would have deemed it chained and fast.

Above the blue and fleecy sky:
Below, the waves that quivering lie,
Like crispèd curls of greenery.

"A sail!" resounds from every lip.
Mizzen, no, square-sail – ah, you trip!
Edith, it cannot be a ship!

So home again from sea and beach,
One nameless feeling thrilling each.   20
A sense of beauty, passing speech.

Let lens and tripod be unslung!
"Dolly!"'s the word on every tongue;
Dolly must sit, for she is young!

Photography shall change her face,
Distort it with uncouth grimace –
Make her bloodthirsty, fierce, and base.

I end my song while scarce begun;
For I should want, ere all was done,
Four weeks to tell the tale of one: 30

And I should need as large a hand,
To paint a scene so wild and grand,
As he who traversed Egypt's land.

What say you, Edith? Will it suit ye?
Reject it, if it fails in beauty:
You know your literary duty!

On the rail between Torquay and Guildford, Sep. 28, 1869.

[Double Acrostic for Agnes and Emily]

Two little maids were heard to *say*
   (They dwell in London city)
"This summers-day's too hot to *play,*
   And picture-books are pretty."

So, curling up like little mice,
   And clasping hand in hand,
They read (& whispered "Ain't it nice?")
   The tale of *Wonderland.*

Bright streamed the sunlight on the floor,
   To tempt them out to run;
But they (like mice, I've said before)
   Loved *shadow* more than sun.

And one cried "Sister! Let's invent
   A dream – and plan to go
Where Mr. Dodgson says he went –
   That *Russian* fair, you know."

The other said "It's nearly three:
   Papa will call us soon,
His picture's in the *stand*, and we
   Must sit this afternoon."

"And if we sit extremely good"
   The younger cried in haste,
"He'll give us *wine* – he said he would –
   A little tiny taste."

["Two little girls near London dwell"]

Two little girls near London dwell,
More naughty than I like to tell.

Upon the lawn the hoops are seen:
The balls are rolling on the green.

The Thames is running deep and wide:
And boats are rowing on the tide.

In winter-time, all in a row,
The happy skaters come and go.

"Papa!" they cry, "Do let us stay!"
He does not speak, but says they may.   10

"There is a land," he says, "my dear,
Which is too hot to skate, I fear."

["Thanks, thanks, fair Cousins, for your gift"]

Thanks, thanks, fair Cousins, for your gift
    So swiftly borne to Albion's isle –
Though angry waves their crests uplift
    Between our shores, for many a league!

("So far, so good," you say: "but how
    Your Cousins?" Let me tell you, Madam.
We're both descended, you'll allow,
    From one great-great-great-grandsire, Noah.)

Your picture shall adorn the book
    That's bound, so neatly and moroccoly,   10
With that bright green which every cook
    Delights to see in beds of cauliflower.

The carte is very good, but pray
      Send me the larger one as well!
"A cool request!" I hear you say.
        "Give him an inch, he takes an acre!

"But we'll be generous, because
      We well remember, in the story,
How good and gentle Alice was,
20   The day she argued with the Parrot!"

["I saw a child; even if blind"]

I saw a child; even if blind,
I could have seen she was not kind.

"My child," said I, "don't make that noise!
Here, choose among this heap of toys."

She said "I've tumbled in the river:
And that's what makes me shake and shiver."

"And what's your name, my child?" said I.
"It's Juliet, sir," she made reply.

"You know," said she, "I hates my pa –
10 Never says nothing to my ma" –

"My child," I cried, "you make me sad.
How can you be so very bad?"

At which she laughed in such a way,
I lost my hearing from that day.

A Day in the Country

Come, pack my things, and let the clothes
   Be neatly brushed and folded well:
The friends I visit all suppose
   That I'm a perfect London swell.

I wield a magic art, whose skill
   Would make you open both your eyes:
And any friend of mine, who will,
   I'm ready to immortalise.

"But is there water?" I demand,
   "Water in limitless supplies?"   10
They say " 'Tis ready to your hand,
   And in prodigious quantities."

"Our long-legged Johnnie shall attend:
   He'll fetch it for you at a word."
I said "My worthy long-legged friend,
   You're very like a monstrous bird!"

"Arrange the group! Our eldest boy
   As Shakespeare's lover shall be dressed;
And it shall be his sole employ
   To roll his eyes and thump his chest."   20

"He *has* such genius!" says Momma.
   "He got the fortieth prize at Eton!
In tragedy he's best, by far –
   As Hamlet he can *not* be beaten

"And don't forget to write below
   Some neat Shakespearian quotation –
The picture'll strike our friend, I know
   All of a heap with admiration.

"But is it really *here* you mean
    To group the family together?
You really *must* devise a screen –
    The sun will bake us brown as leather!"

'Tis done. This happy English home
    Is now immortalised securely:
The great historian of Rome
    Could not have done it half as surely!

But evening's now drawing on,
    So for today we'll give it up:
The light, you see is nearly gone –
    But come indoors and take a cup.

"Our larger cups are broken all,
    So this must do – it's made of chiney."
"Indeed," said I, "it's very small:
    I never saw a cup so tiny!"

I've taken pictures bad and good:
    But that, I think, was worse than any
The great Logician never could
    Have proved it worth a single penny!

They tell me it is turning green –
    All change, I'm sure, will be a blessing:
For never, never was there seen
    A thing so hideous, so distressing!

Maggie's Visit to Oxford
(June 9th to 13th, 1889)

When Maggie once to Oxford came,
    On tour as "Bootles' Baby,"
She said, "I'll see this place of fame,
    However dull the day be."

So with her friend she visited
The sights that it was rich in:
And first of all she popped her head
Inside the Christ Church kitchen.
The Cooks around that little child
Stood waiting in a ring: 10
And every time that Maggie smiled
Those Cooks began to sing –
Shouting the Battle-cry of Freedom!

"Roast, boil and bake,
For Maggie's sake:
Bring cutlets fine
For *her* to dine,
Meringues so sweet
For her to eat –
For Maggie may be   20
Bootles' Baby!"

Then hand in hand in pleasant talk
They wandered and admired
The Hall, Cathedral and Broad Walk,
Till Maggie's feet were tired:
To Worcester Garden next they strolled,
Admired its quiet lake:
Then to St. John, a college old,
Their devious way they take.
In idle mood they sauntered round   30
Its lawn so green and flat,
And in that garden Maggie found
A lovely Pussy-Cat!
A quarter of an hour they spent
In wandering to and fro:
And everywhere that Maggie went,
The Cat was sure to go –
Shouting the Battle-cry of Freedom!

"Maiow! Maiow!
40   Come, make your bow,
Take off your hats,
Ye Pussy-Cats!
And purr and purr,
To welcome *her*,
For Maggie may be
Bootles' Baby!"

So back to Christ Church, not too late
For them to go and see
A Christ Church undergraduate,
50   Who gave them cakes and tea.
Next day she entered with her guide
The garden called "Botanic,"
And there a fierce Wild Boar she spied,
Enough to cause a panic:
But Maggie didn't mind, not she,
She would have faced, alone,
That fierce wild boar, because, you see,
The thing was made of stone.
On Magdalen walls they saw a face
60   That filled her with delight,
A giant face, that made grimace
And grinned with all its might.
A little friend, industrious,
Pulled upwards all the while
The corner of its mouth, and thus
He helped that face to smile!
"How nice," thought Maggie, "it would be
If *I* could have a friend
To do that very thing for *me*
70   And make my mouth turn up with glee,
By pulling at one end."
In Magdalen Park the deer are wild
With joy, that Maggie brings
Some bread a friend had given the child,
To feed the pretty things.

They flock round Maggie without fear:
They breakfast and they lunch,
They dine, they sup, those happy deer –
Still, as they munch and munch,
Shouting the Battle-cry of Freedom!   80

"Yes, Deer are we,
And dear is she!
We love this child
So sweet and mild:
We all rejoice
At Maggie's voice:
We all are fed
With Maggie's bread . . .
For Maggie may be
Bootles' Baby!"   90

They met a Bishop on their way . . .
A Bishop large as life,
With loving smile that seemed to say
"Will Maggie be my wife?"
Maggie thought *not*, because, you see,
She was so *very* young,
And he was old as old could be . . .
So Maggie held her tongue.
"My Lord, she's Bootles' Baby, we
Are going up and down,"   100
Her friend explained, "that she may see
The sights of Oxford Town."
"Now say what kind of place it is,"
The Bishop gaily cried.
"The best place in the Provinces!"
That little maid replied.
Away, next morning, Maggie went
From Oxford town: but yet
The happy hours she there had spent
She could not soon forget.   110

The train is gone, it rumbles on:
The engine-whistle screams;
But Maggie deep in rosy sleep . . .
And softly in her dreams,
Whispers the Battle-cry of Freedom.

"Oxford, good-bye!"
She seems to sigh.
"You dear old City,
With gardens pretty,
And lanes and flowers,
And college-towers,
And Tom's great Bell . . .
Farewell – farewell:
For Maggie may be
Bootles' Baby!"

A Lesson in Latin

Our Latin books, in motley row,
Invite us to our task –
Gay Horace, stately Cicero:
Yet there's one verb, when once we know,
No higher skill we ask:
This ranks all other lore above –
We've learned "'*Amare*' means '*to love*'!"
So, hour by hour, from flower to flower,
We sip the sweets of Life:
Till, all too soon, the clouds arise,
And flaming cheeks and flashing eyes
Proclaim the dawn of strife:

With half a smile and half a sigh,
"*Amare! Bitter One!*" we cry.
Last night we owned, with looks forlorn,
"Too well the scholar knows
There is no rose without a thorn" –

But peace is made! We sing, this morn,
"No thorn without a rose!"
Our Latin lesson is complete: 20
We've learned that Love is Bitter-Sweet!

May 1888.

["My First has no beard – but its whiskers abound"]

My First has no beard – but its whiskers abound:
My Next has a beard – but no eyes:
My whole has two eyes – and a nourishing sound
That reminds me of puddings and pies.

To Miss Véra Beringer

There was a young lady of station,
"I love man" was her sole exclamation;
But when men cried, "You flatter,"
She replied, "Oh! no matter,
Isle of Man is the true explanation."

Riddle Poem

VIOLET
VIOLET
   VIOLET
    VIOLET
VIOLET

To find the eldest of the pets,
Go search among the violets!

My First is a berry:
        My Second is sorrow:
My Third from the cherry
        Its sweetness doth borrow:
My Whole is too merry
        To care for the morrow!

[*Some Poems to accompany Photographs*]

The Castle Builder

We are building little homes on the sands;
We are making little rooms very gay;
We are busy with our hearts and hands;
We are sorry the time flits away.

[*"No sooner does the sun appear"*]

No sooner does the sun appear
From out the vapours hazy
Than, first bright offerings to the year,
Expands the little Daisy.

Sweet, all sweets above,
Is a Mother's love,
Deep as death her love
Even for a Daisy.

*

Going a-shrimping

Pretty little legs
Paddling in the waters,
Knees, as smooth as eggs,
Belonging to my daughters.

["Breathes there the man with soul so dead"]

Breathes there the man with soul so dead,
Who never to himself hath said,
"I'll build a studio!
And every day for evermore
I'll photograph my children four
All sitting in a row!"

Ode addressed to a Young Lady
who expressed a Wish for a recent photograph of the Poet

"How deftly you flatter!
Yet what can it matter
Whether former or latter?
Whether thinner or fatter?
Whether dumpish as batter,
Or mad as a Hatter?
But a truce to this chatter!
My verses I scatter
Like ——"

Here the poem broke down, and remains an exquisite
fragment: the Poet not being handy in Similes.

Who Killed Cock Robin?

Who caused the Boer rebellion?
    "I", said the people's Willy,
    "With my speeches all so silly:
I caused the Boer Rebellion".

Who sent out reinforcements?
    "I", said Childers, blandly:
    "And I did it very grandly:
I sent out reinforcements".

Who advised surrender!
10   "I", said Quaker Bright:
    "For I never meant to fight:
I advised surrender".

Who went out to lead them?
    "I", said Roberts of Cabul:
    "And was made an April-fool:
I went out to lead them".

Who tried negotiation?
    "I", said Kimberly, sadly:
    "And I did it very badly:
20 I tried negotiation".

Who signed the treaty?
    "I", said Evelyn Wood,
    "This I never thought I could.
I signed the treaty".

Who spoke up against it?
    "I", said Cairns, profoundly:
    "And I gave it to them roundly:
I spoke up against it".

Who said 'twas honourable?
    "I", said Selbourne glib,   30
     "Though I knew it was a fib.
I said 'twas honourable".

Who cried "Shame"! upon it?
    "We", said Whig and Tory,
     "Who care for England's glory:
We cried 'Shame!' upon it".

Who approved it strongly?
    "We", say all the Rads
     And the mean-spirited cads.
"We approve it strongly".   40

Who will pay the piper?
    "I", says poor John Bull:
     "For, whoever plays the fool,
I always pay the piper!"

"Sylvie and Bruno" (1889) and
"Sylvie and Bruno Concluded"
(1893)

Sylvie and Bruno

["Who sins in hope, who, sinning, says"]

Who sins in hope, who, sinning, says,
"Sorrow for sin God's judgement stays!"
Against God's Spirit he lies; quite stops
Mercy with insult; dares, and drops,
Like a scorch'd fly, that spins in vain
Upon the axis of its pain,
Then takes its doom, to limp and crawl,
Blind and forgot, from fall to fall.

["Is all our Life, then, but a dream"]

Is all our Life, then, but a dream
Seen faintly in the golden gleam
Athwart Time's dark resistless stream?

Bowed to the earth with bitter woe,
Or laughing at some raree-show,
We flutter idly to and fro.

Man's little Day in haste we spend,
And, from its merry noontide, send
No glance to meet the silent end.

[A Beggar's Palace]

From sackcloth couch the Monk arose,
    With toil his stiffen'd limbs he rear'd;
A hundred years had flung their snows
    On his thin locks and floating beard.

[The Gardener's Song]

He thought he saw an Elephant,
    That practised on a fife:
He looked again, and found it was
    A letter from his wife.
"At length I realise," he said,
    "The bitterness of Life."

***

He thought he saw a Buffalo
    Upon the chimney-piece:
He looked again, and found it was
    His Sister's Husband's Niece.
"Unless you leave this house," he said,
    "I'll send for the Police!"

He thought he saw a Rattlesnake
    That questioned him in Greek:
He looked again, and found it was
    The Middle of Next Week.
"The one thing I regret," he said,
    "Is that it cannot speak!"

***

He thought he saw a Banker's Clerk
    Descending from the bus:

He looked again, and found it was
    A Hippopotamus:
"If this should stay to dine," he said,
    "There won't be much for us!"

* * *

He thought he saw a Kangaroo
    That worked a coffee-mill:
He looked again, and found it was
    A Vegetable-Pill.
"Were I to swallow this," he said,
    "I should be very ill!"   30

* * *

He thought he saw a Coach-and-Four
    That stood beside his bed:
He looked again, and found it was
    A Bear without a Head.
"Poor thing," he said, "poor silly thing!
    It's waiting to be fed!"

* * *

He thought he saw an Albatross
    That fluttered round the lamp:
He looked again, and found it was
    A Penny-Postage-Stamp.   40
"You'd best be getting home," he said:
    "The nights are very damp!"

He thought he saw a Garden-Door
    That opened with a key:
He looked again, and found it was
    A Double Rule of Three:
"And all its mystery," he said,
    "Is clear as day to me!"

He thought he saw an Argument
        That proved he was the Pope:
He looked again, and found it was
        A Bar of Mottled Soap.
"A fact so dread," he faintly said,
        "Extinguishes all hope!"

The Old Man's Incantation

Let craft, ambition, spite,
Be quenched in Reason's night,
Till weakness turn to might,
Till what is dark be light,
Till what is wrong be right!

Peter and Paul

"Peter is poor," said noble Paul,
        "And I have always been his friend:
And, though my means to give are small,
        At least I can afford to lend.
How few, in this cold age of greed,
        Do good, except on selfish grounds!
But I can feel for Peter's need,
        And I WILL LEND HIM FIFTY POUNDS!"

How great was Peter's joy to find
        His friend in such a genial vein!
How cheerfully the bond he signed,
        To pay the money back again!
"We can't," said Paul, "be too precise:
        'Tis best to fix the very day:
So, by a learned friend's advice,
        I've made it Noon, the Fourth of May."

"But this is April!" Peter said.
     "The First of April, as I think.
Five little weeks will soon be fled:
     One scarcely will have time to wink!   20
Give me a year to speculate –
     To buy and sell – to drive a trade –"
Said Paul "I cannot change the date.
     On May the Fourth it must be paid."

"Well, well!" said Peter, with a sigh.
     "Hand me the cash, and I will go.
I'll form a Joint-Stock Company,
     And turn an honest pound or so."
"I'm grieved," said Paul, "to seem unkind:
     The money shall of course be lent: 30
But, for a week or two, I find
     It will not be convenient."

So, week by week, poor Peter came
     And turned in heaviness away;
For still the answer was the same,
     "I cannot manage it to-day."
And now the April showers were dry –
     The five short weeks were nearly spent –
Yet still he got the old reply,
     "It is not quite convenient!"   40

The Fourth arrived, and punctual Paul
     Came, with his legal friend, at noon.
"I thought it best," said he, "to call:
     One cannot settle things too soon."
Poor Peter shuddered in despair:
     His flowing locks he wildly tore:
And very soon his yellow hair
     Was lying all about the floor.

The legal friend was standing by,
     With sudden pity half unmanned:
The tear-drop trembled in his eye,
     The signed agreement in his hand:
But when at length the legal soul
     Resumed its customary force,
"The Law," he said, "we can't control:
     Pay, or the Law must take its course!"

Said Paul "How bitterly I rue
     That fatal morning when I called!
Consider, Peter, what you do!
     You won't be richer when you're bald!
Think you, by rending curls away,
     To make your difficulties less?
Forbear this violence, I pray:
     You do but add to my distress!"

"Not willingly would I inflict,"
     Said Peter, "on that noble heart
One needless pang. Yet why so strict?
     Is this to act a friendly part?
However legal it may be
     To pay what never has been lent,
This style of business seems to me
     Extremely inconvenient!

"No Nobleness of soul have I,
     Like some that in this Age are found!"
(Paul blushed in sheer humility,
     And cast his eyes upon the ground.)
"This debt will simply swallow all,
     And make my life a life of woe!"
"Nay, nay, my Peter!" answered Paul.
     "You must not rail on Fortune so!

"You have enough to eat and drink:
      You are respected in the world:
And at the barber's, as I think,
      You often get your whiskers curled.
Though Nobleness you can't attain –
      To any very great extent –
The path of Honesty is plain,
      However inconvenient!"

" 'Tis true," said Peter, "I'm alive:
      I keep my station in the world: 90
Once in the week I just contrive
      To get my whiskers oiled and curled.
But my assets are very low:
      My little income's overspent:
To trench on capital, you know,
      Is always inconvenient!"

"But pay your debts!" cried honest Paul.
      "My gentle Peter, pay your debts!
What matter if it swallows all
      That you describe as your 'assets'?   100
Already you're an hour behind:
      Yet Generosity is best.
It pinches me – but never mind!
      I WILL NOT CHARGE YOU INTEREST!"

"How good! How great!" poor Peter cried.
      "Yet I must sell my Sunday wig –
The scarf-pin that has been my pride –
      My grand piano – and my pig!"
Full soon his property took wings:
      And daily, as each treasure went,   110
He sighed to find the state of things
      Grow less and less convenient.

Weeks grew to months, and months to years:
     Peter was worn to skin and bone:
And once he even said, with tears,
     "Remember, Paul, that promised Loan!"
Said Paul "I'll lend you, when I can,
     All the spare money I have got –
Ah, Peter, you're a happy man!
120   Yours is an enviable lot!

"I'm getting stout, as you may see:
     It is but seldom I am well:
I cannot feel my ancient glee
     In listening to the dinner-bell:
But you, you gambol like a boy,
     Your figure is so spare and light:
The dinner-bell's a note of joy
     To such a healthy appetite!"

Said Peter "I am well aware
130   Mine is a state of happiness:
And yet how gladly could I spare
     Some of the comforts I possess!
What you call healthy appetite
     I feel as Hunger's savage tooth:
And, when no dinner is in sight,
     The dinner-bell's a sound of ruth!

"No scare-crow would accept this coat:
     Such boots as these you seldom see.
Ah, Paul, a single five-pound-note
140   Would make another man of me!"
Said Paul "It fills me with surprise
     To hear you talk in such a tone:
I fear you scarcely realise
     The blessings that are all your own!

"You're safe from being overfed:
     You're sweetly picturesque in rags:
You never know the aching head
     That comes along with money-bags:
And you have time to cultivate
     That best of qualities, Content –   150
For which you'll find your present state
     Remarkably convenient!"

Said Peter "Though I cannot sound
     The depths of such a man as you,
Yet in your character I've found
     An inconsistency or two.
You seem to have long years to spare
     When there's a promise to fulfil:
And yet how punctual you were
     In calling with that little bill!"   160

"One can't be too deliberate,"
     Said Paul, "in parting with one's pelf.
With bills, as you correctly state,
     I'm punctuality itself.
A man may surely claim his dues:
     But, when there's money to be lent,
A man must be allowed to choose
     Such times as are convenient!"

It chanced one day, as Peter sat
     Gnawing a crust – his usual meal –   170
Paul bustled in to have a chat,
     And grasped his hand with friendly zeal.
"I knew," said he, "your frugal ways:
     So, that I might not wound your pride
By bringing strangers in to gaze,
     I've left my legal friend outside!"

"You well remember, I am sure,
        When first your wealth began to go,
And people sneered at one so poor,
180   I never used my Peter so!
And when you'd lost your little all,
        And found yourself a thing despised,
I need not ask you to recall
        How tenderly I sympathised!

"Then the advice I've poured on you,
        So full of wisdom and of wit:
All given gratis, though 'tis true
        I might have fairly charged for it!
But I refrain from mentioning
190   Full many a deed I might relate –
For boasting is a kind of thing
        That I particularly hate.

"How vast the total sum appears
        Of all the kindnesses I've done,
From Childhood's half-forgotten years
        Down to that Loan of April One!
That Fifty Pounds! You little guessed
        How deep it drained my slender store:
But there's a heart within this breast,
200   And I WILL LEND YOU FIFTY MORE!"

"Not so," was Peter's mild reply,
        His cheeks all wet with grateful tears:
"No man recalls, so well as I,
        Your services in bygone years:
And this new offer, I admit,
        Is very very kindly meant –
Still, to avail myself of it
        Would not be quite convenient!"

["He either fears his fate too much"]

He either fears his fate too much
    Or his desert is small,
Who dares not put it to the touch,
    To win or lose it all.

Fairies' Song

Rise, oh, rise! The daylight dies:
    The owls are hooting, ting, ting, ting!
Wake, oh, wake! Beside the lake
    The elves are fluting, ting, ting, ting!
Welcoming our Fairy King,
    We sing, sing, sing.

Hear, oh, hear! From far and near
    The music stealing, ting, ting, ting!
Fairy bells adown the dells
    Are merrily pealing, ting, ting, ting!   10
Welcoming our Fairy King,
    We ring, ring, ring.

See, oh, see! On every tree
    What lamps are shining, ting, ting, ting!
They are eyes of fiery flies
    To light our dining, ting, ting, ting!
Welcoming our Fairy King
    They swing, swing, swing.

Haste, oh, haste, to take and taste
    The dainties waiting, ting, ting, ting!   20
Honey-dew is stored———

The Three Badgers

There be three Badgers on a mossy stone,
    Beside a dark and covered way:
Each dreams himself a monarch on his throne,
    And so they stay and stay –
Though their old Father languishes alone,
    They stay, and stay, and stay.

There be three Herrings loitering around,
    Longing to share that mossy seat:
Each Herring tries to sing what she has found
10   That makes Life seem so sweet.
Thus, with a grating and uncertain sound,
    They bleat, and bleat, and bleat.

The Mother-Herring, on the salt sea-wave,
    Sought vainly for her absent ones:
The Father-Badger, writhing in a cave,
    Shrieked out "Return, my sons!
You shall have buns," he shrieked, "if you'll behave!
    Yea, buns, and buns, and buns!"

"I fear," said she, "your sons have gone astray?
20   My daughters left me while I slept."
"Yes'm," the Badger said: "it's as you say.
    "They should be better kept."
Thus the poor parents talked the time away,
    And wept, and wept, and wept.

Oh, dear beyond our dearest dreams,
Fairer than all that fairest seems!
To feast the rosy hours away,
To revel in a roundelay!

How blest would be
A life so free –   30
Ipwergis-Pudding to consume,
And drink the subtle Azzigoom!

And if, in other days and hours,
Mid other fluffs and other flowers,
The choice were given me how to dine –
"Name what thou wilt: it shall be thine!"
Oh, then I see
The life for me –
Ipwergis-Pudding to consume,
And drink the subtle Azzigoom!   40

The Badgers did not care to talk to Fish:
They did not dote on Herrings' songs:
They never had experienced the dish
To which that name belongs:
"And oh, to pinch their tails," (this was their wish,)
"With tongs, yea, tongs, and tongs!"

"And are not these the Fish," the Eldest sighed,
"Whose Mother dwells beneath the foam?"
"They are the Fish!" the Second one replied.
"And they have left their home!"   50
"Oh wicked Fish," the Youngest Badger cried,
"To roam, yea, roam, and roam!"

Gently the Badgers trotted to the shore——
The sandy shore that fringed the bay:
Each in his mouth a living Herring bore –
Those aged ones waxed gay:
Clear rang their voices through the ocean's roar,
"Hooray, hooray, hooray!"

Light Come, Light Go

He steps so lightly to the land,
    All in his manly pride:
He kissed her cheek, he pressed her hand,
    Yet still she glanced aside.
"Too gay he seems," she darkly dreams,
    "Too gallant and too gay
To think of me – poor simple me –
    When he is far away!"

"I bring my Love this goodly pearl
    Across the seas," he said:
"A gem to deck the dearest girl
    That ever sailor wed!"
She clasps it tight: her eyes are bright:
    Her throbbing heart would say
"He thought of me – he thought of me –
    When he was far away!"

The ship has sailed into the West:
    Her ocean-bird is flown.
A dull dead pain is in her breast,
    And she is weak and lone:
Yet there's a smile upon her face,
    A smile that seems to say
"He'll think of me – he'll think of me –
    When he is far away!

"Though waters wide between us glide,
    Our lives are warm and near:
No distance parts two faithful hearts –
    Two hearts that love so dear:
And I will trust my sailor-lad,
    For ever and a day,
To think of me – to think of me –
    When he is far away!"

Sylvie and Bruno Concluded

["Dreams, that elude the Maker's frenzied grasp"]

Dreams, that elude the Maker's frenzied grasp –
Hands, stark and still, on a dead Mother's breast,
Which nevermore shall render clasp for clasp,
Or deftly soothe a weeping Child to rest –
In suchlike forms me listeth to portray
My Tale, here ended. Thou delicious Fay –
The guardian of a Sprite that lives to tease thee –
Loving in earnest, chiding but in play
The merry mocking Bruno! Who, that sees thee,
Can fail to love thee, Darling, even as I? –   10
My sweetest Sylvie, we must say "Good-bye!"

["King Fisher courted Lady Bird"]

King Fisher courted Lady Bird –
Sing Beans, sing Bones, sing Butterflies!
    "Find me my match," he said,
    "With such a noble head –
With such a beard, as white as curd –
    With such expressive eyes!"

"Yet pins have heads," said Lady Bird –
Sing Prunes, sing Prawns, sing Primrose-Hill!
    "And, where you stick them in,
      They stay, and thus a pin
Is very much to be preferred
      To one that's never still!"

"Oysters have beards," said Lady Bird –
Sing Flies, sing Frogs, sing Fiddle-strings!
    "I love them, for I know
      They never chatter so:
They would not say one single word –
      Not if you crowned them Kings!"

"Needles have eyes," said Lady Bird –
Sing Cats, sing Corks, sing Cowslip-tea!
    "And they are sharp – just what
      Your Majesty is not:
So get you gone – 'tis too absurd
      To come a-courting me!"

[Streaks of Dawn]

Take, O boatman, thrice thy fee;
Take, I give it willingly;
For, invisible to thee,
Spirits twain have crossed with me!

Matilda Jane

Matilda Jane, you never look
At any toy or picture-book:
I show you pretty things in vain –
You must be blind, Matilda Jane!

I ask you riddles, tell you tales,
But all our conversation fails:
You never answer me again –
I fear you're dumb, Matilda Jane!

Matilda, darling, when I call,
You never seem to hear at all: 10
I shout with all my might and main –
But you're so deaf, Matilda Jane!

Matilda Jane, you needn't mind:
For, though you're deaf, and dumb, and blind,
There's some one loves you, it is plain –
And that is me, Matilda Jane!

The Revellers' Song

There's him, an' yo', an' me,
        Roarin' laddies!
We loves a bit o' spree,
Roarin' laddies we,
        Roarin' laddies
        Roarin' laddies!

What Tottles Meant

"One thousand pounds per annuum
Is not so bad a figure, come!"
Cried Tottles. "And I tell you, flat,
A man may marry well on that!
To say 'the Husband needs the Wife'
Is not the way to represent it.
The crowning joy of Woman's life
Is *Man*!" said Tottles (and he meant it).

The blissful Honey-moon is past:
The Pair have settled down at last:
Mamma-in-law their home will share,
And make their happiness her care.
"Your income is an ample one:
Go it, my children!" (And they went it).
"I *rayther* think this kind of fun
Won't last!" said Tottles (and he meant it).

They took a little country-box –
A box at Covent Garden also:
They lived a life of double-knocks,
Acquaintances began to call so:
Their London house was much the same
(It took three hundred, clear, to rent it):
"Life is a very jolly game!"
Cried happy Tottles (and he meant it).

"Contented with a frugal lot"
(He always used that phrase at Gunter's),
He bought a handy little yacht –
A dozen serviceable hunters –
The fishing of a Highland Loch –
A sailing-boat to circumvent it –
"The sounding of that Gaelic 'och'
Beats me!" said Tottles (and he meant it).

But oh, the worst of human ills
(Poor Tottles found) are "little bills"!
And, with no balance in the Bank,
What wonder that his spirits sank?
Still, as the money flowed away,
He wondered how on earth she spent it.
"You cost me twenty pounds a day,
At *least*!" cried Tottles (and he meant it).

She sighed. "Those Drawing Rooms, you know!
I really never thought about it:
Mamma declared we ought to go –
We should be Nobodies without it.
That diamond-circlet for my brow –
I quite believed that she had sent it,
Until the Bill came in just now –"
"*Viper*!" cried Tottles (and he meant it).

Poor Mrs. T. could bear no more,
But fainted flat upon the floor.
Mamma-in-law, with anguish wild,
Seeks, all in vain, to rouse her child.
"Quick! Take this box of smelling-salts!
Don't scold her, James, or you'll repent it,
She's a *dear* girl, with all her faults——"
"She is!" groaned Tottles (and he meant it).

"I was a donkey," Tottles cried,
"To choose your daughter for my bride!
'Twas you that bid us cut a dash!
'Tis *you* have brought us to this smash!
You don't suggest one single thing
That can in any way prevent it –"
"Then what's the use of arguing?"
"*Shut up*!" cried Tottles (and he meant it).

"And, now the mischief's done, perhaps
You'll kindly go and pack your traps?
Since *two* (your daughter and your son)
Are Company, but *three* are none.
A course of saving we'll begin:
When change is needed, *I'll* invent it:
Don't think to put your finger in
This pie!" cried Tottles (and he meant it).

See now this couple settled down
In quiet lodgings, out of town:
Submissively the tearful wife
Accepts a plain and humble life:
Yet begs one boon on bended knee:
"My ducky-darling, don't resent it!
Mamma might come for two or three –"
80   "NEVER!" yelled Tottles. And he meant it.

[The Earl's Poem]

"We doubt not that, for one so true,
There must be other, nobler work to do,
Than when he fought at Waterloo,
                And Victor he must ever be!"

["In stature the Manlet was dwarfish"]

In stature the Manlet was dwarfish –
        No burly big Blunderbore he:
And he wearily gazed on the crawfish
        His Wifelet had dressed for his tea.
"Now reach me, sweet Atom, my gunlet,
        And hurl the old shoelet for luck:
Let me hie to the bank of the runlet,
                And shoot thee a Duck!"

She has reached him his minikin gunlet:
10   She has hurled the old shoelet for luck:
She is busily baking a bunlet,
        To welcome him home with his Duck.
On he speeds, never wasting a wordlet,
        Though thoughtlets cling, closely as wax,
To the spot where the beautiful birdlet
                So quietly quacks.

Where the Lobsterlet lurks, and the Crablet
     So slowly and sleepily crawls:
Where the Dolphin's at home, and the Dablet
     Pays long ceremonious calls: 20
Where the Grublet is sought by the Froglet:
     Where the Frog is pursued by the Duck:
Where the Ducklet is chased by the Doglet –
     So runs the world's luck!

He has loaded with bullet and powder:
     His footfall is noiseless as air:
But the Voices grow louder and louder,
     And bellow, and bluster, and blare.
They bristle before him and after,
     They flutter above and below,   30
Shrill shriekings of lubberly laughter,
     Weird wailings of woe!

They echo without him, within him:
     They thrill through his whiskers and beard:
Like a teetotum seeming to spin him,
     With sneers never hitherto sneered.
"Avengement," they cry, "on our Foelet!
     Let the Manikin weep for our wrongs!
Let us drench him, from toplet to toelet,
     With Nursery-Songs!   40

"He shall muse upon 'Hey! Diddle! Diddle!'
     On the Cow that surmounted the Moon:
He shall rave of the Cat and the Fiddle,
     And the Dish that eloped with the Spoon:
And his soul shall be sad for the Spider,
     When Miss Muffet was sipping her whey,
That so tenderly sat down beside her,
     And scared her away!

"The music of Midsummer-madness
50   Shall sting him with many a bite,
Till, in rapture of rollicking sadness,
                He shall groan with a gloomy delight:
He shall swathe him, like mists of the morning,
                In platitudes luscious and limp,
Such as deck, with a deathless adorning,
                The Song of the Shrimp!

"When the Ducklet's dark doom is decided,
                We will trundle him home in a trice:
And the banquet, so plainly provided,
60   Shall round into rose-buds and rice:
In a blaze of pragmatic invention
                He shall wrestle with Fate, and shall reign:
But he has not a friend fit to mention,
                So hit him again!"

He has shot it, the delicate darling!
                And the Voices have ceased from their strife:
Not a whisper of sneering or snarling,
                As he carries it home to his wife:
Then, cheerily champing the bunlet
70   His spouse was so skilful to bake,
He hies him once more to the runlet,
                To fetch her the Drake!

A Fairy-Duet

"Say, what is the spell, when her fledgelings are cheeping,
                That lures the bird home to her nest?
Or wakes the tired mother, whose infant is weeping,
                To cuddle and croon it to rest?
What's the magic that charms the glad babe in her arms,
                Till it cooes with the voice of the dove?"

" 'Tis a secret, and so let us whisper it low –
    And the name of the secret is Love!"

      "For I think it is Love,
        For I feel it is Love,   10
For I'm sure it is nothing but Love!"

"Say, whence is the voice that, when anger is burning,
    Bids the whirl of the tempest to cease?
That stirs the vexed soul with an aching – a yearning
    For the brotherly hand-grip of peace?
Whence the music that fills all our being – that thrills
    Around us, beneath, and above?"

" 'Tis a secret: none knows how it comes, how it goes:
    But the name of the secret is Love!"

      "For I think it is Love,   20
        For I feel it is Love,
For I'm sure it is nothing but Love!"

"Say whose is the skill that paints valley and hill,
    Like a picture so fair to the sight?
That flecks the green meadow with sunshine and shadow,
    Till the little lambs leap with delight?

" 'Tis a secret untold to hearts cruel and cold,
    Though 'tis sung, by the angels above,
In notes that ring clear for the ears that can hear –
    And the name of the secret is Love!"   30

      "For I think it is Love,
        For I feel it is Love,
For I'm sure it is nothing but Love!"

The Pig-Tale

Little Birds are dining
      Warily and well,
      Hid in mossy cell:
Hid, I say, by waiters
Gorgeous in their gaiters –
      I've a Tale to tell.

Little Birds are feeding
      Justices with jam,
      Rich in frizzled ham:
Rich, I say, in oysters
Haunting shady cloisters –
      That is what I am.

Little Birds are teaching
      Tigresses to smile,
      Innocent of guile:
Smile, I say, not smirkle –
Mouth a semicircle,
      That's the proper style.

Little Birds are sleeping
      All among the pins,
      Where the loser wins:
Where, I say, he sneezes
When and how he pleases –
      So the Tale begins.

There was a Pig that sat alone
      Beside a ruined Pump:
By day and night he made his moan –
It would have stirred a heart of stone
To see him wring his hoofs and groan,
      Because he could not jump.

10

20

30

A certain Camel heard him shout –
    A Camel with a hump.
"Oh, is it Grief, or is it Gout?
What is this bellowing about?"
That Pig replied, with quivering snout,
    "Because I cannot jump!"

That Camel scanned him, dreamy-eyed.
    "Methinks you are too plump.
I never knew a Pig so wide –
That wobbled so from side to side –   40
Who could, however much he tried,
    Do such a thing as *jump*!

"Yet mark those trees, two miles away,
    All clustered in a clump:
If you could trot there twice a day,
Nor ever pause for rest or play,
In the far future – Who can say? –
    You may be fit to jump."

That Camel passed, and left him there,
    Beside the ruined Pump.   50
Oh, horrid was that Pig's despair!
His shrieks of anguish filled the air.
He wrung his hoofs, he rent his hair,
    Because he could not jump.

There was a Frog that wandered by –
    A sleek and shining lump:
Inspected him with fishy eye,
And said "O Pig, what makes you cry?"
And bitter was that Pig's reply,
    "Because I cannot jump!"   60

That Frog he grinned a grin of glee,
      And hit his chest a thump.
"O Pig," he said, "be ruled by me,
And you shall see what you shall see.
This minute, for a trifling fee,
      I'll teach you how to jump!

"You may be faint from many a fall,
      And bruised by many a bump:
But, if you persevere through all,
And practise first on something small,
Concluding with a ten-foot wall,
      You'll find that you can jump!"

That Pig looked up with joyful start:
      "Oh Frog, you are a trump!
Your words have healed my inward smart –
Come, name your fee and do your part:
Bring comfort to a broken heart,
      By teaching me to jump!"

"My fee shall be a mutton-chop,
      My goal this ruined Pump.
Observe with what an airy flop
I plant myself upon the top!
Now bend your knees and take a hop,
      For that's the way to jump!"

Uprose that Pig, and rushed, full whack,
      Against the ruined Pump:
Rolled over like an empty sack,
And settled down upon his back,
While all his bones at once went "Crack!"
      It was a fatal jump.

Little Birds are writing
    Interesting books,
     To be read by cooks:
Read, I say, not roasted –
Letterpress, when toasted,
    Loses its good looks.

Little Birds are playing
    Bagpipes on the shore,
     Where the tourists snore:
"Thanks!" they cry. " 'Tis thrilling!
Take, oh take this shilling!
    Let us have no more!"

Little Birds are bathing
    Crocodiles in cream,
     Like a happy dream:
Like, but not so lasting –
Crocodiles, when fasting,
    Are not all they seem!

That Camel passed, as Day grew dim
    Around the ruined Pump.
"O broken heart! O broken limb!
It needs," that Camel said to him,
"Something more fairy-like and slim,
    To execute a jump!"

That Pig lay still as any stone,
    And could not stir a stump:
Nor ever, if the truth were known,
Was he again observed to moan,
Nor ever wring his hoofs and groan,
    Because he could not jump.

That Frog made no remark, for he
　　　　Was dismal as a dump:
He knew the consequence must be
That he would never get his fee –
And still he sits, in miserie,
　　　　Upon that ruined Pump!

Little Birds are choking
　　　　Baronets with bun,
　　　　Taught to fire a gun:
Taught, I say, to splinter
Salmon in the winter –
　　　　Merely for the fun.

Little Birds are hiding
　　　　Crimes in carpet-bags,
　　　　Blessed by happy stags:
Blessed, I say, though beaten –
Since our friends are eaten
　　　　When the memory flags.

Little Birds are tasting
　　　　Gratitude and gold,
　　　　Pale with sudden cold
Pale, I say, and wrinkled –
When the bells have tinkled,
　　　　And the Tale is told.

Late Collections

Rhyme? And Reason?
(1883)

Echoes

Lady Clara Vere de Vere
Was eight years old, she said:
Every ringlet, lightly shaken, ran itself in golden thread.

She took her little porringer:
Of me she shall not win renown:
For the baseness of its nature shall have strength to drag her
down.

"Sisters and brothers, little Maid?
There stands the Inspector at thy door:
Like a dog, he hunts for boys who know not two and two are
four."

"Kind words are more than coronets,"   10
She said, and wondering looked at me:
"It is the dead unhappy night, and I must hurry home to tea."

A Game of Fives

Five little girls, of Five, Four, Three, Two, One:
Rolling on the hearthrug, full of tricks and fun.
Five rosy girls, in years from Ten to Six:
Sitting down to lessons – no more time for tricks.

Five growing girls, from Fifteen to Eleven:
Music, Drawing, Languages, and food enough for seven!
Five winsome girls, from Twenty to Sixteen:
Each young man that calls, I say "Now tell me which you
    mean!"
Five dashing girls, the youngest Twenty-one:
10 But, if nobody proposes, what is there to be done?

Five showy girls – but Thirty is an age
When girls may be *engaging*, but they somehow don't *engage*.
Five dressy girls, of Thirty-one or more:
So gracious to the shy young men they snubbed so much
    before!

Five *passé* girls – Their age? Well, never mind!
We jog along together, like the rest of human kind:
But the quondam "careless bachelor" begins to think he knows
The answer to that ancient problem "how the money goes"!

Four Riddles

*No. I. was written at the request of some young friends,
who had gone to a ball at an Oxford Commemoration –
and also as a specimen of what might be done by making
the Double Acrostic A CONNECTED POEM instead
of what it has hitherto been, a string of disjointed stanzas,
on every conceivable subject, and about as interesting to
read straight through as a page of a Cyclopaedia. The first
two stanzas describe the two main words, and each subse-
quent stanza one of the cross "lights." [See pp. 150–53]*

*No. II. was written after seeing Miss Ellen Terry per-
form in the play of "Hamlet." In this case the first stanza
describes the two main words.*

No. III. was written after seeing Miss Marion Terry

perform in Mr. Gilbert's play of "Pygmalion and Galatea."
The three stanzas respectively describe "My First," "My
Second," and "My Whole."

II.

Empress of Art, for thee I twine
This wreath with all too slender skill.
Forgive my Muse each halting line,
And for the deed accept the will!

———————————

O day of tears! Whence comes this spectre grim,
Parting, like Death's cold river, souls that love?
Is not he bound to thee, as thou to him,
By vows, unwhispered here, yet heard above?

And still it lives, that keen and heavenward flame,
Lives in his eye, and trembles in his tone: 10
And these wild words of fury but proclaim
A heart that beats for thee, for thee alone!

But all is lost: that mighty mind o'erthrown,
Like sweet bells jangled, piteous sight to see!
"Doubt that the stars are fire," so runs his moan,
"Doubt Truth herself, but not my love for thee!"

A sadder vision yet: thine aged sire
Shaming his hoary locks with treacherous wile!
And dost thou now doubt Truth to be a liar?
And wilt thou die, that hast forgot to smile?   20

Nay, get thee hence! Leave all thy winsome ways
And the faint fragrance of thy scattered flowers:
In holy silence wait the appointed days,
And weep away the leaden-footed hours.

III.

The air is bright with hues of light
And rich with laughter and with singing:
Young hearts beat high in ecstasy,
And banners wave, and bells are ringing:
But silence falls with fading day,
And there's an end to mirth and play.
Ah, well-a-day!

Rest your old bones, ye wrinkled crones!
The kettle sings, the firelight dances.
Deep be it quaffed, the magic draught
That fills the soul with golden fancies!
For Youth and Pleasance will not stay,
And ye are withered, worn, and grey.
Ah, well-a-day!

O fair cold face! O form of grace,
For human passion madly yearning!
O weary air of dumb despair,
From marble won, to marble turning!
"Leave us not thus!" we fondly pray.
"We cannot let thee pass away!"
Ah, well-a-day!

IV.

My First is singular at best:
More plural is my Second:
My Third is far the pluralest –
So plural-plural, I protest
It scarcely can be reckoned!

My First is followed by a bird:
My Second by believers
In magic art: my simple Third
Follows, too often, hopes absurd
And plausible deceivers.   10

My First to get at wisdom tries –
A failure melancholy!
My Second men revered as wise:
My Third from heights of wisdom flies
To depths of frantic folly.

My First is ageing day by day:
My Second's age is ended:
My Third enjoys an age, they say,
That never seems to fade away,
Through centuries extended.   20

My Whole? I need a poet's pen
To paint her myriad phases:
The monarch, and the slave, of men –
A mountain-summit, and a den
Of dark and deadly mazes –

A flashing light – a fleeting shade –
Beginning, end, and middle
Of all that human art hath made
Or wit devised! Go, seek HER aid,
If you would read my riddle!   30

Fame's Penny-Trumpet

Affectionately dedicated to all "original researchers" who
pant for "endowment."

Blow, blow your trumpets till they crack,
Ye little men of little souls!
And bid them huddle at your back –
Gold-sucking leeches, shoals on shoals!

Fill all the air with hungry wails –
"Reward us, ere we think or write!
Without your Gold mere Knowledge fails
To sate the swinish appetite!"

And, where great Plato paced serene,
Or Newton paused with wistful eye,
Rush to the chace with hoofs unclean
And Babel-clamour of the sty.

Be yours the pay: be theirs the praise:
We will not rob them of their due,
Nor vex the ghosts of other days
By naming them along with you.

They sought and found undying fame:
They toiled not for reward nor thanks:
Their cheeks are hot with honest shame
For you, the modern mountebanks!

Who preach of Justice – plead with tears
That Love and Mercy should abound –
While marking with complacent ears
The moaning of some tortured hound:

Who prate of Wisdom – nay, forbear,
Lest Wisdom turn on you in wrath,
Trampling, with heel that will not spare,
The vermin that beset her path!

Go, throng each other's drawing-rooms,
Ye idols of a petty clique: 30
Strut your brief hour in borrowed plumes,
And make your penny-trumpets squeak.

Deck your dull talk with pilfered shreds
Of learning from a nobler time,
And oil each other's little heads
With mutual Flattery's golden slime:

And when the topmost height ye gain,
And stand in Glory's ether clear,
And grasp the prize of all your pain –
So many hundred pounds a year –   40

Then let Fame's banner be unfurled!
Sing Paeans for a victory won!
Ye tapers, that would light the world,
And cast a shadow on the Sun –

Who still shall pour His rays sublime,
One crystal flood, from East to West,
When YE have burned your little time
And feebly flickered into rest!

A Tangled Tale
(1885)

A Tangled Tale

The elder and the younger knight
They sallied forth at three;
How far they went on level ground
It matters not to me;
What time they reached the foot of hill,
When they began to mount,
Are problems which I hold to be
Of very small account.
The moment that each waved his hat
Upon the topmost peak –
To trivial query such as this
No answer will I seek.
Yet can I tell the distance well
They must have travelled o'er:
On hill and plain, 'twixt three and nine,
The miles were twenty-four.
Four miles an hour their steady pace
Along the level track,
Three when they climbed – but six when they
Came swiftly striding back
Adown the hill; and little skill
It needs, methinks, to show,
Up hill and down together told,
Four miles an hour they go.
For whether long or short the time
Upon the hill they spent,

Two thirds were passed in going up,
One third in the descent.
Two thirds at three, one third at six,
If rightly reckoned o'er,   30
Will make one whole at four – the tale
Is tangled now no more.

Three Sunsets and Other Poems
(1898)

Puck Lost and Found

"Inscribed in two books ... presented to a little girl and boy, as a sort of memento of a visit paid by them to the author one day, on which occasion he taught them the pastime of folding paper 'pistols.'"

Puck has fled the haunts of men:
Ridicule has made him wary:
In the woods, and down the glen,
No one meets a Fairy!

"Cream!" the greedy Goblin cries –
Empties the deserted dairy –
Steals the spoons, and off he flies.
Still we see our Fairy!

Ah! What form is entering?
Lovelit eyes and laughter airy!
Is not this a better thing,
Child, whose visit thus I sing,
Even than a Fairy?

Nov. 22, 1891.

Puck has ventured back agen:
Ridicule no more affrights him
In the very haunts of men
Newer sport delights him.

Capering lightly to and fro,
Ever frolicking and funning –
"Crack!" the mimic pistols go!
Hark! The noise is stunning!

All too soon will Childhood gay
Realise Life's sober sadness.   10
Let's be merry while we may,
Innocent and happy Fay!
Elves were made for gladness!

Nov. 25, 1891.

Appendix
Poems Doubtfully Attributed
to Lewis Carroll

Sequel to The Shepherd of Salisbury Plain

But supposing this sheep, when he entered the fold,
    Had solemnly taken a vow
To shape all his bleats to one definite mould,
    Pray what can be said for him now?
Must the rules we hold binding in business and trade
    Be ignored in the Church's domain?
And need promises never be kept that are made
    To the Shepherd of Salisbury Plain?
Though freedom of bleat is withholden from none
    Of the flock, be his wool black or white,
Yet the freedom of breaking your promise is one
    To which few would insist on their right.
So, my friend, without wishing to charge upon *you*
    The quibble your verses maintain,
I but say, would that all were as honest and true
    As the Shepherd of Salisbury Plain!

Audi alteram partem.

[*Solutions to Puzzles from Wonderland,
probably from another hand*]

I

If ten the number dreamed of, why 'tis clear
That in the dream ten apples would appear.

II

In Shylock's bargain for the flesh was found
No mention of the blood that flowed around:
So when the stick was sawed in eight,
The sawdust lost diminished from the weight.

III

As curly-wigged Jemmy was sleeping in bed,
His brother John gave him a blow on the head;
James opened his eyelids, and spying his brother,
Doubled his fist, and gave him another.
This kind of box then is not so rare;
The lids are the eyelids, the locks are the hair,
And so every schoolboy can tell to his cost,
The key to the tangles is constantly lost.

IV

'Twixt "Perhaps" and "May be"
Little difference we see:
Let the question go round,
The answer is found.

V

That salmon and sole Puss should think very grand
Is no such remarkable thing.
For more of these dainties Puss took up her stand;
But when the third sister stretched out her fair hand
Pray why should Puss swallow her ring?

VI

"In these degenerate days," we oft hear said,
"Manners are lost and chivalry is dead!"
No wonder, since in high exalted spheres
The same degeneracy, in fact, appears.
The Moon, in social matters interfering,
Scolded the Sun, when early in appearing;
And the rude Sun, her gentle sex ignoring,
Called her a fool, thus her pretensions flooring.

VII

Five seeing, and seven blind
Give us twelve, in all, we find;
But all of these, 'tis very plain,
Come into account again.
For take notice, it may be true,
That those blind of one eye are blind for two;
And consider contrariwise,
That to see with your eye you may have your eyes;
So setting one against the other –
For a mathematician no great bother –   10
And working the sum, you will understand
That sixteen wise men still trouble the land.

Notes

Poems from Family Magazines

Useful and Instructive Poetry (1845)

This volume is the earliest surviving work by Charles Dodgson, written when he was thirteen. The manuscript has the poems written on 29 right-hand pages – with lively illustrations (some unfinished) on the left-hand pages (Berol).

My Fairy

Poems with a moral tag are a constant butt for the young Dodgson.

Punctuality

The punctilious instructions are undermined by the flowery moral, a nice double take.

Charity

For once, a useful if unsympathetic moral: throughout his life LC mocked the moralism beloved by pedagogic poets writing for children.

Melodies

There is only one other recorded limerick by LC, a form made famous by his contemporary Edward Lear. There is no account of the two ever having met or even of their knowing about each other. See "To Miss Véra Beringer".

A quotation from Shakespeare with slight improvements

The scene is from *Henry IV, Part 2*, iv, 5, in which the young Prince Henry sits beside his sleeping father and is tempted to try on the crown: "biggin" does indeed mean a woollen nightcap while "rigol" (30) means a circle or diadem. The 13-year-old poet perfectly follows the iambic pentameters of the original and achieves a conversational effect, as he does also in the next poem, "Brother and Sister".

The Juvenile Jenkins

The Dodgson family moved from Daresbury to the Rectory at Croft-on-Tees when LC was eleven years old. Young Jenkins has not been identified.

The Angler's Adventure

29–36. *Buffon's history ... Plesiosaurus*: Georges-Louis Leclerc, Comte de Buffon, published *Histoire naturelle*, 36 vols. (1749–88); Thomas Bewick published *History of British Birds*, 2 vols. (1797–1804); Izaak Walton published *The Compleat Angler* in 1653. Fluxions is Isaac Newton's term for differential calculus; the first Plesiosaur skeleton fossils were found by Mary Anning in the earlier nineteenth century. All these pseudo-learned references are, of course, there to be reversed by the maid who knows a toad when she sees one.

Rules and Regulations

LC was a life-long sufferer from stuttering as were several of his siblings; hence, perhaps, the twice-repeated injunction among these absurdist rules of behaviour not to stammer or stutter.

Clara

The Gothic deflated, with a glance at Tennyson.

The Rectory Magazine (c. 1848)

The second of the family magazines, with contributions from several of the Dodgson children. Lewis Carroll (C.L.D.) wrote under a range of pseudonymous initials (see Introduction), listed in his key to "Names of Authors with their assumed initials". Only his poems are included here.

Terrors

The railway continued to be a source of fascination and comedy (see, e.g., "Prologue to 'La Guida di Bragia'"). The mingling of astronomical,

Gothic, medieval and contemporary terrors give this poem a mysterious quality despite its prosaic ending.

The Rectory Umbrella (c. 1850–53)

The seventh of the Dodgson family domestic magazines. Between it and *The Rectory Magazine* were four of which no copies appear to have survived (see Introduction). As he describes in "The Poet's Farewell", LC wrote the whole of this particular magazine himself, including the footnotes. Some of the poems were later collected in the next magazine, *Mischmasch*.

Ye Fatalle Cheyse

title: *Cheyse*: Chase not cheese: the pseudo-medieval spelling throughout is for the fun of obscurity, added to by the footnotes.

The Storm

note 9. *murderous*: Reads "murdurous" in *Rectory Umbrella*.

Lays of Sorrow – Number 1
Lays of Sorrow – Number 2

The verses about the cannibal hen and the obstinate donkey in the "Lays of Sorrow", are clearly drawn direct from family experiences re-cast in mock-heroic style.

Number 2, note 3 *"Moans from the Miserable"*: In this little prose piece the domestic rabbits complain of being affectionately carried about by their ears, and it includes a ditty:

> "Oh ye whose hearts have nerves,
>   Oh ye whose ears have tears,
> It is not your love you are wearing out,
>   But living victim's ears!"

The Poet's Farewell

LC's complaint about writing the whole volume himself (38–40) seems to indicate that the missing earlier volumes included some contributions from his siblings.

6.   *shone*: Reads "shon" in *Rectory Umbrella*.

Mischmasch (*c.* 1855–62)

The last of the domestic magazines and rather different in nature from the earlier volumes. In *Mischmasch* are gathered a considerable number of LC's early poems that had already been published and that he thought worth preserving when in his twenties, from *Whitby Gazette*, *Comic Times*, *The Train*, *Temple Bar*, *All the Year Round* and *College Rhymes*. Some of them are cut out from these magazines and pasted in. Also included are a poem each by Louisa and Wilfred (see Introduction).

Many of the poems were later collected in *Phantasmagoria* (1869) and so appear there in this edition, often in revised form. Notable is the "Stanza of [pseudo-]Anglo-Saxon Poetry".

The poems first collected in *Mischmasch* were "The Two Brothers", "The Dear Gazelle", "She's All My Fancy Painted Him", "The Lady of the Ladle", "The Palace of Humbug", "Stanza of Anglo-Saxon Poetry", "The Three Voices", "Tommy's Dead", "Ode to Damon", "A Monument – all men agree", "Melancholetta", "The Willow Tree" (later titled "Stanzas for Music"), "Lines" (revised as "A Valentine"), "Blogg's Woe" (later titled "Size and Tears"), "Faces in the Fire". The prose pieces "Photography Extraordinary" and "Wilhelm Von Schmidt" also contain poems, which are printed here.

The Two Brothers

Another take-off of the idiom of Border Ballads: here their deadpan violence and ear for dialogue and for mismatched question-and-answer is transferred into fantasy sibling quarrels among the Dodgsons.

98. *Than*: Reads "Then" in *Mischmasch*.

The Dear Gazelle

This poem is introduced by a page headed "Poetry for the Million". The joke is set out in the first two paragraphs:

> The nineteenth century has produced a new school of music, bearing about as much relation to the genuine article, which the hash or stew of Monday does to the joint of Sunday.
>
> We allude of course to the prevalent practice of diluting the works of earlier composers with washy modern variations, so as to suit the weak-ened and depraved taste of this generation.

The third paragraph suggests that the other arts will copy this musical trend and ends: "Poetry must follow." The poem is treated as a musical lyric, with expression, tempo and expansion signs, such as D.C.: da capo – again from the start. The first line of each stanza plays on Thomas Moore's poem "Lalla Rookh":

> I never nurs'd a dear gazelle,
>   To glad me with its soft black eye,
> But when it came to know me well,
>   And love me, it was sure to die!

First published *Comic Times*, 18 August 1855.

She's All My Fancy Painted Him

A shorter and considerably revised version of this poem is offered as evidence in the courtroom scene in *Alice in Wonderland*: "[The White Rabbit's Evidence]". William Mee's popular ballad "She's all my fancy painted her" (music by Mrs Philip Millard) turns up a number of times, revised and parodied, in LC's poetry.
First published *Comic Times*, 8 September 1855.

From *"Photography Extraordinary"*

The essay plays with the idea that just as photographs are "developed", so "the ideas of the feeblest intellect, when once received on properly prepared paper, could be 'developed' up to any required degree of intensity". The different styles achieved are demonstrated in prose passages and in the three poems.
First published *Comic Times*, 3 November 1855.

From "Wilhelm Von Schmitz", chapters 3 and 4

All four chapters were first published in the *Whitby Gazette* (7 September 1854), hence the various allusions to Whitby in the "novel". This was Carroll's second published piece. In the *Mischmasch* version this absurd tale lacks chapters one and two; it is written in a spirited Gothic style. Its main characters are the Poet, the Waiter, Muggle and Sukie, and it has a happy ending. The three poems are all supposedly the production of the "Poet", Wilhelm Von Schmitz.

[*"My Sukie! he hath bought, yea, Muggle's self"*]

4.   *its*: Reads "it's" in *Wilhelm Von Schmitz*.

The Lady of the Ladle

LC's first published poem; the opening parodies Walter Scott's "The Lady of the Lake":

> The stag at eve had drunk his fill,
> Where danced the moon on Monan's rill,
> And deep his midnight lair had made
> In lone Glenartney's hazel shade.

20. *pomatum*: A perfumed hair-oil originally made from apples.
30. *Coronach*: This is a lament with bagpipes and parodies Scott's "Coronach" in Canto iii of his "Lady of the Lake", beginning: "He is gone on the mountain".

First published *Whitby Gazette*, 31 August 1854.

Lays of Mystery, Imagination, and Humour

Number 1
The Palace of Humbug

The first line recalls the song "The Gypsy Girl's Dream" from *The Bohemian Girl* (1843), the opera by Michael William Balfe, with libretto by Alfred Bunn. Richard Roe and John Doe (34, 36) are the substitute names used to protect the identities of witnesses in a lawsuit. All the legal terms in the poem, such as "suit", "plea" and "law", are punned against common speech, and "Sue" is a suitably legal name, though pronounced differently.

First published *Oxford Critic and University Magazine*, no. 1, June 1857, having been rejected by other comic journals.

Stanza of Anglo-Saxon Poetry

Readers will recognise this as the opening verse of "Jabberwocky", eventually published in *Through the Looking-Glass* (1872). These 1855 notes by LC do not entirely square with Humpty Dumpty's explanations there to Alice! ("Ed." in text is LC himself.)

Tommy's Dead

Sydney Dobell's tragic poem (1856) of age and bereavement here turns jaunty, by the device of making the speaker a particularly cantankerous old father and by pretending that Tommy was a cat.

Dobell's "Tommy's Dead" probably alludes to the Crimean war and opens:

> You may give over the plough, boys,
> You may take the gear to the stead,
> All the sweat o' your brow, boys,
> Will never get beer and bread.
> The seed's waste, I know, boys,
> There's not a blade will grow, boys,
> 'Tis cropped out, I trow, boys,
> And Tommy's dead.

Ode to Damon

Damon and Chloe, typical pastoral names, are here transposed to London everyday life. The Lowther Arcade opposite Charing Cross was a market for bric-a-brac while the 1851 Great Exhibition (18) took place in Hyde Park, a good step away, which gives point to Damon's mistaken "short cut".

First published *College Rhymes*, iii, October 1862.

[Riddle]

The solution offered in *Handbook*, p. 9, is 'tablet'.

Other Early Verse

Prologue to "La Guida di Bragia"

For an operetta written for LC's own Marionette Theatre, perhaps around 1855 when he was much occupied with performances and was also planning a book with "practical hints for constructing Marionettes and a theatre" (see *Diaries*, i, 81–2). No other marionette plays by LC are extant. Bradshaw's railway timetable guide ("La Guida di Bragia") is mentioned quite frequently in the diaries, and of course the railway figures in *Through the Looking-Glass*. LC was very interested by the new train network and, being a sociable man, used it frequently to visit friends all over the country. Indeed, a number of his friendships began in railway carriages, as with the Drury family (see note to "[To the three Misses Drury 1]"). In the little play manuscript, he imagines the mayhem that would ensue if the timetable decided to play tricks on its passengers by altering the times in secret (Berol).

First published *Queen*, clxx, 18 November 1931, pp. 37–40, 66.

The Ligniad, in two Books

This mock-epic was written while LC was an undergraduate at Christ Church, addressed to his earliest friend at the college, George Girdlestone Woodhouse, the first person to speak to him in the dining-hall. The title suggests a "wooden" quality, drawing on "*Wood*house": "lignum" means wood; the wooden hero cannot rise to poetry, though he is here celebrated in mock-heroic form. The "wood" also alludes to his bat, since Woodhouse was distinguished not only for his devotion to Greek and Latin but for his powers as a cricketer. LC is following in the mock-heroic tradition of Pope's *Dunciad* without his acrimony.

9.   *Doric reeds*: Pastoral shepherds' pipes.
10.   *Scapula*: A printer's term; here, the page printed from a plate.
12.   *Attic salt*: Athenian wit.
17.   *Greek Iambics*: A popular exercise for public schoolboys and undergraduates was the translation of English poetry into Greek verse. The Gaisford Prize at Oxford, from 1857, was awarded for this.
20.   "*'ώμοι, πέπληγμαι*": "Ah me, I am smitten" (Aeschylus, *Agamemnon*, line 1343).
40.   *Plays Euripides*: He is believed to have written over ninety plays of which eighteen survive.
48.   *A fragment from our Poet Laureate*: From Tennyson's "Edward Gray" (1842):

> Love may come and love may go,
>   And fly like bird from tree to tree;
> But I will love no more, no more,
>   Till Ellen Adair come back to me.

101. "*short slip*": Fielder positioned behind the batsman. Perhaps the poem celebrated a recent cricket-match in which Woodhouse excelled as batsman, bowler AND fielder.

See Roger Lancelyn Green, "Carroll's 'The Ligniad': an early mock-epic in facsimile", in Guiliano, pp. 81–91.

[*From a letter to his younger sister and brother Henrietta and Edwin, 31 January 1855*]

These exuberant Chinese whispers were written when LC had just begun teaching at Christ Church in 1855 at the age of 23 (*Letters*, i, 31). He jokes about dignity and distance between teacher and pupil and about the other hierarchies of college life. A "Scout" was a college servant.

Upon the Lonely Moor

This is the early version of what would sixteen years later become the White Knight's song in *Through the Looking-Glass* (1872).
First published (unsigned) *Train*, ii, 1856, pp. 255–6.

From "*Novelty and Romancement: A broken spell*"

["*'When Desolation snatched her tearful prey*"]

The rodomontade of this poem is part of a burlesque prose invention in which the glamorous "Romancement" turns out to be "Roman Cement".
First published *Train*, ii, 1856, pp. 249–54.

Alice, daughter of C. Murdoch, Esq

Addressed to the four-year-old daughter of William Clinton Murdoch and his wife Isabella, probably during a visit to London in June 1856 when LC invented a "story-charade" with some of the younger family members (see *Letters*, i, 33 note 1).

From "*The Legend of Scotland*"

This short story with verses was finished on 16 January 1858, having been promised for several months to the children of Charles Longley, Bishop of Durham. The ghostly tale was based on Auckland castle where they lived (*Diaries*, iii, 151–2). It's not clear why the victim changes from a medieval Scot into an Irishman in the final two lines.

[*"Into the wood – the dark, dark wood"*]

This poem was written to go with LC's photograph of Agnes Grace Weld as Little Red Riding-Hood in his photograph album, 6 January 1858 (*Diaries*, iii, 148).

*

In the early 1860s LC published fourteen poems in *College Rhymes*, an Oxford and Cambridge magazine with many contributions from

Christ Church. He was the Editor from July 1862 until March 1863. He later collected six of his poems with some changes in *Phantasmagoria* and this section has only those poems that he did not include there.

Disillusionised

31. *She's all my fancy painted her*: See poem with this title (pp. 51–2).
First published *College Rhymes*, iii, 1862, pp. 129–30.

Those Horrid Hurdy-Gurdies!

The first line of each stanza (except the last) is from enduringly popular songs: "My mother bids me bind my hair" by Anne Hunter was set to music by Haydn; "My lodging" goes back to the seventeenth century and was adapted by Thomas Moore for his "Believe me if all those endearing young charms"; "Ever of Thee I'm fondly dreaming" seems to have been first published in the early 1850s. The organ grinder's songs were endlessly repeated as he turned the handle of his hurdy-gurdy.
First published *College Rhymes*, iii, 1862, pp. 112–16. Reprinted in *Three Sunsets*.

[Prologue]

LC adapted this poem, first written in 1853 for a proposed volume of verse, as the Prologue to volume 4 of *College Rhymes* (1863).

The Majesty of Justice

The Vice-Chancellor of Oxford University had his own court, not part of the general system of justice in the land. The dialogue in the poem satirically questions whether only ceremonial can ratify justice. R.W.G. was one of LC's noms-de-plume.
First published *College Rhymes*, iv, 1863, pp. 96–9.

Miss Jones

This is a medley of twenty-two songs was written in 1862 at Croft together with LC's sisters Margaret and Henrietta, the "tunes running into each other" (*Diaries*, iv, 139). Margaret listed the titles: "The Captain and his Whiskers", "Willie we have missed you", "Cherry Ripe", "Kate's Letter", "Irish Emigrant", "Annie Laurie", "Irish Jig", "Wait for the Waggon", "Oft in the stilly night", "Lucy Long", "Reuben Wright", "Oh charming May", "Oh weel may the keel row", "So early in the morning", "Some love to reason", "I gave my hand", "I will marry my own love", "The girl I left behind me", "The perfect cure", "the Minstrel boy", "Beautiful Rhine", "Rule Britannia" (reduced facsimile, *Collected Verse*, pp. 47–9). There was a hope that it would be performed at "the Egyptian Hall" in London, but this came to nothing.

Alice's Adventures in Wonderland (1865)

I have drawn on *Handbook* (1979) and *Annotated Alice* for much of the information concerning the parodies in the *Alice* books below.

[*"All in the golden afternoon"*]

These prefatory verses recall the river expeditions on 17 June and 4 July 1862 when LC began to invent what became *Alice's Adventures in Wonderland* (*Diaries*, iv, 81–2). The three Liddell sisters present were Lorina, aged thirteen (Prima), Alice, ten (Secunda), and Edith, eight (Tertia). Notice the change from present to past tense in stanza 5.

[*"How doth the little crocodile"*]

For the full text of the Isaac Watts poem "Against Idleness and Mischief" from his *Divine Songs for Children* (1715), here parodied, see Introduction.

[*Mouse Tails*]
[*"We lived beneath the mat"*]

This poem appears in the original manuscript for *Alice's Adventures Under Ground* (1886), and refers directly to cats, unlike the mouse's tale below. Both mouse poems are set out as a tail.

[*"Fury said to"*]

The unjust trial presages the courtroom scene at the end of *Wonderland*.

[*" 'You are old, Father William', the young man said"*]

A direct parody of Robert Southey's didactic poem "The Old Man's Comforts and How He Gained Them" (1799), which begins:

> "You are old, father William," the young man cried,
> "The few locks which are left you are grey;
> You are hale, father William, a hearty old man,
>   Now tell me the reason I pray."

"In the days of my youth," father William replied,
"I remembered that youth would fly fast,
And abus'd not my health and my vigour at first,
    That I never might need them at last."

LC has picked up and exaggerated the energy implied in the cantering metre of the original.

[*The Duchess's Lullaby*]

The Duchess's "sort of lullaby" during which she "kept tossing the baby violently up and down" parodies a poem almost certainly by David Bates that became very popular after its (anonymous) appearance in *Sharpe's Magazine* (1848): see Introduction. The unexceptionable advice in Bates's poem becomes oddly menacing by repetition across nine verses: here are stanzas one and three:

Speak Gently! It is better far
    To rule by love than fear;
Speak gently, let no harsh words mar
    The good we might do here!
. . .
Speak gently to the little child!
    Its love be sure to gain;
Teach it in accents soft and mild;
    It may not long remain.

As Alice comments: "'If I don't take this child away with me,' thought Alice 'they're sure to kill it in a day or two.'" See Introduction, p. xxx.

["*Twinkle, twinkle, little bat*"]

The original poem by Jane Taylor, first published in *Rhymes for the Nursery* (1806), is one of the few that survive LC's parody. The first of its five stanzas runs:

Twinkle, twinkle, little star,
How I wonder what you are!
Up above the world so high,
Like a diamond in the sky.

[*The Mock Turtle's Song: I*]

This poem parodies Mary Howitt's "The Spider and the Fly", based on an older song, in *Sketches of Natural History* (1834). Her fly in the first stanza shows the same canny demurring as LC's snail:

> "Will you walk into my parlour?" said the spider to the fly,
> " 'Tis the prettiest little parlour that ever you did spy,
> The way into my parlour is up a winding stair,
> And I've got many curious things to show when you are there."
> "Oh, no, no," said the little fly, "to ask me is in vain,
> For who goes up your winding stair can ne'er come down again."

[*The Mock Turtle's Song in "Alice's Adventures Under Ground"*]

In the manuscript of *Alice's Adventures Under Ground*, the Mock Turtle sings a different song: "Salmon come up!" a parody of a Negro Minstrel song that LC had heard the Liddell sisters sing on 3 July, the day before the river expedition that most immediately sparked *Alice* (*Annotated Alice*, p. 133). The chorus of that song begins:

> Sally come up! Sally go down!
> Sally come twist your heel around!

[" *'Tis the voice of the Lobster: I heard him declare*"]

In the Old Testament Song of Songs "the voice of the turtle" (2:10) means the turtle-dove; LC is here playing on the Mock Turtle's presence, which seems to lie behind Alice's elision of "turtle" to "lobster". The poem parodies another of Isaac Watts's didactic verses, "The Sluggard", from his *Divine Songs for Children*, which begins:

> 'Tis the voice of the sluggard; I heard him complain,
> "You have wak'd me too soon, I must slumber again."

The third stanza runs:

> I pass'd by his garden, and saw the wild brier,
> The thorn and the thistle grow broader and higher;
> The clothes that hang on him are turning to rags;
> And his money still wastes as he starves or he begs.

LC fiddled with this parody a number of times. In 1870 he wrote an alternative stanza for William Boyd's *Songs from Alice in Wonderland*:

> I passed by his garden, and marked, with one eye,
> How the owl and the oyster were sharing a pie,
> While the duck and the Dodo, the lizard and cat
> Were swimming in milk round the brim of a hat.

The 1886 completion "eating the owl" (finishing the couplet in the text) appeared in Savile Clark's operetta on *Alice*, while Stuart Collingwood's biography offers:

> But the panther obtained both the fork and the knife,
> So, when *he* lost his temper, the owl lost his life.

[*The Mock Turtle's Song: II*]

Another song that the Liddell sisters sang is the basis for this parody: James M. Sayles's "Star of the Evening" opens:

> Beautiful star in heav'n so bright,
> Softly falls thy silv'ry light,
> As thou movest from earth afar,
> Star of the evening, beautiful star.
>
> Chorus: Beautiful star,
>   Beautiful star,
> Star of the evening, beautiful star.

LC's printed elongation of the words evokes the swoop of the soupy music.

[*The White Rabbit's Evidence*]

Here LC adapts his own "She's All My Fancy Painted Him", and see also "Disillusionised". William Mee's song "Alice Gray" bemoans an impossible love and opens:

> She's all my fancy painted her,
>   She's lovely, she's divine,
> But her heart it is another's,
>   She never can be mine.

> Yet loved I as man never loved,
>   A love without decay,
> O, my heart, my heart is breaking
>   For the love of Alice Gray.

Phantasmagoria and Other Poems (1869)

[*Part 1*]
Phantasmagoria

The titles of the Cantos jokingly set medieval courtly speech and Gothic "horror" (customary for ghost stories) against the modern down-to-earth bonhomie and banter in the conversations between Ghost and Householder.

title   *I – The Trystyng*: The Meeting.

title   *II – Hys Fyve Rules*: Five Rules of Etiquette for Ghosts.

161. *Tare and Tret*: A weight allowance for packaging or dust, etc.; and an extra allowance.

title   *III – Scarmoges*: Skirmishes.

231. *Kobold*: A German folklore apparition that can manifest as animal, object or human being.

241. *Brocken*: A Brocken spectre is a phenomenon of misty mountains when an enormous shadow seems to appear. The ghost found the mountain air too cold.

285. *Ruskin*: John Ruskin, the art critic who established the fashion for Gothic architecture. He was well known to LC (see Introduction); he appears also in "Hiawatha's Photographing" (see line 74 and note).

title   *IV – Hys Nouryture*: His Upbringing.

328. *Bradshaw's Guide*: A guide to railway timetables and a favourite allusion for LC. See note to "Prologue to 'La Guida di Bragia'".

333–5. *'Three little . . . toastesses'*: "seven little ghostses . . . sitting on postses . . . eating buttered toastses" was a popular Hallowe'en song, which the ghost here claims to have invented.

411–14. *Shakespeare . . . in sheets*: "the sheeted dead/Did squeak and gibber in the Roman streets" (*Hamlet*, i, 1, 115–16).

title *V – Byckerment*: A LC nonce word: bickering, quarrelling.

549–50. *'The man ... pocket!'*: Dr Samuel Johnson is usually cred-
ited with this remark comparing punsters and pickpockets.

title *VI – Dyscomfyture*: Embarrassment, disappointment.

title *VII – Sad Souvenaunce*: Remembrance, nostalgia.

700. *Coronach*: A dirge played on bagpipes.

710. *parallelepiped*: A geometric solid whose six faces are parallelo-
grams, a favourite with LC who jokingly suggested that one of
his little sisters use it as the name for her rabbit, but here useful
as an odd rhyme word.

Reprinted, with some variations, in *Rhyme? And Reason?*

A Valentine

14. *dolorum omnium*: Mors dolorum omnium exsolutio est: Death
is the resolution of all woes (Seneca, *De Consolatione*, XIX, 5).

32. *"Jonson's learned sock be on"*: John Milton, "L'Allegro", line 131.

The original version was copied into *Mischmasch*.

A Sea Dirge

22. *"thoughts ... free"*: From Lord Byron, *The Corsair*, Canto 1,
stanza 1:

> O'er the glad waters of the dark blue sea,
> Our thoughts as boundless, and our souls as free,
> Far as the breeze can bear, the billows foam,
> Survey our empire, and behold our home!

Carroll ruefully changes the triumphalism of Byron into sea-sickness.

27–8. *B sharp ... natural C*: On the piano keyboard the note B sharp
is the same pitch (and ivory key) as C natural. So C becomes sea
and the rest follows in this argument.

First published *College Rhymes*, ii, October 1860, pp. 56–8.

Ye Carpette Knyghte

A clothes horse, a saddle of mutton and a bit of rhyme instead of the
chivalric accoutrements of the knight cavalier, all disguised in mock-
medieval spelling.

First published *Train*, i, March 1856, p. 191.

Hiawatha's Photographing

The metre is identical both in the quietly comic introduction and in the poem itself with that of Henry Wadsworth Longfellow's epic *The Song of Hiawatha* (1855), for example:

> Thus departed Hiawatha
> To the land of the Dacotahs,
> To the land of handsome women;
> Striding over moor and meadow,
> Through interminable forests,
> Through uninterrupted silence.

The trochaic tetrameters lope along easily and are based on the Finnish poem *Kalevala*. Longfellow's poem draws on Native American legends; LC's on English bourgeois life viewed through a sceptical camera's lens. LC was an early adept of photography and he includes in this version of the poem three stanzas (lines 16–33) that precisely describe the laborious processes necessary, while brilliantly conforming to the demands of the metre. In 1856, the year before LC wrote this poem, Mary Cowden Clark (under the pseudonym Harry Wandsworth Shortfellow) published a parody, *The Song of a Drop o' Wather: A London Legend, A Companion to Longfellow's "Hiawatha"*, which LC owned (Lovett, no. 1837, p. 281).

11. *Euclid*: Greek mathematician active around 300 BC and still fundamental to the teaching of geometry at the time LC was writing. LC wrote a defence of Euclid in the form of a comic five-act drama, *Euclid and His Modern Rivals* (1879).

74. *curves of beauty*: In *Modern Painters II*, Ruskin wrote that "all forms of acknowledged beauty are composed exclusively of curves" (*The Works of John Ruskin*, ed. E. T. Cook and Alexander Wedderburn, Library Edition, 39 vols. (London: George Allen, 1903–12), iv, p. 88).

91. *"passive beauty"*: Cf. Wordsworth's poem "Address to my Infant Daughter", his month-old daughter Dora: "to enliven with the mind's regard / Thy passive beauty".

First published *Train*, iv, December 1857, pp. 332–5.

The Lang Coortin'

The poem mimics the locutions and the laconically doom-laden stories of the old Border Ballads, just then fashionable again, as in Walter Scott's *Minstrelsy of the Border* (1832).

7.   *popinjay*: An old word for a parrot; also a dandy.

First published *College Rhymes*, iv, 1863, pp. 32–9.

Melancholetta

The performance they take "his" sister to was Shakespeare, *King John*, followed by the burlesque opera by William Barnes Rhodes, *Bombastes Furioso* (1810). But even the burlesque cannot make her laugh: she still finds tears in *things* (hounds, whales, tiers) in a materialist version of "Lacrimae rerum". LC copied into *Mischmasch* several extra verses, the last of which is:

> The other night I tried a slice
>   Of melon, and I eat a
> Large quantity, it proved so nice –
>   That night in dreams I met her,
> Green as a melon, cold as ice,
>   "Dearest!" she moaned, "art better?
> Thy melon I – will that suffice?
>   Or must I add -choletta?"

Signed B.B., a frequent pseudonym for his comic poems from the time of the family magazines on.

First published *College Rhymes*, iii, 1862, pp. 67–71.

The Three Voices

The three-lined, three-rhymed stanzas follow the metre of Tennyson's "The Two Voices" (1842), originally titled "The Thoughts of a Suicide", written when Tennyson was in despair after the death of his friend, Arthur Hallam. The parody picks up the grand generalisations that in the original have the weight of misery but here become pompous and absurd; for one example, see Introduction, p. xxxi, and for another:

> Heaven opens inward, chasms yawn.
> Vast images in glimmering dawn,
> Half shown, are broken and withdrawn.

The metaphysical extremes of the lady's speech also pick up on the "Spasmodic" poets of the period whom LC also mocked in "Poeta Fit Non Nascitur" (see p. 376 note to line 17). LC copied the poem into *Mischmasch* and then revised it for its first publication in *Train*, ii,

November 1856, pp. 278–84, where it has a very different opening from this *Phantasmagoria* version:

> He trilled a carol fresh and free,
> He laughed aloud for very glee:
> There came a breeze from off the sea:

A Double Acrostic

LC disliked dancing and is here mocking the follies of the Christ Church Commemoration Ball (25 June 1867), which excludes him and leaves him penning acrostic verses. He includes an in-joke: the poem harks back to the very first number of *College Rhymes*, i, 1861, p. 3, where the first poem opens with praise of Oxford:

> There stands an ancient city by the side
> Of a broad river, and her palace-towers
> Rise royally, by wisdom sanctified,
> From out her leafy bowers.

Here, instead of "by wisdom sanctified", "No words of wisdom flow" (60).

The answer to this double acrostic might be (as suggested in *The Collected Verse of Lewis Carroll* (1932)): Commemoration; Monstrosities. But a better solution is that of H. Cuthbert Scott: Quasi-Insanity; Commemoration: see Edward Wakeling and Kazunari Takaya who worked out the cross-lights: Quadratic, Undergo, Alarm, Stream, Ice, Interim, No, Supper, Arena, Night, I, Two, Yawn in *Mischmasch: The Journal of the Lewis Carroll Society of Japan*, ix, 2007, pp. 152–71. See also Fisher, p. 49, for various solutions. Most of LC's double acrostics are found in "Poems for Friends" and "Late Collections".

11–12. There is no value for x in the final equation. Gardner, *Universe* (p. 15) suggests that this may be a whimsical self-portrait by LC since he has no place in the dance.

Size and Tears

Written November 1862. LC was slim.
First published *College Rhymes*, iv, 1863, pp. 113–15, signed R. W. G.

Poeta Fit Non Nascitur

title   *Poeta ... Nascitur*: Poeta fit, non nascitur: a poet is made, not born (Latin).

17. *spasmodic*: A bombastic school of poetry, fashionable in the 1840s and 50s, and mocked by William Edmonstoune Aytoun in his parody, *Firmilian: A Spasmodic Tragedy* (1854): see "The Three Voices" and note. Aytoun was one of the two writers combined in the pen name Bon Gaultier whose ballads influenced LC (see Introduction and note 10).

84. *'Exempli gratiâ'*: For example (Latin).

91. *Boucicault*: Dion Boucicault, Irish actor and playwright famed for his melodramas, especially *The Coleen Bawn* (1859).

First published *College Rhymes*, iii, 1862, pp. 112–16, signed K.

Atalanta in Camden Town

Algernon Swinburne published his verse tragedy "Atalanta in Calydon" in 1865. LC admired Swinburne's work and knew him personally. The first verse of the Chorus may have given LC hints for the metre but there is no absolute resemblance, rather the joke lies in the transposing of rapturous language to more mundane circumstances. "When the foam of the bride-cake is white, and the fierce orange-blossoms are yellow" (25) instead of:

> When the hounds of spring are on winter's traces,
>> The mother of months in meadow or plain
>> Fills the shadows and windy places
>> With lisp of leaves and ripple of rain;
>> And the brown bright nightingale amorous
>> Is half assuaged for Itylus,
>> For the Thracian ships and the foreign faces,
>> The tongueless vigil, and all the pain.

15. *Dundreary*: A foolish aristocratic character given to malapropisms and extreme sideburns in Tom Taylor's play *Our American Cousin* (1858).

First published *Punch*, 27 July 1867, LC's only publication there: see Introduction.

The Elections to The Hebdomadal Council
The Hebdomadal Council

This poem is satirically written in the person of a liberal (Goldwin Smith) objecting to the victory of the conservatives on the Oxford University Hebdomadal Council, by a majority of one, and purports to be a second edition of the letter LC objects to. From LC's note 23 on, the voice is that of the anonymous poet responding to the unrealistic proposals of his opponent. The manner is much closer to Pope's satires, including the use of heroic couplets, than elsewhere in LC's work.

title   *Hebdomadal Council*: The executive council of Oxford University from 1854 until 2003.

   epigraph   *"Now is the Winter of our discontent"*: Shakespeare, *Richard the Third*, i, 1, 1. On Dr Wynter, see LC's note I (p. 166).

24. *Jowett*: Benjamin Jowett was in 1862 charged with heresy by Edward Pusey, though this was not pursued, and in 1865 Jowett was elected to the Regius Chair of Greek at Oxford. His suggestions for university reform promised to open admission to many less wealthy students, emphasising intellectual ability, not gentlemanly manners or forebears. Hence the allusion (165) to Fagin, the cunning master-thief in Dickens's *Oliver Twist* who trains the boys as pickpockets: "brain, and brain alone, shall rule the world". LC was among those who objected to Jowett's salary being raised from a meagre sum and he was here on the side of those who opposed any change in the statutes towards meritocracy.

27. *Who would ... blow!*: From Lord Byron, *Childe Harold's Pilgrimage*, Canto 2, stanza 76: "Hereditary bondsmen! know ye not,/Who would be free, themselves must strike the blow?"

45. *caucus-meeting*: A caucus is a closed meeting of like-minded electors: taken further, a conspiracy. LC was suspicious of this method of consultation: in the caucus race in *Alice in Wonderland*, all the creatures chase round and round without a clear outcome.

First published anonymously as a pamphlet in 1866. For other of LC's satirical poems on Oxford controversies, see "Oxford Poems".

Phantasmagoria: Part 2

The poems in Part 2 are all more earnest in tone and together show LC's quite considerable capacity as a serious writer concerned with issues of life and death and with women's dilemmas, particularly in "The Path of Roses" and "The Sailor's Wife".

The Valley of the Shadow of Death

Written April 1868. Reprinted in *Three Sunsets*.

Beatrice

Written 4 December 1862. The second Beatrice is Dante's beloved (19–21, 34), the first is the young girl martyr of the first century AD whose body had been exhumed in 1822 and passed into the care of nuns in Rome (22–8). The poem is probably addressed to LC's five year-old child-friend Beatrice Ellison.
First published *College Rhymes*, iv, 1863, pp. 46–9, signed C.L.D.

[Acrostic Lines to Lorina, Alice and Edith]

The first letters of each line compose the given names of three of the Liddell sisters. The poem was inscribed in his present to them of Catherine Sinclair's *Holiday House* (1839; 2nd edition, 1856) and was dated Christmas 1861. Sinclair's children are unruly and naughty but not wicked, and are described with wit and affection: a book to LC's taste. This is the only single-acrostic poem in *Phantasmagoria*; see "Poems for Friends" for many more examples.

The Path of Roses

This serious poem was written in tribute to Florence Nightingale under the sorrow of the ravages wrought by the Crimean War, 1853–6. First published *Train*, i, May 1856, pp. 286–8.

79.   *Azrael*: The Archangel of Death occurs in several religious traditions.

The Sailor's Wife

One of several of LC's serious poems from the 1850s and early 60s that express themselves as dream or nightmare (cf. "In Three Days", "Stolen Waters" and "The Path of Roses"). Here the watchdog's bark welcomes home the lost sailor.
First published *Train*, iii, April 1857, pp. 231–3.

Stolen Waters

The poem recalls John Keats's "La Belle Dame Sans Merci", though in this case a child redeems the speaker. It may also have been a response to Christina Rossetti's "Goblin Market" (1862), which LC especially admired.
title   *Stolen Waters*: "Stolen waters are sweet, and bread eaten in secret is pleasant" (Proverbs 9:17 (King James)).
First published *College Rhymes*, iii, 1862, pp. 106–11, signed C.L.D.

Stanzas for Music

The original title in *Mischmasch* was "The Willow Tree". When reprinted in *Three Sunsets*, it is dated 1859. Set to music by William Boyd in 1870 as "The Bridal".

Solitude

Despite the reference to "years hath piled" (37), LC was 21 years old when he wrote this poem. It may have been prompted by memories of his mother's sudden death two years earlier at the age of 47, two days after he began his Oxford degree, and by the impossibility of returning to the intact childhood family. When reprinted in *Three Sunsets*, it is dated 16 March 1853.

First published *Train*, i, March 1856, pp. 154–5, under the name Lewis Carroll, the first time that the pseudonym appears.

Only a Woman's Hair

Jonathan Swift, author of *Gulliver's Travels* (1726): the hair may have been that of Esther Johnson, the Stella to whom he was devoted, and Swift's "Only a woman's hair" was probably ironic or defensive. LC's imagining of different women and their hair concludes with the scene at Bethany (24–34) when the woman who had sinned wiped Christ's feet with her hair in her devotion (Luke 7:36-50). When reprinted in *Three Sunsets*, it has the date 17 February 1862.

First published *College Rhymes*, iii, 1862, pp. 59–60, signed C.L.D.

Three Sunsets

First published as "The Dream of Fame", *College Rhymes*, iii, 1862, pp. 3–7, signed C.L.D. Reprinted as title poem in *Three Sunsets*.

Christmas Greetings

Written at Christmas 1867. In *Phantasmagoria* this poem is printed in minute "diamond"-size type as befits a message from a fairy. It was reissued separately in 1884 in "pearl" (one size larger) and included in editions of *Alice in Wonderland* after that date and in *Alice's Adventures Under Ground* (1886). It was later inscribed in the "Alice" window at All Saint's Church, in Daresbury, LC's birthplace (dedicated 1935).

After Three Days

Holman Hunt's painting *The Finding of the Saviour in the Temple* presented a new naturalism in the treatment of religious subjects and hotly divided opinion in 1861 when it was first exhibited at a private viewing in London. LC wrote to his sister Mary that "it is about the most wonderful picture I ever saw" (*Letters*, i, 42–3). Cf. Luke 2:42–51. He was in sympathy with the Pre-Raphaelite painters and their desire to bring experience close through accurate and homely detail. When reprinted in *Three Sunsets*, it is dated 16 February 1861. First published *Temple Bar*, ii, July 1861, pp. 566–8.

Faces in the Fire

Copied into *Mischmasch* and dated January 1860, just before LC's 28th birthday on 27 January. In the early versions it has a less melancholy opening stanza:

> I watch the drowsy night expire,
> And Fancy paints at my desire
> Her magic pictures in the fire.

An extra verse after stanza five imagines the lost beloved as a mother. First published Dickens's *All the Year Round*, 11 February 1860. Reprinted in *Three Sunsets*.

Puzzles from Wonderland (1870)

First published Christmas 1870 number of *Aunt Judy's Magazine* (*Aunt Judy's Christmas Volume*, 1871), pp. 101–2.

VI

5.   *Full*: Northern pronunciation as "fool".

Through the Looking-Glass, and What Alice Found There (1872)

[*Prologue to "Through the Looking-Glass"*]

33.   *"happy summer days"*: The last words of *Alice in Wonderland*.
36.   *pleasance*: Alice Liddell's second name, meaning delight.

Jabberwocky

The first verse of "Jabberwocky" appeared in *Mischmasch* in 1855, accompanied by various definitions of the words (see "Stanza of Anglo-Saxon Poetry"). In Chapter VI, Humpty Dumpty gives his own, sometimes different, definitions: *brillig* = "four o'clock in the afternoon – the time when you begin *broiling* things for dinner"; *slithy* = "lithe and slimy . . . a portmanteau – there are two meanings packed up into one word"; *toves* = "something like badgers – they're something like lizards – and they're something like corkscrews"; *gyre* = "to go round and round like a gyroscope"; *gimble* = "to make holes like a gimblet"; *the wabe* is " 'the grass-plot round a sun-dial, I suppose?' said Alice, surprised at her own ingenuity"; *mimsy* = "flimsy and miserable"; *mome rath* = " '*rath*' is a sort of green pig but '*mome*' I'm not certain about. I think it's short for 'from home' – meaning they'd lost their way, you know"; *outgrabe* = " '*outgribing*' is something between bellowing and whistling, with a sort of sneeze in the middle". LC introduces a number of these words into *The Hunting of the Snark*: mimsy, borogoves, outgrabe, Jubjub, frumious, Bandersnatch. The syntax in "Jabberwocky" is stable although the semantics are odd; so the story is compelling though its elements are obscure.

The reversed stanza (and title) is found in *Through the Looking-Glass* (1872).

["Tweedledum and Tweedledee"]

This is a nursery rhyme slightly varied by LC. Two other nursery rhymes in *Looking-Glass* also control the fates of their heroes ("Humpty Dumpty's Song", "The Lion and the Unicorn"). In *Wonderland* only the "Queen of Hearts" nursery rhyme functions in this way.

The Walrus and the Carpenter

For the 1887 production of Savile Clarke's operetta based on the *Alice* books, LC wrote an extra verse at the end of the poem as well as songs for two ghostly oysters:

> The Carpenter he ceased to sob;
>   The Walrus ceased to weep;
> They'd finished all the oysters;
>   And they laid them down to sleep –
> And of their craft and cruelty
>   The punishment to reap.

The first oyster sings:

> The Carpenter is sleeping, the butter's on his face,
> The vinegar and pepper are all about the place!
> Let oysters rock your cradle and lull you into rest;
> And if that will not do it, we'll sit upon your chest! [line repeated as chorus]

The second oyster sings:

> O woeful, weeping Walrus, your tears are all a sham!
> You're greedier for Oysters than children are for jam.
> You like to have an Oyster to give the meal a zest –
> Excuse me, wicked Walrus, for stamping on your chest! [line repeated as chorus]

See Introduction.

[*Humpty Dumpty's Song*]

Humpty Dumpty flouts the usual rules of sentence structure by repeatedly ending with a conjunction: see Introduction. Fishes and shell-fish haunt the *Alice* poems as well as LC's earlier verse.

[*The White Knight's Song*]

For an earlier and shorter version of this poem, see "Upon the Lonely Moor". Its subject matter parodies Wordsworth's poem "Resolution and Independence": see Introduction. The metre of LC's poem derives from Thomas Moore's "My heart and lute", which begins: "I give thee all – I can give no more", and Alice recognises it. That allusion would have signalled a more poignant undersong to the first readers.

30. *Rowland's Macassar-Oil*: A gentleman's hair product, hence the "anti-macassar" covers placed over chair backs in the period and later.

59. *Menai bridge*: Between Anglesey and the mainland, it was a prodigious feat of early-nineteenth-century engineering, which opened in 1826; it needed frequent repair. During its construction the iron was soaked in warm linseed oil (rather than wine).

[*The Red Queen's Lullaby*]

1. *Hush-a-by lady*: "Hushaby baby, on the tree top": for once a less alarming version than the original, "Down will come baby and cradle and all".

["To the Looking-Glass world it was
Alice that said"]

A parody of Walter Scott's "Bonny Dundee", whose first verse and chorus run:

> To the Lords of Convention 'twas Claver'se who spoke,
> 'Ere the King's crown shall fall there are crowns to be broke;
> So let each Cavalier who loves honour and me,
> Come follow the bonnet of Bonny Dundee.
>
> Come fill up my cup, come fill up my can,
> Come saddle your horses, and call up your men:
> Come open the West Port, and let me gang free,
> And it's room for the bonnets of Bonny Dundee.

[The White Queen's Riddle]

The answer is "an oyster", which sits in its own dish and seals its cover up tight.

Wasp in a Wig

This song appears in the "Wasp in a Wig" episode that LC dropped from the final version because Tenniel objected to it both as a weak link and because he could not think how to illustrate it.

First published 'Wasp in a Wig': a 'suppressed' episode of 'Through the Looking-Glass, and what Alice found there', with a preface, introduction and notes by Martin Gardner (London: Macmillan, 1977).

["A boat beneath a sunny sky"]

This poem is placed at the end of Looking-Glass: the first letters of each line spell Alice Pleasance Liddell. "Life what is it but a dream" recalls the last line of the well-known round, perhaps another of the songs the young Liddell sisters sang:

> Row, row, row your boat
> Gently down the stream
> Merrily, merrily, merrily, merrily,
> Life is but a dream.

Oxford Poems, with some Memoria Technica

Examination Statute

LC wrote this just before a vote on a proposal to adopt a new statute which, he felt, would damage mathematics and classics by lowering the requirements. The statute was passed on 25 February 1865. A facsimile of the 1864 Oxford print, showing all the names, is in the *Parrish Catalogue*, p. 102, in Princeton University; see also *Handbook*, p. 24. First published as a pamphlet, Oxford, 1866.

The Deserted Parks

The poem was part of a campaign to keep the university parks from being used as college cricket grounds and so excluding the citizens of Oxford from their enjoyment. The poem, very aptly, takes Goldsmith's "The Deserted Village" (1770) as its model, a poem that mourns the enclosing of common ground for a rich man's garden. The campaign was successful.

epigraph   *"Solitudinem ... appellant"*: The emended Latin motto is from Tacitus, *Agricola*, 30: Atque ubi solitudinem faciunt, *pacem appellant*: And where they make a desolation they call it peace (*Parcum* = park, LC's jokey correlation of *pacem* = peace).
First published anonymously in 100 copies, 1867.

The New Belfry of Christ Church, Oxford

The anonymously published pamphlet (1872), which included the satirical poems included here as well as a "Hamlet" skit, was prompted by Dean Liddell's rebuilding programme at Christ Church for which the well-known architect George Gilbert Scott was employed. It had been discovered that the tower at the cathedral was unstable and there was a risk that the bells might fall, so they were removed and a new belfry built for them. LC was under the impression that the wooden structure ("tea-chest") employed during the building of the belfry was to be the finished product. What he called "the blot" (26) still exists unseen within the finished Wolsey Tower completed 1878.

Song and Chorus

See note to "The New Belfry of Christ Church, Oxford" and Introduction. For commentary, see *Pamphlets*, i, pp. 67–79.

From *The Vision of the Three T's: A Threnody by the Author of "The New Belfry"* (1873)

The "Three T's" are "Tunnel, Trench, and Tea-Chest". (Cf. "A Bacchanalian Ode", line 28). On "Tea-Chest", see note to "The New Belfry of Christ Church, Oxford". Published anonymously by James Parker and Co., Oxford, 1873.

The Wandering Burgess

Another satirical go at the Belfry, cast in LC's favourite mode of a Border Ballad. Willie is William Gladstone, sometime British prime minister, a frequent butt in LC's satirical verses, and here mocked for his trailing around the country seeking a parliamentary seat; but even Gladstone is shocked by the "Tea-chest" in the Quad.

A Bachanalian Ode

This second poem from *The Three T's* concerns a performance of Bach's St Matthew Passion to be given in Christ Church Cathedral. LC objected on two grounds: that a charge was to be made whereas he believed that the cathedral as a place of worship must be open to all, and because, though the music was religious, he did not approve of the cathedral being a place of entertainment.

[*The Wine Committee*]

First published (with the following two poems) *Twelve Months in a Curatorship By One Who has Tried It* (1884).

[*"I love my love with a T"*]

This poem, the following one and the prose pamphlet in which they appear express the irritations LC felt in his role as Curator of the Common Room during his first year in office (1884), in particular the problems of dealing with other committee members. For first publication, see note to "[The Wine Committee]" above.

[*"He took a second-story flat"*]

LC took an apartment at 6 Brewer Street to supplement his rooms in college, probably in 1890. In a letter to his niece Edith, 28 February 1890, he tells her that "one is so cramped in one's tiny College rooms; but, by having a house in Brewer Street *as well*, one really has enough room to swing a cat" (*Letters*, ii, 1071).

Memoria Technica

According to his nephew Stuart Dodgson Collingwood, LC had a "wonderfully good memory except for faces and dates" (Collingwood, pp. 268–9). Partly in order to compensate for this, in 1877 he devised a system for recalling dates, but also for "logarithms of all primes under 100", "pi to 71 decimal places", the specific gravity of metals, foundation of colleges and other facts. His system built on that of Dr Richard Grey (1730). Being a skilled and addicted rhymester, LC produced rhymed couplets to represent the equivalent in letters of the numbers to be recollected. See Introduction and *Letters*, i, 790. *Handbook*, p. 97 has the clearest explanation of the scheme: "dates are fixed in the memory by the last letters of the fact to be dated being altered into letters representing numbers. Dodgson represents 1–9,0 by two alternative consonants each, and fills in with vowels to make a word. Thus the Discovery of America was in 1492. The 1 may be disregarded; 4,9,2 can be represented by *f,n,d* (or *q,g,w*): so you compose a rhyme, 'Columbus sailed the world around / Until America was FOUND.'"

The "Memoria Technica" (pp. 232–3) are dated 16 October 1894: see *Diaries*, ix, 177–8 note 298. Other examples remind LC of the date of the foundation of colleges, for example:

> You may ring Big Tom if you please.
> We only charge very small fees.   [1546, l,f,s]

Christ Church.

> They must have a bevel
> To keep them so level.   [1555, l,v,l]

Based on the level lawns of St John's College.

The Hunting of the Snark (1876)

In the Preface Carroll remarks that "this poem is to some extent connected with the lay of the Jabberwock", and he includes the nonce words "beamish" (Fit 3), "uffish" and "galumphing" (Fit 4), "Jubjub" (Fits 4 and 5), "outgrabe" (Fit 5), "Bandersnatch", "frumious" and "mimsiest" (Fit 7) from it.

[*"Girt with a boyish garb for boyish task"*]

This dedicatory poem is addressed to Gertrude Chataway, then aged nine. On 24 October 1875, LC had the idea of suggesting a Christmas publication for the *Snark* though in the event the poem was not published until April 1876. That same day he thought of "writing an acrostic on Gertrude Chataway ... and did the same night" (*Diaries*, vi, 421, 427). The initial letters of each line spell her name and, with a further ingenious twist, the syllables of her name form the opening of each stanza: Girt, Rude, Chat, Away.

Fit the First

13. *A Billiard-marker*: "All billiard-players know the really good marker, who, so to speak, 'fields' for us round the table, who invariably puts the balls ready in the bottom pockets when put in previously at pool, who is always at hand with a lighted spill directly we have filled our pipes or opened our cigar-case, whose friendly hand assists us at leaving in that awful struggle with our great coat" (*Billiard News*, 25 December 1875).

Fit the Second

25. *the bowsprit got mixed with the rudder*: In his Preface, LC provides this useful explanation:

> The Bellman, who was almost morbidly sensitive about appearances, used to have the bowsprit unshipped once or twice a week to be revarnished, and it more than once happened, when the time came for replacing it, that no one on board could remember which end of the ship it belonged to. They knew it was not of the slightest use to appeal to the Bellman about it – he would only refer to his Naval Code, and read out in pathetic tones Admiralty Instructions which none of them had ever been able to understand – so it generally ended in its being fastened on, anyhow, across the rudder. The helmsman used to stand by with tears in his eyes; he knew it was all wrong, but alas! Rule 42 of the Code, "No one shall speak to the Man at the Helm," had been completed by the Bellman himself with the words "and the Man at the Helm shall speak to no one." So remonstrance was impossible, and no steering could be done till the next varnishing day. During these bewildering intervals the ship usually sailed backwards.

73. *bathing-machines*: Cabins for changing into swimwear.

Fit the Fourth

37. *England expects*: "England expects every man to do his duty":
     Admiral Nelson's message to the fleet just before he was killed.

Fit the Fifth

61–8. *Taking Three as the subject to reason about . . . perfectly true*:
      The calculation remains true for any number.

> When the Butcher . . . tries to convince the Beaver that 2 plus 1 is 3,
> he adopts a procedure that starts with 3 and ends with 3. It is not
> apparent, unless you write an algebraic expression for the operations,
> that the process must end with the same number you start with. The
> algebraic expression is:
>
> $$\frac{(x+7+10)(1,000-8)}{992} - 17$$
>
> (This expression simplifies to x) . . .

> (Gardner, *Universe*, p. 10)

Fit the Sixth

9. *a shadowy Court*: A law court scene as chaotic as the scene at the
    end of *Wonderland* but more preoccupied with the niceties
    of legal language: e.g. "never indebted" (32) or "nil debet" and
    "transportation" (57): the common penalty of sending criminals
    to colonies far off had already ceased when LC was writing.

Poems for Friends, including acrostics, riddles,
"charades" and a cipher-poem

Particularly in his later years many of LC's verses were addressed to
people he knew and liked. In this section are gathered two prologues
he wrote for amateur performances by his friends of plays by other
people, a poem emerging from a friend's dream experience, birthday
verses and a good many acrostics, double-acrostics, "charades" and
riddles. Some of these were written on the flyleaves of books he was
giving as a present, while many of them appear in letters to young
friends.

[*Two Prologues*]

LC's *Diaries* are full of visits to the theatre, indeed it has been calculated that over the span of forty years he visited the theatre 479 times, seeing 686 plays. (See note on "Prologue to 'La Guida di Bragia'".) His reluctance to take full orders as a cleric has been linked with his desire to continue theatre-going, an entertainment disapproved by the Bishop of Oxford. LC was a great admirer of the distinguished actress Ellen Terry and her actress sisters Kate and Marion, and became good friends with the whole family. See also "The Lyceum", "To M. A. B.", "['Breathes there the man with soul so dead']" and "Four Riddles: II".

[*Prologue to "The Loan of a Lover"*]

The Loan of a Lover was a musical comedy by James Robinson Planché, associated with the acting of Madame Vestris. This prologue was specially written by LC for an amateur performance by the Hatch family in November 1871.

47. *"Whitebait at Greenwich"*: A farce by J. Morton. Victorian theatres habitually included several theatrical items in one evening's entertainment.

[*Prologue to "Checkmate"*]

Checkmate was a comedy by Andrew Halliday. The prologue was specially written by LC for a performance by the Hatch family, February 1873.

[*Some poems to Colleagues and Friends*]

[*A Request*]

Composed 5 March 1872. Augustus Harcourt (2) was a friend and colleague of LC at Christ Church. He was the Lee's Reader in Chemistry and a Fellow of the Royal Society, which may help to explain his requested assistance in illuminating LC's darkroom. See *Letters*, i, 475.

[*Winter Birthday*]

A birthday poem for LC's friend Robert Holford Macdowall Bosanquet, who was a mathematician and physicist, Fellow of St John's College, Oxford and an accomplished musician. The syncopated lines suggest a sneeze or a shiver (Grace Lawless Lee, *The Story of the Bosanquets* (Canterbury: Phillimore, 1966), p. 84).

Dreamland

LC's friend Charles Hutchinson had a dream during which he saw heroes of old passing by, each of whom turned to look at him. The dream was accompanied by a melody for a four-line stanza that Hutchinson still heard on waking. LC wrote the poem to fit the music and the vision that Hutchinson had experienced.

First published Oxford University Press in 1882 and *Aunt Judy's Magazine*, i (n.s.), July 1882, p. 547.

To "Hallie"

Clara Halyburton Cunnynghame and her family lived in Ripon where LC's family lived for some time. He accompanied the poem when Haly, or Hally or Hallie, was 16 with the message: "Dedicated with profound respect, to Miss Clara Hallyburton [*sic*] Cunnynghame from her humble Servant . . . The Author, In remembrance of January 1868" (see *Letters*, i, 110). Her younger sister Maggie (Margaret) was also a recipient of Carroll's verses.

["*My dear Christie*"]

The correspondent has been identified by Edward Wakeling: "Christie is almost certainly Sophia Christiana 'Christie' Taylor (b. 1859), daughter of Henry Sharp Taylor (1817–1896), doctor at Guildford, and his wife, Sophia Russel (b. 1820)" (private communication).

6.   "*pour rire*": Entertainment (French). Morton Cohen suggests a date of October 1869 because of a postscript reference to Ina Watson (see *Letters*, i, 141).

[*Letter to Maggie Cunnynghame*]

LC wrote out this letter on 30 January 1868 as prose, but the rhyming words are ingeniously concealed in the sentences throughout and were there as a riddle for Maggie to solve. Hatch (pp. 41–5) has set it out as a poem as given here. For Maggie, see note to "To 'Hallie'".

To Three Puzzled Little Girls, From the Author
[*To the three Misses Drury 1*]

On 2 August 1869 LC met the Drury family on a train, an encounter that began an enduring friendship. This poem was inscribed in a copy of *Alice's Adventures in Wonderland* that he sent them the next day. The daughters were Minnie, Ella and Emmie (Mary, Isabella, Emily).

After Dodgson's death, Minnie and her daughter Audrey Fuller were largely responsible for establishing by subscription the *Alice in Wonderland Cot* at Great Ormond Street Hospital (*Letters*, i, 136 note 2).

[*To the three Misses Drury 2*]

LC wrote this on the flyleaf of *Phantasmagoria* for the three sisters, after they had together visited German Reed's theatrical entertainment where the triple bill was *Happy Arcadia, All Abroad* and *Very Catching* (Collingwood, p. 419).

[*To the three Misses Drury 3*]

Written 11 January 1872, in a copy of *Looking-Glass* inscribed to the three sisters.

[" '*No mind!' the little maiden cried*"]

Sent on 17 December 1870, with a teasing letter to Janet Merriman, daughter of Henry G. Merriman, headmaster of the Royal Grammar School at Guildford, after LC had taken a photograph of her (Letters, i, 158–9).

To Miss Mary Watson

The three Watson girls, Ina, Hartie and Mary (Georgina, Harriet, Mary) inspired many of LC's most playful and inventive photographs, puzzles and poems from 1869. He concocted a portmanteau name for them, Harmarina, and visited the family frequently over twenty years.

[*Two Poems to Rachel Daniel*]

I [*"Oh pudgy podgy pup"*]
II [*"What hand may wreathe thy natal crown"*]

LC first offered the playful "Oh pudgy podgy pup" when invited in November 1880 (*Letters*, i, 392–3) to contribute to a set of seventeen poems for the arrival of Rachel, first daughter of Charles Daniel, founder of the Daniel Press. He remarked parenthetically in that letter, "I hate babies, but that is irrelevant." He was later persuaded to compose the more florid rhyme ["What hand may wreathe thy natal crown"], which was published in *The Garland of Rachel*, printed at the private press of H. Daniel, Oxford (1881), and accompanied by a Latin metrical version of his composition by Sir Richard Harington.

The Lyceum

LC presented the poem to Agnes Georgina Hull, written 25 March 1881, in a mock-tattered form with some rhyme words missing: "Ellen Terry" (l. 12) and all the repeats of "the Lyceum" (ll. 8, 16, 24; l. 8 could also be "per diem"). Agnes was by this time fourteen years old and strains were emerging in their relationship. See also note to "['Around my lonely hearth to-night']".

LC starts the letter with a joke revision of Tennyson's lines that run

> It is the miller's daughter,
> And she is grown so dear, so dear

He claims to have found an original manuscript of Tennyson's poem that has a different title:

"The first title was 'How an Elderly Person took a Young Person to the Play, but could not get her away again.' And he had begun it in quite a different metre:

> Two went one day
> To visit the play:
> One came away:
> The other would stay.

And then he seems to have changed his mind, and written it as I have given it to you.'

"Dear" ceases to mean "affection and comes to mean "expense" in LC's somewhat irascible version of the poem.

9.   "*The Cup*": A favourite vehicle for Ellen Terry's acting partner and manager Henry Irving.

17.   *Two Brothers*: "The [Two] Corsican Brothers" was one of the many stage adaptations of Alexandre Dumas's novella (1844).

[*"Something fails"*]

Written to Edith Blakemore, 1 February 1881. She has sent LC scales for his birthday which still haven't arrived; are they "medicine-scales", "scales to practice on the pianoforte" or "a *fish*" See Hatch, p. 159.

[*Letter to Violet Dodgson*]

Another rhymed letter, 6 May 1889, sent to LC's niece Violet Dodgson as prose for her to puzzle out. See Hatch, pp. 204–6, where it is set out as a poem as here.

[*Acrostics, riddles and a cipher-poem*]

Most of LC's acrostics, double-acrostics and riddles are gathered in this section but see also: "Little maidens, when you look"; the ingenious dedication to *The Hunting of the Snark*; and "Is all our life, then, but a dream" and "Dreams, that elude the Maker's frenzied grasp".

[*Cipher-poem and translation*]

These were enclosed in a letter to Edith Argles, 29 April 1868, for the amusement of Edith and her sister Dolly. Lily and Fox were two dogs. The verse is in the Telegraph Cipher invented by Dodgson (see Hatch, pp. 53–6). No other such extended cipher poem by LC is extant.

A Riddle

Riddle addressed to Harriet, Mary and Georgina Watson (see note to "To Miss Mary Watson"), ?Summer 1870 (see *Letters*, i, 157). The clues seem to be all English plant names: e.g. maidenhair fern, goat's beard, mouse ear plant, foxtail, dandelion, ox-eye daisy.

[*Puzzle*]

The missing letters spell out: 1 Mary, Ina, Hartie; 2 creature, wings; 3 Hartie, fairy, Ina, Mary; 5 Mary, Ina; 7 Hartie, party; 8 arithmetic.

[*Acrostic for Ruth Dymes*]

Inscribed in Charlotte Yonge's *Little Lucy's Wonderful Globe* (1871), sent as a present to Ruth Dymes (see next note).

To Miss Margaret Dymes

LC met the large Dymes family in 1877 and the friendship continued into the 1880s.

[*"No, no! I cannot write a line"*]

Sent to Margaret Cunnynghame, 10 April 1871 (see *Letters*, i, 163). See note to "To 'Hallie'".

[*" 'Are you deaf, Father William?' the young man said"*]

This acrostic for Adelaide Paine was written on the flyleaf of *The Hunting of the Snark*, sent as a present to her in 1876 (see *Letters*, i, 251–2).

To the Misses Drury

Acrostic poem to Minnie, Ella and Emmie Drury (see note to "[To the three Misses Drury 1]"), laid into a copy of the *Snark* given to them by LC on 6 April 1876 (*Letters*, i, 249). Minnie asked if the verses had a "hidden meaning", but Carroll replied that they were only "acrostical".

[*"Alice dear, will you join me in hunting the Snark"*]

Acrostic addressed to Alice Crompton, 7 April 1876 (*Letters*, i, 247). She was ten years old. It seems that she and LC never actually met but had a friendship by correspondence. She later became a leader in the movement for women's suffrage and education.

[*"Alice dreamed one night that she"*]

On the same day that LC sent Alice Crompton the acrostic (see note above), he composed another, for another "unseen" Alice, Alice Pratt (see *Letters*, i, 248).

[*"From the air do they come"*]

In a presentation copy to Florence Louise (known as "Boofy") Beaton who LC met at Sandown in August 1876 (*Diaries*, vi, 482) (Widener Library, Harvard University).

[*"Love-lighted eyes, that will not start"*]

Acrostic for Laura Isabel Plomer, who was fourteen at the time of their friendship in the mid-70s.

Madrigal

Sent to May Forshall, Christmas 1877; she meanwhile had sent him a mat (Hatch, p. 121).

[*Anagrammatic Sonnet*]

In a letter to Maud Standen, 18 December 1877 (*Letters*, i, 293-4), LC explains the composition of the "sonnet": "Each line has 4 feet, and each foot is an anagram, i.e. the letters of it can be rearranged so as to make one word. Thus there are 24 anagrams, which will occupy your leisure moments for some time, I hope."

Handbook (p. 210) suggests:

> Oats. Wreath. Myrtle. Tidier.
> Weight. Antics. Twine. Editor.
> Syringe. Gnawer. Plaster. Wonted.

Whose. Wither. Yeast. Snoweth.
Weasel. Merino. Yonder. Hewest.
Myriad. Forego. Tougher. Yawneth.

Other versions are possible. For example, Edward Wakeling offers
Myrtle or Termly, Editor or Rioted, Wither or Whiter, Snoweth or
New Shot: for further suggestions, see his *Rediscovered Lewis Carroll
Puzzles*, p. 69.

[*"They both make a roaring – a roaring all night"*]

Sent in a letter to Agnes Hull, 10 December 1877, in which LC is jok-
ing about forgetting names. The youngest sister Jessie always adds
herself: "and Jessie", so he disguises the last rhyme. Answer: Sea-son
(Hatch, pp. 133–4). See also note to "The Lyceum".

Love Among the Roses

Acrostic for Sarah Sinclair, 'the infant Cerito', the young actress
daughter of the actor Joseph Scrivener who used the stage-name Henry
Sinclair. LC saw her performing as Cupid in the Adelphi Pantomime
on New Year's Eve 1877 and wrote the poem three days later (see
Diaries, vii, 75 and 91). He later helped to raise money for the three
young children after their father died.

[*"Around my lonely hearth to-night"*]

Acrostic for Agnes Georgina Hull. Carroll made the family's acquaint-
ance in 1877 and a warm friendship prospered, which broke down
in September 1882 (see *Diaries*, vii, 471–4). See also note to 'The
Lyceum'.

[*Poem for Dolly Draper*]

Acrostic poem addressed to Dorothy (Dolly) Draper, 20 May 1876,
sent with an inscribed copy of *Looking-Glass,* and revealing LC's
birthday, 27 January (see *Diaries*, vi, 462).

To M. A. B.

The second part ("Maiden, though thy heart may quail") is an acros-
tic for Marion Terry, 15 August 1876. She was the sister of Ellen and
Kate Terry and became a very successful actress in her own right.
Queen Mab is traditionally the Queen of the fairies.

To Miss Gaynor Simpson

LC sent this riddle to Gaynor Simpson, ?February 1880, with two separate joke solutions: the first produced her name. "'My first': *Gain*. 'Who would go into trade if there were no gain in it?'; 'My second' *Or* (the French for 'gold'): 'Your jollifications would be very limited if you had no money;' 'My whole': *Gaynor*. 'Because she will be an ornament to the Shakespeare charades – only she must be "laid on thinnish," that is, *there mustn't be too much of her.*'"

Then he apologised for sending "a sham answer" and proposed: "My first – *Sea*: 'It carries the ships of the merchants.'; my second: *Weed*: 'That is, a cigar, an article much used in jollification.'" He then offers an absurd "whole": "*Seaweed*, because if you laid that on a newly painted picture that would 'finish' it" (*Letters*, i, 367). He had earlier offered the riddle to Mrs George Macdonald without a solution, with the first line as: "My first lends its aid when I plunge into trade" (*Letters*, i, 221). Collingwood (pp. 377-9) says the correct solution is "Copal".

LC rarely gave solutions and seems often to have had several possible ones in mind for his riddles and for the double-acrostics. Edward Wakeling remarks: "He would always accept an alternative reasonable answer" (private correspondence).

For Alexandra Kitchin

Alexandra Kitchin was known as Xie (LC sometimes called her "dear multiplication sign"). The clues are: Ale ("resembling wine"); x ("follows nine"); and ("sentences combine"); ra (Royal Academy): "the line", at eye-level – the most advantageous position for a picture to be exhibited. LC took a great many photographs of Xie over several years and was close friends with her whole family. See *Lewis Carroll and the Kitchins*, ed. Morton N. Cohen (New York: Lewis Carroll Society of North America, 1980).

A Charade

The product of an awkward incident on 5 February 1880 when LC gave a goodbye kiss to a young woman Harriet (Atty) Owen, who with her little brother had been visiting his rooms while her father was busy elsewhere in college. "She does not look 14 yet, and when, having kissed her at parting, I learned (from Owen) that she is 17, I was astonished" (letter to Mrs Kitchin, *Diaries*, vii, 240). Atty Owen's mother was deeply offended, perhaps particularly by LC's light-hearted letter of apology, and all contact was for a time broken off. The reversal between manners then and now is striking: now kissing a child might well be looked at askance, then a young lady. This casts an interesting light on his society's views of the propriety of LC's conduct. The riddle is: AT/rocity; atroci/TY; t/OW/n; EN/ding.

Dedicated to a tea-tea. Why? Oh, when?

The title gives her name: A-t-t-y O-wen. Written 16 March 1880. Perhaps an attempt at mollifying (see preceding poem and note) by emphasising Atty's youth "her small head" (11).

To my Pupil

Acrostic dedication in a copy of LC's *A Tangled Tale* (1885) given to Edith Rix (born 1866): the second letter of each line spells her name. They met because she answered one of the mathematical "knots" in *Tangled Tale* when it originally appeared in Charlotte M. Yonge's magazine *Monthly Packet*, April 1880 (*Handbook*, pp. 108, 136–8 and *Diaries*, viii, 204).

To My Child-Friend

Written 1886. Acrostic dedication to Climène Mary Holiday, niece of Henry Holiday, illustrator of *The Hunting of the Snark*. The second letter of each line spells her name.

To Miss Emmie Drury

This combines her name with LC's volume *Rhyme? Or Reason?* See note to "[To the three Misses Drury 1]".

A Nursery Darling

Dedicatory acrostic to Marie Van der Gucht, an eleven-year-old LC met through the Holiday family in 1885 and entertained frequently. The second letter of each line spells her name.

["Girlie to whom in perennial bloom"]

Written 1891, acrostic for Gladys Baly. *Diaries*, viii, 586 quotes from her reminiscences of LC published in the *Christian Science Monitor* (23 February 1932), which is the source of this acrostic.

[Double Acrostics]
(To Miss E. M. Argles)

LC became friends with the Argles family and spent a week with them at Torquay adjacent to Babbacombe. The first two stanzas praise

Babbacombe; each succeeding stanza gives a clue with an answer that generates the first and last letters needed to form the words running downwards: Babbacombe Friendship. The answers are 9 BlufF, 12 AnchoR, 15 BroccolI, 18 BarquE, 21 AppreciatioN, 24 ChilD, 27 OdiouS, 30 MontH, 33 BelzonI, 36 EditorshiP.

33. *BelzonI*: Giovanni Battista Belzoni, Venetian explorer and engineer. His drawings of the royal tombs at Thebes were published by his widow in 1829.

[*Double Acrostic for Agnes and Emily*]

In a letter sent to Amy Hughes, 4 April 1871, LC declares he wrote a previous riddle specifically for her, then:

> I set to work on getting your letter to make a double acrostic for Agnes and Emily. Here it is. The first verse describes the two "upright" words (each has five letters) & the others describe the horizontal words – The words underlined are to help you in guessing.

LC's underlining is printed as italic in this edition.

The answers are 1–4 [Agnes and Emily], 8 AlicE, 12 GlooM, 16 NinjI, 20 EaseL, 24 SherrY.

16. *Russian fair*: The only allusion in his poems to LC's one expedition outside the British Isles, all the way across Europe to Russia, leaving in July 1867.

20. *sit*: The children are to "sit" for their father, the Pre-Raphaelite painter and illustrator, Arthur Hughes. LC purchased his *The Lady with the Lilacs*.

[*"Two little girls near London dwell"*]

For Trina and Freda Bremer, written while on a visit to their mother Elizabeth Bremer, October 1870. The answers are 4 TurF, 6 RiveR, 8 IcE, 10 NoD, 12 AfricA.

[*"Thanks, thanks, fair Cousins, for your gift"*]

Written for Mabel and Emily Kerr, 20 May 1871, nieces of Mrs Edwin Hatch, who were living in Canada and had sent LC a "carte" (*carte-de-visite*-sized photograph) of themselves. This ingenious double-acrostic includes a joke substitution in each of the rhymes ("league" for mile, "Noah" for Adam, "cauliflower" for broccoli, "acre" for ell, "parrot" for Lory (see *Wonderland*, chapter 3)). The correct rhyme words run downwards to form their names, Mabel and Emily.

[*"I saw a child; even if blind"*]

Sent to Edith Argles; Dolly was her little sister. See also note to "(To Miss E. M. Argles.)" The answers are 1 CrueL, 3 DollY, 5 ColD, 7 RomeO, 9 UnfiliaL, 11 EviL, 13 LoudlY.

A Day in the Country

Woolf (pp. 59–61) prints this poem and her suggested solutions are given here. She describes its double-acrostic structure: each verse is a riddle "and the puzzler must figure out the two 'column-words' which relate to the entire poem and whose letters in order begin and end each riddle's solution" (p. 59). The puzzle has never been completely solved and some of Woolf's suggestions are doubtful. The more certain answers are 4 PortmanteaU, 8 PhotographY, 12 PumP, 16 OstricH, 20 RomeO, 32 AssemblinG (?), 40 TeA, 44 EggcuP, 52 UglY. My own added suggestions would be: 24 T—T: Tait; 28 M—O Malvolio; 36 N—R Napier? (48 A—H). Edward Wakeling has passed on the information, from Alan Tannenbaum (private communication) that the acrostic was addressed to Professor Henry Wall, a logician, so that several of the clues may be the names of logicians. Wakeling's further suggestions are: Talent, Memento, Awning, Nestler or Number, Arch.

37. *evening's*: Reads "evening" in MS.

Maggie's Visit to Oxford

Maggie Bowman was the younger sister of Isa, one of LC's favourite friends. She and her three sisters all became successful actresses. All the episodes in the poem are also recorded in his diary. Maggie was touring in *Bootles' Baby*, a comedy by Hugh Moss (1888); it was made into a film in 1914.

A Lesson in Latin

This poem was written in May 1888 for the fourth class of the Latin School for Girls in Boston, Massachusetts. LC had given them permission to name their school magazine *Jabberwock*. The poem plays the Latin infinitive "to love" or the imperative "be loved" – amare – against the adverb – amare – "bitterly".

[*"My First has no beard – but its whiskers abound"*]

Solution: A Kit/chin = A. Kitchin, (*Letters*, i, 384). See note to "For Alexandra Kitchin".

To Miss Véra Beringer

Sent while Véra Beringer was on holiday on the Isle of Man (probably July 1888), this limerick is a rare example of the form for LC (see "Melodies" and note). She was an actress who in 1888 at the age of nine performed Lord Fauntleroy "with wonderful naturalness and spirit" (*Diaries*, viii, 400).

Riddle Poem

Sent to Olive, Ruth and Violet Butler, 29 December 1892. Read down from O in the first line for the name "Olive". The "berry" is Olive, "sorrow" is Ruth, the "Third" is Violet (obscurely). Is Butler a reference to butlers' tipsy reputation?

[*Some Poems to accompany Photographs*]
The Castle Builder

Poem written to accompany the 9 July 1875 photograph of Edith Morley, daughter of Henry Morley, professor of English literature at University College London, and his wife, Mary. Edith was photographed in beachwear with a spade (*Diaries*, vi, 404).

[*"No sooner does the sun appear"*]

Poems to accompany two photographs in Henry Holiday's album of Daisy Whiteside and of Daisy and her mother, taken 10 July 1875 (*Diaries*, vi, 404–5, 407).

Going a-shrimping

Poem to accompany photograph in Henry Holiday's album of Honor, Evelyn and Olive Brooke, children of Stopford Brooke, then a widower, 13 July 1875. Honor later recounted how she and Winifred Holiday "climbed a tree and discussed how I would like to be taken with naked toes": see *Diaries*, vi, 406 note 666. See also note to "To My Child-Friend".

[*"Breathes there the man with soul so dead"*]

Sent in a letter to Arthur Lewis, 21 April 1880 (*Diaries*, vii, 261 note 472). Lewis was married to Kate Terry and they had four daughters. LC wrote: "This is the sort of think [*sic*] Scott would have written if he had lived in our day." Cf. Scott's *Lay of the Last Minstrel* (1805):

Breathes there a man, with soul so dead,
Who never to himself has said,
This is my own, my native land!

Ode addressed to a Young Lady

Sent in a letter to Albina (Lily) Falle, 23 May 1884 (*Diaries*, viii, 111–12).

Who Killed Cock Robin?

LC sent this poem in his own handwriting to Mrs E. L. Shute on 18 February 1887, and she believed it to be by him. But it is unusual in taking a strong political position outside his Oxford concerns and does not employ LC's more usual tactics in his parodies, though the rewriting of a nursery rhyme is like him. R. B. Shaberman in *Under the Quizzing-Glass* suggests that LC may have hoped, unsuccessfully, to publish it in *Punch* for which its content would have been suitable.

The First Boer war took place in 1880–81. "Willy" is the Prime Minister William Gladstone. The hasty political settlement in March 1881 was deplored by many commentators.

A possible source of personal interest for LC was that his child-friend Hallie (Clara Halyburton Cunnynghame) (see "To 'Hallie'") later married Robert Oxley who was Commander of the Gordon Highlanders at Kabul in 1879.

Sylvie and Bruno (1889) and Sylvie and Bruno Concluded (1893)

Sylvie and Bruno

This long and complex work was seeded as early as 1867 by the short story "Bruno's Revenge", which includes the fairy song beginning "Rise, Oh rise! The daylight dies". Chapter references for the poems are given below because of the length of the work. In the Preface LC declares that he wrote it "in the hope of supplying, for the children whom I love, some thoughts that may suit those hours of innocent merriment which are the very life of childhood: and also, in the hope of suggesting, to them and to others, some thoughts that may prove, I would fain hope, not wholly out of harmony with the graver cadences of life". See Introduction, pp. xxi–xxiii.

[*"Who sins in hope, who, sinning, says"*]

Included in the Preface, this poem suggests the much graver tone: God is not mocked.

[*"Is all our Life, then, but a dream"*]

The dedicatory poem is addressed to Isa Bowman and the initial letters of each line spell her name. The poem muses on the final line of the poem that concludes *Looking-Glass*: "Life, what is it but a dream?" See also note to "Maggie's Visit to Oxford".

5.   *raree-show*: A peepbox: LC loved toy theatres, marionettes and peep shows as well as the stage.

[*A Beggar's Palace*]

Chapter 5.

[*The Gardener's Song*]

The stanzas appear at irregular intervals (stanza 1, chapter 5; 2–3, chapter 6, etc.) throughout *Sylvie and Bruno*; stanza 9 is from *Sylvie and Bruno Concluded*, chapter 20.

The Old Man's Incantation

Chapter 9.

Peter and Paul

Chapter 11. This relentless, comic and sardonic tale reworks the meaning of the old saying "Robbing Peter to pay Paul". The money never gets lent but the debt must be repaid.

[*"He either fears his fate too much"*]

Chapter 14.

Fairies' Song

Chapter 15. The song is interrupted by the arrival of Sylvie (and never finished).

The Three Badgers

Chapter 17. Another ruthless rhyme reminiscent of "The Walrus and the Carpenter".

Light Come, Light Go

Chapter 20. The title implies a sadder outcome than the poem relates.

Sylvie and Bruno Concluded

["Dreams, that elude the Maker's frenzied grasp"]

This dedicatory poem of farewell to his *Sylvie and Bruno* books is addressed to Enid Stevens, an Oxford child-friend, and the third letter of each line spells her name.

["King Fisher courted Lady Bird"]

Chapter 1.

[Streaks of Dawn]

Chapter 3.

Matilda Jane

Chapter 5. This poem was first sent with a copy of *Wonderland* in French to Mrs Holiday on 7 June 1870, though it was written for his cousin Menella (Nella) Wilcox about her doll Matilda Jane, necessarily "deaf, and dumb, and blind" (14), but beloved (*Handbook*, p. 185 and Hatch, p. 125).

The Revellers' Song

Chapter 5.

What Tottles Meant

This poem is spread across several chapters (13–16). It uses a fixed refrain ("and he meant it"), which changes meaning in the course of the tale.

[The Earl's Poem]

Chapter 16.

["In stature the Manlet was dwarfish"]

Chapter 17.

A Fairy-Duet

Chapter 19.

The Pig-Tale

Chapter 23. This poem, as Bruno remarks, "begins miserably, and it ends miserablier". It is one of the "Other Professor's" endless tales. Lurking in it is LC's loathing of hunting. (Stanza 5 first appeared in *Sylvie and Bruno*, chapter 10.)

Late Collections

Rhyme? And Reason? (1883)

This collection largely consists of previously published poems, illustrated by Henry Holiday and Arthur Frost. Only the new ones are printed here.

Echoes

The poem combines fragments from Wordsworth's "We are Seven" with some from Tennyson's "Lady Clara Vere de Vere" and his "Locksley Hall".

A Game of Fives

Possibly an ungallant reference to LC's responsibility towards his unmarried sisters.

Four Riddles

No. I. "There was an ancient city" is printed in *Phantasmagoria*.

II.

Edward Wakeling and Kazunari Takaya have worked out this double-acrostic, based on Ellen Terry as Ophelia: cross-lights: ENGAGEMENT, LOVE, LETTER, EQUIVOCATOR, NUNNERY (*Mischmasch: The Journal of the Lewis Carroll Society of Japan*, ix, 2007, pp. 152–71).

III.

In W. S. Gilbert's very successful blank-verse drama *Pygmalion and Galatea* (1871), Pygmalion is married to Cynisca who at first is happy for him to be fond of his statue of Galatea, but when she comes to life

Cynisca grows jealous and after twenty-four hours of life Galatea thinks it best to return to her statue state. So, Gala-tea: Galatea.

IV.

Answer: I-magi-nation.

Fame's Penny-Trumpet

This poem is particularly directed against experimenters using vivisection. In 1875 LC published a letter in the *Pall Mall Gazette* (12 February), and his powerful anti-vivisectionist article "Some Popular Fallacies about Vivisection" in *Fortnightly Review* in June (xvii (n.s.), pp. 847–54) was also published under the name "Lewis Carroll", despite his distaste for mingling his private person and career with that of his pseudonym.
First privately printed in 1876, signed "An Unendowed Researcher, July 1876".

A Tangled Tale (1885)

A Tangled Tale

Illustrated by Arthur B. Frost. "Excelsior": the first "knot" or mathematical problem (the hill and the tangled knot). See also note to "To my Pupil".

Three Sunsets and Other Poems (1898)

This collection appeared posthumously after LC's unexpected death at the age of 65 in January 1898. Almost all the poems had been previously published: some in the second, serious part of *Phantasmagoria*, two in *Sylvie and Bruno*, one in *Jabberwock* in 1888. The only newly published items were the two acrostics "Puck Lost and Found" from 1891. The illustrations "Twelve Fairy-Fancies by E. Gertrude Thomson" are not tied in to the text.

Puck Lost and Found

Acrostics for Princess Alice and Prince Charlie, children of the Duchess of Albany. They visited LC twice on 19 November 1891, and he taught them "to fold paper pistols, and to blot their names in creased paper, and showed them the machine which, by rapid spinning, turns the edging of a cup etc. into a filmy solid" (*Diaries*, viii, 596, also *Letters*, ii, 749–50).

Appendix

Poems Doubtfully Attributed to Lewis Carroll

Sequel to The Shepherd of Salisbury Plain

A poem "The Shepherd of Salisbury Plain", published in *Punch*, xlii, 1 February 1862, is pasted into LC's scrapbook (Library of Congress), and this "Sequel" is a reply (*Handbook*, p. 20). Edward Wakeling comments, in his notes on the Scrapbook:

> – This poem, which borrowed its title from Hannah More, was an attack on Walter Keir Hamilton, Bishop of Salisbury, who was in dispute with one of his clergy. Two eight-line stanzas in manuscript replying to this poem, and entitled "Sequel to The Shepherd of Salisbury Plain," was found at Christ Church in 1952 among the Common Room papers of C. L. Dodgson. It was thought to be by Dodgson. However, the hand-writing suggests that the author may have been his friend and colleague, Thomas Vere Bayne.

The presence of the original *Punch* poem in LC's scrapbook and of the "Sequel" among his Common Room papers suggests a further feasible explanation: that Vere Bayne copied out this text but that the poem was by LC. Although I incline to Edward Wakeling's view on the authorship, I have decided to put the poem in an appendix since some doubt exists and readers may like to form an opinion.

17. *Audi alteram partem*: Hear the other side of the question (Latin).

[Solutions to Puzzles from Wonderland, probably from another hand]

Contributed by "Eadgyth" to the January 1871 number of *Aunt Judy's Magazine*, the solutions are probably not by LC since "Eadgyth" made a number of contributions that are certainly not by LC, but may be by Mrs Gatty, editor of the magazine (*Handbook*, pp. 56–7). How-ever, they serve well as rhymed responses.

Index of Titles

Index of First Lines